THE FOG

The Fog

JAMES HERBERT

NEW ENGLISH LIBRARY
TIMES MIRROR

First published in Great Britain by New English Library in 1975
© 1975 by James Herbert

*

Open market edition December 1975
First NEL edition July 1976
Reprinted July 1976
Reprinted August 1976
Reprinted October 1976
New edition March 1977
Reprinted June 1977
Reprinted September 1977
Reprinted November 1977
This new edition June 1978

*

NEL Books are published by
New English Library Limited from Barnard's Inn, Holborn, London EC1N 2JR.
Made and printed in Great Britain by Hunt Barnard Printing Ltd., Aylesbury, Bucks.

45004278 2

One

The village slowly began to shake off its slumber and come to life. Slowly because nothing ever happened with speed in that part of Wiltshire; a mood of timelessness carefully cultivated by the villagers over the centuries prevailed. Newcomers had soon fallen into the leisurely pace and welcomed the security it created. Restless youngsters never stayed long but always remembered, and many missed, the protective quiet of the village. The occasional tourist discovered it by accident and delighted in its weathered charm, but within minutes its quaintness would be explored to the full and the traveller would move on, sighing for the peace of it, but a little afraid of the boredom it might bring.

Jessie opened her grocery shop at precisely 8.30 as she had been doing for the past twenty years. Her first customer, Mrs Thackery, wouldn't be in till 8.45, but to break the routine of early opening would never be considered. Even when Tom, her late husband, had died, the shop had still been opened on the dot of 8.30 and two days later when he'd been buried it was only shut for an hour between 10.00 and 11.00. Jessie enjoyed her morning chat with Mrs Thackery, who always called whether she needed to buy something or not. She'd been a great comfort since Tom had died and never missed her morning cup of tea with Jessie. They never got bored by each other's gossip; one topic could last two weeks and a death in the village would get them through three.

She waved to Mr Papworth, the butcher across the street who was sweeping the pavement outside his shop. Nice man, Mr Papworth. Much nicer since his wife had left him. That had caused a stir in the village and no mistake, when she'd walked out after six years of marriage. She hadn't been his sort anyway. Much too young for him, too flighty; couldn't stand the quiet life. He'd brought her back from his holiday in

5

Bournemouth and after all the years, when everybody had thought him a confirmed bachelor, had announced her as his bride. It could never have lasted, they all knew that at the outset, but he had tried. Still, all that was in the past. His visits from across the road were becoming more and more frequent and the whole village knew what was in the wind and that the butcher's and grocery shop would eventually become a combined family business. There was no rush; things would take their course.

'Good morning, Mrs Bundock!'

Her reverie was interrupted by two young voices in unison. She looked down and smiled at little Freddy Gravies and his even smaller sister, Clara.

'Hello, you two. Just off to school?'

'Yep,' replied Freddy, craning his neck to look at the jars of sweets on the shelves behind her.

'And how are you, Clara?' Jessie beamed at the five-year-old who had only recently started school.

'Fine, thank you,' came the shy reply.

'I'm surprised to see you two today. Saturday's usually your pocket-money day, isn't it?'

'Yep. But we polished all Daddy's boots yesterday, so he gave us a special treat,' was Freddy's bright-faced reply. Their father was a policeman whose station was in the next town. He was a gruff-spoken but pleasant man who adored his two children, but dealt with them strictly.

'Well, what are you going to buy?' Jessie asked, knowing they wouldn't have much to spend. 'You'd better hurry or you'll miss your bus.'

Clara pointed at the Penny-chews and Freddy nodded his head in agreement. 'Three each, please,' he said.

'Well now, Penny-chews are cheaper on Mondays. You get four each for six p today.'

They beamed up at her as she reached for the jar and took out the sweets.

'Thank you,' said Clara as she put three in her pocket and began to unwrap the fourth. Freddy gave Jessie the money, took his four and followed his sister's example.

'Bye bye now. Have a nice day!' she called after them as they ran from the shop, Freddy clutching Clara's hand.

'Morning Jessie.' The postman was leaning his bike up outside the door.

6

'Hello, Tom. Something for me?'

'Airmail, 'spect it's from your boy,' he replied, entering the shop. 'S'going to be another lovely day today. Beautiful clear sky out.' He handed her the blue and red envelope, noticing the shadow of sadness that seemed to pass over her face. 'Been in the army nearly a year now, hasn't he?'

She nodded, studying the stamps on the envelope.

'Ah well, Jessie, it was only to be expected. Young boy like that. Couldn't stay cooped up in a village like this all his life, could he? Needed to see places, did Andy. Always liked to get about, always up to some mischief. Having the time of his life now, I reckon.'

She nodded again, sighing as she began to open the envelope.

'Yes, I suppose you're right. But I do miss him. He was a good boy.'

The postman shook his head once then shrugged his shoulders.

'Well, see you tomorrow, Jessie. Must be off.'

'Yes. Bye, Tom.' She unfolded the thin blue writing paper and began to read the letter, a smile spreading across her face as Andy's natural boisterousness shone through the written words.

Suddenly she felt giddy and lurched against the counter. She put her hand to her forehead, alarmed at the strange stomach-rising feeling. Then she heard a deep rumbling noise, a sound that came from below, under her feet. The floor began to quiver causing her to clutch at the counter again; the quiver became a trembling. Jars began to rattle on their shelves, cans began to tumble. The rumbling grew louder, deeper. It began to fill her head. She dropped her letter and clapped both hands to her ears. The ground shook. She lost her balance and fell to her knees. The whole shop seemed to be moving. The large glass window cracked and then fell in. Shelves collapsed. The noise became deafening. Jessie screamed and stumbled towards the doorway; every time she tried to rise she was thrown to her knees. She crawled to the entrance, terror of the building collapsing in on her forcing her on. Vibrations ran through her body, at times the shaking almost making her lose contact with the floor.

She reached the door, and looked out at the road that ran through the village. She couldn't believe what her eyes told her.

The postman stood in the middle of the road holding on to

his bike. A huge crack appeared at his feet and suddenly as the ground opened up, he disappeared. The crack snaked along the length of the street to where young Freddy and Clara stood transfixed, clutching one another, and on towards Mrs Thackery who had been making her way to Jessie's shop. Suddenly it seemed as though the whole village had been wrenched apart. The road disappeared as the ground opened up like a gigantic yawning mouth.

Jessie looked across the road and just caught sight of the terrified face of Mr Papworth as he and the whole row of shops and houses on his side were swallowed up by the earth.

Two

John Holman wearily changed gear to take the car around the bend in the narrow country road. He was unshaven and his clothes were still damp from the morning dew. He'd spent half the night trying to sleep inside a thicket out of sight of the army patrols that practised their manoeuvres on a large but secluded part of Salisbury Plain. The area was owned by the Ministry of Defence and trespassers were severely dealt with if caught. The grounds could never be entered by accident; high fences and many warning notices took care of that. The fences travelled many miles around the territory's perimeter and a heavy screen of trees and undergrowth successfully concealed what lay beyond.

Holman shook his head in disgust at the danger and discomfort he'd had to go through to maintain secrecy when he himself worked for the same government. It was idiotic that the two departments, the Ministry of Defence and the Department of the Environment, couldn't work hand in hand, but held back information, guarded against intrusion, as if they were two different countries. He had been recruited into a new office specially formed by the Department of the Environment, to investigate anything from polluted rivers to outbreaks of disease. It was a special unit because nearly all the investigations were carried out secretly. If a company was suspected of illegally dumping dangerous waste product, be it into the sea, into a river, or on to a tip, but no proof could be found by direct methods, then Holman was sent in to probe further.

He usually worked alone and often under a cover; more than once he'd taken on manual labour to get inside a factory to find the information needed. Hospitals, a mental home – even an experimental home-range factory farm; he'd worked in many places and, often as not, in government institutions to get at the source of suspected malpractice. His one big frustration was that the transgressions he unearthed were not always acted upon. When politics – business or governmental – became involved, he knew the chances of prosecution against the offenders were slim. At thirty-two, Holman was still young enough to be angered by the seeming lack of resolution shown by his superiors when he himself had taken great risks to ferret out the proof they had asked him to provide.

However, he could also be quite unscrupulous in achieving his aims and more than once had seriously infringed the law, causing alarm among the few superiors who knew about his activities. At the moment his project was to investigate land owned by the Ministry of Defence, used by them for military purposes and protected for them by the Official Secrets Act. Vast areas of land, much of it appropriated during the Napoleonic war and more recently, World War II, was used as a training ground for the army. Most of it was in the south because of invasion fears. Holman knew that much of it was going to waste, areas of great natural beauty, rich arable soil being allowed to spoil. At a time when good land and open spaces were becoming more and more scarce, valuable country could not be allowed to be misused. The Ministry of Defence was holding tightly on to over 750,000 acres for training or test purposes and his department was demanding at least 30,000 of those acres be handed back to the people. There was every reason for the Ministry of Defence to retain a good part of this private land, but suspicions were that only a fraction of it was necessary.

The Ministry had been approached, but a tight security net had been drawn over any enquiries. So Holman had been given the job of seeing just how much land was being used and if for valid purposes. The war between different government departments was ridiculous in his eyes, but he accepted it as a fact of life.

He had spent two rigorous days dodging patrols, taking photographs, gathering information about the enormous woodland area owned by the Ministry on Salisbury Plain. Had he been caught the consequences could have been quite severe, but he knew the risk involved and even enjoyed it. His employers knew this and played on the streak in his character that demanded risk, an element of danger, a gamble.

Now, as he rounded the bend, he saw a village ahead. One of the small, barely known villages that dotted the Plain, he

10

decided. Maybe he could get some breakfast here.

He drew nearer and suddenly became aware of a strange vibration running through the car, then of a deep rumbling noise as the vehicle began to shake. By the time he reached the main street running through the village his vision was becoming too blurred for him to travel further. And what he could see, he found hard to comprehend.

A gigantic crack appeared directly ahead of him then grew longer and wider, reaching towards him in a jagged, fast-moving line. His shocked brain just had time to register two children and a woman, and beyond them a man with a bicycle, before the ground opened up and they disappeared into the black chasm it created. The shops on his left began to collapse into the widening hole. The noise was deafening as the earth was wrenched apart, climaxing in a sound like an explosive thunderclap. Through his horror he realised that the ground below his car was beginning to split. He opened the door but too late – the car lurched forward and began to fall. The door was forced shut and Holman was trapped inside.

For a moment the car was stuck, but as the hole widened, it slid forward again. Panic seized him. He cried out in terror. Down it plunged at an acute angle, the rough sides of the earth preventing it from free-falling. After what must have been only a few sickening seconds, the car became wedged again and he found himself pressed up against the steering wheel, staring down into a frightening black void. His body was frozen, his mind almost paralysed with the horror of what was happening. Slowly, his brain began to function. He must be at the end of the opening, where the sides were narrowest. If it widened further, the car would plunge into the black depths below. He tried to look up towards ground level but couldn't see through the swirling dust.

Panic drove him into action. He frantically pushed himself away from the steering wheel but the sudden movement caused the car to slide a terrifying two feet farther down. He forced himself to keep calm, his breath coming in short gasps, the sounds of falling masonry, glass and dislodged earth filling his ears. More cautiously, he began to edge himself over into the back seat. He froze as the car shifted again, but this time the movement was fractional. He kept his position for a few tense moments then started to ease himself back again.

Gaining the back seat, he turned round into a position where

11

he could wind down a rear side window. He saw there was just sufficient gap between the car and the side of the chasm for him to squeeze through. Loose earth fell through the open window adding more weight to the precariously balanced vehicle.

Abandoning caution, he scrambled through and clung to the crumbling wall of rock and earth, expecting to hear the wrenching sound of the car tearing itself loose to fall into the depths below. For a full five minutes he stayed there, his head tight against the earth, clutching desperately to the treacherous surface.

The unsettled dust began to clear slightly and he looked around him fearfully. From the jagged outline above he guessed the eruption was at least five hundred yards long. The sides seemed steady now although shales of earth still showered down into what seemed a bottomless pit. He peered into the darkness below and shuddered at the awesome sight. It was as though the very bowels of the earth had opened up; the blackness seemed infinite.

A slight tremor made him bury his hands and face into the earth again, his heart pounding wildly, expecting at any moment to be dislodged from his insecure perch.

A sudden cry forced his eyes open once more. He peered through the disturbed dust and saw what looked like a tiny figure lying on a narrow sloping ledge about fifty feet away on the opposite wall of earth. With shock, he realised it was one of the children he'd seen in the street above. The little girl. Of the boy who'd been with her, there was no sign. She began to whimper piteously.

Holman knew he had to reach her or she would soon slide down the incline into the deep chasm. He called out to her, but she didn't seem to hear. He looked around, wondering how he would cross the gorge to get to her. She was about ten feet above him and thirty feet below ground level. Climbing to her shouldn't be too difficult providing he took great care; the sides were full of protuberances and old roots. The problem was to get across – and quickly.

Another thought struck him; what if the gap should close? The thought of being crushed to death as though in a giant nutcracker spurred him into action.

The car would have to act as a bridge. Two steps and he would be on the other side. It was dangerous but the only course of action he could take. Tentatively he placed a foot on the roof of the car. It held. He put his weight on it, still holding on to the wall on his side. The roof slanted downward and the thought of slipping on its smooth surface terrified him. Before he could allow himself to think further he took two bounds across the gap, almost willing himself to fly.

But the second step caused the car to lose its grip on the sides of the walls and it slipped forward and down, taking Holman with it. Desperately he grabbed at the side he had been making for and with more luck than judgement, managed to grasp a dead tree root. It cracked and broke, but thin tendons held it together and swung him inwards.

The child looked up at the sound of the crashing car and screamed when she saw the man hanging there. Rivers of earth, disturbed by her feet, ran over the ledge and showered into the gaping hole. She buried her head in her hands and sobbed, calling for her lost brother.

Holman hung there, thin strands of rotted wood between him and death. His feet sought support from the crumbling earth and one hand grabbed at solid rock. He managed to find a hand-hold and eased his weight from the broken root. He raised his feet until they found a more solid rest. Gulping in lungfuls of dusty air he looked towards the little girl.

'It's all right,' he shouted across. 'Stay perfectly still and you'll be all right. I'm coming to get you!'

He didn't know if she heard him or not but, he knew she would not last long on the precarious ledge. Again the thought of the ground closing up drove him on. He inched forward, testing every handhold, every foothold, and gradually came within eight feet of her and found himself on a fairly solid outcrop of rock. He didn't know how much time had elapsed; it could have been hours, but more likely it was no longer than minutes. Surely help would come soon, someone would try to see if anyone was trapped in the hole. He looked for a way to reach the girl.

There was a narrow crack running along the wall almost from where he stood to four feet below the ledge the girl was on. If he used it for footholds and used his hands to cling to the rock above his head, he should be able to reach the ledge, lean over it from the side and grab her. Her little body shook from the sobs but she didn't look up.

Carefully, he began to feel his way along, keeping his eyes on

13

the girl, ready to warn her not to move. As he drew nearer, her sobbing stopped and she looked up at him, her tiny face a mask of sheer horror. God, what must he look like coming towards her like this? With all the terror she'd been through, now to see this shape, filthy with dust, eyes wide and staring, clambering towards her.

'It's okay, it's okay,' he said, softly but urgently. 'I'm coming to help you. Don't move.'

She began to back away.

'No, no, don't move!' he couldn't help but shout.

She began to slide down, and, realising her predicament, dug her hands into the soft earth, crying out in fright.

Holman took a chance and lurched forward, hoping the side of the ledge would hold his weight. One foot stayed in the crack, the other dangled in space, one hand shot towards the girl, the other grabbed at the rock face. He managed to grab her outstretched hand and prevent her from sliding further. Her legs were over the edge now, her feet kicking at the empty air. His left hand found a crevice in the wall and he clung to it grimly, knowing if he lost his grip, both he and the girl would plunge to their deaths. She was screaming now, but her hand grabbed his as she realised the danger behind her.

For a few moments, all he could do was cling there, looking into her frightened face, clutching her struggling limbs. He whispered to her to be still, kindly, trying to keep panic from his voice. Slowly, her struggles died down and her body went limp, as though she knew nothing more could happen to her, her young mind going blank to protect her. He began to pull her up, her slight body no weight, but difficult because of his awkward position. Finally, she was completely back on the ledge but still he dragged her towards his chest.

'Hold on to me, sweetheart,' he told her gently. 'Put your arms around my neck and hold tight.'

He pulled her down between the ledge and his body, telling her to put her legs around his waist. Numbly she complied, her short legs resting on his hips.

'Now don't let go and everything will be fine,' he whispered, easing himself back along the crack, the shape of the girl pushing him outwards. His arm and leg muscles were rigid with the strain, but endurance was one of his assets.

Finally, exhausted, he reached the more solid outcrop of rock. He sank to his knees, still holding the child close, his

14

shoulders heaving with the exertion. Turning slowly, still clutching the girl, he leaned back against the cliff wall and rested his aching limbs.

For a few minutes his brain registered no more than the blessed relief from exertion but, as his strength returned and his breathing grew more even, he began to wonder at what had happened.

He remembered entering the village and then – and then the ground, the very earth opening up. First the crack snaking its jagged way along the concrete, then the noise, the deep rumble, the build-up to the cracking stone, and then the incredible sight of the ground opening up, the enormous split in the earth. The two sides moving apart, their edges crashing inwards, down, down into God knows where. The sight of the two children, the man and his bike – had he seen a woman too? – disappearing into the hole. The shops collapsing – he remembered seeing the shops on one side collapsing – and then the ragged mouth reaching towards him. The tilt of the car, the lurch as it slid forward.

It all seemed to have happened in slow motion. And yet it had all happened so fast. He stroked the girl's head, trying to still her sobs, reassuring her that they'd be all right, but the cries for her brother stung his heart.

He looked up towards the daylight, hoping he would see someone up there, someone looking for survivors. Survivors? Survivors of what? The question exploded in his brain. An earthquake? It was incredible. Earthquakes had occurred in England before, and minor tremors were frequent. But an eruption of this size? The incredible, the unbelievable, had happened. In a crazy world, the most crazy thing had happened. Wiltshire had suffered an earthquake! He laughed aloud at the thought, startling the child. He pulled her raised head back to his chest, gently, and rocked her comfortingly.

What had caused it? It certainly wasn't any gas-mains explosion; not with this devastation. The hole was too deep, too long. No, it had certainly been an earth tremor, not as serious as those suffered in other countries of course, but of just as great a magnitude because it had happened in England! Why? Had the nearby military installation been testing some underground explosives? He had evidence of some pretty strange goings-on from his discreet weekend visit, but doubted they had anything to do with this. A chain reaction, perhaps, from one of their experiments. But probably nothing to do with them for, after all, they had vast areas of British-occupied wasteland in far off countries to carry out their tests in. England was no place for experiments of this kind. It was more likely a freak of nature, a disturbance below that had been building up for centuries, probably thousands of years. And today had been the day for it to erupt.

But still the doubt lingered.

Just then Holman noticed movement at his feet. At first he thought it was dust caused by the disturbance, but then saw it was billowing up from below. It was like a mist, slowly rising in a sluggish swirling motion, slightly yellowish although he couldn't be sure in the gloom. It seemed to spread along the length of the split, moving up towards his chest, covering the girl's head. She started to cough, then looked up and her whimpers became stronger when she saw the mist. He lifted her higher so her head was level with his shoulder. Then the mist reached his nostrils. It had a slightly acidy smell to it, unpleasant but not choking. He got to his knees, wondering what it could be. Gas? A ruptured main? He doubted it – gas was generally colourless, this had some substance to it. It was more like – well, a fog. It had body, the yellowish tinge, a slight but distinct odour. A vapour probably released by the eruption from deep underground, trapped for centuries, finally finding its way to the surface.

It was above his head now and he found it difficult to see through. He got to his feet, lifting the child with him. Once above the rising cloud, an immense fear overcame him. For some reason his horror of the swirling mist was more intense than the horror he'd just been through. Perhaps it was because this was happening slowly, whereas everything else had been so fast, leaving so little time for thought. This somehow seemed more evil, more sinister; he didn't know why, but it filled him with a great sense of foreboding.

'Help! Is there anybody up there? Can anyone hear me?' He called out urgently, no panic in his voice yet, but he could feel hysteria rising. There was no answer. Maybe it was too dangerous to approach the edge of the hole. Perhaps there were too many injured up there anyway.

'I want you to get on my back, darling, and put your arms around my neck,' he told the girl, lifting her chin so he could look at her face. 'We're going to climb up now.'

16

'I – I want my brother,' she whimpered, no longer afraid of him, but still not trusting.

'I know, darling, I know. But your Mummy and Daddy will be waiting for you up there.'

She burst into tears again, burying her head into his shoulder. The thick blanket of fog was now up to his chin. Moving her around to his back, he took off his belt and tied her wrists together just below his neck, tucking her legs around his waist. He began to climb.

As he did so, moving slowly with the added weight and because the going was treacherous, the mist kept pace with him, finally overtaking and swirling above his head.

The people above heard the cry for help coming from the huge hole that had wrecked the village. They'd assumed that anyone who had plunged into it must surely be dead, but now gained new heart at the sound of a voice, a chance to react against the tragedy. The policeman whose children were thought to have been lost in the eruption, was lowered over the edge of the crack. He would not give up. He had searched the rubble and still half-collapsed, potentially dangerous buildings, but hadn't found his youngsters yet. When they heard the cry for help, he was already tying a stout rope to his waist to be lowered into the hole to search for survivors.

When he emerged five minutes later, he held a small unconscious girl in his arms. He laid her on the ground to be taken care of by the elderly but competent doctor, he kissed her once, tears from his eyes falling on her face, then dashed back to the hole and was lowered again. This time, he brought up a man. A man covered from head to foot with dust and dirt. A man who gibbered and screamed, a man who had to be restrained by four others from running back and throwing himself into the black depths. A man who was insane.

The villagers watched the mist rise from the hole, not billowing over the edges, but rising in a densely-packed steady column, the centre of which seemed to glow faintly – or was it merely the strong sun shining through it? – rising high into the air to form a heavy, yellowish cloud. It looked like the aftermath of a hydrogen bomb, only a much smaller mushroom shape, the lower column finally ending and joining the cloud in the sky. It was soon forgotten when the winds blew it away; not dispersing it, but moving it in a huge, almost solid-looking mass, across the sky, away from the ruined village.

Three

The Reverend Martin Hurdle trudged across the fields with a heavy heart. His thoughts were on the nearby village that had suffered the great disaster, the peaceful little village that had virtually been demolished by the freak earthquake. It had been the main story in the newspapers all that week. The great shock was that it had happened in England, not some far off, remote country that people had scarcely heard of. This was on their own doorstep, the British people could relate to it, not viewing it distantly through the news media and the press, thereby finding true sympathy hard to arouse. This had happened to their own kind. For the people of his village, they were neighbours, relatives; for the people in the rest of Britain, they were countrymen. This would be the basis of his sermon today: that through this tragic event they could now perhaps truly understand and feel compassion for the plight of other nations all over the world who suffered misfortune as a normal part of their lives. People were concerned too much with their own mundane, day-to-day problems: money worries, job worries, affair-of-the-heart worries, disputes with family, with neighbours, with life itself – all petty, insulated, but only shown to be so when some major disaster happened.

This tragic event would force people to look outward, to see what was happening in the world around them, to realise just how insignificant their selfish, introverted problems were. If only he could use this distressing event to show his congregation just how big life was, that the world did not revolve around individuals but around the great mass of humanity itself. This was the very reason that one had to help not just oneself, not just one's neighbours, but every person had to help *everybody*, help them to exist, to survive. That the catastrophe had happened to *their* neighbouring village proved it could strike anywhere at any time; no one, no community, no nation was immune.

The words ran vigorously through his mind. He knew just how he would tell his congregation that Sunday morning, just when his voice would soften almost to a whisper, to allow him to build up to a loud, heart-stirring climax. After thirty years as a clergyman he now knew the subtle inflections his voice could use, and the times he had to boom out to reach his parishioners. At fifty-two he had not yet quite despaired of human nature. There was good in the worst people, just as there was hypocrisy in the most devout, but sometimes –

He shrugged his shoulders helplessly. He usually enjoyed his early Sunday morning walk across the fields, his pace brisk, his mind running through the sermon he would deliver that day, but he supposed the tragedy of the eruption still bore heavily on him. Having heard the news, he'd driven to the village to try to help, to administer the Last Rites to the dying, to comfort the injured. The last war had been the only experience he'd had of death and injury in these proportions and he had believed he'd got over the horror of it, but old memories had been resurrected, scars he'd thought healed were opened freshly.

He looked up from the ground abruptly, realising he'd walked into a mist. Early morning mists were familiar to him but this seemed different. It had a yellowish tinge to it and was thick, suddenly very thick as it swept over him. Strange smell, too. Goodness, he thought, better retrace my steps and get clear of this. Wouldn't want to get lost and be late for service.

He walked back in the direction he'd come, for some reason becoming nervous as his steps didn't bring him clear of the dense mist. No, this wasn't a mist, he thought. It was fog. How strange to run into fog on a summer morning as brilliant as it had been when he'd set out. This was as bad as some of the old London 'pea-soupers'. He looked skyward and could just make out the faint haze of the sun. He wondered now if he were walking in the right direction.

'Goodness,' he muttered aloud, 'I'm lost!' What was that? His heart pounded as a dark, nebulous shape approached him.

It was large, not as tall as him, but bulky. And silent.

It seemed to drift towards him suspended in mid-air, its size increasing as it drew nearer. Then, oh God! – another. Another joined it, seeming to dissolve into it, becoming one huge shape, still approaching, almost on top of him. It, whatever it was, knew he was there! He backed away steadily, his mouth opening and closing soundlessly. He began to move faster, not turning but walking backwards, afraid to take his eyes off the shapes that loomed larger before him.

Suddenly, he bumped into something solid. He whirled, falling to his knees in his fright. Another black shape hovered over him, menacingly silent.

And then, he laughed. Tears of relief ran down his face and he pounded the earth in near-hysterical amusement.

He had walked into a herd of cows. He laughed louder, occasionally choking as he breathed deep mouthfuls of the murky air, the cows observing him in dumb vacuity, an occasional restless ululation their only comment.

It took him a full five minutes to recover his wits and admonish himself for his foolishness. Frightened by a herd of cows! Old George Ross, who owned them, would roar with laughter when he told him the story. No wonder he thought the shapes had been floating above the ground. The fog was so thick one could hardly see the cows' legs!

Yes, he'd learned a lesson himself today. The unknown was always more fearful than the reality.

It took him another twenty minutes to find his way clear of the fog.

The man crouched low in the bushes when he heard a rustle of leaves to his left. Human or animal? Tom Abbot had to be careful. If he was caught poaching on the Colonel's land again he'd be in serious trouble. Colonel Meredith had caught him red-handed last time and given him a 'sound thrashing' as the Colonel liked to boast in the village pub, then warned him if it ever happened again he'd 'march him off to the police station, toute suite'. Toute suite! Him and his fancy language. Well, he'd never catch Tom again. Last time it had only been because he'd lingered too long into the morning on account of his poor catch in the early hours. The Colonel had spotted him hiding in the bushes and crept up on him, then used his thick walking stick to beat him about the head and shoulders. Too surprised and hurt to offer resistance, he'd been dragged along by his collar as though he were riff-raff and booted off the estate with the threat of police action and 'another bloody good hiding' if he set foot on that land again.

Well, Colonel Meredith, you won't get old Tom again, he repeated to himself. Too wily for the likes of you, with your fancy house and fancy cars and fancy friends. Nice little pheasant I've got here and I'll get myself another before I leave. It's still too early for you to be about, I've got a good hour before you're up and around. Three months I've laid off, fooled you into thinking you'd frightened me off, but oh no, old Tom don't give up that easy. Nice price I'll get for this pheasant and no questions asked.

The poacher crept forward again, still cursing the land-owner in his mind, peering into the bushes ahead. He froze. Yes, there was something there and not a man. He kept perfectly still, not wanting to frighten it away, to let it come out in its own time, whatever it was. Another pheasant, I'll warrant, Tom told himself. Woods were full of them, all under the sanctuary of bloody Colonel Meredith. Well, Tom had patience. Tom would wait for it to show itself. Tom could wait for nearly an hour without so much as twitching a muscle. Come on, my beauty, take your time, Tom can wait.

He crouched there for a full ten minutes before he became aware of the yellowy tentacles of mist creeping around his legs. My Gawd, that's all I need, he cursed silently. He looked behind him and was surprised to see a solid blanket of fog almost on top of him. Queer, he'd never experienced fog here before. Well, he'd wait a while longer in the hope that whatever was in the bushes would make a move and show itself before the fog grew too dense.

Soon, he was completely enveloped in it and began to curse, realising if the bird or animal didn't make a move soon he wouldn't be able to see it anyway. Still nothing happened and the heavy mist crept forward till eventually he couldn't even see the bush. Only then did he hear a rustle and the sound of something scampering away. He cursed aloud this time and stood up, kicking at the ground in disgust.

Ah well, one was better than nothing at all. He turned back and walked deeper into the fog. It didn't bother him, he knew the area so well he could find his way back blindfold.

The Reverend Martin Hurdle prepared himself for his Sunday morning service. As he donned his cassock he smiled at the thought of the panic he'd been in earlier when he'd got lost in

22

the fog. Usually one of the joys of the week, his early morning walk had almost turned into a nightmare. He couldn't explain the lift he'd felt when he'd emerged again into the sun, the sense of relief, the delight of being released from that sinister cloud. He had a slight headache now but otherwise he'd got over the unpleasant experience and no doubt would chuckle when he recounted the story to his friends.

The church was fairly full today, the pleasantness of the weather helping, but the tragedy of the neighbouring village accounting primarily for the large attendance. The vicar greeted his parishioners at the door of the church as they went in, chatting briefly with some, smiling and nodding at others. When it was time for the service to begin, he entered through a side door into the sacristy, hurried his altar boys along, and walked briskly with them into the church.

The service began as normal, pleasurable to some, boring to others, but today, because of the tragedy, meaningful for most. A few people near the front noticed the vicar occasionally put his hand to his forehead as though he were tired or had a headache, but the service continued smoothly enough.

They sat and looked up at him when he climbed the steps to his pulpit, anxious to be comforted by his words in their time of sadness. He looked down at their upturned, expectant faces, eyes focused on him, eager for him to speak.

Then the Reverend Martin Hurdle, Vicar of St Augustine's for eighteen years, lifted his cassock, undid his trousers, took out his penis, and urinated over his congregation.

'Now where have those blessed cows got to?' George Ross asked himself aloud, a frown wrinkling his already multi-wrinkled, weathered face even more. 'Bet they've got through that gap again.'

The farmer was used to his herd breaking through the fence of bushes and trees that surrounded their meadow and wandering off into the next. He plodded down towards the spot they'd most likely have broken through. 'As if I haven't got enough to do without chasing those silly creatures all mornin'. I'll give 'em what for!' he cursed angrily.

He reached the gap and pushed his way through. 'Now where are yer'?' He stood looking around, then his mouth dropped open at the sight of the fog at the other end of his field. 'Well I'll be! Never noticed that.' He scratched his bristly chin, puzzled.

He began to walk towards the murky cloud and grinned as he saw his cows emerging from it. 'Trust you!' he shouted at them. 'Trust you to get yourselves lost in that. Stupid bloody creatures!'

Funny, having a fog down here, he pondered. Too heavy to be a mist. All this bloomin' p'lution. 'Come on, me beauties!' he called out as they trudged towards him. The fog, he noticed, was drifting off into the adjoining field. Strange that he could see the edges of it, like a solid block of smoke moving across the countryside, not at all like the normal widespread blanket of grey.

The cows were up to him now and the leaders passed him.

'Come on now, up to the sheds!' he bellowed at them, slapping one hard on the rump as it passed.

It stopped and turned its head towards him. 'Move yourself,' the farmer said gruffly, slapping it again. The cow stood silently watching him.

George cursed it more loudly, then turned to see what progress the rest of the herd was making. They had all stopped and were turned towards him, watching.

'What's this, then?' For some inexplicable reason, he had begun to feel nervous. There was a tension about his herd that he couldn't understand. 'Move yourselves. Get on 'ome!' He waved his arms at them, trying to startle them into movement. They watched him.

Then they began to close in on him.

He realised he was surrounded by the cows and the ring was drawing tighter around him. What was happening? He could not understand the menacing air these dumb, gentle animals had taken on. He felt himself jostled from behind. He turned and lashed out at the cow he'd slapped before. 'Get back!' he shouted, logic telling him his rising fear was unreasonable.

He heard a pounding of hooves and again felt himself pushed from behind, this time more violently. He fell to the ground.

'Get away, get away!' He scrambled about on his hands and knees trying to rise, but every time he raised himself, he was knocked off his feet again. Suddenly, one of the cows turned and kicked out with its hind legs, catching him an agonising blow in the ribs, sending him flying forward.

He began to scream as he received more kicks. They seemed to be taking it in turns to run forward and lash out at him. One kick caught him full in the face, breaking his nose, blinding him for a few seconds. When he could see once more, it was like opening his eyes to a bad dream.

The cows were racing round him, their eyes bulging almost out of their sockets, froth and slime running from their mouths. They trampled over him. If he rose, they crushed him with their bodies. They used their heads to knock him off his knees. They began to bite him, snapping off his fingers as he raised his arms to protect himself. A scream ended in a gurgling, choking noise as a kick broke his jaw and blood ran down his throat.

When at last he lay sprawled semi-conscious on the muddied grass, they herded together, and crushed the life from his battered body with their hooves.

The poacher gazed at the house from his hiding place in the undergrowth. He'd emerged from the fog, but instead of returning to his ramshackle house on the outskirts of the village he'd walked along the main road towards the gates of the Colonel's huge country home. He'd skulked up the long, winding drive and hidden in the bushes, waiting and peering through the leaves at the house. After a while his eyes, strangely glazed, looked from left to right. He rose and crept stealthily towards the back of the building. He knew where to go for he'd done casual work for the Colonel's head gardener years before. That was how he knew the grounds so well, the best places to poach, the best places to hide. He walked down towards a wooden hut at the end of the long garden. He pushed open the door, his eyes now developing a fixed stare, no longer worrying about the noise he was making, his movements controlled, steady. He reached for an axe, rusted with time, but the blade still sharp. As he turned to leave the hut, his gaze fell on a box of three inch nails used for fencing. He scooped up a handful and put them in his pocket.

He walked back up the garden, not bothering to hide, walking in a straight line towards the house. As he reached the back door, the Merediths' cook was just opening it to let the steam from her kitchen escape. She'd just cooked the Colonel and his wife breakfast and the maid had taken it up to them. Now it was time for her morning tea before she started to make preparations for their lunch. There were lots of guests coming, so there was much to do.

She had no chance to scream before the axe hit her, only a fleeting look into the eyes of a madman, a chance for fear to begin to rise but never to reach its peak, for in the next instant, she was dead.

Tom Abbot entered the kitchen and climbed the stairs that led to the hall. He'd never been in the house before and only the sound of voices drew him towards the dining-room. He opened the first door he came to and went in, not stopping till he was in the middle of a large sitting-room, bigger than the whole of the ground floor of his tiny house. He stood there, gazing ahead.

The sound of footsteps passing the open door caused him to turn and retrace his steps. He heard the sound of voices again and walked towards another door.

The maid hummed to herself as she descended the stairs to the kitchen, holding her tray with half-eaten grapefruit and crusts of toast aloft so that she could see the steps beneath her.

'Put the kettle on, Mrs Peabody,' she called out as she approached the kitchen door. 'Let's have a nice cuppa' while they're noshing their bacon and eggs.'

Discovering the kitchen empty, she looked around curiously. The kettle was already steaming away. She put down her tray and walked over to the gas stove to turn the kettle off. The door to the garden was open so she assumed the cook had stepped outside for a breath of fresh air or to empty some food scraps into one of the dustbins. She walked around the large centre table to the door so she could call for her. A scream broke from her lips as she saw the body, lying there just outside the door-way, its skull cleaved open to the bridge of the nose. Before she fainted, she realised it was the cook, recognisable only because of her build and clothes, her face covered in blood, her features in a frozen grimace of terror, bearing no resemblance to the face it had once been. As she collapsed, the maid's brain just registered the other scream, the scream from upstairs that pierced the still air.

When she regained consciousness, she couldn't at first recollect what had happened. Then her body stiffened as she remembered. She saw the corpse, her foot almost touching it, and she backed away shuddering, trying to call for help but her vocal cords paralysed with fear. She somehow got to her feet and

26

staggered towards the stairs, clambering up them, falling and sobbing, nothing preventing her from getting away from that kitchen. She gained the hallway and ran down it towards the dining-room, gasping for air, trying to call out.

She stumbled through the open door and stopped short at the sight confronting her.

Her mistress lay sprawled on the floor in a pool of blood, only a few tendons in her neck holding her head to her body. It lay parallel to her left shoulder, grinning up at her. The Colonel lay spreadeagled on the huge dining table, long nails through the palms of his hands and the flesh of his ankles to pin him there. A man stood over him, an axe dripping with blood in his hands.

As the maid watched, dumb-struck, unable to move with the horror of it, the man raised the axe above his head and brought it down with all his strength. It severed a hand and splintered the wood beneath. The man struggled to free the weapon from the table and raised it again. By the time he'd cut off the other hand, the Colonel was unconscious. By the time he'd hacked off both feet, the Colonel was dead.

The maid finally began to scream when the man with the axe turned his head and looked at her.

Four

'Hello, John.'

John Holman looked up at the girl and smiled. 'Hello, Casey.'

'How do you feel?'

'Okay.'

He was sitting on the steps of the hospital, unwilling to wait inside. He found hospitals depressing.

'They said you'd need at least another couple of weeks.' She sat next to him on the steps.

'No, I'm all right now. Any longer in there and I'd have gone mad again.'

She flinched at the words, remembering how he had been the first time she'd visited.

The news of the eruption had stunned the country, spreading alarm, causing dismay among geologists, panic in the neighbouring towns and villages. She hadn't even known Holman was in that area for he was very secretive about his job; she wasn't even sure of his department. All she knew was that he had an 'assignment' for the weekend, that no, he couldn't tell her where he was going, and *no*, she definitely could *not* go with him. Had she known he had been in the village that suffered the earthquake, she – she refused to think about it. It had been bad enough when she had rung his office the following day to find out why he hadn't called her on his return and had learnt of his involvement. The department knew he'd been in the area and as they hadn't heard from him since, assumed he either couldn't get back because the roads leading to the disaster were completely blocked by rescue and medical services and the hordes of curious sightseers – the usual ghoulish element that flocked to any disaster – or he had stayed to help. They didn't reveal to her that they were concerned that perhaps he was being held by the military on their Salisbury Plain base and they were now anxiously expecting the Ministry of Defence to come roaring down their necks. She was asked to ring back later when no doubt they would have some news and was advised not to make the trip down to Wiltshire because of the mounting traffic and the impossibility of finding him anyway.

The rest of the day had been spent in a fear-ridden daze. She rang her employer, an exclusive antique-dealer in one of the side streets off Bond Street, and told him she felt too ill to come in. A fussy little man, who considered women necessary only for business purposes, he brusquely hoped she would be well enough to do her job tomorrow. For the rest of the day she wandered listlessly around the house, afraid to go out in case the phone rang. She barely ate and listened to the radio only to find out more news of the earthquake.

Casey had known Holman for nearly a year now and was becoming more and more aware that if he ever left her, she would be lost. Her dependence on him was now stronger even than her dependence on her father had been. When her mother had divorced her father eight years ago, she had turned to him to provide the comfort and guidance every child needs from a mother, and he had coped extraordinarily well. Too well, in fact, for by overcompensating for the lack of his wife, he had tied the daughter almost irrevocably to him. Holman had begun to break the bonds between them, unconsciously at first, but when he realised just how strong the ties were he began to gently, but purposefully, draw Casey away from her father. He did this not so much out of love for her, but because he cared about her as a person. He knew she had a strong mind and a will of her own, but she was too tightly enmeshed in her father's domineering love. If the relationship developed any further then she would never be free to live her own life. Besides, the closeness between father and daughter made him feel uneasy.

Holman had tried to get Casey – her real name was Christine, but he had invented the nickname for reasons he hadn't told her of yet – to leave her father's house and get a flat of her own. This she would have done had he allowed her to live with him, but there he'd drawn the line. After two previous disastrous affairs he had resolved never to become too entangled with one person again. He had been near to it many times and even proposed marriage once, but the girl backed out because she knew, and realised she had always known, that he didn't love her. That had been years before, and now he wondered if he were really capable of love. He had gradually lost most of his

29

cynicism on that topic during the months he had known Casey. He still resisted, but guessed he was fighting a losing battle. Maybe he was getting old, resigning himself to the fact he needed a companion, that although he'd never been quite alone, he hadn't shared for a long, long time.

Casey was breaking down that barrier just as he was breaking down the closeness between her and her father. The process was gradual, but inevitable. Still, each of them offered resistance. She would not leave her father without the assurance of someone taking his place; he refused to be that someone, the move had to come from her *before* she had the guarantee of someone to run to. Holman was older than Casey, but had no intention of becoming a father-figure. At the moment, it was deadlock.

Now, in her anxiety, as she waited for the phone to ring, Casey knew she would do as he asked. She understood his reasons. It would hurt her father terribly, but it wasn't as though she would never see him again. And perhaps when he realised she was determined, his iciness towards John would begin to thaw. If it didn't, then she knew she would have to go through the agony of choosing again, but this time for keeps. And she knew it would be her father who would lose.

She waited till three pm, then rang Holman's office again. This time they had some news. They apologised for not having let her know sooner but all hell had broken loose in their department because of the earthquake. These things just weren't *meant* to happen in England! A man identified as John Holman whose papers showed he worked for the Department of the Environment, had been taken to Salisbury General Hospital, where he was in an extreme state of shock. When Casey pressed them for details, her heart pounding, her thoughts racing, they became evasive, but assured her that John had suffered no physical damage. Again, they advised her to keep clear of the area and promised they would keep her informed of any developments.

Casey thanked them and replaced the receiver. Then she rang the hosital itself. The operator apologised, told her that the hospital was jammed with calls and suggested she try later.

Numbed, she scribbled a note to her father, looked for the town on a road-map, and hurried out to her bright yellow saloon car, a present from her father. She avoided driving through London by going north and then around on the North Circular.

She bypassed Basingstoke and Andover, taking minor roads, knowing the towns would be jammed with traffic. On the outskirts of Salisbury, she ran into heavy traffic being held up by the police. Drivers of cars were being cross-examined as to their destinations, and unless their reasons for travel were genuine and not just to satisfy ghoulish curiosity about the earthquake, they were turned back. When it was Casey's turn, she explained about John and was allowed to continue her journey with the undertaking that on no account would she try to travel beyond the town to the disaster area. On their advice, she parked her car on the outskirts of the town and walked to the hospital which she found in a state of turmoil. Having enquired about Holman, she was asked to wait with the many other anxious relatives or friends who had come to the hospital for news of victims of the catastrophe.

It was not until eight that evening and after several attempts to obtain news of Holman that a weary looking doctor came down to see her. He took her aside and told her in a low voice that it would be better if she did not see John that night; he was suffering from shock and had sustained an injury that, although not too serious, required him to be given a blood transfusion and at that moment, he was under heavy sedation. Observing the girl was in a highly emotional state, he chose not to explain the nature of Holman's sickness at that time. Tomorrow, when she'd calmed down, would be time enough to explain that her lover, boyfriend, whatever he was to her, had gone totally mad, and at that moment was strapped to a bed, even though he was under sedation, so he could not harm himself or anybody else. It was strange how the man had been bent on killing himself. He'd had to be tied down in the ambulance on the way to the hospital, and once there he'd broken free, smashed a glass window and tried to drive a long, knife-like shard of glass through his neck. Only the intervention of the burly ambulance driver who now suffered from a broken jaw caused in the ensuing struggle had saved him from cutting himself too deeply. Holman had gone completely berserk and two porters and a doctor had been injured before he could be restrained and finally sedated. Even then he was fitful and had to be strapped down. No, the doctor decided, now was not the time to tell her. Tomorrow she could see for herself.

Casey spent the night in a hotel crowded with journalists and also people who lived near the wrecked village and thought it wise to be a little further away from the area. By careful listening Casey learned more details of the earthquake. At least a third of the village's tiny population of four hundred had been killed, at least another third injured. Many of the old houses and cottages that were not even near the enormous split in the earth had been demolished, killing or maiming their occupants. The most remarkable story was of the little girl and the man who had been rescued from the very jaws of the eruption. They'd been discovered alive inside the gigantic hole and had been pulled to the surface, the girl unconscious, the man in a state of shock, but nevertheless, very much alive. Only much later did Casey realise they had been talking of John Holman.

The next morning she went back to the hospital and was told she would be able to see him later on in the day, but to be prepared for a shock. The doctor she'd seen the night before explained quietly to her that Holman was no longer the man she had known, that he had gone uncontrollably insane. When the girl broke down, the doctor hastened to add that the illness could be short-term, that the experience he'd suffered might have only temporarily snapped his mind and given time it could heal itself. She went back to the hotel and cried her way through the day until it was time to go back to the hospital. They advised her not to see him, but she insisted – and then regretted her insistence.

The doctor had been right – he wasn't the man she knew. And loved. He was an animal. A foul-mouthed, raging animal. Heavy leather straps tied him to a bed. A bed in a special room for it contained only the bed; there were no windows and the walls were covered in a soft, plastic-like material. Only his head, hands and feet could move, and this they did in a constant, violent motion, his head thrashing from side to side, his throat bandaged, thick wadding secured in his mouth to prevent him from biting off his own tongue, his hands clenching and unclenching, like claws. And his eyes. She would never forget the maniac look in those enlarged, staring eyes. He had worked the wadding in his mouth loose and began to scream. She couldn't believe the obscenity she heard, that any human being could harbour the thoughts that flowed verbally from his lips. Although his eyes looked at her, he didn't see her. A nurse ran forward and once again stuffed the wadding back into his mouth carefully avoiding his snapping teeth.

Casey left in a wretched daze, tears blurring her vision. At first, she hadn't been sure if it even was John, his physical appearance had seemed so different, and now she wanted to tell herself that it hadn't been. But it was useless to pretend. She had to face up to the facts if she were to help him recover – and if he didn't? Could she go on loving the thing she'd just seen?

She returned to the hotel, her mind in a turmoil, her emotions confused. A conflict began deep inside her. After hours of weeping, of fighting the repulsion she felt for his madness, she began to lose the battle. She rang her father. He urged her to come home immediately and she had to resist the impulse to agree to it; she wanted his protection, his comforting words, the words that would take the responsibility away from her.

But no. She owed it to John to stay near him while there was a chance – the flimsiest chance. The illness couldn't destroy what had been, the closeness that had been theirs. She told her father she would stay until she knew about John one way or the other. She was adamant that he shouldn't come down, that she would come home only when satisfied John was beyond help.

Casey's wretchedness increased that evening when she visited Holman again. The doctor felt that she should know about the young child rescued with him who had died that afternoon without ever coming out of the unusual coma she'd been in since the eruption. They now thought she'd been affected by gas released from below the ground. It was possible that Holman also had been affected and this, in some strange way, was the cause of his madness. The next few days would tell if the brain damage was permanent or would pass. Or if the effects were fatal.

She hardly slept that night. Now that death had to be considered, her emotions had become clearer: if he lived, even if he were still insane, she would never leave him. Reality told her that her love could not be the same as before, that it would be a different kind of love, a love born out of his need for her. If he died – she forced her mind to accept the words – if he died, then she would forget the creature she had seen these last two days and remember only what he'd been, what they'd shared. In the early hours of the morning she finally fell into an exhausted and dream-filled sleep.

When she returned to the hospital in the morning, dread in her heart but still hopeful, Holman was completely sane. Weak, ashen-faced, but totally sane. And one week later, he was ready to go home.

3   33

Sitting on the steps next to him, Casey took Holman's hand. He kissed her cheek and smiled at her. 'Thanks,' he said.

'For what?'

'For being here. For not running away.'

She was silent.

'The doctors told me how I was,' he continued. 'It must have been frightening for you.'

'It was. Very.'

'They're still trying to work out how a complete maniac could become normal again so quickly. They say the gas, whatever it was, must have been responsible. It temporarily affected the brain then wore off. I was lucky. It killed the little girl.' He stared at the ground, unable to hide his grief.

She squeezed his hand and asked, 'Are you sure it's all right for you to leave the hospital so soon?'

'Oh, they wanted me to stay. Wanted to do more tests, find out if there'd be any permanent damage. But I've had enough. Reporters, television interviewers – they've hounded the survivors that are well enough, and I've been a prime target. Even Spiers came down yesterday to interrogate me.'

Spiers was Holman's immediate boss at his Ministry, a man he both admired and hated. Their many disputes arose mainly after Holman's various assignments had been completed, when he had provided all the evidence he could lay his hands on, presented all the facts to Spiers who had engineered the assignment, and then the man would take no action against the offenders. 'It will go on file,' he would say. What Holman never knew was the battle his superior went through to get action taken, but his power was limited against the overriding strength of wealth and politics.

'What did he want to know?' asked Casey.

'Whether I'd completed my weekend's assignment.' He couldn't tell her Spiers had come to find out if he had found any evidence that could connect the earthquake with experiments being carried out on the military base. Holman thought it unlikely and had no such proof anyway.

'Fat little toad! I don't like him,' said Casey.

'He's not really too bad. Bit cold, a bit hard – but he can be okay. Anyway, I've got to report to him tomorrow – ' he put up his hand at her protests, 'just to give him a debrief on the weekend job, then I'm on a week's leave.'

'I should think so too, after all you've been through.

'Yes, but honestly, I feel fine now. Throat's still a little sore, but they tell me I was lucky – the cut wasn't too deep – and God knows, I've had a good enough rest in here. Come on, let's leave before I go out of my mind again.'

He laughed at her frown.

It was just before Weyhill that they ran into the fog again. The roads had been fairly quiet, the weather fine. They kept to the smaller roads purposely, not wanting to rush back to London but to enjoy the passing countryside, the peaceful warmth of the summer morning.

When they saw the heavy cloud ahead of them it was about half-a-mile away, looking depressingly ominous. They could see its outermost edges quite clearly, but its top was more like the usual fuzzy-edged fog shape.

'Strange,' said Holman, stopping the car. 'Is it smoke or just a mist?'

'It's too heavy for mist,' replied Casey, staring ahead. 'It's fog. Let's go back, John, it's creepy.'

'It's too much of a detour to go back. Anyway, it isn't much of a fog, we'll soon pass through it. Funny, it's just like a wall, the sides are so straight.'

They both jumped at the sound of a horn as a coach sped past them heading towards Weyhill. Six small boys stuck their tongues out and waggled their hands at them from the back window as the school bus swung back into the proper lane.

'Bloody fool,' muttered Holman. 'He's heading right into it.' They watched it disappear down the road and then get swallowed up by the fog. 'He must be bloody blind!'

They suddenly realised the fog had crept much nearer to them. 'Christ, it moves fast,' said Holman. 'Come on then, let's go through it. It'll be okay if I take it easy.'

He put Casey's car into first and drove on, unaware that the girl at his side was becoming unnaturally nervous. She couldn't rationalise her apprehension, it was just that the black cloud somehow seemed pregnant with menace, like the heavy dark clouds just before a storm broke. She said nothing to Holman, but her hands gripped the sides of her seat tightly.

Very soon, they entered the fog.

It was much thicker than Holman had anticipated. He could barely see the road ahead. He drove cautiously, keeping in

35

second, using dipped headlights. He leaned close to the wind-screen for better vision, occasionally using his wipers to clear the heavy smog from the glass, keeping his side window open to look through now and again. The fog seemed to be tinged with yellow, or was it just the throwback glare from his head-lights? As the slightly acrid smell reached his nostrils, a tiny nerve twitched in his memory cells. It was something to do with the earthquake the week before. He still couldn't remember much about it – the doctors informed him this was perfectly normal, a certain part of his mind was still in a state of shock – but somehow the smell, the yellowish colour, the very atmos-phere stirred something inside him. He broke into a cold sweat and stopped the car.

'What's the matter, John?' Casey asked, alarm in her voice.

'I don't know. It's just a feeling. The fog – it seems familiar.'

'John, the papers said a cloud of dust or smoke came from the eruption; they thought it had been caused by a blast beneath the ground. This isn't a normal fog we're in. Could this be it?'

'No, surely not. It would have been dispersed by the wind by now, not hanging around in a great lump.'

'How do you know? If it came from deep underground, how do you know how it would act?'

'All right, maybe it is. Anyway, let's not sit here discussing it, let's try and get clear first.' He wound up the side window, hoping the action would not throw any fear into her. 'At the rate it's moving, I reckon it will be easier to try and go on through it rather than turn back.'

'Okay,' she answered, 'but please be careful.'

He edged forward, his eyes peering ahead into the gloom. They had made a hundred yards' slow progress when they came upon the coach lying half in a ditch alongside the road. They had nearly run into a small group of boys who had been stand-ing at the rear of the coach before Holman jammed on his brakes. Fortunately, they had been travelling so slowly they were able to stop almost immediately.

'Now come along boys, I've already told you to keep to the side, away from the road,' they heard a voice bellow.

Holman opened his door and climbed out of the car, telling Casey to remain inside. The slight but distinct odour of the fog disturbed him again as he closed the door behind him.

'Is anyone hurt?' he asked the spectral shape of the man he assumed was the boys' master.

36

'A few bruises here and there among the boys,' came the reply as the figure approached him, 'but I'm afraid our driver has suffered a nasty blow on the head.'

When the teacher was only three feet away Holman saw he was a tall, gaunt-looking man, with a hooked nose and deep-set eyes. He had only one arm, his right ending just above the wrist. The teacher went on, in a lower tone of voice, 'Mind you, it was all his fault, the idiot. He was so busy joking with the boys he didn't even notice the fog until he was in it and then he hardly slowed down even though I warned him.' He looked down at the pupils who had now clustered around him. 'Boys! I told you to get to the side of the road. Now the next boy who disobeys me gets a flogging. Move yourselves!'

They scattered, enjoying the fun now that they'd got over their initial shock.

'Let's have a look at the driver,' said Holman, 'maybe I can help.'

They walked to the front of the coach where they found the driver sitting on the grass beside the ditch nursing his head in his hands. He held a bloody handkerchief to his forehead and occasionally moaned as he rocked backwards and forwards. A group of boys stood around him, watching him both anxiously and curiously.

'Now, Mr Hodges, how are we feeling?' asked the teacher, hardly a trace of sympathy in his tone.

'Fucking awful,' came the muffled reply.

The boys tittered and hid smiles of delight behind shaking hands.

The teacher cleared his throat and stiffly ordered his pupils to go to the back of the coach and stay out of the road. 'Yes, well, let's have a look at the cut Mr Hodges, and perhaps we can do something about it.'

Holman bent down and brought the hand holding the blood-stained handkerchief away from the damaged forehead. The gash looked worse than it probably was. He took out his own handkerchief and pressed it to the cut telling the driver to hold it in place.

'I don't think it's serious, but we'd better get you to a hospital right away.'

'There's a doctor's surgery in the town ahead. I'm sure they'll look after Mr Hodges,' said the impatient teacher. 'The only problem is getting him there.'

'We'll take him and inform the police at the same time. They'll soon get a breakdown lorry to you and arrange other transport for the boys. Are you sure none of them are hurt badly?'

'Yes, quite sure, thank you. It's really very kind of you. I do hope we won't have to wait too long, this damp fog won't be good for the boys.'

As they helped the injured Hodges back to the car, the teacher explained the coach journey to Holman. 'We're from Redbrook House, a private boarding school in Andover. We were just on our way back from a nature ramble on the Plain, you know. It was a beautiful morning and the boys get so restless towards the end of term, I had to get them out into the fresh air. I cannot for the life of me imagine where this fog came from.'

Holman cast an anxious eye around him. The fog seemed as dense as ever.

'Of course, many of the boys' parents wanted me to send them home when that dreadful earth tremor occurred,' the master continued, 'but I was insistent that they remain and finish off the term. Freaks of nature, I told them, happen only rarely, perhaps once in a lifetime, and Redbrook certainly was not going to close down because of hysterical howlings of over-anxious parents. A few of them persisted of course, and I had no choice but to let their offspring go – but I can tell you, they took a very stiff letter with them!'

Holman smiled to himself at the prattling of the one-armed teacher. The old die-hard, traditionalist teachers still flourished despite the new wave of long-haired, liberal-minded younger educationalists. Well, there was good and bad to be said for both sides.

As the trio approached the yellow car, easily visible in the murky fog, Holman saw Casey's white face apprehensively watching them through the windscreen. She opened her door and made as if to get out to help them.

'No, stay there, don't get out!' he shouted at her.

Puzzled, she remained where she was, half in, half out.

'Close the door,' he told her, less sharply. She complied, the puzzled expression still on her face.

He opened the door on his side, pulled the seat forward and helped the injured driver to climb through into the back. Then he turned back to the teacher.

'If I were you, I'd get all the boys back into the coach and keep the door and windows closed.'

'Whatever for?' the teacher asked.

'Let's just say the fog can't be good for them. I'll get someone back to you as soon as possible, so just sit tight.' He got into the car and turned the ignition. Before he closed the door he reiterated his advice. 'Keep them inside and close all the windows.'

'Very well, Mr, er . . . ?'

'Holman.'

' . . . Holman, but I'm sure we'll be warm enough and a little fog can't do too much harm.' Oh can't it? thought Holman as he gunned the engine and cautiously moved off. I wonder? He still wasn't quite sure of his uneasiness about the fog. The doctors had said his breakdown could have been caused in some way as released gas from the cracked earth. It was a pretty far-fetched possibility, but that smell had seemed familiar some-how and he knew he'd never experienced it before the eruption. It was more instinct than judgement, but he had learned to trust his instincts implicitly. A groan from behind interrupted his thoughts.

'Ooh, 'ave I got a headache,' Hodges moaned loudly.

'We'll soon get you to a doctor,' Casey reassured him, reluc-tantly taking her eyes off the murky road ahead to examine the unfortunate coach driver.

'I'll get the blame for this,' he went on woefully. 'Summers'll make sure of that. Miserable bastard. Oh, sorry, miss,' he excused himself.

Summers, they assumed, was the teacher they'd just left with the boys.

'Never did like me. Didn't like the way I got on with the boys.'

'Is Redbrook his school?' asked Holman.

'Nah! 'e's only Deputy Head, but the way he carries on you'd think it was. The kids call him Captain Hook.' He laughed and winced at the effort. 'It was all his fault, any road.'

'What do you mean?'

'Wal', I was driving along, 'aving a bit of a laugh with the boys, y'know, showin' off a bit I suppose, and 'e starts snappin' at me like I was one of the kids. Wal', I turns round to give 'im the right answer, and wallop – we're in the ditch. Lucky I didn't go right through the windscreen, I can tell you. Anyway, I blacks out and the next thing I know, I wake up, blood pourin' down me face, and 'e's still going on at me. Ain't right, is it?'

Holman chuckled and said nothing. His amusement soon vanished when he realised the fog was becoming thicker. He slowed down to a crawling pace and leaned even further towards the windscreen.

'John, what's that?' Casey clutched at his arm, her eyes staring across him at something to his right.

He looked through his side window but saw only the swirling mist. 'What? I can't see anything.'

'It's gone. It may have been nothing, but I thought I saw a glow. Something white, shining through the fog, but it vanished almost immediately. I think a heavier bank of fog must have swept by, I can't see it anymore.'

'It might have just been a clear patch, the sun getting through somewhere.'

'Yes, maybe.'

Their attention was drawn back to their passenger as he began cursing again.

'Bloody weather. Bright one minute, fog the next. Goes with the times, it does.'

'What d'you mean?' Holman asked.

'Nice peaceful summer we've had, couldn't 'ave been better. Then what happens? A bloody earthquake, of all things. Here in Wiltshire!' He rocked forward in pain as his voice rose. 'And then yesterday. Did you hear about yesterday?'

Holman shook his head, still concentrating on the road. Casey replied, 'You mean the axe murders?'

'Yeah. In all the papers this mornin'. 'Appened fairly near the earthquake village, an' all. Rich bloke, Colonel something-or-other, murdered with 'is wife and all 'is staff, cook and a maid, I think. Done in with an axe. And the bloke they reckon done it chopped at 'is own wrists 'till he bled to death. Party of people came over to see this Colonel and found all the bodies just lyin' around. I dunno' what it's comin' to, one thing after another.'

'Yes,' said Holman, 'it's like you said. Sunny one minute, dark the next.'

'And now I suppose I'm goin' to lose me job over this.'

'No, I'm sure you won't,' Casey said sympathetically.

'Oh, you don't know old Captain Hook. Never 'as liked me.

Still, I know a few little secrets about him.' Hodges groaned again. 'How much further?'

For another painfully slow fifteen minutes they were immersed in the dense fog then, suddenly, they were clear. It was like passing through a door, the change was so abrupt.

'Christ,' muttered Holman in surprise. He'd been squinting into the mist and just had time to register it becoming slightly lighter when at once they were driving in bright sunlight. He and Casey looked over their shoulders at the thick yellowish-grey blanket behind them. Hodges was too busy nursing his own pain and grievances to take any notice. As they watched, it seemed to move away from them like a dark shroud being drawn across the countryside. Casey shivered and Holman smiled at her with a reassurance he hardly felt.

'It isn't natural,' the girl whispered.

Holman shook his head, but had no answer to give. He switched off the car lights and moved forward again, picking up welcome speed as he went. The village was soon reached and Hodges directed him to the police-station. He ran up the steps and quickly told them what had happened to the coach. The police sergeant couldn't quite understand Holman's anxiety when he learnt that none of the boys was seriously hurt. He was surprised and almost disbelieving about the fog, it certainly hadn't passed through the village and he'd had no reports of it from around the surrounding countryside. Nevertheless, he reassured Holman, he would get in touch with the garage and send one of his men out there right away. He gave him directions for the doctor's surgery and thanked him for the trouble he'd taken.

When Holman left the police-station he had a faint feeling of dissatisfaction. Perhaps he was making more of it than the situation warranted, after all, fog in England certainly wasn't unusual although at this time of year it was a little strange. It was difficult to conjure up the menacing atmosphere of the cloudy yellow-greyness in his mind now that he was in the bright sunshine. The fog seemed unreal, as though it had never really happened. Could it be he wasn't well yet? Was his mind still a bit 'disturbed'? He knew Casey had also been uneasy about the experience they'd been through, but was that merely the transference of his fears? He knew how easy it was for tension from one person to be passed on to another until a whole group of people were infected. He needed to relax. The

41

strain of the past hour had already drained him, left him feeling agitated and restless. Why hadn't he wanted Casey to get out of the car? Did he really think this fog had something to do with his own recent illness? He wasn't at all sure of his motives, but hadn't wanted her to be subjected to too much of the smoke-like substance. Maybe the feeling of apprehension would pass once his body – and his mind – had fully rested.

They drove the still grumbling Hodges to the doctor's surgery, left him in capable and friendly hands, then drove on to London.

Five

A few hours later, after stopping for a pub lunch on the way, they reached Holman's flat in St John's Wood Road, opposite Lord's cricket ground. He parked the car in the forecourt and wearily they took the lift to his flat at the top of the old but well-kept building. His flat was sparsely furnished, uncluttered and comfortable. A few original paintings hung on the walls, but otherwise the decorations were kept to a minimum. In one corner stood the tall, long stem of a plant, its length completely bare, but with thick rich foliage sprouting from its top. He claimed laughingly that it had climbed over the wall of the London Botanical Gardens and found its way to his flat because it was looking for someone to love. The truth was Holman had stolen it one night many years before on a drunken raid on the Gardens with some equally inebriated friends. He had no idea of the correct name for it so he called it George.

His bedroom window looked out on to a flat roof where he had spent many a peaceful summer's evening just gazing at the stars, a contrast to the side of him that demanded excitement, to be involved in trouble. The one big luxury he had allowed himself to indulge in was his bed. He liked to sleep, he liked to make love; when he slept he hated to feel cramped by a partner; when he made love, he hated to feel cramped by a bed. So it was logical his bed should take up most of the space in his medium-sized bedroom. On first seeing it, Casey had giggled; on sharing its luxury, she had become immensely jealous of Holman's past. But in the time she had known him, she had matured enough to accept the life he had obviously once led.

She made him coffee while he slumped in a chair, pulling his shoes off for greater comfort. She brought the cups in and sat at his feet, placing the coffee on the floor.

'How do you feel now, John?' she asked gently.

'Oh, a little bit tired, that's all. Post-hospital depression I think it's called.'

She rubbed the soles of his feet abstractedly. 'I've decided to leave Theo.' She always called her father by his first name, another habit Holman unreasonably found irritating.

'Leave him?' He sat up in surprise, studying her face as if her expression would confirm or deny her statement.

'Yes. I discovered a lot of things about myself when you were in hospital, John, the most important being that I love you more than I could have imagined possible. More than Theo. More than anything. I nearly gave up, darling. I nearly left you there when I thought you were beyond help.'

He leaned closer to her, taking her face in his hands, saying nothing.

'The way you were,' she continued, 'things you said. It frightened me – I couldn't believe it was you.'

'It wasn't really me, Casey,' he said softly.

'I know, John. But it was like a nightmare. Not knowing if you'd ever recover, ever be close to me again – ever hold me like this. I went home and rang Theo. I was going to leave you, to go home. But as I spoke to him I realised I couldn't. And when I went back to the hospital the next day and they told me there was the possibility that you could die – I realised I'd be nothing without you. My father could never mean as much to me again, he could never take your place.'

'Casey . . .'

'Believe me, John.'

'Casey, listen. Give it a couple of weeks; don't decide now.'

'I don't need to. I know.'

'All right, do it for me then. You've been through too much recently. I want you to be absolutely certain of how you feel – for both our sakes.'

'And what about you, John? Are you certain of your feelings?'

He lay back heavily in the armchair. 'Don't ask me yet. Too much has happened for me to be sure of anything at the moment.'

'Is that why you want me to think about it – because you need more time?' She bit her lip, now uncertain of his love.

'Partly, yes. I need to sort myself out too.'

Tears began to form in her eyes as she rested her cheek on his knee, not wanting him to see her weeping. He stroked her hair and they sat in silence for a few moments, then she looked up at him and said, 'John, let me stay tonight.'

'What about your father?' he asked.

'I've told you, he doesn't matter. I still love him, I could never lose that, but it's you now. I don't want to leave you. Let me stay for at least tonight.'

'Okay, Casey, why should I fight you off?' he answered, trying to lighten the mood.

'I'll ring Theo later and explain.' She knelt, bringing her face close to his. 'I don't need more time, John, but I'll take it. I want you to be sure, too, and if you should decide you don't really want me that badly . . . ' she hesitated, forcing herself to say the next words, ' . . . I'll go away.'

He kissed her lips, suddenly laughing at her sorrowful face. 'Okay, Casey,' he said, 'you've got a deal!'

They drank their coffee, both lost for a while in their own thoughts. Gradually, Holman began to relax. He pushed thoughts of the earthquake, the fog, and now Casey's decision from his mind. He never walked away from a problem, but occasionally liked to bury it and dig it up later. His moods changed as easily as traffic lights, a quality the girl sometimes adored, sometimes hated. This time, because she too needed some relief, she was gladly susceptible to it.

'You know, a week in that hospital, and not seeing you the weekend before . . . ' he looked down at her, a hint of a leer in his smile.

'Yes?' She smiled back at him.

'Well, I feel a bit like a monk. Celibate.'

'It's good for you.'

'I could go blind.'

She laughed and said, 'I thought you needed rest.'

'Quite right. Let's go to bed.'

'Promise me one thing.'

'Anything.' He began to unbutton her blouse, becoming impatient as the second button stuck. She undid it for him.

'Promise me you'll come back tomorrow after seeing Spiers. You won't get involved in another assignment.'

'You must be joking. I'm taking the rest of the week off even if the whole country cracks in half!'

He pulled her blouse free of her skirt and cupped her breast with his hand, sliding one finger inside the lacy material of her bra.

'What about you?' he asked. 'You won't be able to get any more time off, will you?'

'Oh, yes I will,' she answered, now unbuttoning his shirt. 'I've been sacked.'

His restless hand rested.

'What?'

'When I rang the boss and informed him I was staying near you for the week he politely told me not to come back, I would be replaced.'

'The little bastard,' Holman cursed.

'It's a relief,' she laughed. 'He was too jealous of my clothes anyway; I think he thought they'd look better on him.'

Holman got to his feet, discarding his unbuttoned shirt. 'I think you need comforting,' he said, taking her hand and leading her into the bedroom.

Holman strolled along Marsham Street enjoying the bustle, glad to be among normal, active people after the subdued confinement of the hospital. They flowed into their offices like ants into cracks beneath a stone, regretfully leaving the bright morning sun for the artificial glare of fluorescent tubes, allowing their personalities to emerge once again after brief hibernation during their journey to work. Holman entered the gloom of the large Environment building and took the lift to the eighth floor. He greeted Mrs Tribshaw, a middle-aged fluttery secretary he shared with a colleague, assuring her he was in the best of health after his misadventure with the earthquake, entered his office and closed the door on her excited queries as to the extent of his injuries.

'Hello, John.' His colleague, a cheerful Scot with only a trace of accent, looked up and greeted him with a quizzical grin. 'What the hell happened to you?'

'It's a long story, Mac, I'll tell you over a drink when we get the chance.'

McLellan continued to stare at Holman, still grinning inanely. They had often shared the same assignment and knew they could depend on each other in a tricky situation. He was slightly older than Holman, but a little more idealistic. Although he pretended to envy Holman's bachelor life-style, he secretly relished his own family life. Three kids – two boys, one girl – a fiery-tempered but good-natured red-headed wife, and a semi-detached in the better part of Wimbledon; not a lot he had to admit, but enough to keep him content. His one release was his job. Although Holman handled the more risky assignments, occasionally he was sent on one requiring subterfuge, a little deviousness. But on the whole, his tasks were fairly routine, yet even these he rarely found boring. He often laughingly explained to Holman it was the fact that he, a little Jock from Glasgow, could help to bring the arrogant, money-conscious, filth-disposing capitalists into line. Or that he, a modestly paid, underprivileged civil servant could find a flaw in the land-destroying schemes of his own government, his own bosses. True, his information was not always acted upon, in fact, he would grudgingly admit, in fifty per cent of the cases it was *not* acted upon, but he got a great kick on the occasions he succeeded. Holman called him a Communist infiltrator and he would laughingly admit it was true, although both knew it was far from the truth. When they worked together they enjoyed each other's company immensely, McLellan because he had the chance to lead the bachelor life for a brief time, Holman because he liked the Scot's dry sense of humour.

'Spiers has been calling for you,' Mac finally said, having satisfied himself that physically, at least, Holman seemed okay. 'He rang down about half-nine wanting to know where the hell you were.'

Holman walked around his desk and sat down, quickly looking through the memos that had piled up during his absence.

'Nothing changes, does it,' he observed, sifting through a stack of grey report pages. 'You're away for a week and you think everything's altered in that time; you come back feeling a stranger and within five minutes you've caught up with everything and you're back in the old routine.'

'Yes, well, if I were you, I'd get back into the old routine of seeing Spiers right away.'

'Right. I'll see you later, Mac, then I'm off for the rest of the week.'

'Lucky bleeder,' Mac grinned, and then his smile faded for an instant. 'I'm glad you're okay, John. Spiers didn't say much about it, but I gather you went through a rough time. You take it easy.'

'Sure, Mac. Thanks.'

Holman winked at Mrs Tribshaw as he strode through the outer office raising his hand to still her fretful questions and climbed the stairs to the ninth floor to Spiers' office.

'Is he in?' he asked the secretary, who stopped typing and looked up startled.

'John! Are you better?' He felt slightly embarrassed at her obvious joy at seeing him.

'I'm fine. Is he in?'

'What? Oh, yes, you can go right in. What happened, John? We heard you were involved in that awful earthquake.'

'Tell you later.' He knocked on the door and entered the inner office.

Spiers looked up from his papers, peering at him through thick-lensed glasses. 'Ah, John. Feeling okay? Good. Take a seat, I'll be with you in a moment.'

Holman sat, studying the bald head his chief presented to him as he continued to read through his papers. Finally, Spiers shuffled them together and put them neatly to one side of his desk.

'Well, John,' he said, staring at Holman with eyes that penetrated yet seemed to see nothing. 'I've had your films processed and examined the contacts. There do seem to be a few strange items among them, but they really don't affect us in any way. Now, the shots of the countryside within the perimeter are very interesting, but we'll get to that later. First, I'd like you to tell me again about the earthquake, right from the beginning, leave nothing out.'

Holman told him as much as he could remember, but his mind went blank as he reached the point where he had rescued the girl.

Spiers leaned forward on his desk. 'John, try to think. Did you hear an explosion before the ground opened?'

'No, definitely not. I heard the rumble, that's all, and then the crack as the ground split, but I'm sure there wasn't an explosion.'

Spiers slumped back in his chair, taking off his glasses and polishing them with his handkerchief. He cleared his throat sharply and rubbed the bridge of his nose with finger and thumb, as though tired. He replaced his glasses and leaned forward again. 'You see,' he said, 'a cloud of smoke was reported rising out of the ground just after they'd brought you up.'

'You think there was an explosion then?'

'Possibly.'

'Connected with the military base?'

'No, no. We've absolutely no grounds to suspect anything like that. You said you thought it was unlikely yourself.'

'Yes, I know, but I'm beginning to wonder now. Who knows what they're doing out there? On the way back yesterday, I ran into fog. Fog – on a hot summer's day! Are they using some new kind of smoke-screen device that they've just let drift off their patch into the rest of the countryside?'

'Oh, come now. That could have been caused by anything – a change in temperature, a factory near-by. I ran into some fog myself when I came down to see you. Salisbury Plain is full of mists at any time of year; we can't blame the military for everything, you know.'

'But you think they had something to do with the eruption?'

'Certainly not. I know there are certain aspects of the Ministry of Defence which we both dislike, but you can be sure they would never be as irresponsible as to have caused a disaster like this.'

'What about the photographs? They show some pretty strange things. You saw the dome?'

'They prove nothing!' Spiers was becoming angry and realised it. Once again he slumped back in his chair and went on more quietly, 'Anyway, I've had them destroyed.'

'What?'

'Do you realise the trouble you could be in – the department could be in – if it was discovered we held photographs of secret military installations?'

'But what was the point in going down there?'

'To take photographs, yes! But not to be used by us. I merely wanted proof for myself, so that I knew there was rich land being wasted, acres of arable soil, beauty spots, so that I was in a stronger position to argue that the area should be given back to us. My God, we could be put away for years for the sort of photographs you took!'

A seed of suspicion was planted in Holman's mind. 'You suspect something, don't you?' he asked Spiers quietly.

Spiers spoke wearily: 'Look, I've been on to the Ministry of Defence. There is a massive clampdown in security – I don't know if it means anything, and I'm powerless if it does. I have a meeting arranged for this afternoon with the Defence Minister and Sir Trevor Chambers, and we hope to get some answers.'
Sir Trevor Chambers was their department's Parliamentary

Under-Secretary, a gruff, forceful man, who indeed liked to get answers. 'Needless to say, this is strictly between you and me.'

'And if you do discover the army is involved?'

'We shall have to wait and see.'

'Oh yes, the usual answer. I suppose it'll go on file, will it?'

'Damn your belligerence! Just who do you think you are? I think . . . ' He began to falter and without thinking Holman took advantage of the break in his words.

'For once, let's slay them! If they are responsible, let's break their bloody arms, let's –'

Spiers seemed to regain his composure and said, 'Let's remain calm. There is nothing to gain . . . ' Once again, his voice trailed off in mid-sentence.

Still unaware in his anger of the change that seemed to be taking place in his chief, Holman raged on, until finally there was no ignoring the strange, vacant look that had come into the eyes of Spiers behind the heavy glasses.

'What's wrong?' Holman asked, concerned. 'What's – ' He broke off as Spiers rose from his chair, staring over Holman's head. Spiers turned and walked to the window; Holman was still too puzzled to move. Spiers opened the window and turned again to look at the surprised younger man, his eyes for a second almost losing their blankness, a flicker of recognition returning to them but lost again in an instant. Then he turned back to the window, climbed on to the sill, and before Holman could make a move towards him, jumped out.

Holman was stunned. He sat rigid, his mouth open, unable to take in what he had just witnessed. Then, shouting Spiers' name, he rushed to the window. He saw the crumpled figure lying on the pavement nine floors below, a pool of blood spreading swiftly from beneath the smashed head. From that distance, he could just make out one hand curiously raised in the air, the elbow resting on the ground, the fingers of the hand clenching and unclenching in a twitching, spasmodic motion. Then the whole body arched upwards in a violent jerk and just as suddenly collapsed again, this time to lie perfectly still, the twitching hand finally resting.

Holman drew in a long, uneven breath and leaned against the window frame. People were rushing towards the broken body, others keeping well away, averting their eyes. He turned

50

back in towards the room and saw Spiers' secretary standing in the doorway, a frightened look on her face.

'He – he jumped,' Holman managed to say at last.

She backed away from him into her own office. The door burst open behind her and several people rushed in. 'What's happened?' one of the men demanded to know. 'Who was it?'

Holman sank into the chair Spiers had occupied only moments ago, strangely, perversely, noting it was still warm. He didn't answer the people who crowded around him; he just sat staring at the desk top. What had happened? Why had he jumped? What had unhinged his mind so suddenly? The feeling came over Holman again. The sense of his skin crawling, the feeling he'd had when they'd entered the fog. It couldn't be, there was no reason to it. But his brain needed no reason, the feeling was enough. He sprang to his feet and pushed past the startled people crowding into the office. He had to get to Casey.

Six

Redbrook House stood in its own grounds in one of the quieter roads in Andover. A long gravel drive with trees on either side separated it from the outside world, the large red-bricked building looming frighteningly for any young newcomer taking his first journey down to it. Though built long before, it was established in 1910 as a school for only the privileged classes. It flourished successfully until the 1930s when it suddenly fell out of favour with the very rich who had begun to notice that some of the boys admitted were not quite as well-bred as their own offspring, though the parents were obviously wealthy enough to afford the exorbitant fees the school demanded; but then, money was not just a matter of inheritance anymore. The school declined in stature over the next fifteen years until the arrival of an eager, energetic and young deputy headmaster who managed to sweep away the old traditions and teaching methods maintained from Lord Redbrook's days, and to introduce new, more exciting ways of training, more vigorous approaches to the old and often boring subjects. Within five years he had established himself as headmaster and rejuvenated the school into a modern, forward-looking college, still private, but not quite as exclusive. His name was Hayward, and now, after over thirty years, the very methods he had introduced were the old, tired ways.

Five years before Hayward had taken on a deputy headmaster in hope of breathing new life into the school, knowing his methods were out of date but loving the old place too much to leave it himself. And, after all those years, perhaps too afraid to leave. The Governors of the school had, over the last few years, frequently urged him to retire, but felt too much compassion for the old man to make it a directive. It was they who had suggested he take on a new deputy head, the old one

52

having died two years before and never been replaced. Hayward would have considered a much younger man for the job, a man perhaps in his late twenties as he had been when he had joined the school, fresh-minded and eager to experiment, but such teachers were hard to find for a school like this. The younger men were more ambitious. They sought the more outward-going establishments where they could reap the glory without a long, uphill struggle. And Mr Summers came highly recommended by one of the Governing Committee's members.

Summers had been a captain in the army during World War II and had lost an arm in the course of it. He never talked about his injury or how he had acquired it. Indeed, he rarely spoke of his war-time exploits at all, and even less of his career as a schoolmaster. Although Hayward was disappointed by his assistant's narrow-minded educational theories, he had to admit the man was generally very competent. Disliked by the boys, he was sure, but he did show an extreme interest in and devotion to the school and would no doubt take over his position as head eventually. But his constant carping was becoming increasingly irritating.

Summers had turned the business of the crashed coach into a major issue, condemning poor Hodges out of hand, demanding his instant dismissal. The blame belonged entirely to Hodges, he had informed the headmaster, for speeding in such dangerous weather, showing off in front of the boys. He was too friendly with the boys anyway.

When Hayward had confronted the wretched-looking driver, who acted as janitor, gardener, and performed countless other tasks around the school, he had admitted it was true, but had gone on in a surly tone to imply certain notions about the deputy head. It was because of these implications that Hayward had decided to sack Hodges, not because of the misadventure in the fog. He could not allow the man to go around spreading these allegations against one of the members of his staff, particularly as he could provide no proof of them. As for Summers, Hayward would not even question the man; it would be too embarrassing for both of them. But he would certainly keep an eye on him.

Tomorrow Hayward would send for Hodges and tell him of his decision to let him go and warn him, warn him forcefully, not to spread any malicious slander which would cause him to end up in court. He thanked God the crash itself hadn't been serious; none of the thirty-six boys taken along had been hurt badly, a few bruises here and there, nothing to worry about. Only the unfortunate Hodges had sustained a nasty knock on the head, but even he, after a good night's rest, seemed physically sound. It was such a pity he had to get rid of the man, thought Hayward with a sigh, but good teachers were harder to replace than odd-job men.

Hodges sat on the old broken armchair in the basement storeroom he called his office and sipped at his strongly brewed tea. He poured some Scotch into the tin mug, swirling it around to mix with the hot liquid. He grunted several times as he stared into the thick brew, shrugging his shoulders and clucking his tongue.

That's cooked his goose for 'im, he told himself with a grin. Thought 'e'd got me in trouble, did'e? Oh, yes, well I soon turned the tables on 'im, didn't I? He sniggered aloud. He wasn't at all drunk; the whisky with his tea was his usual mid-morning break. Old Captain Hook is really goin' to pay for it this time. Didn't recognise me when 'e first came to the school, did 'e? But I recognised 'im all right. I was just a corporal then, 'e was a smart-arsed captain, but word gets around on an army camp. Oh, yes, we knew about 'im.

He thought back to the old days: to the huge army installation at Aldershot, the rough training ground for thousands of raw recruits. There had been tension in the air in those days; the war was in its third year, every week more and more soldiers were being shipped abroad, and each week they seemed younger, less experienced. Hodges was a corporal in the cookhouse and was content to idle away the war as such. He knew of Captain Summers, had heard the rumours about him, sniggered with his cronies each time they saw the thin, waspish figure march by, saluting but wriggling their little fingers at him when he had passed. But Summers hadn't been the only one; in a camp that size and with so many raw young men, homosexuality was not too unusual. It was sneered at, true, despised by most, but many had secretly indulged in its illicit pleasure. Hodges had even tried it himself once, but found it painful and 'too much like bloody hard work!' for his liking. The rumoured 'bromide in the tea' didn't seem to do much good. He used to chuckle to himself when on night duty at the thought of all those pricks raised

54

secretly towards the stars, pumped by thousands of hands all over the camp.

But Summers had propositioned the wrong new recruit one day. He had looked fresh-faced and girlish enough, but too late, the Captain discovered he had been conscripted with a bunch of his mates from North London. The boy had told him what he could go and do with himself and then applied some threatening blackmail to gain himself and his friends special privileges as well as the odd quid or two.

After only a few months, when the boy learnt he was going to be shipped abroad and suspecting that Summers had something to do with the arrangement, he and three of his bunch had waited one night on a quiet stretch of road leading to the camp, knowing that Summers would be returning alone on his bike. He often had assignations with young men from the town or arranged to meet a soldier there, always returning alone, always using the second-hand bike he had bought himself rather than taking the bus or begging a lift from one of his motor-possessing fellow officers. The group waited patiently, drinking beer and giggling as they described what they would do to the Captain when they got hold of him.

And then, after an hour's wait, they caught sight of him coming towards them along the dark road. They waited for him to draw level and then pounced, restraining their shouts of glee and anger for fear of being heard by anyone else who might be coming along in the distance. They began to beat him viciously, giving him no chance to recognise any one of them. His cries of fright and pain were cut off by a vicious kick to the throat. He drew his legs up and covered his head with his arms to protect himself, but the constant kicks and punches forced him to try to crawl away. Suddenly, over the screams of the terrified man, they heard the roar of an approaching lorry and saw the side lights in the not-too-far distance.

Taking advantage of the sudden break in their assault, Summers scrambled to his feet and staggered across the road, falling rather than jumping over a fence before they realised what had happened. With a shout, two of them chased after him, the other two deeming it wiser to take the opposite direction and hide in the bushes until the lorry had passed. The aggrieved boy was one of the pursuers and he had no intention of allowing the officer to escape so lightly.

Summers stumbled across the open field, panic lending him

55

speed, the dull thud of boots on grass behind him giving him strength. Without seeing where he was going, or caring, he ran headlong into a barbed-wire fence. He did not see the warning signs spaced at regular intervals along the cruel wire fence, nor would he have understood them if he had – his terror was greater than his rationality. His cry of pain as a barb gashed his cheek brought renewed shouting and cursing from behind. He climbed through the fence, ripping his uniform, wickedly tearing his flesh, and ran headlong into the minefield.

The boy behind, ignoring the warnings in his rage, followed him through, pulling a knife from his trouser pocket, knowing he would soon catch up with his quarry. His companion called after him, warning him of the danger, shouting for him to come back, but he was too close to Summers now. The Captain had fallen to his knees and had raised one arm towards the boy as though to ward him off, blubbering like a baby, pleading.

The boy grinned. It didn't matter that the queer had recognised him. He hadn't intended it to go this far, but now he decided. He would be overseas soon, probably killed in this fucking war, so the Captain was going to pay. No one would know who'd done it, he was a known poof. It could've been anyone. He raised the knife so the officer could see it clearly, enjoying the new paralytic fear in the other's eyes. He grinned nastily as he walked towards the officer.

The explosion killed the boy instantly, throwing his body into the air as though it were a leaf blown by the wind. The Captain was knocked back by the blast and when he tried to sit up, his right arm would not support him. When he tried to see why, he dully registered that part of his arm wasn't there any longer.

They found him a little later, sitting in the middle of the minefield, holding the bloody stump of his right arm, still wondering what had happened to the rest of it.

Everyone in camp knew what had happened all right, even though it had been hushed up. It had caused quite a stir and Hodges had relished every minute of it along with a thousand others. Summers had been discharged, of course, but on medical grounds; a one-armed captain was no use in a war. Hodges himself, to his regret, had been shipped off abroad a few months later and had soon forgotten the incident, his dim mind concentrating only on survival. It was not until five years ago when he'd shown the new deputy head into Mr Hayward's study that he'd remembered. Summers hadn't recognised him of course, but the one arm, the thin waspish figure, had brought it all back. He debated with himself whether he should inform the headmaster or not; a man like that shouldn't be around young boys. He decided not to, feeling that somehow the knowledge might be put to his advantage eventually. Well, he had been right about that – today had proven it. Occasionally, he had enjoyed himself by hinting to Summers that he knew of his past. Nothing direct, of course, just a seemingly casual remark about his army days, about the war, the 'queer' things that had happened. Hints as subtle as a kick in the groin, but Summers would merely look at him as though he were something the dog had neglected to bury.

He drained the brownish tea, took a swig from the whisky bottle for good measure, wiped his mouth with the back of his hand, and picked up the garden shears with the intention of trimming the hedges outside the front gate. He ignored the headache, blaming it on the blow on the head he'd received the day before. He went upstairs.

Summers sat in his study engaged in writing a full report of the coach incident for the school governors. He implicated Hodges, the driver, as wholly responsible because of reckless driving in extremely adverse weather. He finally put down his pen and sat back in his chair with a satisfied smile, quickly scanning the report then picking it up again to add a few words here and there, occasionally deleting a sentence, adding another, until he was sure that he was completely vindicated from any blame. After all, it was the headmaster's idea that he should take his form out to the Plain in the first place. End-of-term restlessness, indeed. If he had had his way, the boys would have had a twenty-times-around-the-playing-fields trot to work off any restlessness they might feel. He rubbed his eyes vigorously, blinking rapidly when he took his hand away. Dratted headache! Throughout the morning, he'd felt a sharp pain across his eyes, only lasting a few seconds at a time, but nevertheless, extremely painful.

He shuffled the pages of his lengthy report together, now completely satisfied that it was ready to be typed by Miss Thorson, the school's secretary and administrative clerk. Only the fact that it would be signed by the headmaster as well as himself prevented him from adding a few derogatory comments concerning other matters relating to the running of the school. However, he could always filter these through verbally to the Board via his personal contact.

And that my friend, he smiled to himself as he rose from his desk, is your goose cooked at any rate. He walked to the window, thinking of the despicable coach driver, Hodges. He was sure he had known the man years ago when he'd been in the army, but could not remember from which camp. Something in the man's manner disturbed him, the seemingly casual remark, the sly look that crossed his face when he mentioned the war. Did he imagine he could intimidate him in some way? What exactly did Hodges know of his past? Well, whatever the loathsome man knew or did not know, he was a reminder of the past. And the past was something Summers wanted desperately to forget.

He raised the stump of his arm, the sight of it reviving memories of pain and humiliation. Had Hodges known the full story? Had his crafty comments alluded to the terrible incident and the reason for it? No, the army had been discreet. The few brother officers that had known of his weakness, and indeed, some of whom shared it, had covered up the affair as only the services could. He, himself, could not remember much about that night, but even now, thirty-odd years later, he could still feel the pain in his hand as though it were still there. The nights he had lain awake because of the dull, throbbing ache in a non-existent limb, the pain not coming from the healed over stump, but from below it, where there was nothing.

And the damage had been much greater than just the maiming of his body. The maiming of his mind had caused him even greater suffering. Although the desire had still been there for a while after the accident, he discovered his body could no longer fulfil his needs. The discovery had frightened him, filling him with suicidal despair. But to kill himself required more courage than he would ever possess, so he had survived the mental torture and the physical wound, not because he was courageous, defiant to adversity, but because he was afraid to die.

Then, mercifully, after a few years, even the desire began to fade as though his mind had accepted the disability, not just compromised, but given in completely to the impotence of his body. He felt no yearning towards the young boys he taught, or attraction to the young men he came in contact with, although

58

he still liked to be around them. The sight of youthful bodies no longer stirred him, but he could appreciate their beauty, like a man without sense of smell could continue to appreciate the sight of a rose.

Out of the corner of his eye, Summers caught sight of a figure lumbering along the driveway towards the main gate. Hodges. The hunched, shuffling gait was unmistakable. Summers smiled to himself, feeling a sense of agreeable pleasure in the knowledge that soon the man would no longer be an annoyance to him. He noted the bandaged head, glad that the injury had been inflicted. You deserve worse, he thought to himself, and that's just what you are going to get. Old Hayward was too soft, but this time he would not be able to dismiss his recommendation that Hodges be sacked. The report would have to go before the Governing Committee and they certainly would not tolerate the irresponsible actions of the driver-cum-odd-job man.

He abruptly turned from the window and glanced at his watch. Time to do a round of the school before his next lesson. He often did a quick tour of the school in his free period, feeling it was his duty as deputy head to make a regular inspection of the classes while lessons were in progress, even visiting the empty dormitories to ensure the boys had left them neat and tidy, beds made, side-lockers carefully packed. Many a boy had been punished for leaving a discarded sock under a bed. He secretly enjoyed going through their lockers, seeking out pornographic photographs or books, various items that could be confiscated, even sniffing at dirty handkerchiefs for signs of masturbation.

The boys, from bitter experience, knew of his quirks and were careful not to leave any incriminating evidence lying around. One had foolishly left a drawing of a one-armed man, crudely resembling Summers, on his knees peeping through a keyhole, the caption reading: 'Beware, beware, Captain Hook is always there – especially if you are bare.' The culprit had been severely dealt with by Summers personally, the headmaster not even being informed of the matter.

Summers left his study, ignoring the sudden pain again before his eyes, carrying the report under his arm. As he walked along the corridor he listened at each classroom door, almost wishing to hear the sounds of rowdiness. When he reached the head-master's outer office he handed over the document to the busy Miss Thorson. Satisfied with her guarantee to type it before lunch, he continued his round of the school. His own form, he knew, would be in the gymnasium, a comparatively new addition to the old school, a building that stood across the small playground away from the main building itself. They had all fully recovered from their shake-up of the previous day, a few proudly displaying their bruises to the other boys in the school who had not been on the outing to the Plain, and all glorifying the event beyond the facts. As Summers crossed the playground, unconsciously eager to see the boys performing their physical exercises, he hummed a tune to himself.

Hodges had almost reached the main gate when he suddenly stopped. He stood there for several minutes before he sank to his knees, dropping the cutting shears, holding his hands to his face. He rocked backwards and forwards for a few moments then fell forward so that he was on all fours, staring at the ground. The shears lay beneath him, glowing dully in the shadow of his body. He crouched back on his knees and grasped the handles bringing the implement up before his eyes, staring at the shears without comprehension. He opened and closed them with one sharp snapping movement, then slowly rose to his feet. He turned and walked back towards the school, holding the shears before him with both hands as though they were a water diviner. He entered the main entrance to the old building and passed the open doorway to the headmaster's outer office. Miss Thorson barely gave him a glance as she busily tapped away at her typewriter. As he walked down the corridor towards the rear of the school he caught sight through the open doorway to the playground of a black-gowned figure walking briskly towards the gymnasium. The thin, waspish figure, the stump of one arm swinging at his side, told him who the figure belonged to. He followed.

The boys had stopped halfway through the PE exercises leaving Osborne, their burly physical training master, jumping on the spot alone, arms and legs snapping in-out, in-out. One boy had ceased jumping first, then all the others, as one, had followed suit. They stood rigid, staring at the energetic teacher, their arms at their sides, no words passing between them, but somehow mentally in tune with one another. Osborne finally stopped his prancing and glared at the boys.

'Who told you to stop?' he thundered at them. 'Well?'

The boys just stared.

'Get cracking right away!' He began jumping on the spot again but stopped as he realised they were not following his example. He marched angrily towards the boy nearest to him, unable to understand this sudden attitude, suspecting he might be the victim of some practical joke. Although a big bluff man who liked to shout and always reacted swiftly and roughly to any insolence, he was popular among the pupils and to some, a kind of hero. His prowess at all forms of athletics and sports had won him the respect even of his fellow teachers.

'What's the game, Jenkins?' he demanded of the blank-faced boy before him. The boy's lips moved but no sound came from them. He pushed roughly past him to the next boy.

'Come on, Clark, what's all this about, eh?'

Clark, one of his personal favourites because of his promising ability as a sportsman, said nothing, but stared at the teacher as though he'd never seen him before.

'All right, all right, you've had your little prank, but I'm going to give you five seconds to get weaving again!' He strode into the middle of them. 'One . . . '

He failed to notice Clark, now behind him, walk towards a cricket bat lying on one of the benches at the side of the gym.

' . . . two . . . I'm warning you boys, you're all going to be punished for this! Three . . . '

Clark picked up the bat and walked back with it towards the angry teacher.

'Four. This is your last chance . . . '

As his lips formed the word 'five', Clark raised the bat high and brought it crashing down on the back of Osborne's head. The teacher staggered forward as the hall filled with the crack of the impact between wood and skull. Clutching the back of his head, bent double, almost blind with pain, he turned in time to see the heavy bat swinging down towards him again. He cried out in horror, the look of questioning on his face barely registering before it was erased under the impact of the second blow.

He sank to the ground, still conscious but painfully stunned. He sprawled forward as the bat landed again, blood now running down his neck, staining his blue track-suit. The boys surged forward as one, shouting in a wild fury, stamping on the limp man with plimsoled feet. They tore the trousers of his track-suit from his body and turned him over on to his back, grabbing and kicking at his exposed testicles. Several tore off their own shorts and vests and began rubbing at their own already enlarged penises. One of the smaller boys jumped on the teacher and tried to enter him as though he were a woman, but was dragged off and beaten to the ground by the others. They pulled the top half of the track suit off so Osborne was completely naked, then dragged him towards the wall-bars. The bars were of the type that swung away from the wall when in use, so that climbing ropes hung from the tops of their frames.

The boys lifted Osborne and viciously pushed him back against the bars, two climbing either side of him to loop the hanging ropes through the wooden bars and lashing his wrists to them high above his head. Then his feet were pushed through the lower rungs so that they were trapped by the ankles.

While some spat, kicked, punched or just jeered at the hanging man, others ran towards the huge sports chest and brought out wicket stumps, skipping ropes, more bats. One boy struggled with a heavy medicine ball. Their laughter and shouting stopped as they formed a semi-circle around the moaning figure. Blood from Osborne's head wounds spread down his body as he writhed feebly in his agonising position. Then, in turn, they began to beat him with the wicket stumps, lashing him with the wooden ends of the skipping ropes, striking him with the bats. His genitals were crushed by one of the stronger boys who systematically hit at Osborne's knee caps and private parts. Clark took the medicine ball and aimed it at Osborne's head, making it crack back against the wall bars under the impact of the throw. The boys all bore the same animal look of madness on their faces, their eyes wide, their mouths slack and drooling, the insane excitement of their actions making them scarcely human. All except one. One small boy crouched shivering in a far corner, too terrified to run away, too paralysed to take his eyes off the incredible scene taking place. A boy who had not been allowed to accompany the others on their coach trip the day before because he was recovering from an illness. He crouched there in a tight ball, his legs drawn up, clutching them with his arms, his nose buried into his knees – hoping, praying that the others would not notice him.

Summers reached the entrance to the gymnasium and paused; the pain in his head was becoming more severe. He dabbed a handkerchief to his forehead, wiping away the beads of sweat that had broken out. Perhaps I'm coming down with something, he thought. Perhaps the crash yesterday had more effect on me than I imagined. Oh well, it will soon be end of term and then I'll have a couple of months to rest and forget about these wretched boys for a while.

He opened the door and stopped again, this time with shock. His mouth dropped open in a soundless scream, his legs almost gave way beneath him. The boys, most of them naked, were milling around something red and pink hanging from the wall bars. It looked like a carcass, a bloody, butcher's carcass – and then he realised it was Osborne. Surely dead; the head hung loosely down towards his chest, the hands hung limply from the ropes that bound them. He saw now that the body was a mass of bruises and contusions, blood flowing down from a head wound. He could see that some of the boys' feet were red from the pool that had formed on the ground. They turned to stare at him as he stepped forward, still unable to speak. He saw that some of the boys lay on the floor writhing in their own private ecstasy as they masturbated, and others were coupled together. He saw the damage they had done to the obscene-looking body, the beating they had dealt it. He saw the boys watching him, *his* boys, so pure in their innocence, so evil in their deviation. Standing before him, magnificent in their nakedness!

He suddenly felt a stirring. A stirring in a region that had lain dormant for so many years. He looked down, amazed at the thrusting bulge from between his legs. A cloud seemed to haze over his eyes and he shook his head jerkily. Then a smile formed on his lips.

He strode forward towards the silent boys.

'Yes,' he said urgently. 'Yes, yes!'

Hodges walked across the playground, still holding the shears before him, his eyes focused only on the door ahead. He reached it and pushed it open. There was no reaction on his face as his eyes fell upon the bizarre scene before him, and only a dull reaction in his brain. Two men were tied to the wall bars on the far wall; one hanging still and quiet, his body now hardly recognisable as that of a man, as the other writhed and squirmed and moaned, not with pain, but with the pleasure pain brought. One arm was tied by the wrist to the wooden struts of the wall bars, the other was tied between the shoulder and elbow because there was no wrist. His feet were trapped inside the lower rungs, bent slightly at the knees so that the pelvis was thrust forward. Both men were naked so Hodges could see the huge, erect penis of the one who appeared to be alive. The boys were beating at the organ with wooden sticks, while others were lashing at the man with ropes. The man was Summers. His eyes gleamed with the excitement, his head twisted with ecstasy.

'Captain Hook,' said Hodges aloud.

All eyes turned towards him. Even Summers stopped his squirming to look. He walked forward, brandishing the large garden shears, snapping them open and shut. 'Captain Hook, Captain Hook,' he repeated over and over again as he walked towards the helpless figure, an evil grin spread across his features.

Summers also smiled as Hodges stood before him, saliva running from his mouth. His breath came in short, sharp heaves as he looked expectantly at the odd-job man. Hodges' eyes travelled down the bare torso before him until they reached the huge, swollen penis. He grasped it with one hand and chuckled throatily, the laugh becoming insanely loud. Summers grinned back at him, his head nodding in a seemingly meaningless gesture.

Hodges released the throbbing member and slowly raised the shears, so that it was between the two sharp blades.

'Yes, yes,' Summers cried, his whole body now quivering with excitement.

The boys watched in silence as the two blades snapped together and the scream echoed around the gymnasium.

Seven

Holman impatiently stabbed at the lift button. He was breathing hard, having left the taxi in which he'd raced back to St John's Wood, trapped in the inevitable traffic jam. The taxi driver's look of astonishment had turned into one of delight as he clutched the couple of pound notes Holman had hastily thrust into his hand. Fortunately the snarl-up had not been far from Holman's flat, but the sprint down the road had left him breathless and with a painful stitch in his side. He jiggled with the button, knowing it wouldn't make the lift come any sooner, but unable to stand there inactive. It finally arrived just when he was considering using the stairs and he abruptly pushed past the middle-aged, blue-haired woman who emerged. She gave him a look of disgust as the door closed telling the Pekinese at her heels that rude young men like that should be birched and made to sweep the streets.

Holman thumped the side of the lift with the soft underside of his fist as it began its slow ascent. Surely Casey would be all right. She had stayed in the car during the incident with the fog so it may have had no effect on her at all. And what about himself? He felt okay and he'd been fully exposed to it. But Spiers? He'd said he'd run into some fog when he'd been down to visit him. Could it have been the same fog? Then he remembered the slightly acrid smell, the tinge of yellow in the mist; it had seemed familiar at the time, and now he began to remember his experience in the fissure. The mist that had risen from the depths of the crevice – yellow, sharp smelling. Was it the same? Had it caused his madness? Or was he still mad?

The lift jerked to a stop and he gave the slow moving door a helpful shove sliding through when the opening was wide enough. He reached the door of his flat fumbling for the key, trying to calm himself, only too willing to appear foolish if she was perfectly all right. He opened the door and a chill ran

5

through him as he saw the place was in darkness. Perhaps she was still sleeping and had not bothered to draw the curtains. No, he had drawn them open himself that morning. He stood in the doorway and called out her name, not too loudly, not wanting to alarm her. He walked to the half-open door to the lounge. Pushing the door wider, he reached in and switched on the light. The room was empty. Everything was as he'd left it except for the closed curtains. He tried the kitchen. Empty. He walked softly to the bedroom door, grasped the handle, and gently pushed it open.

'Casey?'

Silence.

He could see the bed through the gloom but could not tell if its ruffled blankets covered a sleeping body. He stepped into the room and walked towards it.

Only the harsh, dry chuckle he heard behind him saved his life. He whirled around at the sound, the movement causing the kitchen knife Casey was plunging down towards his back to miss and slew through the material of his coat sleeve. He gasped with pain as the blade cut a fine line across the muscle of his arm, but the shock caused him to fall back and so avoid the knife on its return journey. She stood before him, familiar, but a stranger. Her eyes were cold, her mouth was drawn back in a grimace that resembled the frozen smile he'd seen on dead animals. Her brown-blonde hair hung limply across her face as though she'd been caught in the rain, there were long scratch marks on her cheeks where she'd raked them with her fingernails. A stream of saliva glistened on her delicate chin. She held the knife above her head and the dry, harsh chuckle came again from her throat. She plunged down once more with the knife, but this time Holman was ready. He stepped back and tried to grab her wrist, but missed. As the knife swept up again, the long, wicked-looking blade aimed at his stomach, he caught her arm and moved in towards her, his other arm encircling her waist.

Their heads were close together, almost touching, and suddenly she sank her teeth into his cheek, biting deep and hard. He wrenched his head away, feeling the skin tear, but oblivious to any pain. They fell backwards, on to the bed. Snarling noises came from her lips as they struggled for the knife and the fingernails of her free hand tried to rake his face. He twisted her wrist, trying to make her release the weapon, but her strength was incredible. He got his other arm underneath her chin, not wanting to hurt her but knowing he had no choice. He pushed up, forcing her head back, stretching her neck, causing her to choke. As she emitted an almost animal whine, he almost released her, afraid to hurt her too much. Aware of the slight relaxation in his muscles, she brought her knee up full into his groin. He cried out at the sudden agonising pain and doubled up, his grip on her wrist weakening considerably. She pulled it free and sprang away from him laughing triumphantly.

She knelt on the bed beside him as he gasped for air and raised the knife above her head again, holding it with both hands. The sight made him forget his pain and he kicked out at her stomach, viciously sending her crashing off the bed to land in a heap on the floor. He struggled up on one elbow, both of them now heaving, trying to draw air back into their bodies. The knife lay somewhere in the gloom, he couldn't see where. She raised herself to her knees, glaring maliciously at him, her teeth bared in a snarl of rage, then leapt towards him, her arms flailing, fingers clawing to tear at his eyes. He caught her arms as her full weight landed on him, then arched his body to try to throw her off, but was only partially successful. They rolled over on the bed, their bodies becoming entangled in the bedclothes, restricting their movements. She spat at him, her eyes gleaming with fury, muted growling noises coming from deep down in her throat. He fought back desperately, still afraid to hurt her but knowing he would have to if he were to prevent her harming him and possibly herself.

They fell to the floor, taking the bedclothes with them, landing in a struggling, mixed-up heap on the floor. She managed to free herself from his grasp and raise herself to one knee, the sheets from the bed impeding her efforts. He grabbed for her again and caught at her blouse. It tore as she pulled herself away, exposing her small breasts, the sight causing Holman to hesitate, to freeze momentarily, dangerously. It was as though her sudden nakedness, the sight of her soft defenceless flesh made her vulnerable. Helpless.

But her laugh quickly swept pity from his mind, and he struggled to free himself of the sheets. It was a laugh that chilled him; the empty cackle of a crazy woman. He sprang at her.

She dodged his outstretched arms and leapt across the bed with an agility that surprised him. He clumsily scrambled after her, his feet still caught in the sheets on the floor, and managed to roll to one side as she brought the bedside lamp crashing down towards his head. He gasped as it struck his already injured shoulder, crying out her name as though it would bring her to her senses. Swinging his feet round, dragging some of the bedclothes with them, he crouched on the floor beside her. She kicked him in the face, catching his jaw, stunning him. He fell back against the side of the bed, the restraint of not wanting to hurt her now completely gone from his mind. He would have to fight her as he would fight a man – or a mad dog. He saw her grab for something on the floor and realised it must be the knife. As she came towards him again he pushed himself from the bed and backed away, never taking his eyes off her, fighting down his emotion for her, regarding her as the crazed stranger she now was. She advanced slowly, no longer chuckling, but the smiling grimace still there on her face, the look of hatred still distorting her features. Their movements were slow, measured, the movements of a cat stalking a terrified mouse. Suddenly, she ran forward, raising the knife high for the death strike, a scream of anticipation escaping from her lips. He ducked beneath the descending arm and was behind her. As she whirled, he made for the bedroom door, feeling terror of the blade he knew was a few feet from his exposed back. He reached the door, grabbed the handle and twisted his body to slam it shut behind him. He heard the thunk of the knife as it sank into the wood then the thud of her body as it followed through and struck the door. He immediately pushed the door open again, all his strength behind the thrust, the whole action in one fluid movement. It slammed into the girl, knocking her back violently, causing her to lose her grip of the knife handle. She fell to the floor with a scream more of rage than hurt, her skirt rising high to her thighs, the sight exciting Holman despite his predicament. He leapt on to her, his whole weight pinning her to the floor, but still she struggled, her continuing strength amazing him. Her legs opened in her efforts to free herself and he lay between them, his face next to hers, his arms pinning hers above her head. He could feel himself growing stiff, the position of love making and the excitement of his fright combining to distract his mind from the danger towards the more primitive urge of his body. 'Casey,' he breathed as he moved his body against her, 'Casey!'

She bit into his already wounded neck, deep and hard, drawing blood and savouring it. He cried out and tried to pull away, but she clung to him, her head rising with him. He could feel his flesh break again as her teeth sank deeper. He released one of her arms, which immediately clawed at his hair, and drew his fist back. He punched her hard in her ribs but still she would not let go. Desperately, ignoring the pain, he pulled one knee up so it rested high between her legs, causing his back to make a hole between their bodies. Then he raised his fist again and slammed it low into her stomach.

Her head fell back to the floor and she lay there gasping in air through blood-stained lips, her legs drawn up, her free hand clutching her stomach. Then he slapped her. A hard, cruel, swiping blow that threw her head to one side. He pulled her half to her feet and hit her again, knocking her to the floor once more. At the sight of her lying there, moaning, tiny whimpering noises coming through tears of pain, his rage vanished.

He knelt beside her and cradled her in his arms, tenderly rocking her to and fro.

'Oh, Casey, I'm sorry, darling,' he said softly, forgetting her madness, thinking only of the pain he had caused her. But even as he held her and her breathing became more even, he could feel her body stiffening, her whimpers becoming low murmurings. He looked around quickly and caught sight of the rumpled sheets on the floor. He lowered her body, praying she was still too helpless to move, and grabbed for them, pulling them towards him. Her shoulders began to heave now, not from breathlessness but from insane anger building up. She raised herself on one elbow. Hastily, he pushed her down and rolled her over, pulling her hands behind her back. She began to kick out but he sat heavily on her to make her helpless. As he tied her hands with the rolled up sheet, she thrashed her head from side to side, scraping it on the hard floor, oblivious to the pain. Then, without warning, her body went limp, her eyes became glazed as though she were in a deep cataleptic trance, and saliva, pink from Holman's blood, drooled from her once-sweet lips to the floor.

He turned her over and anxiously wiped away the thin layer of moisture from her brow. She stared ahead unseeingly. Lifting her gently, he took her over to the bed, and laid her on it, propping her head and shoulders up with two pillows. He drew the sides of her ripped blouse together, covering her breasts, the proud little breasts he had lovingly kissed so often and arranged her skirt to cover her thighs, the soft thighs he had also lovingly kissed so many times before. Then he wiped the spittle and blood from around her mouth with the edge of a sheet, reminding himself of the wound she had re-opened with her sharp teeth. He put his handkerchief to his neck and winced at the pain now that he had become conscious of it. There was quite a lot of blood on the handkerchief when he drew it away, but he didn't think too much damage had been done.

He sat there in the gloom staring at the girl, one hand with the handkerchief to his throat, the other resting lightly on her knee. She was unresponsive when he quietly spoke her name. How much had the gas, the fog – whatever it was – how much had it affected her? Would she ever be normal again. Would she try to kill herself as Spiers had done? Even he, Holman, had tried to throw himself back down the fissure and later cut his own throat with glass. The little girl had died because of the fog. But she had been heavily subjected to it, as had he, inside the hole, and her young mind had been unable to cope with the effects. His only hope was that Casey had not been exposed too much. She'd been inside the car most of the time. Did it make any difference though? Was such a short exposure still as lethal? The next few days would tell. His only hope was to get her to a hospital where they could keep her under restraint until she got over it, or – He pushed the thought from his mind. The doctors had told him there was little they had been able to do but keep him on drugs to pacify him while the struggle had gone on inside his brain, an area they could not enter unless they used drastic surgery which may have proved fatal anyway. Would her mind be strong enough to resist whatever was eating into it?

He was still sitting there in the semi-darkness when the police pounded on the door ten minutes later.

Holman went to the door quickly, afraid to leave Casey alone for too long. He was surprised to see the police and immediately assumed a neighbour had been concerned about the sounds of the struggle. There were two, one uniformed, the other in plain-clothes. He didn't know there was yet another guarding the stairs on the ground floor.

'John Holman?' the man in plain-clothes asked brusquely.

'Yes. Good thing you came . . . '

He was cut off as the detective pushed his way in, flashing a

70

card in Holman's face and pocketing it immediately. 'Detective Inspector Barrow, we've been told to pick you up.'

'What? Oh, Spiers. Look, get an amb . . .'

'We understand that you were the only witness present at, er, an incident at the Department of the Environment building a short while ago.' The detective was young and very unlike Holman's idea of a detective. He wore a poloneck jumper and a long suede jacket; his hair, though not exactly long, was certainly no 'short back and sides'. He glanced around the flat, visibly puzzled by the absence of daylight.

'Yes, that's right. My boss committed suicide, but . . .'

'Why did you leave?' The detective was walking away from him, opening doors and looking in as he went. Holman turned towards the burly policeman standing in the doorway. 'Look we've got to get an ambulance right away,' he said, ignoring the detective's question.

'Christ!' he heard and turned again to see the plain-clothes policeman standing at the door to his bedroom, a look of astonishment on his face.

'Hold him, Turner!' the detective shouted over his shoulder as he disappeared into the room. A heavy hand clamped on to Holman's upper arm as he made towards the bedroom.

'You don't understand,' Holman said angrily. 'We've got to get her to a hospital immediately.' He wrenched his arm free and ran down the short passage. He saw the young detective sitting on the bed untying Casey's hands. 'No, wait! Don't release her – she's not sane!' The words hurt him to say, but he had to make them understand. A rough hand went around his neck and his right arm was yanked behind him and up.

'You don't understand!' he managed to gasp.

'Oh, we understand all right,' said the CID man, turning to eye him coolly. 'Your colleagues told us *you* hadn't been well. Don't give us any trouble, mate, I'm just in the mood for a bastard like you.' He spoke quietly, but the menace was unmistakable.

Holman relaxed his muscles, unafraid of the threat, but realising there was nothing he could do for the moment.

'All right, let's take it easy. But you've got to get her to a hospital,' he said, trying to keep his voice calm. 'I was in the earthquake in Wiltshire last week. There was a gas released, it affects the brain . . .'

'It certainly affected yours,' said the detective, helping the girl to her feet. 'I don't know what you've done to her, but look at her, look at those eyes . . .'

'No, no. It wasn't me. It was the fog. Spiers was caught up in it too. It affects the brain.'

'As far as we know, there've been no reports of gas during any damage at the earthquake.'

'But I was inside it. Inside the eruption where the gas was!'

'Yes, we heard about a man and a child being rescued. The kid's dead, we'll take your word for it that you were the man. But there's been no mention of anybody else being down there.'

'They weren't down there.' Holman was beginning to lose his temper, but fought hard to control it knowing no good would come from a shouting match. 'This was later, at different times.'

'All right, Sergeant, get him out of here, we've got plenty of time for questions.'

'Wait a minute, there's something else!' Holman resisted the strong arms of the policeman holding him. 'The school! Listen to me. There was a bus-load of kids caught in the fog. I can't remember the name of the school, but it was in Andover. You've got to find it and quickly. God knows what's happened there by now!'

Holman impatiently drummed his fingers on the hard top of the bare table in one of New Scotland Yard's many 'interview' rooms. The stone-faced policeman who stood by the door watching him said nothing, bored by his duty, but ready to spring into action at the least sign of aggressiveness from his charge.

'What have they done with the girl?' Holman asked him for the third time. As before, there was no reply. 'You could at least tell me that!' Holman slumped back in his seat, knowing it was useless to argue with this zombie. He'd been kept at the police headquarters for well over three hours now, wearily answering the same questions over and over again. Their disbelief was evident and when he'd been left alone with his guard and given time to reflect, he realised he could not blame them. He had been the only other person in the office when Spiers had jumped and they had been heard arguing beforehand; the police had discovered him with a bound and beaten girl in his flat; he'd only just been released from hospital after suffering a mental breakdown. The facts spoke for themselves and his anger at their repeated questions had not improved their opinion of his sanity. The girl was in a state of shock it seemed, unable to tell them of her ordeal, but they were sure she would be able to answer their questions later. They had finally agreed to check on the schools in Andover; if there was some abnormality with the pupils then maybe his story could begin to take on some credence.

He looked up sharply as the door suddenly opened and two men walked briskly into the room. One was the young detective who had brought him in. He stood back, icily regarding Holman, as the other, an older, more genial-looking man, sat in the chair facing him on the other side of the table. Chief Superintendent Wreford had skilfully interrogated Holman, allowing his younger colleague to be antagonistic while he played the more sympathetic role. Holman had soon realised this was an act and that the mild-mannered, soft-spoken policeman was in fact a shrewd and perceptive interrogator. Wreford had tried to determine whether Holman was a dangerous lunatic or a clever liar with some obscure but sinister motive. So far, he wasn't sure.

'We've been checking on the schools in Andover . . . ' he paused to study Holman's reaction.

'Yes?' said Holman leaning forward.

' . . . and found nothing.'

Holman's look of frustration was too natural to be forced.

'However,' the Chief Superintendent went on, 'we've had a report of a serious fire in a school just on the outskirts of the town.'

'That must be it! It has to be!'

'Well, there's no way of knowing yet. Apparently the fire was in a gymnasium adjoining the school and they believe there could have been thirty-or-so boys trapped inside. The survivors are in a state of shock, and can't be questioned just yet. We haven't got all the facts, but at least we know the name of the school.' His gaze became imperceptibly more intense. 'It was Crayton's.'

Holman looked down at the table and frowned as he tried to remember. 'No, no, I don't think that was it. The teacher told me the name, but I just can't remember it. I do remember the teacher only had one arm, but that's not much use to you.'

The Chief Superintendent studied Holman's face for a few moments and then said, 'All right, that wasn't the real name. I'm going to show you a list – let's see if you recognise any of the names on it.'

He handed a sheet of paper to Holman who quickly scanned the typewritten list. He shook his head and read through it again, this time more slowly. 'It's no good,' he said finally, 'I don't recognise any. One or two sound familiar but . . . ' Again, he shook his head.

'The name of the school is Redbrook. Redbrook House, to be exact. Ring a bell?'

'It sounds right, but I couldn't honestly swear to it.'

'I bet you couldn't,' the younger policeman broke in harshly.

'Let me handle this, Barrow,' Wreford said sharply, becoming a little tired now of his subordinate's ruthlessness. Although he often used him as a balance against his assumed mildness, he had begun to wonder if Barrow didn't relish the role he played just a little too much.

'All right, Mr Holman,' he said, his voice quickly becoming more even, 'we'll have to hold you for a short time while we're making further investigations.'

'Are you arresting me?' Holman's tone was incredulous.

'Certainly not. But you must admit, the circumstances are suspicious, to say the least.'

'I suppose so. But what about Casey? She'll need me.'

'Miss Simmons will be well looked after.'

'Where is she?'

'At the moment, she's in Middlesex Hospital under sedation. It seems she's still in a state of shock.'

'But don't you see, that's because of the fog. It's a reaction to it!'

'Whether it is or not, we'll soon find out. And tell me something, Mr Holman, if this fog is drifting around the country sending people mad, why haven't we had reports of it? Why aren't all the people living in that part of the country raving lunatics?' A slight edge of anger had appeared in the policeman's last question.

'I don't know! I suppose it's because the fog doesn't cover such a wide area. And don't forget, there's a lot of open land around there. It may be that not too many people have come in contact with it as yet. And there seems to be some sort of delayed reaction. We came in contact with it yesterday, Spiers the day before. It must take time to work its way into the system!'

74

'But you told us you were mad when they dragged you from the hole!' said Barrow, annoyed that his superior should even listen to such drivel.

'I was subjected to a massive dose of it! I was its first victim!' Holman angrily banged his hand on the table.

'Then tell us, Mr Holman,' said Wreford calmly, 'why you are not mad now. Or are you?'

There was an abrupt silence in the small room. Three pairs of eyes looked intently into Holman's, the three policemen waiting for his reply.

'Look,' he said wearily, 'I just don't know. I'm not a doctor, I'm not a scientist – maybe the Ministry of Defence can tell you.'

The two CID men looked at one another. 'What do you mean by that?' asked the Chief Superintendent quietly.

'They've got military installations down on Salisbury Plain. They conduct experiments – dangerous experiments – in the interest of the nation! Maybe they've got some answers.'

'Oh, come on . . . ' began Barrow, a sneering grin on his face, but he was cut off by the older man.

'Are you saying the Ministry of Defence is responsible for this? That they've released some sort of . . . ' Wreford paused, ' . . . some sort of nerve gas?'

'For God's sake, I don't know! It's a possibility though!'

'Oh, sir, do we have to listen to this?' Barrow looked as though he were ready to pounce on Holman.

'No, we don't. If what you say is true, Mr Holman, then we should know very shortly. Until we do, I'm afraid we have to hold you.'

'Okay, okay. But see they look after Casey. She's got to be watched constantly.'

'She'll be in safe hands, Mr Holman, I can assure you of that.'

Eight

Herbert Brown was worried about his pigeons. He drained his whisky and stared at the empty glass for a few moments.

'Another one, Herby?' asked the barman, reaching for a new glass, knowing his customer would not drink from the old.

'Yes, Harry. Have another one y'self.'

Harry knew the offer would come, which was why he was always eager to serve Herbert.

'Ta. I'll have a small light,' he said, smiling through cigarette-stained teeth. He was a runt of a man, insignificant to most of his customers, but always treated well by Herbert Brown.

'Nah, have a short.'

'All right, Herby. I'll have a gin and tonic.' He poured the drinks and took the pound note from the bar where Herbert had nonchalantly laid it. He rang up the till and swiftly scraped out the change, a ten pence piece finding its way into his own pocket.

'Here you are, Herby. Cheers.' He raised his glass and sipped his gin. He was a good sort, Herby. Always ready to buy a drink. Never checked his change. He spent at least three evenings a week in the pub opposite his shop in Hackney Road, and most lunchtimes. Herbert usually rose early, about five or six, and went to the market to buy stock for his fruit shop. By eleven, he considered his day was done and a trip to the betting shop was always followed by a visit to the pub, leaving his hard-working wife to cope with the selling of the fruit. She had long ago resigned herself to the fact that Herbert would never change, but this did not stop her acid-tongued beratement of him. And the more he was nagged, the more he drank. And the more he drank, the more he was nagged. The circle was never-ending, but neither of them could see it. It was a way of life.

'I shouldn't worry about them, Herb. They'll turn up.' Harry leaned forward on the bar, a false look of sympathy on his face.

He couldn't understand how anyone could worry about bloody pigeons, let alone breed them. He'd once been up to Herby's coop, a dangerously perched hut built on a side roof at the back of his shop. The house itself was large, as were most of the houses along London's Hackney Road; their backyards dropped a floor below road level, providing extra habitable basement rooms and giving the houses concealed depth. An extension had been built by the shop's previous occupiers, extending most of the length of the backyard and reaching the second floor level. The roof, which was flat, could be reached from a landing window, and on it Herbert had built his pigeon coop.

The smell inside the hut had made Harry feel nauseous, and Herbert's drunken clucking had filled him with barely concealed disgust. For the life of him he could not understand what Herby saw in the fat, cooing creatures. Puffing themselves up, messing all over the place. They weren't good for anything – even pigeon pie was out of style nowadays. Herby raced them, Harry knew that. But he'd never won anything from it. When he'd cautiously broached the subject to him, the only reply he'd got was, 'Have you ever watched them fly?' Just the silly sort of answer you'd expect from an old drunk. Still, apart from his stinking pigeons, Herby was all right. Always good for a drink, always good for a tap.

'They should've been back before now,' Herbert was saying mournfully. 'Only took them down to Salisbury in the van. Got some new ones, y'see, you've got to go easy on 'em at first. Mustn't take 'em too far or they'll never find their way home. Some of the older ones were with 'em so they should've been all right. And Claude never gets lost!'

Harry had to hide a grin as he thought of the ridiculously-named pigeon which was Herbert's favourite. He'd had it for many years, a scruffy old bird that always looked as though it had just escaped from the clutches of a cat. He treated it like a baby. The time Harry had been up there, Herby had held it to his cheek and spoken to it as though it could understand every word. Not baby-talk though, but sensibly, man-to-man. When Harry had held it, it had shit in his hand.

'Took 'em on Sunday,' Herbert continued, his words slurring slightly. 'Should be back by now. Trouble is y'see, they need the sun to guide them.'

'Well, maybe they got back earlier this evening Herb, just after you got here. You wait, when you get home, they'll all be

77

sitting up waiting for you.' He caught another customer's eye and looked heavenward, careful that Herbert didn't see. The man, who had been eavesdropping, winked back.

'You taking the piss, Harry?' Herbert's words were challenging.

Harry knew that after a few Scotches his friend could quickly turn nasty at the slightest hint of sarcasm. 'No, no,' he said hastily. 'I just meant they'll all be up there on the roof waiting for you. I'm sure they will. Here, it's about time you had one on me.' He turned to reach for a new glass and breathed a sigh of relief when he heard Herbert's voice droning on, now sentimental again. He didn't want to upset Herby.

'Thing is with birds, Harry, they don't demand nothing. You feed 'em, an' that's it, they're yours. They're not like dogs or cats that creep around you, begging. They're proud, y'see. They come to you for food and that's it. If you don't feed 'em, sod ya', they're off.' He leaned forward and pointed a rigid finger at the barman. 'But if you look after them right, they'll always come back to you. They're loyal, y'see. Independent, but loyal.'

He sat back as though satisfied with his statement. Harry placed the whisky on the bar before him, nodding his agreement, but annoyed that he'd been forced to buy him a drink. The landlord had eagle eyes so he couldn't take too many chances with the till. He'd have to pay for it.

'Claude'll bring 'em back, I know he will.' Herbert emptied the glass in two swift swallows, causing Harry to wince at the thought of the fiery liquid burning its way down his throat to eat away at the lining of his stomach. His insides must be made of cast-iron.

'Can't understand why they've been gone so long though.' Herbert stood up, swaying slightly. 'I'm off, Harry.'

'Okay, Herb, see you tomorrow,' grinned the barman and added maliciously, 'Give my love to the old lady.'

He almost regretted his words when Herbert turned back to the bar and eyed him for three long seconds, his befuddled brain unsure of the tone of the last remark.

'Fuck 'er,' Herbert finally said, and weaved his way unsteadily out of the pub.

Once outside, he leaned against the wall for a few moments. He'd taken the last drink too fast and could feel the bile rising inside him. It was the thought that his beloved birds might be waiting for him that had suddenly caused his haste. He fought

78

down the sickness and lurched across the wide main road, stopping at its centre to allow a No 6 bus to crawl slowly by.

His wife watched him from their bedroom window above the shop.

She'd done it so many times before, had spent long, solitary hours gazing out at the busy main road from the darkened room, driven there not to watch for him coming home but by loneliness. She would study the people walking by, the young couples, the customers she knew, wondering where they were going, what they would do when they got there. The strangers, who were they, what were they doing in this neighbourhood? Sometimes her mind would go off into strange, often sordid, fantasies at the sight of them. There had been a time when the sight of one coloured person was enough to send her off into a frenzy of fancies, but now she was filled only with angry indignation. She could look directly into the brightly lit upper decks of the double-decker buses that regularly passed by her window. Although the glimpses were fleeting, they filled her mind with curiosity. And enhanced her loneliness.

Since the boys had left, she found she had too much time to herself, too much time to ponder over her marriage and the hard years it had brought her. They had their own lives to make, it was true, but you'd think they would visit more often even though they both lived a little way out now. She loved to see the babies, her grandchildren. It was Herbert who'd driven the boys away with his drinking, his belligerence. What affection had he shown them? What interest? But his pigeons were another matter. Oh yes, nothing was too good for his bloody pigeons! Look how worried he was when he thought they were lost, how anxious he'd been the last couple of days. What could he see in them?

Look at him now, standing in the middle of the road in a drunken stupor. God, how she wished that bus had knocked him down! She was the one who had made the business a success; it was all due to the hard work she'd put into it. All right, so he did get to the market very early in the mornings, but why should that excuse him for the rest of the day? They could have been well off if he didn't squander every penny they made on drink and gambling. And giving it away. Oh yes, all his cronies knew where to come when they were short of a few bob! Good old Herby – the paupers' friend. Well, she'd sifted a bit away out of the takings; she had to, otherwise they'd soon be out on the

79

street if business suddenly went bad. It wasn't stealing – how could you steal money you earned yourself? But there was no reason he should know about it. Look at him, staggering across the road! I just hope none of the customers see him, the rotten bastard.

Tears glistened in Lena Brown's eyes, not tears of self-pity or sorrow, but tears of hate.

'I wish you'd die,' she said aloud, her breath causing the window-pane to mist up. 'I wish you'd fucking die.'

Herbert reached the side door to his shop and fumbled for his key. His wife had once bolted the door from the inside. Only once, never again. The police had been called because of the commotion he'd made, but she'd never dared to lock him out of his own house again. He found his key and had no difficulty in placing it in its metal womb, turning it viciously and pushing the door open. He closed it loudly behind him, not caring if he disturbed his wife upstairs. Not that she'd be asleep. Oh no, she'd be waiting for him no matter what time it was. You'd think she'd get sick at the sound of her own voice by now. Well, fuck 'er! She wasn't important!

He felt his way along the dark passageway and down the steps to the backyard, not bothering to turn on the lights. Unbolting the heavy back door, he stepped out into the cool night air, breathing in great mouthfuls of it. He unzipped his trousers and pissed on the hard concrete ground, enjoying the sound as the yellow stream spattered off it. He never knew why he did this, their toilet stood directly opposite him and it had cost him a small fortune to have the one upstairs put in. But it was one of life's little pleasures, he told himself. And it infuriated Lena.

As the stream of urine lost its impetus and retreated back towards his shoes, he became conscious of another sound. It was the sound of cooing.

He looked up towards the roof. His pigeons – they'd come back, bless 'em! He laughed aloud and quickly zipped up his trousers, getting his fingers wet in the process. Wiping his hands on his jacket, he lurched back into the house, leaving the door wide open behind him. He staggered up the stairs, cursing as he tripped, using his hands on the stairs ahead of him. As he reached the landing window, he heard his wife's voice coming from the bedroom.

'You dirty bastard!' she called. 'You're a bloody animal! Why don't you use the lavatory like any normal man.'

'Shut your noise,' he shouted back, reaching one knee up to the window sill. He had to be careful now. More than once he'd lost his grip and gone tumbling down the stairs. She always said he'd go walking off the roof one of these nights, and good riddance too. But he knew he'd never get that drunk because if he did, he would never be able to get out the bleedin' window.

He scrambled through, his hands resting on the floor of the roof, supporting his upper body. He could still hear her voice from inside the house, shrill, unpleasant. But he could also hear the cooing now, much louder, and the sounds of movement inside the coop as the birds shuffled on their perches, excited by the noise he was making.

'I'm coming, my darlings,' he called out, drunkenly conscious of the silly grin on his face. He was careful to keep well away from the edge of the flat roof; he didn't fancy the drop on to the concrete thirty feet below. 'I knew you'd get back, Claude. I knew I could depend on you. What happened, get lost did you?'

He struggled with the latch on the door, noticing that some of the newer birds were still on the roof of the wooden hut. They always took a little while to learn how to get back inside the coop. They'd soon follow the example of the others. 'Claude, come on, darling, where are you?' He switched on the bicycle lamp he kept hanging up inside the hut, the sudden light causing several of the birds to flutter around in panic.

'It's all right, darlings, it's only me. I won't hurt you.' Herbert closed the door behind him so that none of the pigeons could escape. He had to crouch low as the sloping roof of the hut was not high enough to allow a grown man to stand. He quickly checked over the birds, counting them, making sure none had received any injuries. He finally spotted Claude, perched high in the corner of the hut, not moving, but a gentle cooing coming from its throat.

'Hello, old Claude. D'you miss me?' He lurched towards the older pigeon trying not to disturb the others. He was unaware of the sudden silence that had descended upon them, or that they were now all perfectly still.

'Well, Claude, what have you got to say for yourself, eh?' He reached for the pigeon and gently picked it up. Holding it close to his face, he began to stroke its breast, making soft clucking noises. 'You know who's boss, don't you? You know who'll look after you.'

The bird's head suddenly shot forward and its beak pecked

at Herbert's bleary eye. He screamed out in pain and fell back among the perches, releasing his grip on his pet bird. The whole hut erupted into a whirlwind of screeching, fluttering bodies as the birds flew at him from all sides. He raised his arms to protect his face, but they pecked at his hands viciously, causing thin trickles of blood to run down them. He swiped at them wildly, sending their frail bodies crashing into the sides of the coop, several falling to the floor again, unable to rise, feebly fluttering their broken wings in a useless attempt to reach him. But still the others continued their attack, flapping their wings at his head, pecking at his crouched body, finding exposed flesh, drawing tiny dots of blood.

Suddenly, part in rage, part in panic, Herbert grabbed at one of the feathered bodies and with a cry of anguish, crushed its tiny bones with his hands. But the movement had left his face exposed and three of the pigeons immediately flew at it, one clinging to his neck, the other two striking at his cheeks and eyes. He was already half-blinded and now felt his other eye pop as he released the dead bird and tried to protect his face again. The shock forced him to his feet, thrashing out violently, smashing the birds to the ground, crushing them with his feet as he staggered blindly towards the small doorway. But in the turmoil, in the confusion of flying bodies, beating wings, the shrieks of the birds, his own cries of fear, his pain, he had lost all sense of direction and crashed into the side of the hut, knocking himself to the ground.

As he lay there, arms outstretched, stunned by the fall, the pigeons flurried on to his heaving chest and continued their combined onslaught. He kicked out, sobbing with the horror of it, and managed to roll over in the confined space, squashing the birds that still clung to him. Raising himself to one knee, feeling the sharp pecks at his neck and shoulders, but now almost oblivious to the pain, he stretched out one hand towards the side of the coop. His fingers curled through and round the wire mesh of one of its windows and he slowly pulled himself to his feet, ignoring the pigeon that had settled on his hand and was biting at his raw knuckles. Some inner sense informed him of the direction of the door based on the position of the wire window he clung to. The pain now was on its second wave and it broke through the protective barrier his fear had set up.

He screamed aloud, shaking, shuddering his entire body, flailing his limbs and lumbered towards the small exit, still covered in feathered, tormenting bodies. Unable to see the torch, he sent it flying as he stumbled through the door, his brain as well as his eyes blind now.

His wife stared at him from the landing window, her face white in the moonlight, her hands clutching the window-sill. She had heard the commotion from her bedroom, at first ignoring it, assuming her husband was in one of his fits of rage. But then the urgency, the terror in the screams had reached her and she had flung herself from the bed, fearful at what she might find when she reached the landing window. And what she'd found had left her in open-mouthed disbelief.

A figure had emerged from the coop at the end of the small roof, a figure that seemed scarcely human in the moonlight. It moved in crouched, lurching steps and was surrounded by wildly-beating wings. She drew in her breath in horror as she realised it was her husband, just recognisable, and he was being attacked by the pigeons he loved. She stood there, her mouth agape, for once in her life speechless, unable to move, unable to help him. His next cry broke the spell and she struggled to climb through the window, her heavy body hindering her progress. When she was halfway through, her hands on the roof, her buttocks high in the air on the window ledge, she looked up to see her husband stumble towards the edge. She opened her mouth to scream his name, but no sound came. Her lips silently opened and closed twice and only when he stepped off into space did any sound emerge.

'Herby!' she screamed, and the scream covered the squelching thud as his body hit the concrete thirty feet below.

She crawled towards the edge of the parapet, sobbing and calling his name over and over again. She lay flat and peered into the darkness below. His body was barely visible, a dark form lying perfectly still, legs twisted outwards at odd angles. A sudden movement gave her hope, but she saw it was the weak fluttering of a dying bird that had plunged to the ground with him. She knew he was dead.

'Oh, Herby, my poor darling. Oh Herby,' she wept.

Above her, on the roof of the coop, the pigeons had gathered. They gazed down at her and were still. The one called Claude cooed softly.

Much earlier, on that same day, Edward Smallwood had been

fishing. He was a tall, nervous man, prematurely balding and, at the age of thirty-five, still living with his parents. His nervousness was largely due to his domineering father, a man much smaller than himself, but a man with strict principles and harsh ideals, who made no effort to hide his disappointment in his 'weakling' son. Edward's even smaller mother doted on her son and kindly, but misguidedly, tried to shield him from the discordances of life and the severity of his father. Nevertheless, both parents loved their gangling, stoop-shouldered 'boy' in different ways, and both as damagingly. They supervised his life to an intimidating degree so that any spark of initiative, any mood of impulsiveness had been carefully drained from his nature at a very early age, not maliciously, but in a kindly, patronising way. And because it was done in kindness, albeit a stricter kindness from his father, the effects were more lasting. They had guided him into his first and only job at the age of sixteen, a job in the bank managed by a friend of the family; a good job, 'safe, respectable'. There he had stayed and worked his way up to the position of assistant manager through dogged perseverance rather than natural ability. He had refused any transfers that had cropped up from time to time, not wanting to move from the busy but pleasant enough town of Ringwood on the borders of the New Forest, and knowing his parents would not allow it anyway. He had not even felt disappointment when the manager, the friend of his family, had died two years before and he had not been offered the appointment. It hadn't even occurred to him that he should and was puzzled by his father's beratement over the matter.

Edward had never really hated anyone before that; disliked, certainly, been afraid of, most definitely, but the feeling of hate had never before intruded upon his life. But Norman Symes, the new bank manager, had aroused passions in him that had never even been tickled before. Symes' philosophy in life seemed to be, if each day, I can bring a little unhappiness into the life of Edward Smallwood, then that day has not been in vain. Edward had mentioned it only once to his parents and the scolding of his father and the twittering sympathy of his mother prevented him from ever doing so again. So he had borne the misery alone, a misery only experienced before in his schooldays. He was well aware of how others on the staff enjoyed his discomfort in the presence of the manager, and so was Symes; that was half the trouble. The manager seemed to go out of

84

his way to humiliate him in front of the others, as though his own prestige was enhanced by these spiteful remarks. Edward sighed at the thought of the little but nasty tribulations the day would bring. With a bit of luck, Symes would be on one of his 'get out and meet the local businessmen' exercises that day, and they would see little of one another.

Edward pushed back the bedclothes and groped for his glasses, hidden somewhere on the small bedside table. He tutted as he knocked over the half-drunk cup of weak tea his mother had brought up to him earlier. His day had already been ruined by the fog which had suddenly descended upon him while he was fishing on a remote bank of the River Avon at six o'clock that morning. Twice a week he cycled out to his favourite spot to fish, a pleasure of which even his parents approved. His doctor recommended early morning fresh air to help rid him of his constant catarrh, an ailment that caused him to snuffle most of his way through the day. He hadn't noticed the early morning fresh air relieving his congestion much, but had found great pleasure in the quiet solitude of the river bank and it helped him to steel himself against the oncoming day. He even regretted catching any fish and rarely baited his hook. Now and again he had to, to satisfy the serious enquiries of his father, but to pull a life from its watery existence left him with a feeling of sorrow.

But that particular morning, engrossed in his own thoughts, the yellowy mist had stealthily crept around him and it was only when he suddenly realised he could hardly see the end of his line that he became aware of the fog surrounding him. A little frightened by the suddenness of it, he had quickly packed away his flask and fishing tackle and tried to find his way back to the main road. It had taken him a good ten minutes of bumping into trees, becoming entangled in low-lying bushes to do this. Fortunately, the fog did not extend as far as the main road and, more by luck than judgement, he found himself back in bright sunlight. His mother was, as usual, overly sympathetic when he reached home, and packed him off to bed for an extra hour's rest before he went off to work. He was surprised to find later that he'd actually dozed off for that hour, but the fog had left a nasty taste in his mouth which his mother's weak tea did little to dispel.

He found his glasses and rubbed his eyes before putting them on, frowning with a headache that he had just become aware of.

He made his way to the bathroom, bidding his father good morning as he passed his door, knowing the old man would be propped up in bed reading the *Telegraph*, munching toast, sipping tea.

'Good morning, Edward!' came the brisk reply, and Edward repeated his 'Good morning, Father.'

After a more thorough toilet than his earlier effort, he went back to his room and dressed, putting on the clothes his mother had carefully laid out for him the night before. He went downstairs, kissed his mother's proffered cheek, and sat down at the table, not feeling very hungry, despite his early morning exercise. He made an attempt to eat but had to push the plate away after a short while. His mother looked at the remnants of his bacon and eggs and then peered anxiously into his face.

'Aren't you feeling well, dear?' she asked.

'I'm all right, Mother, just not feeling very hungry, that's all.' He sipped his tea, looking down into his cup rather than at her concerned face.

'It's probably that nasty fog, got on to your chest.'

'No, I don't think so, Mother.'

'You know how weak your chest is,' she went on, ignoring him. 'Perhaps you shouldn't be out in the cold air first thing in the morning after all.'

He pulled away as she reached towards his forehead.

'No, really Mother, it's nothing at all. I'm just not hungry, that's all.'

'Have you been to the toilet?'

'Yes, Mother.'

'Let me get you some of your father's laxative pills.'

'No, Mother, I've been.'

'Well, where does it hurt then, dear?'

'It doesn't hurt. I'm just not hungry!'

'There's no need to snap, Edward, I'm only trying . . . '

'I'm not snapping, Mother.'

'Just because you're not feeling well, there's no need to take it out on Mother.'

'But I am feeling well, Mother. I don't feel like breakfast, that's all. I've got a bit of a headache.'

'Well, why didn't you say so. I'll get you some paracetamols, they'll soon shift it.'

'No, it's not that bad . . . ' But she was gone, returning seconds later with two white tablets in her hand.

'Now, take those with your tea. You'll soon feel better.' She would have actually popped them into his mouth had he not grabbed them and swallowed them quickly. 'Your father thinks it might be wise if you stayed home today in case you get worse.'

'Oh for goodness sake, Mother, it's only a slight headache!' Edward rose from the table, his face going a blotchy red from anger.

'Sit down, Edward.'

'Yes, Mother.' He sat down.

'You know how frightful you look when you lose your temper.'

'I didn't lose my temper,' he sulked.

'There's no need to make others suffer just because you're not well.'

He sat in broody silence now, knowing any further words from him would only prolong the conversation and his mother would begin to snuffle at his ingratitude.

'Very well, Edward. You may go off to work, but please don't come home complaining that you're worse at lunchtime.'

'No, Mother.'

'Try to eat something in your tea break.'

'Yes, Mother.'

'A biscuit or something.'

'Yes, Mother.'

Mrs Smallwood softened at the look of misery on her son's face. What would he do when they were no longer there to care for him? He was so dependent on them, needed them so much. She knew she would go first and Father really didn't understand the boy too well. Who would comfort Edward when his father scolded him? To whom would Edward turn? She bravely fought back the tears of pity and reached a hand kindly towards him and patted his head.

'Off you go now, Edward, or you'll be late.'

'Yes, Mother.' He rose again from the table and buttoned his jacket.

His mother looked up at him, forcing a smile, trying to hide the sorrow she felt. 'We love you, dear,' she said.

'Yes, Mother,' he answered.

The dull throbbing in his head increased as he walked through the town towards his branch of the Midland Bank. Several people who knew him wished him good morning and he returned their nods with a polite but strained smile. He loved his parents dearly, but did wish they wouldn't fuss so, especially Mother. She would worry herself into an early grave if she didn't learn not to fret over him so much. He choked at the thought. Goodness, he must remember to buy her a box of chocolates on his way home to lunch to make up for this morning's rudeness. He knew she would be upset for the rest of the week if he didn't. He thought of his father and how, since his early retirement, he'd seemed to have become even more domineering, as though the running of their lives had replaced the running of his old office with the insurance company. Still, Edward knew his father had his interests at heart.

As he stepped off the kerb, the beep of a car startled him into reality. He jumped back, his heels catching on the kerb, and sat down heavily on the pavement, managing to cling to his briefcase. Edward stared up at the passing car and saw the driver's mouth moving vehemently through the closed window. The car's horn sounded angrily again as the vehicle sped onwards. He heard the sniggers of passers-by as he sat there, his knees together, ankles far-stretched, holding his briefcase into his lap. They turned away as he looked at them, none offering to help him to his feet. He stood up, brushing at the back of his trousers with his hand, a huge blush sweeping over his face to the top of his balding scalp. Making sure the road was clear, he crossed it, his embarrassment giving his stride added length.

Damn them, he cursed inwardly, years of bitter resentment welling up inside him. Damn them for laughing, damn the driver for swearing at him! Damn the whole town. Damn the Midland Bank! Damn Symes!

He saw a man ahead of him stoop to pat the upturned head of a friend's dog. Edward strode briskly up to him and gave the offered bottom a hearty kick. The man jumped up with an astonished yelp, the dog holding on to his hand with its teeth in fright. He yelped again and turned back to the dog, smacking its head with the palm of his other hand. Edward marched on, ignoring the confused barking and shouting he'd left behind. A trader came out of his shop to see what the disturbance was about and as Edward passed him, he whirled and dealt the inquisitive shopkeeper a swift kick to his seat.

The man turned, using both hands to rub his smarting bottom, and stared after the retreating assistant bank manager, not quite sure of what had happened. Edward made his way along the street kicking bottoms at random, his victims too astonished to do anything but stare after his tall, foot-thrusting figure. He rounded a corner and spotted the most enormous backside he'd ever seen trundling along ahead of him. It belonged to a neatly and, of course, expansively dressed businessman, whose wide neck bulged over a spotlessly white collar. He was the proprietor of one of the costlier hotels in Ringwood, a pompous man and a perfectionist in his trade; this morning he was on his way to complain about the quality of yesterday's lamb to the owner of the large wholesale butcher who supplied most of the hotels in the area with their fresh meat.

The sharp blow to his rear startled him from his irascible thoughts. He turned quickly to discover the source of his rude surprise, and to his amazement found a tall, bespectacled man glaring challengingly into his face.

The fat man was too dumbfounded to muster up much vehemence in his indignant demand 'What do you think you're doing?' he asked.

Edward did not reply but raised his leg to kick the side of the fat man's thigh, his foot curling round in an attempt to reach the ample backside.

'Here, stop that!' The man backed away nervously.

Edward manoeuvred himself into a more favourable position for reaching the man's rear.

'Stop it!' But the blow had already landed. The hotel proprietor rubbed his reddening bottom with both hands, using friction to dull the smarting. 'I'll have the law on you! Who are you . . . ' He half-turned to trundle away, frightened by the gleam in the advancing Edward's eye. 'Get away!' he spluttered, his fat legs increasing their pace, finally breaking into a lumbering run. Edward followed, his longer legs easily enabling him to keep up and deal out more kicks to the large wobbling target before him.

They left a trail of bewildered onlookers behind them, who stared and then chuckled at one another in delight. It made a fine comedy, the contrasting figures of the two men – one tall and thin, the other, short and rolly – adding to the ridiculousness of it.

The hotel proprietor was becoming winded, his bottom sore and bruised. His pleas for help from the people he passed met only with incredulity turning to amusement. Finally he saw what he had been praying for. A policeman was just emerging from a shop and striding across the pavement to his Panda patrol car.

'Help!' the fat man panted. 'Help me!'

Fortunately for Edward, he'd seen the policeman too and had slowed down to a casual stroll. The fat man grabbed the policeman by the arm and was stabbing an agitated finger towards the now-passing assistant bank manager.

'"That man! That man has been chasing me!' The policeman calmly turned and looked down at the fat man tugging at his shirt sleeve then at the passer-by he was gesticulating towards. 'Stop him!' the fat man went on excitedly, fuming at the policeman's apparent casualness. 'He's been attacking me! Arrest him!'

The policeman had learned long ago never to accept anybody's word unless there were at least one or two unbiased witnesses to back up their story There were plenty of nutcases around who loved to create a scene and involve perfectly innocent bystanders and this little fat man didn't seem at all right in the head. However, these matters had to be investigated and feelings soothed. 'Just a moment, sir,' he called to Edward.

'That's it, constable,' the proprietor said with some feeling of satisfaction. 'He's a madman. You lock him up.'

'Yes, officer?' Edward walked calmly over to the two men, a faint look of surprise on his face.

The policeman immediately became suspicious of the fat man still tugging at his elbow. It seemed pretty obvious who the madman was.

'Er, this man says you assaulted him, sir,' he said, almost apologetically.

'I beg your pardon?' Edward replied, slightly indignant, not ruffled, but as though curious about the insinuation.

'He says you attacked him, sir.'

'He did. He's been chasing me all the way down the street, kicking me.' The fat man stood immediately behind the policeman, as though expecting another kick at any moment.

'But officer, there must be some mistake,' said Edward. 'I've never seen this man before.'

The policeman tried to calm the fat man who was hopping up and down behind him. 'He's kicked my bottom black and blue. Do something constable!'

'Kicked his – ? Oh, really, officer.' Edward smiled benignly. 'I do have to be on my way or I'll be late for work, but if I can assist you in any way . . . ?'

'Er, just a moment, sir.' The policeman turned to face the dismayed hotel proprietor. 'Have you any witnesses?'

'Well, of course, yes!' The fat man pointed at the onlookers. Unfortunately, they only chuckled and shook their heads at the policeman.

'I see,' the policeman said, putting away his notebook, a weary look on his face.

'But he did kick me!' wailed the fat man.

'I did not,' said Edward calmly.

'Well, I'm afraid sir, there's nothing I can do unless you have witnesses,' said the policeman. 'Now why don't you go on about your business and let this gentleman go on about his.' He ignored the outraged spluttering of the proprietor and turned back to Edward, speaking in a confidential tone. 'I'm sorry about this, sir. It often happens with these people. They see a uniform and immediately use it to make themselves feel important. He's harmless enough.'

'I understand, officer,' said Edward, with concern. 'It's quite all right. Really.'

'They want to be noticed, that's all.' The policeman smiled. 'It's certainly original, though, saying you kicked his bottom all the way down the street.'

Edward smiled back. 'Yes, it certainly is.' Both men shook their heads in wonder.

'Well, good day to you, sir,' the policeman half-saluted. 'He won't bother you again.'

'Thank you, officer. Good day.'

As the policeman turned and walked towards his car Edward took two brisk steps after him, swung his foot back, and gave him a hefty kick in the seat of his pants.

Symes looked up at the clock on the wall for the fourth time that morning. Half-past-ten and still Smallwood had not shown! The scowling bank manager expected the telephone to ring at any moment and Smallwood's distraught mother to pour out excuses about the condition of her son's ill-health as soon as he picked up the receiver. Well, he was coming to the end of his tether with that boy. Boy! He was a grown man, but he acted as though he were sixteen! True, he was conscientious enough, rarely made a mistake in his figures, but he was so godawful slow! And at the slightest sign of illness his mother kept him at home. He knew the previous manager had coddled the big, over-grown schoolboy because he knew the boy's father, but *he* certainly was not going to tolerate much more of his constant absenteeism, even though it was a treat not to have him snuffling around him all day It was his irritating mannerisms more than his lack of initiative that annoyed Symes: the way he chewed on his fingers, the way he apologised for everything, the way he bowed and scraped to the customers. And the rest of the staff had no respect for him; they regarded him as a joke.

Anyway, his being away so often was a good excuse to get rid of him. Balmer could take his place, he was a good lad, always quick with an answer, always ready to take on more work. And with Symes getting out and about more, meeting the people as it were, he needed a good backup man to handle the steady influx of routine work. It was a good policy to go out and contact the local businessmen and developers personally, rather than wait for them to come to him. See them in their offices, visit the sites, talk business over a good three-hour lunch – that was the way to treat good clients and drum up new ones. Now that the word had been whispered down from Head Office that the world of banking no longer sat on its backside and waited for the corporations to come to them, but went out and searched for promising enterprises themselves, they expected the managers of their local branches to do the same. He was sure that his own activities would soon come to their notice, and, unlike many of his counterparts in other branches, he relished the thought of being called to Head Office to build his reputation in the very fountain-head of the bank. Today he had some extremely important appointments to keep and the thought of Smallwood letting him down again filled him with annoyance.

There was a light tap on the door and his secretary poked her head through the smallest gap possible and said, 'Mr Small-wood's in, Mr Symes. I thought you might like to know.' She smiled smugly.

Symes looked up in surprise. It was usual for his assistant to be away, but very unusual for him to be late. 'Is he indeed? Well, would you inform him I'd like to see him right away, Mrs Platt.'

His secretary's head disappeared from view and seconds later, the door opened again to reveal Smallwood standing outside.

'Come in, come in. Don't just stand there,' said Symes, irritably. 'Why are you so late?'

Edward closed the door behind him and walked up to the manager's desk, not answering.

'Well, I asked you a question and I expect an answer.'

Edward rubbed his forehead with his hand and looked at Symes as though he'd never seen him before. 'I – I ran into a little trouble, sir.'

The little trouble had in fact amounted to being charged with causing a breach of the peace and assaulting an officer of the law, a charge he would have to answer to in court the following morning. A kindly police sergeant who knew his parents had advised him to return home and rest, knowing there was nothing malicious about him, and putting the morning's event down as 'nervous exhaustion or something like that'. But Edward hadn't gone home. He had something to do.

Symes studied his assistant's face and sighed resignedly. He supposed he was lucky that Smallwood had turned up at all – he certainly *looked* rather pale.

'All right, you know I've got a busy day on, tell me later. I've got an appointment at eleven and want to go down to the vault before I leave.' He gathered up some papers and put them away in his drawer. 'Reverend Peters made rather a large deposit today for his Restoration Fund. The man's an idiot – keeps his collections at the vicarage until he has a sizeable amount, then deposits it. Doesn't like to trouble me too often, he says.' He walked around his desk to the wall-safe. 'I've told him so many times he'll get robbed one day. Three hundred pounds he brought in today!' He dialled the combination and swung the safe door open, reaching inside for a brown envelope and the keys to the vault room. 'I don't want this lying around while I'm out all day, even though its safe enough in here. You can never be *too* careful, Smallwood. Besides, as I told Mrs Platt, if all goes well, I may not even be back at all today.' He had arranged to meet his last client of the day on the golf course.

He closed the safe door again and twirled the dial. Walking towards the door of his office he glanced back over his shoulder at Edward who was watching him silently.

'Come along, man, I haven't got all day!'

They descended the steps to the basement room that contained the vault. Symes unlocked the heavy metal door and they entered the room full of small lockers, each containing confidential papers belonging to the bank's clients. The vault itself stood at one end, fairly small but large enough for a bank of that size. The bank manager hummed as he walked towards it, anticipating the pleasant day he had before him. Edward followed.

'Now, Smallwood,' said Symes, handing him the brown envelope containing the vicar's money, 'you've got a busy day ahead of you and I don't want to find any work left over till tomorrow. Get Balmer to give you a hand if you need it.' He was silent as he dialled the combination to the vault, concentrating on the figures, enjoying the position of trust he had. The last numeral clicked into place and he stood straight, a smile of satisfaction on his face. He swung the heavy, metal door open and turned to retrieve the envelope from his assistant. He frowned at the blank look on Edward's face.

'I want to have a word with you tomorrow, Smallwood. It concerns your future with the bank, so don't be away.'

He turned back and placed one foot inside the vault, crouching slightly because of its smallness, and reaching for a black box marked 'St Andrew's Vicarage, Rev Anthony Stephen Peters'.

'Did you hear me, Smallwood?' came his muffled voice. 'I don't know what's the matter with you today.'

Edward stepped forward and pushed at his employer's back violently. Symes fell forward, striking his head on the back wall of the vault, his legs buckling beneath him. He was just in time to turn over and through the daze in his head see the heavy door swing shut, leaving him in a frightening black void.

Edward twisted the dial several times then leaned his aching forehead against the cold metal. The air inside the vault would not last long. Certainly for not more than a night.

He walked from the room, locking the door behind him, and climbed the stairs to the ground floor. When he passed Mrs Platt's desk, she looked up enquiringly.

'Where's Mr Symes?' he asked.

'Oh, he's gone for the day,' answered Edward. 'He went out the back way to his car, said he was late.'

'But what about his briefcase?'

'Said he didn't need it.'

Mrs Platt clucked in annoyance. 'He kept me late yesterday typing those papers. He said they were important for today.' She banged her keyboard, huffily.

'Mrs Platt,' said Edward.

She looked up at him.

'I'm going home now. I don't feel well.' He walked away from her. 'I doubt if I'll be back.'

Nine

'It seems we may owe you an apology, Mr Holman.' Wreford looked across his desk at Holman, indicating that he should take the seat opposite.

'You mean you've had more news from the school?'

Chief Superintendent Wreford paused before he spoke, a worried frown on his face. 'Indeed, we have,' he said.

Holman let a weary sigh escape from his lips. It was four am and he had spent a restless night in a small detention room, furnished only with a chair and a hard bed. He'd been woken from his fitful doze by Barrow who had brought him up to Wreford's office without saying a word. Both CID men looked tired for they had spent much of the night talking with various police stations around the Salisbury area in an effort to find out if any unusual incidents had occurred in their areas recently. And if anyone had reported fog.

The report from Andover concerning Redbrook House had spurred them into this activity.

'Tell me what's happened,' said Holman.

'From a class of thirty-seven, one boy managed to escape without any serious injury from the fire. He was in a state of shock – it was assumed that the fire was responsible – but later, he began to say some strange things.' Wreford swivelled his chair so he faced away from Holman. 'At first, the doctors thought he was hysterical, but certain peculiarities about the bodies brought out caused them to listen more closely to what the boy was saying.'

Barrow broke in. 'Some of the bodies were naked; although the fire would have burnt the clothes there would have still been bits of material charred into the skin.'

Wreford continued: 'It looks as though the fire had been deliberately started; a can of petrol was found near one of the bodies – the body of a man. The man had one arm. They're sure it was the deputy headmaster, a man named Summers.'

Holman felt sick; could *he* have prevented it?

'It also seems that many of the bodies had been mutilated,' said Barrow, grimly.

Wreford turned his chair back to Holman. 'From what they can gather from the boy, it started out as a normal PE lesson. Then the boys turned on their sports master and beat him unconscious. Then the other teacher – Summers – came in, and they attacked him. The boy gets hysterical at this point and it's not very clear what happened next, but apparently the other boys seemed to have gone completely berserk, beating and – ' he paused. 'And mutilating each other.'

'Oh, Jesus. If only I'd got to you sooner.'

'You're not to blame, Mr Holman. It happened fairly early in the day. You couldn't have known.'

Holman shook his head. 'No, but it was in the back of my head. Something disturbed me when we were actually in the fog. But what about this boy – is he insane?'

'The doctors think not. Hysterical, yes, and who knows what effect this experience will have on him? But they're sure he's not mad. And so are we.'

'Why? What makes you think so?'

'Something that helps confirm your story about the fog.'

Barrow, sitting on the edge of his Chief Superintendent's desk, spoke: 'He was ill on the day of the outing. The matron wouldn't let him go because he was just getting over a chill. He was in the gym yesterday, but wasn't taking part in the exercises because he wasn't considered well enough. He was sitting at the back, watching his friends. Luckily, they took no notice of him, but he witnessed the whole bizarre episode! Poor little sod.'

The room was quiet for a few moments before Holman asked, 'What happens now?'

'We've spent most of the night talking to police stations in the area, trying to trace the whereabouts of the fog now, enquiring about any unusual events occurring recently on their patches.' Wreford held up several sheets of paper containing scribbled notes. 'There are plenty of strange things that have been happening, but then there always are. Our problem is which of them we can attribute to the fog.'

'Then you do believe me?'

'Let's say we don't disbelieve you. We needed more evidence – '

7   97

'More evidence?' Holman exploded, but Wreford held up his hand.

'We think we have that evidence. A hatchet murder a few days ago: a man named Abbott chopped up a wealthy landowner, his wife and his two women staff, then he cut his own wrists. He had a slight grievance against the landowner, we understand, but hardly enough to account for this butchery. In the same area, a farmer was trampled to death by his cattle, a vicar ran amok in his church. A few other incidents, relatively minor, but nevertheless, they could all add up to the same thing. We've asked for any further reports to be sent directly to us and we're now trying to locate the fog.'

'But it could be anywhere.'

'We'll soon find it.'

'All right, so what's your next move?'

'We compile all the facts, then I contact the Commissioner with a view to presenting the evidence to the Home Secretary.'

'But in the meantime, half the countryside will have been affected.'

'No, Mr Holman. I intend to move fast.' He leaned towards Holman and said sternly, 'But I must have the evidence to show.'

'You've got it!'

'I have a few scribbled notes and reports on their way to me.'

'Then make a verbal report!'

'I intend to. But I have to have a clear case to get to the Home Secretary!'

'A clear case? You're waiting for something else to happen, aren't you?'

'Frankly, yes.'

Holman was dismayed. His mouth dropped open in disbelief.

'But that doesn't mean I'm not taking any action,' Wreford added quickly. 'I've alerted all our forces in the West Country – '

'Telling them what?'

'Telling them to be on the lookout for a dangerous gas and to move in immediately they hear of any disturbances, big or small.'

'But the people should be warned. They should be cleared from the path of the fog!'

'First we have to locate the fog, Mr Holman. And then we have to make sure it *is* responsible for these outbreaks.'

'But you said you believed me!'

'And so I do, but I have no power to do as you ask. And to get any authorisation at all, I have to convince my superiors of the danger.'

'So you're going to wait for more people to die.'

'Within the next few hours, the fog or gas – whatever it may be – will begin to take effect on the people it has already been in contact with and then we should be provided with insurmountable evidence. There would be nothing we could do about these particular people now anyway.'

'Except lock them up for their own good!'

'Be your age, Mr Holman. What would we do? Broadcast a message for anyone who has been in contact with fog recently to please report to their nearest police station? At best, we'd be a laughing stock; at worst, there'd be panic throughout the country. And for what purpose? What if the fog has now dispersed? What if it is now ineffective? What if we find the fog is not to blame after all, that the things that have happened are only unrelated, freak occurrences? What then, Mr Holman? Will you take the responsibility?'

Holman sprang to his feet and thumped the desk with his hand. 'We can't sit around doing nothing!' he shouted.

'I've told you my course of action,' snapped Wreford. 'Now please sit down and try to be reasonable.' He spoke more soothingly. 'Think about it, Mr Holman. We only have your evidence about the fog, and let me be frank, you were only released from hospital the other day after what appeared to be a nervous breakdown. Bear with me, let me assemble the facts before I put forward a case. As it is, I've stretched my neck out by ordering a full alert in the West Country. There'll be all hell to pay when my chiefs hear about it in the morning.' He glanced at his watch. 'I mean later today. I'm just asking you to be a little more patient.'

'I don't have much choice, do I?' said Holman, resting his elbows on his knees and clenching his hands together. 'Very well. But now I want to see Casey. I want to go to the hospital.'

Wreford smiled kindly. 'Of course, but I'd rather you stayed here.'

'Like hell!' Holman sat up again.

'I need you here. Let me get Detective Inspector Barrow to ring the hospital and see how she is. They wouldn't let you see her at this time of the morning, anyway.' Wreford nodded to the young detective, who disappeared from the room.

'I'm sure you understand our position,' Wreford continued smoothly.

'I'm sure I don't,' answered Holman.

Barrow returned a few moments later, a look of concern on his face. He ignored Holman and walked round the Chief Superintendent's desk to whisper in his ear.

'Oh, for God's sake!' stormed Holman.

'It's all right, Mr Holman,' said Wreford, quickly, not wanting the man's temper to boil over again. 'Barrow has rung the hospital and they informed him Miss Simmons was discharged a few hours ago in the care of her father.'

Holman stared blankly at him.

Wreford looked embarrassed. 'I'm sorry. Apparently, there was nothing they could do. The girl seemed perfectly all right, if a little dazed, and her father insisted he took her home despite their protests. They would have liked to have kept her in under observation for a short while, but unfortunately they couldn't prevent her from leaving.'

The blue-green Rover sped through the quiet streets towards Highgate, its three occupants grim and silent. Holman stared blankly out of a window, his tired mind in a frenzy of concern for Casey, an empty, sick feeling in the pit of his stomach. Was she all right? Had the effects of the gas worn off? She really hadn't had too much exposure to it.

Barrow sat beside him in the darkness, his feelings a mixture of disbelief and curiosity. It certainly was an unusual case and he still did not know if he was sitting next to a lunatic or a crusader. The man was certainly hot-tempered, but not exactly raving. And his incredible story certainly had some cold logic to it. You had to take a step back because you found yourself accepting it, and then, when looking at the whole affair objectively, *that* was when you realised how ridiculous it was. He was glad it was Wreford who would be taking responsibility and he would only be carrying out orders. Too soft, was Wreford, always had been. Shrewd, though, no question of that. But he'd made a big mistake this time, trusting this prick! He'd stuck his neck out all right, but not as much as he'd led Holman to believe. Wreford had alerted the local police forces, certainly, but only to be on the lookout for any adverse weather conditions, *particularly* fog, and to report such to him direct. He'd persuaded a friend in the central control room, where information from all over the country was relayed, to keep him informed throughout the night if any reports of an unusual nature came in from Somerset, Wiltshire, Dorset or Hampshire. Unofficially, of course. He'd have to explain his request for weather reports, and he'd better have a good reason ready, but that was as far as he'd risked his reputation. And if – just *if* – Holman's incredible theory was correct, Wreford was covered; he'd acted, with discretion, on the information he'd received.

Barrow glanced at his watch. Ten past five. Jesus, he was tired; A couple of hours kip in one of the detention rooms hadn't done him much good, and all for what? For the benefit of this creep. Still, it had been uncanny about the school. Maybe . . . ? No, now he was falling for it! Holman's voice instructing the driver interrupted his thoughts.

'Straight to the top of Highgate Hill and turn left through the village. Then it's a side-road off to the left. I'll tell you where.'

The police car began its ascent up the long hill, the gradual dawn light giving the streets a lonely and chilly atmosphere. They reached the village and turned left towards Hampstead, Holman peering through the window, anxiously looking for the road Casey and her father lived in. He spotted it and told the driver to turn off, the tension inside him beginning to mount. Again, he asked himself: had the effects of the fog worn off? He would soon find out.

He tapped the driver's shoulder when he saw the house. 'That's it,' he pointed.

It was a large house, set close to the road, the small front garden only nominal, but compensated for by the huge landscaped garden to the rear. Casey's father was a wealthy man, deputy-chairman of one of Britain's biggest Unit Trust Finance Houses and with interests in many other commercial enterprises, not the least of which was property development. On the few occasions they'd met, they had taken a dislike to one another, because both knew they were vying for the same person – Casey. Holman had been surprised at the intensity of Simmons' hostility; he understood his possessiveness after losing his wife, but the affection he displayed towards Casey made Holman feel uncomfortable. It seemed a little too intimate for a father-daughter relationship. When he later questioned her about it, Casey had been genuinely amazed that he should think there was anything odd about her father's attitude. Amazed, then angry at his implication. Holman had backed off, realising his own jealousy could be colouring his view of the situation. But Simmons had made it quite obvious that Holman's interest in his daughter was not at all welcome and on one occasion had gone to great lengths to tell him so while Casey was out of the room. Holman's icy response had done nothing to soothe the situation between the two men and, as a consequence, he'd never been back to the house again while her father was there.

Now as he stared up at the dark windows of the house, he cursed the older man's stupidity in insisting Casey be released from the hospital so soon. It she had harmed herself – He pushed the unwelcome thoughts from his mind.

'Looks like they're all in bed, doesn't it?' remarked Barrow caustically.

Holman ignored him and got out of the car.

'You wait here Tom,' he heard Barrow behind him tell the driver. Holman walked towards the front gate to the house, then stopped to let the Detective Inspector catch up.

'Do you really want to wake them up?' Barrow asked.

'Yes,' answered Holman, and walked towards the impressive white front door. His sense of foreboding increased when he discovered it was open. He pushed at it with a trembling hand.

Ten

At that precise moment, just over a hundred miles away, Mavis Evers stood bare-foot on Bournemouth beach and contemplated suicide. She had driven through the night from London, fighting the tears that welled up, obscuring her vision, threatening to send her red Mini crashing off the road. She did not want to die in the wreckage of a car so that her friends, her parents would never know whether it had been deliberate or accidental. She wanted them to know she had taken her own life. Her death, unlike her life, had to have some meaning. Even if it was only Ronnie who fully understood that reason.

Ronnie had destroyed her. Ronnie had made her fall in love. Ronnie had made her lose her innocence.

Twice she had to pull over to the side of the road and stop, unable to stem the flood of tears that had abruptly burst forth. Once she had to stop as fog drifted into her path, and she had wept as she waited for it to pass.

Why had her lover done this to her? After living together for two years, sharing each other's lives joyfully, excluding anyone else from their intimate happiness. Laughing at the world. Until Ronnie had suddenly, and irrevocably, drifted away. It had taken a mere two weeks, the first signs when Ronnie had sorrowfully but firmly rejected her caresses, then the arguments, the questions, the pleading, and finally, the terrible revelation. Ronnie had fallen in love with someone else. A man. She had fallen in love with a man.

The irony was that it had been Ronnie who had seduced Mavis. Seduced her and introduced her to a kind of love she'd never known. A private kind of love – the kind that can only be shared by two women. A love not acceptable to most, but more binding to those it touched because of its illicitness.

Mavis had known Ronnie years before when they were both children living in Basingstoke. Their parents had been friends and they would often all go off together at weekends to the coast. The times they spent at Bournemouth were the times Mavis treasured most for it was there, in a boarding house where the two young girls had to share a bed, that Ronnie first introduced her to the delights of her own body. She was eleven, Ronnie was twelve. Their parents had gone out for the evening, promising the girls crisps and lemonade if they were good, hoping, in fact, that they'd both be sound asleep when they returned. As the girls lay there, talking over the events of the day, whom they both liked, whom they mutually disliked, Ronnie had suddenly asked Mavis if she had ever touched herself. Perplexed, she had asked where?

Shyly, Ronnie had put her fingers between Mavis' legs, then quickly drew them away. Mavis had been surprised and excited by the strange tingle that had run through her, and touched herself in the same place again, giggling at first and enjoying the sensation. Ronnie had asked if she could feel her there again and she'd agreed, a flush now spreading through her body, but on the condition that she could also touch Ronnie. They'd spent the following two hours in exciting, girlishly innocent, mutual masturbation.

It only happened on two other occasions after that, neither girl placing any significance on the act, both enjoying it for what it was – a happy diversion. They'd seen little of one another in the subsequent years, Ronnie's parents having moved to London, visiting each other perhaps three or four times a year, neither mentioning their earlier intimacies, Mavis at least, realising it was just a stage in development they'd gone through together. Eventually, Ronnie had moved away from her parents, finding a flat for herself further into town, nearer to her job, nearer to her social life. They had corresponded for a while, but even this dwindled to cards on birthdays and at Christmas. And then, not long after her twenty-first birthday, bored by her job, bored by her parents, and bored by her lack of boyfriends, Mavis decided London might be the place for her too. She contacted Ronnie to see if she knew of any reasonably priced flats available, and her friend wrote back suggesting she stayed with her until she found something. So, a little nervous of the sprawling city, Mavis moved in with Ronnie. She was slightly in awe of her friend of long ago when they met at Euston, for Ronnie had developed into a beautiful, sophisticated young woman – on the surface, at any rate. Mavis was soon to learn that she assumed this pose for people she didn't know very well, and this, for a brief time, included Mavis.

Mavis was amazed by Ronnie's wide circle of friends, several of whom were actually *coloured*, and tried desperately to fall in with their cynical and blasé attitudes towards their lives, but after a few weeks, she realised she would never fit naturally into their set. She found their values phoney, their ideals superficial.

She disliked being an imposition on her friend whom she found, underneath the gloss, was the same understanding, lonely girl she'd once known, so she searched for a suitable flat of her own. Disappointed by the depressingly poor accommodation she had been offered, she finally broke down one night after she had returned from another fruitless expedition into gloomy bed-sitter land. The flats she had liked were way above her price range; the ones she could afford were too run-down and seedy for words. She had got soaked to the skin in the steady London drizzle and at the first kind words of sympathy from her friend, her emotions had bubbled to the surface.

Ronnie had perched on the arm of the settee on which Mavis was sitting and put her arm round her distraught friend's shoulders, telling her not to worry, that they would work something out later. She told her to get out of her wet clothes and to take a quick hot bath, then to hop into bed and she would bring her a good stiff drink. After weeping a little while longer, with Ronnie gently stroking her damp hair, she pulled herself together, smiled her thanks through her tears, and went into the tiny room that was used as a dressing-room and spare bedroom. She changed into her dressing-gown as Ronnie ran the bath for her. She soaked for ten minutes, allowing the hot water to warm her body and soothe her distraught nerves. She scrubbed herself and washed her hair, then briskly dried off on one of Ronnie's luxuriously soft towels. Her friend had done well for herself since she'd moved up to London, working as a secretary to the chairman of an American tobacco company, later becoming his personal assistant. The rent for the flat must have been quite high if the prices of the humble flats Mavis had come across were anything to go by. And her clothes were expensive and plentiful, the extent and range of her wardrobe stunning Mavis into open-mouthed admiration. But she was still basically the same sweet friend Mavis had known all those years ago.

She went to her room and heard Ronnie's voice from the

kitchen. 'You get into bed and I'll bring you in some hot chocolate and that stiff drink I promised you!'

'Thank you,' Mavis called back, taking the towel from her wet hair, rubbing her head with it vigorously. She brushed out the knots until it was long and straight, clinging closely to her neck and shoulders. Unwrapping her dressing gown from her body, she caught sight of herself in the full-length mirror, her pink flesh looking round and pure in the soft glow of the reading lamp. She studied herself for a few seconds, content that her figure, although not stunning, was firm yet supple, curvy, but certainly not fat. She ran her hands along her sides and inwards, over her hips and across her soft midriff, then up towards her breasts. As they travelled over the gentle swells, she became aware of Ronnie watching her from the doorway.

She quickly dropped her hands and flushed when she realised her nipples had stiffened to tiny pink points.

'Your body is lovely,' said Ronnie quietly.

Mavis was embarrassed. 'Oh, I'm no Venus, but I suppose it's okay.'

'It's beautiful.' Ronnie moved into the room and set the tray with hot chocolate and two brandies on the small dresser by the side of the bed. She pulled back the blankets and patted the pillow. 'Come on, jump in before you catch cold,' she said, holding the blankets open and moving aside to allow Mavis past.

As Mavis slid between the sheets, Ronnie sat on the edge of the bed, only partially covering her friend's body with the blankets, leaving her breasts and most of her tummy bare. Mavis felt herself reddening even more as Ronnie unashamedly studied her, a faint smile on her lips.

'Remember when we were kids?' Ronnie asked.

Mavis remembered, only now the memory seemed to take on a special meaning. She nodded her head.

'Your body was nice even then,' Ronnie went on, her gaze lingering on the two tiny rosebuds of flesh that were now even more pronounced. Strangely, Mavis no longer felt embarrassed by her look, but began to take pleasure from it, feeling the same rising excitement she'd felt as a child. Her heart was thumping, her nerves trembling. She neither thought of what might happen next, nor denied the thought; her mind was peculiarly alive, yet numb.

Ronnie raised her hand to Mavis' cheek. 'I've missed having

a friend,' she said, her fingertips barely touching the skin, but delicately sensual because of it.

'But I thought you had lots of friends here.' Mavis' voice was small and hesitant.

Ronnie's eyes flickered with sadness for an instant, but the look was barely perceptible. 'Yes, I've lots of friends. But not a real friend – as you were.'

Mavis looked down. 'I'm sorry.'

'Don't be,' Ronnie smiled. 'You're here now.'

Her hand lightly travelled down and rested on Mavis' neck. The grip tightened slightly, then relaxed again.

Mavis found her breath quickening, her small breasts beginning to rise and fall. She raised her own hand to the hand resting at her neck and squeezed the fingers gently, leaving it there.

Ronnie's eyes glistened with what could have been tears and she drew in her breath sharply. Then her hand began to travel down again, tracing the fine skin with feather-like fingers until it found the soft mound she was looking for. Mavis shivered as the palm closed over her breast, and her nipple was trapped between two fingers. Ronnie leaned forward and touched the pink tip with her lips, kissing it gently then moistening it with her tongue.

A glow was enveloping Mavis, starting at her breasts and spreading down to her stomach, then down, down till it was between her thighs. Even the extremities of her limbs were tingling pleasurably, a subdued kind of electricity running through her entire body. She shut her mind from any thoughts of what it all meant. It didn't matter; its meaning wasn't important.

Ronnie had now put her arm around Mavis' back and pulled herself towards her, her lips brushing the naked girl's neck, kissing and biting very, very gently. Mavis slid further down in the bed allowing both of them to lie side by side. As yet, she had not touched Ronnie, a little afraid to do so, a tiny part of her subconscious telling her this would be the final irrevocable relinquishment.

Ronnie's lips finally found hers and they kissed, still softly, all their movements soft, as though passion would make it ugly. Ronnie thrust her tongue between Mavis' lips and was answered by a hesitant counter-thrust. Her hand found Mavis' breast again and this time, its touch was more urgent, gliding from one to the other, not wanting to neglect either. Mavis began to moan slightly as Ronnie's hand began its slow descent down her body towards the place that was so ready – and yearning to receive it. It reached the flat tummy and Ronnie spread it for a moment, feeling Mavis' muscles quiver. Then she continued her unhurried but anxious journey until she reached the little curls of hair, the matted triangle that hid the path to the centre, and her fingertips worked their gentle way through it.

Mavis was disappointed when, instead of descending between her thighs, the hand passed on and stroked the fleshy tops of her legs. She realised it had been an exquisite tease when the fingers began their ascent, this time along the beautifully sensitive inner sides of the thighs. She opened her legs slightly, so that the journey would not be hindered – and then Ronnie was there.

Mavis moaned aloud as Ronnie's fingers crept into her vagina and spread her moistness upwards. She clutched at Ronnie fiercely, finally giving in fully to the passion that had been aroused in her, eager to be touched, to be fondled – even to be hurt. Her fingers pulled at Ronnie's blouse until she found the breasts that Ronnie had so patiently waited to have touched, now wanting her friend's body as much as she had wanted Ronnie to have her own.

Mavis found her hand moving down until it was between her friend's legs. Her lover's legs! The thought increased her desire so that it was almost unbearable, and soon their senses stretched to a frenzy, their cries of joy merged into one long shuddering moan.

They lay naked in the bed and talked into the early hours, each reluctant to sleep, both eager to explore the other's mind and body. They made love many more times that night, in many different ways, but now each way was gentle and had little to do with lust. They discussed the thought that they were lesbians, yet neither could feel any guilt or shame. Ronnie admitted sadly that she had had affairs with women before, but none had touched her emotions as this had, none had been anything other than a means to satisfy passion.

Mavis confessed she had only once been made love to by a man and although she had enjoyed the experience, it had meant nothing emotionally. Both were touched by the other's disclosures; and both realised they had found something unique.

For two years Ronnie and Mavis had been happy sharing a life, not living as man and wife, but just as lovers; neither had any inclination to adopt a masculine role, it wasn't that kind of relationship. Their lovemaking excluded any artificial contrivances; they attained satisfaction only from the other's body, both retaining femininity, both regarding their intimacy as pure.

But then, only two weeks ago, a change had come over Ronnie. It was rapid and alarming. She had rejected Mavis' caresses, falling into long brooding silences, unable to disclose the reason for her sullen moods. Several nights she stayed out, refusing to tell Mavis where she had been, until last night, after being away for three consecutive days, she had come back to the flat and brokenly told her friend that she no longer loved her, that she had met someone who had swept away hidden fears, made her see that the physical love she had always dreaded was a wonderful and deeply moving act. She had fallen in love with a man, and had allowed that man to make love to her.

Ronnie had wept bitterly as she explained that she hadn't wanted it to happen, but Philip had been so kind, so gentle, that her inhibitions about men had melted and, it seemed, her body cleansed. These last words hurt Mavis terribly. Cleansed! Had their love been dirty? Had their sleeping together, holding one another – had it all been revolting? She screamed at Ronnie, implored her not to leave, begged her on her knees. But she had been pushed away, violently, and it was the violence of it that stunned her most, penetrated the part of her that refused to accept her lover's rejection. Ronnie had never used physical force against her before; she had thrown her from her as though this physical action represented the breaking of their ties. Mavis had crawled towards her again, weeping in her own shame, and tried to put her arms around her, tried to bury her head in Ronnie's breasts. Ronnie had allowed her to do so for a moment, but when Mavis' hand reached further in a desperate effort to bring back their previous closeness, she had jumped up, knocking Mavis to the floor, screaming that she must never touch her again.

That was when Mavis knew she had lost. Her sorrow turned to rage when she thought of how she had been cheated. It was Ronnie who had led *her* into this way of life, seduced her! How could she now cast her aside as though it had meant nothing, a phase she had gone through? She had found a 'normal' love and left Mavis unwilling now for any other kind of love. What would she become? A lonely, embittered lesbian? She cried out in self pity.

Ronnie had walked to the door and opened it. Before she left, she had said, 'I'm sorry, Mavis, I'm so sorry. But I have to go, Philip is waiting for me downstairs in his car. He doesn't know about us, and I never want him to. Perhaps someday, when I'm sure of him, I'll tell him. Believe me, Mavis, I didn't want this to happen – I didn't know it ever could – but it's the right thing. I think we were wrong. Forgive me, darling. I hope someday you'll find what I have.'

When Ronnie had left, Mavis remained in a heap on the floor, weeping bitter tears, shocked by her lover's cruelty, appalled at the fate she saw for herself. She finally recognised their affair for what it was – two women living together in an abnormal relationship. She had never accepted the fact that she was homosexual, but somehow, Ronnie's leaving took away all the sensitivity of their mutual inclinations and revealed Mavis in her true light. A lesbian!

It was a fact she now felt unable to live with. The guilt that had lain hidden deep in her mind came to the surface and for the first time she felt remorse. But still she cried for Ronnie, wanted her there in her arms, to be comforted by her, to be possessed by her, and her shame increased because of it. She rose from the floor, her face puffed and blotchy, and curled up on the sofa, her knees drawn up to her chin. She thought back over the two years, the intimacies they'd shared, the plans they'd made. She went back to when they were younger, friends who giggled over their innocent secret. She thought of the first time, in Bournemouth, where now she realised, their union had been unknowingly sealed. Why had everything changed? What was it that caused people to destroy each other?

Then she had decided what she would do. Fighting back her tears, she went down to the little red Mini they had bought, never thinking there would come a day when their possessions would have to be divided as would a divorced couple's.

She drove through the night to Bournemouth, stopping occasionally when she could no longer stem her tears, her only consolation now in what she was going to do. And once, she was forced to stop because of heavy fog.

And now, Mavis stood barefooted on the beach, looking at the moody grey sea in the dawn light. She had stopped crying, her emotions not drained but held in check, because there was no point in tears if she were going to die. She still saw the image of Ronnie before her: her sad-smiling face, her soft brown eyes that reflected sorrow even when they were laughing.

Mavis walked towards the sea, leaving her shoes on the beach behind. The water chilled her with its coldness, but the chill in her spirit was greater. She waded in further, the water rising to her knees, the tide pushing against her as though urging her to go back. It reached her thighs, causing her thin skirt to cling to them, then touched the part of her body that Ronnie had adored and kissed so often. She sank deeper and now the sea seemed to be drawing her in instead of pushing her back, welcoming her into its enveloping, icy depths. She found it difficult to breathe because of the combination of cold and the pressure of the water now around her chest. And the fear she had begun to feel. She stopped, straining to keep her balance against the now unfriendly water.

Death. Death was so absolute. And would there be pain before her body succumbed to the final blackness? Would her body resist the pull of death in those last seconds, panicking to regain the breath of life she'd deliberately let escape? Would her body betray her and fight to preserve its fleeing spirit, causing lingering agony instead of swift and final oblivion? And the pain, the mental anguish she would cause Ronnie, making her responsible for her death. Did she want to destroy Ronnie as well as herself? She still loved Ronnie, she didn't want to hurt her as she had been hurt. Perhaps there was still a chance; perhaps Ronnie would find she wasn't meant for heterosexual love. Perhaps, after a few weeks, she would return to Mavis, disillusioned with his maleness, yearning for the understanding and physical comfort only her friend could give her. There *had* to be a chance! And Mavis would be waiting, ready to forgive her, eager to hold her close while Ronnie pleaded with her to take her back. And their love would be stronger than ever, because both of them would know they were irrevocably tied.

The black sea around her was so frightening!

She struggled to turn around in it, desperate to reach the shore, no longer wanting to die. She nearly lost her balance, and cried out in terror. She was not a good swimmer and if her feet were swept from beneath her she would find it difficult to make her way back to the beach. It would be so pointless to die now, now that she knew that she had not necessarily lost her lover, that their bond could bring them together again.

She staggered back, careful not to lose her footing, feeling as though she were in a nightmare where her legs had become lead and would not allow her to run from the death behind.

She gradually reached a point where the lapping water was only waist deep and stopped for a moment to regain her breath, relieved that she was safe, her mind taking on a curious lightness now that the burden of death had been lifted.

As her chest heaved with the effort, her eyes widened uncomprehendingly.

There were hundreds – could it be thousands? – of people climbing down the steps to the beach and walking towards her, towards the sea!

Was she dreaming? Had her mind become unbalanced because of the distress she had been through? The people of the town were marching in a solid wall out to the sea, making no sound, staring towards the horizon as though something was beckoning to them. Their faces were white, trance-like, barely human. And there were children among them; some walked along on their own, seeming to belong to no one; those who couldn't walk were being carried. Most of the people were in their nightclothes, some were naked, having risen from their beds as though answering a call that Mavis neither heard nor saw. She looked behind her, out towards the brightening horizon, but saw only the black, threatening sea.

They were advancing on her now, and she realised there *were* thousands of them, pouring from houses, hotels, side streets, in a huge moving mass, their footsteps the only sound they made, and these muffled for the majority were barefooted.

Mavis saw an old woman in the front line stumble and fall and she gasped in horror as the crowd passed over her, trampling her into the sand. Their pace did not slow as they entered the sea and they advanced in a solid human wall. She looked to the right and then to the left and saw the wall extended for as far as she could see. The scene, its significance, was too enormous for her to understand. She thought only of getting away from the path of that crushing multitude.

She backed away, but the sea behind was just as threatening. She began to scream at the people as they drew nearer, like a child who is to be punished screaming at an advancing parent. But still they came on, oblivious to her cries, unseeing. She realised her danger and ran towards them in a vain attempt to break through, but they forced her back, heedless to her pleas as she strained and beat against them. She managed to push a short path through them, but the great numbers before her were inconquerable, pushing her back, back into the waiting sea.

Mavis fell and struggled desperately to regain her feet. In doing so, she knocked down a small boy and immediately went down again to pull him to his feet. He stared ahead, not seeing her, not even knowing he had just fallen.

She was knocked again, and this time went under, losing her grip on the boy, her lungs filling with salty water. She emerged fighting for breath, blinded by the salt water, screaming and kicking out in panic. What was happening? Had she killed herself and was this the hell all suicides entered? She fell to her knees again, and this time, as she attempted to rise, other bodies fell on top of her. She squirmed around beneath the water, becoming tangled in other arms and legs. Air escaped from her lungs as she tried to scream and then she felt a tiredness beginning to overcome her. Her struggles became weaker and she finally lay there in the blackness, bodies stumbling over her, some falling on top of her, pinning her to the soft sea floor. Her eyes were open as the last bubble of air escaped from her lips. The terror had gone. There was no pain. There was no recollection of her life, no memories to taunt her in her dying. Just a misty blankness. No thoughts of God. No questions why. Just a descending white veil. Not a veil of peace, nor one of horror. Not even one of emptiness. Nothingness. Free of emotion and free of coldness. She was dead.

The inhabitants and the holidaymakers of Bournemouth came from their homes, hotels and guest houses in their thousands and made for the sea, filling the streets, pouring on to the beach. The fog that had ruined their day yesterday was killing them that morning. They walked into the sea to drown like lemmings, the people behind them climbing over the dead bodies that were heaping up on the sea bed. People who for various reasons, could not walk, killed themselves in other ways. Hundreds could not reach the sea because it was too full of others who had already drowned, and these were later pulled back screaming from the beach by people who rushed to the seaside resort in a vain attempt to minimise the destruction.

The fog rejected the sea either because of its coldness or because the winds were too strong for it. It moved inland again, as though it were a living thing, leaving behind its evil, never settling in one place, always moving, as though searching for something.

Eleven

Holman entered the dark house, trying to make as little noise as possible.

'It would be a better idea to ring the bell and wake them up, wouldn't it?' came Barrow's voice from behind.

'No,' Holman whispered.

'Why the hell not?'

'I don't know. I just don't think it's a good idea.'

'All right. But this is breaking and entering, you know that, don't you?'

'You can wait outside if you want,' Holman whispered back fiercely.

'Oh, no, mate I'm going to hang on to you.'

'Then keep quiet and follow me.'

'I'll keep quiet for now, but later – '

Holman turned away, ignoring the CID man, angered by his arrogance. He moved towards the lounge and quietly pushed the door open. It was empty. He closed the door again and made his way down the hall, towards the room he knew to be Simmons' study. He thought he heard a muffled sound as he turned the handle, but Barrow's urgent whisper distracted him.

'There's a light on upstairs.' Barrow had already begun to climb the stairs and Holman hurried after him. He took the steps two at a time in an effort to catch up with the swift-moving policeman.

'It's her father's bedroom,' he told Barrow as he reached him.

'We're going to look pretty silly when we find him getting dressed for work,' the Detective Inspector sneered.

'Better we look silly than end up with a knife in our throat.'

'My God, and she's *your* girlfriend.'

'I told you, she's not responsible. For the moment, she's out of her mind.'

'Huh!' Barrow snorted. 'Someone is.'

Holman frowned at him. 'You still don't believe me.'

'Listen, mate. I'm under orders from Wreford to play along with you. It doesn't mean I have to believe you!'

'Barrow, you're a bundle of charm.' Holman grinned without humour. 'But you've got your orders – so play along with me.'

He turned away from the fuming policeman, and mounted the rest of their stairs, pausing at the top to listen for any sound. Barrow joined him and they moved stealthily towards the thin bar of light coming from beneath the bedroom door.

Holman slowly turned the handle, involuntarily holding his breath, and gently pushed the door open.

The light came from a small bedside lamp, so its brightness did not hurt their eyes. A figure lay in the bed. All they could see was the head, the eyes looking up towards the ceiling; the face was grey and sunken, the pallor of death about it.

'Simmons!' Holman hurried over to the bed and stopped before the prone figure, his worst fears realised. The shocked eyes slowly turned towards him, and the pale lips moved as though to speak. Barrow pushed past him and leaned towards the older man.

'What's happened, sir? Where are you hurt?'

For a moment the eyes looked at the policeman then swivelled back towards Holman.

'Y-you did this to her,' he said in a weak voice, 'You m-made her do this.'

Holman was too stunned to say anything. Was he now to be blamed for this? He knelt beside the older man.

'Where's Casey – Christine?' he asked.

'Why, why did she do this?' Simmons' eyes looked down as though indicating at something near his stomach.

Barrow yanked back the bedclothes and both men gasped. The end of a pair of scissors protruded from Simmons' stomach, and his pyjamas and the bedsheets were stained with blood.

'Jesus, Jesus!' breathed Barrow. He turned towards Holman. 'I'm going to get Jennings to radio for an ambulance. There's still a chance we can save him if we're quick. Prop his head up with a pillow so he doesn't choke on his own blood. And don't touch those scissors. Don't try and pull them out!' He disappeared through the door and Holman heard him leaping down the stairs, recklessly taking two or three at a time.

115

Holman pulled a blood soaked sheet over the wound, feeling sick, not at the sight of the injury, but at the thought that it had been Casey who had perpetrated it. He bent his head towards her father as he tried to speak, his words only a whisper, barely audible.

'W-why did she do it? I loved her, she knew that.'

'She wasn't responsible,' Holman told him, speaking in a soft voice, as though words could cause the man further injury. 'She came in contact with a – a poisonous gas that affected her mind.' Simmons' eyes looked puzzled for a moment, his brain not understanding the words but then accepting them almost with relief. She had tried to kill him because she was ill – it hadn't been an act of hate; that was enough for his weakened senses for the moment. He began to speak again. 'I brought her home from the hospital. They told me what you'd done to her.' His face became almost fierce, but the effort was too much and its lines fell back into an expression of pain.

'No, I didn't do anything to her,' Holman assured him. 'It was the gas, it made her unwell.'

'I – I brought her home. She seemed dazed. She kept putting her hands to her head as though she were in pain. They didn't want to let her go, but I knew she'd be better off with me. I put her to bed and sat there talking to her. She didn't seem to hear me. I told her things I've never spoken to her about before, but she didn't seem to hear me.'

He began to choke and Holman became worried that blood was rising in his throat. He slid his hand beneath the older man's head in an effort to stop the blood reaching his mouth, not really knowing if it would prevent asphyxiation.

Simmons managed to stop coughing and lay there breathing heavily. 'I loved her,' he went on, 'perhaps too much.'

Holman said nothing.

'And – and I told her something I'd never told her before tonight.'

'Don't talk any more. Try to save your strength.' Holman was hardly listening to him for he'd noticed fresh blood seeping through the sheets.

'No, I must tell you, Holman. You've a right to know – you love her too.' His hands tried to reach the scissors beneath the sheet, but fell back limply to his sides. 'I – I'm not her father, Holman. Her bitch of a mother told me who her real father was just before we were divorced. But it made no difference to

116

me, I loved the child too much. I fought tooth-and-nail for custody, and her mother could never claim in court Christine wasn't mine because she would be admitting her own infidelity. And she was too shrewd and greedy for that.' Holman could almost detect an embittered smile on the pain-wracked face.

That could explain certain things about the man's attitude towards Casey. He looked on her as his daughter, but because he knew she wasn't, another element had crept into their relationship. An element that Casey hadn't been aware of and Holman had only suspected. But it was still sickening, even though there were no real blood ties. Even in his injured state, Holman felt a loathing towards the man.

'I told her tonight – that's why she did this to me,' Simmons murmured, more to himself than Holman.

'No, it wasn't because of that. I told you, it was the gas.'

'It was too much for her I suppose in her shocked state.' He was too deep in his own remorse to listen to the younger man, 'I woke up, I don't know how long ago – a couple of hours, I suppose – and there she was, standing over me. I'd left on the lamp in case she needed me during the night, so I could see her plainly; she was just looking down at me, expressionless, her hands behind her back.' A tear trickled from the corner of his eye. 'I – I put out my arms for her to come to me.' His eyes that had been staring at the ceiling now looked guiltily at Holman. 'I misunderstood.'

Holman frowned. Misunderstood?

'She came towards me, then,' he began to tremble uncontrollably, 'then she pulled back the bedclothes and I saw the scissors slashing down . . . ' His voice broke as he relived the experience.

The younger man's thoughts were not clear. Simmons seemed to be blaming himself. He'd said he'd misunderstood; had he thought? Oh, no, not that. Surely he couldn't have thought Casey had come to him for that kind of love? How stupid, how blind could he be? Poor Casey, to go through that . . . A cry from downstairs interrupted his thoughts. It had sounded like a man's cry, probably Barrow's.

He left the dying man and rushed to the top of the stairs. The sounds seemed to be coming from the study below, sounds of crashing furniture and shouts of alarm. He flew down the stairs and pushed open the study door. And then he stopped.

Barrow was on his hands and knees on the floor, blood oozing from a wound in his scalp. Casey stood above him, a wicked

117

looking shard of glass in her hand. The remnants of the large antique mirror lay shattered around her feet. She raised her arm, ready to plunge the pointed glass down into the back of Barrow's neck.

'Casey!' Holman cried.

She turned to look at him, for an instant, a flicker of recognition showing on her face. Then she smiled and walked towards him. He stopped, still wary, and reached out a hand to her. 'Casey,' he said softly.

With a snarl that changed her smiling face into a grimace of pure hatred she threw herself at him, the weapon slashing for his face.

He ducked under her arm and slammed his elbow into her back knocking her into the wall. He knew from their previous struggle he would have to use force to subdue her. She sprang away from the wall, her clenched fist bleeding from the glass she held, and leapt at him again, the tip of the shard catching his cheek and drawing a thin line of blood. Catching her wrist, Holman smacked her face viciously, sending her to her knees, but still holding on to her. He increased the pressure on her wrist causing her to cry out in pain and to drop the glass. Swiftly pulling her to her feet again, he turned her back to him and pinned her arms behind her. She screamed and fought like the mad woman she was, but this time he showed no mercy and used all his strength to hold her there, bruising her arms with his tight grip.

Barrow had staggered to the door now and was watching them in amazement.

'Christ,' he gasped. 'And to think I didn't believe you.'

'Don't just stand there, you bloody fool!' Holman shouted at him. 'Get something to tie her up with!'

Barrow disappeared from the doorway and returned a moment later with a length of curtain rope. The driver of the police car came through the front door as they were tying the girl's hands.

'Ambulance is on its way, sir,' he said to Barrow, not raising an eyebrow at the scene before him.

'Right. There's an injured man upstairs. Go and stay with him – I think he's had it.' The young detective rubbed the back of his neck. 'Bloody cow,' he groaned. 'I was just coming back into the house when I saw the study door closing. I reckon she was just leaving the house when we drew up and she ducked

118

into the study as we came in. She was probably trying to creep out again as I came back.'

'What happened?' asked Holman, leading the girl into the vast lounge where he sat her down on a long, leather settee. She seemed docile now.

Barrow followed them. 'I ran into the study and then she hit me. She must have been standing behind the door with that bloody mirror in her hands, waiting for me. She knocked me silly, anyway. All I can remember is crawling around the floor trying to get away from her. Bitch!'

'Watch your mouth, Barrow,' said Holman, angrily. He'd had enough of the policeman for one day and was prepared to take a swing at him himself if the man continued in his aggressiveness. He knelt before Casey, taking her pale face in his hands. She stared past him, over his shoulder, her eyes wide and unseeing.

'Casey, darling, can you hear me?' he asked tenderly. 'Can you understand me?'

Her eyes looked at him coldly. 'Bastard,' she said.

It was as though she had hit him. The word was said with such icy vehemence it shocked and hurt him deeply.

'She doesn't know you, Holman, can't you see that,' said Barrow, not unkindly.

'No, she doesn't.' Holman's eyes clouded. 'Will she ever know me again?'

This time, Holman went with Casey to the hospital. Her father was taken by ambulance to the Whittington Hospital on High-gate Hill, while she was returned in the squad car to the Middlesex Hospital. Detective Inspector Barrow left Holman anxiously discussing the girl with the doctor who had treated her previously, and went back to make his report to Chief Superintendent Wreford at New Scotland Yard.

Barrow found the complex building in an uproar and was staggered himself when he caught drift of the news. He hurried to Wreford's office, who confirmed his worst suspicions and sent him rushing back to the hospital to bring in Holman. Reluctantly, Holman agreed to accompany him again to the Yard on the understanding that Casey was to be kept under the strictest supervision and having advised the doctor to get in touch with the hospital in Salisbury where he had been treated,

The doctor had agreed but wanted to know more of Holman's case. Barrow interrupted, telling him he would have to obtain all his information from Salisbury. Holman was needed urgently at New Scotland Yard in a matter which involved more than the well-being of one girl.

He would say no more as they drove back towards Westminster, telling Holman he would find out soon enough and that he himself had yet to hear a full report. Finally, seated in Wreford's office, Holman was told the astonishing and frightening facts.

Wreford wasted no time with preamble. 'We've little time for apologies, Mr Holman,' he began bluntly. 'I've heard briefly what happened to yourself and Detective Inspector Barrow earlier this morning and I sympathise with what you've been through, but events have taken on a greater significance.

'Reports have been flowing in through the night about certain strange occurrences. They weren't channelled through to me of course until I made a request for such reports. I must tell you now, that I did this unofficially.'

He held up his hand at Holman's look of surprise. 'We won't go into it now, but you must understand, I couldn't just take your word for it; I had to play safe.'

'All right,' said Holman bitterly. 'I suppose I should be grateful you even took an interest.'

Wreford cleared his throat and looked down, for a moment embarrassed, then the snap was back in his voice as he went on. 'Well, the reports began to accumulate and pretty soon, it wasn't just me, but the whole building involved. They seemed to be just individual incidents at first, some minor, others a deal more serious, but together they began to take on a pattern. They seemed to be happening in a ragged line between Wiltshire, Dorset and Hampshire. They're pretty curious in our control room of course as to why I had put in an unofficial request for reports around those areas. I'm saving my answer for the Commissioner for Police; we have a meeting in,' he looked at his watch, 'ten minutes. I want you to be there.'

Holman nodded his agreement.

Wreford's face became even more grave as he went on. 'Most of these incidents were isolated, usually concerning one person, occasionally two or three, certainly no more. But just under an hour ago, the most alarming news of all came through. We're all very much in the dark at the moment – we're getting a fuller picture by the minute – but it seems incredible, totally un-believable.'

'For Christ's sake!' said Holman impatiently.

'At around six o'clock this morning, virtually the entire population of Bournemouth left their homes and walked into the sea in a mass suicide attempt. '

Silence filled the room. At last, Holman managed to say, 'It's impossible.'

'Impossible, yes, but it has happened. Over 148,820 people. And that's not counting the thousands that were on holiday there. Men, women, children – all drowned. They're still trying to drag those who couldn't reach the sea back from the beach. Poole Harbour is just crammed with floating bodies, the shores around Bournemouth are littered with corpses.'

Barrow, who had been quiet up to now, spoke. 'What about the fog, sir? Has it been sighted?'

'I've issued instructions to locate it but naturally the local towns have enough on their minds without worrying about fog. I couldn't give them the reason yet without causing a large scale panic. I have to see the Commissioner before I do that. But one thing I did learn: Bournemouth was covered in a thick blanket of fog yesterday.'

The Commissioner for Police wasted no time in getting in contact with the Home Secretary and arranging an immediate meeting. He'd listened grimly to Holman's story occasionally interrupting to ask a relevant question, but not once voicing a negative opinion. Holman asked that the Minister of State for Defence and his own chief, the Parliamentary Under-Secretary of State for the Department of the Environment, be present at their meeting with the Home Secretary, remembering the meeting Spiers had arranged before his death.

Twenty minutes later, he found himself relating his story again in a large, oak-panelled room in Whitehall surrounded by the Ministers and their chiefs-of-staff, having questions fired at him in rapid succession, the Parliamentary Under-Secretary of State for the Army angrily rejecting his insinuations that the military in Salisbury might have some answers as to the cause of the fog.

The Home Secretary banged his fist sharply on the heavy table before them. 'Gentlemen, we will not have arguments at this stage. James, I want a full report on your establishments on Salisbury,' he ordered the Under-Secretary for the Army. 'I want to know of all recent experiments carried out there, particularly the Broadmeyer Experiment.' Holman caught the troubled look that passed between the two men.

'Richard,' the Home Secretary turned to the Minister of State for Defence, 'we'll need troops to clear Bournemouth and to control any panic that is bound to break out in the surrounding area. Commissioner, have your men located the fog yet?'

'No sir, but they have orders to report directly to me as soon as they have.'

'I suggest you get on to the Met. Office and find out shifts in air currents.'

'They're helping us locate the fog now, sir.'

'When you've found it, you'll want to know where it's going, won't you?' the Home Secretary said without a trace of sarcasm in his voice.

'And what do you intend to do once you've found it?' Sir Trevor Chambers, Parliamentary Under-Secretary of State for the Department of the Environment asked dryly. It was a question that had been on all their minds. What could be done against a drifting, insubstantial mass? How could it be confined? How could it be destroyed?

'There are methods,' replied the Minister for Defence. 'Some were developed in the war by the RAF, but the progress of radar has made it unnecessary for this day and age. But the old methods are still usable.'

'Let's find it first,' the Home Secretary said impatiently. 'I want to know in which direction it's heading and *I want its path cleared of people.*'

'My God,' said Sir Trevor, 'that's going to be a massive operation.'

'I'm well aware of that, but what would you suggest?' He allowed no time for an answer. 'Mr Holman, I want you to put yourself at the disposal of the Department of Health's Medical Research Department. You are one victim of the fog who has recovered. I want to know why. It could save the lives of countless others.'

'Er, might I suggest that our chaps from Porton Down work in collusion with the Research Department?' asked the Under-Secretary for the Army.

'Porton Down?' Sir Trevor Chambers raised an eyebrow.

'Yes, our Chemical Defence and Microbiological Research Establishments are based there.'

'Porton Down, Salisbury?' Sir Trevor persisted.

'Yes, that's right.'

'This whole thing is beginning to smell bloody fishy to me!'

The Home Secretary held up his hands to dispel any arguments that might take place. 'Gentlemen, I've asked James for a full report on his work in Salisbury and I will not tolerate any disputes amongst ourselves until I have read that report. For the moment, there are more urgent matters to be put in hand. Now then, we will use the Chemical Defence and the Microbiological Research boys – we'll use anyone who can be of the slightest help in our efforts to combat this menace. Is that understood?'

For the next forty minutes plans were made to deal with the extraordinary situation; plans of action were laid down for the evacuation of people in the path of the threat, and ways of dispersing the fog were discussed. Men left to carry out their urgent duties, others were called in to receive instructions that puzzled them, but which they carried out anyway. The Commissioner was handed a slip of paper and interrupted the proceedings.

'They've located the fog,' he announced sombrely. 'It's moving back north. Towards Winchester.'

Twelve

Captain Joe Ennard took his seat in the cockpit of the giant Boeing 747, greeting his flight officers with a forced grin.

'How was your day off?' his Flight Engineer called out.

'Terrific,' Joe said without enthusiasm. He thought of his day with Sylvia, the day that had started so well and ended so miserably, while he ran through the checks before take off. Pressing his transmit button, he asked Departure Control for permission to start his engines. He was acknowledged and permission granted. He began pulling switches with his First Officer and the Jumbo jet rumbled into life. The noise increased the dull ache he had at a point just above his eyes.

He had spent the previous day in the New Forest with his wife in an attempt to recapture some of the zest they'd had for each other earlier in their marriage. She'd always known about his casual affairs over the past few years but had tried to accept them because of her own shortcomings. At thirty-eight his sexual drive had hardly diminished from the time he was twenty-five. Whether it would have been the same if their marriage had taken a normal course, he didn't know, but the fact that she was so repulsed by the sex act had seemed to strengthen his demand for fulfilment rather than diminish it so, despite the fact that he still loved her, he had been forced to look elsewhere for the important missing part of their marriage.

The irony was that he felt the guilt. She never spoke of his unfaithfulness, never blamed him for his misconduct. Often he found her quietly weeping, but they were never tears of accusation; only tears of regret. It had started two years after their marriage when they'd lost the baby. It hadn't been her fault but nobody, not even the doctors, could convince her of that. Joe had been present at the birth and even now he could see the beautifully formed human being that had emerged from her womb, so tiny, so perfect – so dead. The doctors had all the answers, of course, but answers couldn't bring the baby back.

Afterwards she was afraid that if she ever became pregnant again, the same thing would happen, and this had led to her frigidity. Even the precautions he took could not allay her fears and it wasn't too long before he gave up trying. But they had still loved each other deeply and his casual affairs were just that. There was never any emotional involvement, just a physical act that offered him some release. Was it possible to be unfaithful yet still love your wife? He knew the answer, at least in his case, was yes.

And then yesterday. A day that was meant to bring them closer, to seal the gap that he felt was developing between them. The years of infidelity were finally beginning to take their toll and he had decided that he would no longer look outside his marriage for physical comfort. He had brought her down to the New Forest, where they'd spent so much time before they were married, to pledge his love and loyalty to her, that he would not let his body betray them any more, that there was still enough in their marriage to tie them together, to begin to build on again.

But in the fog that had suddenly enveloped them, she had told him she was leaving. She had found someone else who was prepared to live with her on her terms, who wouldn't need others to satisfy his desires, who would be content to love her for herself and not her body.

He had been too dismayed even to plead with her.

That morning, he had felt a strange relief, almost as if a heavy burden had been lifted from his shoulders. He was free. It wouldn't be him leaving her but the reverse. He didn't have to worry about her breaking down because of the parting, she would be happy now. Perhaps it had been this which had bound him to her all these years; not love, but fear of hurting her when she'd already suffered so much. He even found it in himself to ask about the man. Who was he? Did he know him? Was he married? What did he do? He asked with no malice, with no thoughts of righteous indignation and she sensed this and answered his questions. His name was Kevin – Joe couldn't remember the surname – no, he'd never met him, he was divorced, he was a radar engineer. She'd met him in London while Joe was away on one of his flights. They'd known each other years ago, before Joe, and hadn't seen each other since. She was on a shopping spree and had bumped into him outside

Heal's in Tottenham Court Road. He was in his lunch break and he asked her to join him. She had.

Kevin had told her of his divorce three years before, but she'd said little of her relationship with Joe. At the end of the lunch, they both knew they'd felt a mutual contact with each other, reached out and been met as neither had been for years. He told her proudly of the new field he was helping to develop in radar and that at the moment he was based in London's giant GPO Tower, promising her if she met him the next day he would give her a private tour of the fantastic building.

She broke her promise, but six days later, when Joe was away again, she rang his office at the Tower and arranged to meet him. That had been six months ago, and their feeling for one another had grown till neither wanted to live apart any longer.

She was surprised when Joe smiled at her and wished them both happiness. Was it really so easy to end ten years of marriage?

Joe had left the house and driven to Heathrow airport, the dull headache successfully excluding thoughts of his failed marriage from his mind. He didn't bother to report the headache to the medical officer, considering the dull pain only a minor discomfort.

The 747 trundled towards its appropriated runway, taking its place in the queue behind the other waiting aircraft. The Jumbo, weighing over three hundred and fifty tons and although not fully-loaded, carrying nearly three hundred passengers, quivered with unreleased power.

Joe wiped the moisture from his forehead as he waited for the command from the Control Tower to get his aircraft moving. As always, it was a relief when the order came. The thrust from the four giant engines pushed him back in his seat and the Jumbo rolled down the runway, gathering speed by the second. After six thousand feet he was able to ease back on the stick and bring the nose up, allowing the four main bogies to take up all the weight. Then the huge, clumsy beast was off the ground, gaining height, an impossible spectacle, but a triumph to man's ingenuity.

The crew breathed their sighs of relief as the 747 circled the airport in an effort to increase height. There was always that tense moment when they wondered if the monster would rise or flop back to the ground, despite their years of experience that told them the former would inevitably be true.

Miller, Joe's First Officer, grinned across at him. 'New York City, here I come. And Beryl, my dear, am I going to fly you!' He laughed at his own joke. Beryl was an air hostess belonging to a rival airline he had met at the John F. Kennedy Airport. Her company's over-used slogan always tickled him.

He was surprised at his Captain's lack of response to his joke. 'You okay, Skip?' he asked.

Joe Ennard stared ahead, his hands tightly clutching the stick before him.

'Hey, Captain,' called the nervous young Flight Engineer. It was only his second flight with Captain Ennard and he was still slightly in awe of the man. 'Er, we're a little off course.'

Miller didn't even have to check his instruments. He could tell visually by merely looking down at the ground, still only ten thousand feet below. 'You should be going that way,' he said humorously, pointing over his shoulder with his thumb. 'Skip? Hey, Joe!'

He reached across and shook Ennard's arm. 'You okay? Come on, Joe, snap out of it!' He leaned forward anxiously to look into the rigid man's face. He shook him again.

The blow from the back of Joe Ennard's hand knocked him back into his seat and drew blood from the corner of his mouth.

'Terry, get him!' he yelled at the Second Officer as he turned to his own controls and tried to wrest them from the Captain's iron grip.

The Flight Engineer unbuckled his seat belt and hurried forward, not sure of what he was going to do, reluctant to lay his hands on the Captain.

'Pull him away from the controls!' Miller shouted at him, his efforts to gain control of the giant machine useless without the Captain's co-operation.

Terry grabbed at Joe's hand and tried to yank them away, but the grip was too strong. He put his arm around the Captain's neck and squeezed, pulling back at the same time. The First Officer tried to prise Joe's fingers away from the stick. None of them heard the discreet but urgent tapping on the locked cockpit door; the Chief Steward was also worried about the direction of their flight.

Suddenly, in a swift movement, Captain Ennard released himself from his safety belt and rose as much as his cramped position would allow. A powerful man, and more powerful because of the madness within him, he lashed out at his First Officer, blinding him with his fist, sending him into a heap back in his seat. He drove an elbow into the Flight Engineer's ribs, causing him to lose his grip and double up with pain. With another blow from his forearm, he sent him crashing back down the cockpit.

Miller was holding his head, rubbing his eyes so that he could see again. He screamed at the half-conscious Flight Engineer, 'Get the gun! For God's sake, shoot him!'

They kept the illegal gun hidden behind the transmit unit, a secret agreement among themselves and many other aeroplane crews, as a protection against the increasingly frequent hijackings.

His words were cut off as a two-fisted blow landed on the back of his exposed neck. He slumped forward on to his controls, unconscious.

Joe Ennard took his seat again and reached for the stick. The angry mechanical sound of the voice from Heathrow's Control Tower buzzed through his head, filling the cockpit, but he ignored it. He looked down at London, searching for the tall, familiar landmark, his eyes glazed but still seeing.

A grin of satisfaction spread across his features, a strange grin that bared his teeth, made his face skull-like. He'd found what he'd been looking for.

Terry slowly became aware of the frantic banging on the door. The Chief Steward had heard the commotion and was anxiously demanding that the door be opened, oblivious now to the fact that some of the passengers would hear. The Flight Engineer pulled himself groggily to his knees and looked towards the front of the cockpit. He couldn't see Miller, but he could see the Captain hunched over the controls as though looking through the windows at something below.

He felt the aircraft go into a dive as the pilot pushed forward on his stick, felt all four engines being given full throttle and the great machine thrust forward with unbelievable power. Desperately, he reached for the hidden gun and fumbled with its safety catch. He crawled towards the pilot's seat, holding it before him in a trembling hand.

'Stop!' he called out futilely. 'Pull her out or I'll shoot!'

He staggered to his feet, using the back of Captain Ennard's seat to lever himself up. He raised the gun to the back of the Captain's head, imploring him to pull back on the stick. Then

128

his eyes fell on the building that was rushing towards them. He screamed as he squeezed the trigger.

Before the sound of the gunshot, before the Captain's brains mixed with blood were splattered on to the instrument panel in front of him, Terry thought he heard him say something. It sounded like, 'Good morning, Kevin,' but the Flight Engineer had no time or desire to reflect on the words for his head was filled with its own terror.

The 747 Jumbo jet exploded into the tall GPO Tower with a mighty roar that echoed throughout London, over three hundred and fifty tons of crashing metal that toppled the building as though it were made of children's blocks.

Thirteen

Holman was driven to the Middlesex Hospital to pick up Casey with Detective Inspector Barrow acting as escort. The Home Secretary had made him a valuable man; the one person they had so far who had recovered from the effects of the mysterious fog. He would have to be examined and his brain patterns studied to find out how he had recovered – and if he were now immune. Casey was necessary too, as the nearest person suffering from the effects. Corpses would be flown up from Bournemouth by helicopter for autopsies to be performed on them in an attempt to discover exactly what damage had been done to their brain. Others, still living but insane, would be selected and flown up for further tests. But at that precise moment, John Holman and Casey Simmons were the two most important people in England.

From the hospital, they were taken by ambulance to the Ministry of Health building that was strangely situated at the Elephant and Castle. Holman sat in the ambulance looking down at Casey, who was under sedation, holding her hand in both of his, worried over the paleness of her features. He looked at his watch: 9.45. God, he was tired! He had thought it would be at least around noon. People were still scurrying off to work, their day just beginning, just hearing of the devastating news from the seaside resort. Would they panic? They'd certainly have to be given some answers. Who would they blame? The government? The Russians? The Chinese? Maybe some other countries for a change. Were there any friendly countries left? Even America was becoming hostile.

What excuse would the government give? Pollution? Would that play its part? God knows, he'd found enough evidence of the damage pollution could do in his job, but nothing of this magnitude, obviously. And the public weren't that stupid any more. The media had broadened their minds, given them an insight, however vague, to things that years ago would have been completely unheard of, let alone believed. They would suspect a chemical, a poisonous gas, mistakenly unleashed by some scientific laboratory somewhere, and if they didn't, he felt sure the media would point them in this direction.

If it hadn't been so catastrophic, he might have enjoyed watching the officials trying to worm their way out from the responsibility. But then, there was always the doubt, the doubt that governments all over the world could so cleverly play on. Even he wasn't sure if it was a man-made or freak-of-nature phenomenon; the tiny doubt in the back of his mind would prevent him from going all out to lay the blame on the Ministry of Defence's doorstep. But if he ever found concrete proof . . .

A muffled explosion jerked him from his thoughts. The ambulance pulled to a halt and as he opened the back doors, he saw that all the other traffic crossing Waterloo Bridge had done the same. As he climbed down the steps, Barrow came running around from the police car that had been escorting them.

'Look,' he pointed, 'over there!'

Holman followed his gaze and saw a great ball of smoke and flames rising from the direction of the West End. It snaked up towards the blue sky, a black, billowing cloud, violently red at its base.

'What the hell is it?' Holman asked nobody in particular, his question echoed by the other drivers who had emerged from their cars and were standing perplexed, staring into the sky.

'I'm not sure,' said Barrow, evenly, 'but it's coming from around the area of Tottenham Court Road. It might be just in front of the GPO Tower. If it isn't in front . . . ' He left the sentence unfinished.

Holman turned to stare at him. More muffled explosions came from the same spot and they could see flames shooting into the air.

'It's beginning to happen here,' said Holman quietly.

'What? No; we've had no fog here!' Barrow retorted. 'There's no connection, can't be!'

'I wish we could be sure of that.'

Several groups of people had gathered and were talking excitedly, gesturing towards the black-stained sky. Barrow walked over towards one of the groups and asked some sharp questions. A minute later, he returned to Holman.

'There's your answer,' he said. 'The people over there saw a

131

Jumbo jet circling over London. They said it was very, very low so they realised it was in trouble. Then it went into a dive. They think it hit the Tower, one old boy swears it did.'

Holman shook his head in disbelief. 'It's incredible. The school, Bournemouth – and now this.'

'I just told you, it's probably got nothing to do with the fog!'

'I wish I could believe it, Barrow. I wish I could.'

Even in the bright sunlight, Holman felt a shiver run through him.

He was surprised at the vast basement area that was used for medical research beneath the Alexander Fleming House building. Even as a civil servant himself, he hadn't known of its existence. They were met by the Chief Medical Officer, a fat, jovial man who explained, 'I'm going to take you downstairs and hand you over to Mrs Janet Halstead, Principal Medical Officer for the Research Council. It's a completely different department from ours, but they occupy that part of the building for good reasons. Their divisions of research are spread all over the place, the majority in London, but many as far as Scotland. When they need to get together on a project – and it has happened quite a number of times in the past I can assure you – they get together here. Needless to say, you're bound by the Official Secrets Act to keep this to yourselves.' He laughed at their serious faces. 'It's not that secret, you understand, but there are reasons for not letting it become public knowledge.'

They entered a lift, Casey having been taken through a more private entrance to the rear of the building.

A plump middle-aged woman wearing a white coat greeted them when the doors opened again. She stepped forward and shook Holman's hand without waiting for an introduction.

'You must be Mr Holman,' she said smiling. 'I've been reading about you from your file your department sent me. Your photograph doesn't do you justice.'

Holman smiled back weakly, completely disarmed.

The Chief Medical Officer spoke up. 'This is Mrs Janet Halstead. I'll leave you to it then, Jan?'

She nodded and asked Holman and Barrow to follow her as the lift doors closed on the grinning Ministry of Health man. This was the Principal Medical Officer? Holman couldn't help but smile. She was certainly sweet, but she looked no brighter than the average housewife. The day would prove her to be otherwise.

'I take it Sir Geoffrey has explained why we brought you to this building. There are quite a few people we want to examine you, and it's a bit more convenient to bring them here than to cart you all over the country. I don't know if you've heard yet, but a State of Emergency has been declared. We have to find some answers, very, very quickly.'

She led them into an office and asked them to sit. She perched on the edge of a desk. 'Now, the first thing. Have either of you eaten this morning?' She smiled at their shaking heads. 'Right, we'll soon fix that. Not much for you, I'm afraid Mr Holman. We have a few tests to put you through that won't allow it. However, we'll give you enough to sustain you. We don't want you passing out on us, do we?'

Holman felt himself almost mesmerised by her words and began to relax, a combination of his own tiredness, the soft chair he was sitting in and the easy manner in which she was talking to him.

'While you're eating, you can tell me all that's happened to you – and I'd appreciate it if you tried to leave out nothing. The smallest thing could be of the greatest importance.' She picked up the telephone and pressed a button, then ordered breakfast for them both.

Holman snatched a glance at Barrow who seemed distinctly uneasy in his non-active role.

'Oh, please call me Jan, by the way,' she told them as she replaced the receiver. 'Now, as I've already said, we have an extremely busy day ahead of us here. We have every facility we need and the best medical brains are either already here or on their way. I can promise you, we've wasted no time in the past couple of hours.

'Let me tell you briefly who will examine you. I won't mention all the names because I can't remember half of them myself, but most of them are from these Units: Cellular Disorders; Infectious and Immune Diseases; Psychiatry and Nervous Disorders; Biochemical Parisitology; Neurobiological Studies; Brain Metabolism; Cell Mutation; Molecular Genetics; Immunochemistry and Cellular Immunology; Molecular Pharmacology; Neurological Prostheses and Neuropsychiatry.' She smiled at Holman. 'Two others: Environmental Radiation and I believe the Ministry of Defence is sending us some of their

Chemical Defence and Microbiological researchers.'

He sat there stunned and frightened and she hastily tried to reassure him. 'As you can see a lot of these divisions won't even come into it, we just have to have them at hand in case they're necessary.' She smiled her disarming smile again.

Holman was silent for a moment, a troubled look on his face. Then, he spoke. 'Two Units stuck in my mind, one I think you tried to hide among the others.'

She still smiled. 'And they were?' she asked.

'The obvious one was Environmental Radiation. The other was Cell Mutation.'

She looked at him keenly and said without any hint of patronisation: 'I can see you're very sharp, Mr Holman – may I call you John?'

He nodded.

'Yes, I did bury it among the others, I didn't want to alarm you. As I said, many of these divisions of investigation will be a waste of time. I think Cell Mutation will be one of these – but we have to be sure. You do see that? We can't leave anything to chance. As for Environmental Radiation – well, that's an obvious one in this day and age, isn't it?'

'But what exactly can you find out from me. I mean, I'm cured, aren't I?'

'First of all, information, John. I've already spoken on the phone to the doctors who treated you in Salisbury. Their description of your symptoms was helpful, but I'm afraid very inadequate. By examining you, we can find to what extent your brain was damaged – if it was your brain. I think you are cured, certainly, but we may still find lingering signs of what caused it. Like a blow would leave a bruise, a cut would leave a scar.'

'But wouldn't that necessitate surgery?'

She laughed. 'No, I don't think so, not in your case.' She became serious once more. 'We have plenty of dead bodies we can examine in that way.'

'And what about Casey?'

'Miss Simmons? We'll try to cure her.'

The door opened and their breakfast was wheeled in on a trolley. Janet Halstead reached behind her and switched on a tape recorder.

'Now, John,' she said. 'Take your time and tell us everything you know about this mysterious fog. Start at the beginning and try to leave nothing out.'

The rest of the day was just a blur to Holman. He was probed, tested, examined, interrogated. He was given an electrocardiograph to test his heart; his entire body was x-rayed; a radio-opaque substance was injected into the arterial system of his brain to show up any deformation of the normal pattern in order to trace any space-occupying lesion; electrodes were placed on the surface of his head over the occipital and frontal region to discover any evidence of a tumour; a small amount of cerebrospinal fluid was drained by a needle introduced into the subarachnoid space below the termination of his spinal cord and tested. All these, and many more tests, were carried out on his and Casey's bodies and by late afternoon, he was allowed to fall into an exhausted sleep.

He awoke several hours later to find Barrow slumped in a chair by his bedside, soft snoring noises droning from him. As Holman sat up, the policeman stirred and quickly woke, casting an anxious eye towards the bed. He grinned and rubbed his face.

'You were out for the count,' he said to Holman.

'You weren't doing so bad yourself,' Holman answered flatly.

'Yeah, but I'm a light sleeper.' He looked at Holman ruefully. 'Look, what about calling a truce? I know I was a bit rough on you, but it was pretty fantastic, wasn't it?'

'Yes, it was.'

'Well, I'm sorry.'

'Okay, let's forget it. Actually, I'm surprised you're still around.'

'Special duty, mate. I'm your bodyguard. You're an important person. You've got another one outside.'

'Do they think somebody's going to assassinate me, or – do they think I'm going to run away?' His face took on an incredulous look as he hoisted himself up further in the bed.

Barrow was slightly flustered. With a sigh, he said, 'I'll be honest; they're playing safe. Don't forget the effect this gas has had on others; we don't *really* know if you've recovered yet, do we?'

'All right, I get it,' said Holman, resigned. 'Tell me what's been happening while I've been asleep.'

'Quite a lot. A couple of hours ago the doctors and researchers went into a conflab. I don't know what it was all about but they were having a go at those blokes from Porton Down, the Microbiological Research scientists. They were being evasive and finally refused to answer any more questions until they'd seen their Minister.'

'It all seems to point in the same direction, doesn't it?' Holman commented.

'Yeah,' said Barrow dryly, 'you could say that. Anyway, they went off to the Ministry of Defence about an hour ago, leaving the others in quite a rage. They're carrying on with their work, but they're not very happy about it.'

'How's Casey?'

'I don't know, but I'll get the Medical Officer. She wanted to be informed when you woke.' He walked to the door and gave instructions to the uniformed policeman outside to find Janet Halstead.

'What's happened with the fog?' asked Holman as the Detective Inspector returned to his chair.

'They found it, you know that, and luckily the winds have died down so it's drifting along at a very slow rate. It's an incredible sight, apparently, about a mile wide and a mile high.'

'It's grown.' The fact disturbed Holman. 'When I saw it last, it was half that size.'

'Yeah, they know it's growing. It's becoming thicker in density, too, a sort of dingy yellow colour. They've been spraying it all day to get it to disperse, but I don't know if they've had any success. They're evacuating Winchester anyway, just to be on the safe side, and the Met Office is keeping a constant check on wind shifts.'

'And how has the public reacted?'

'As you'd expect. Panic. Fear. Accusations. The press are having a field day.'

'And what answer have they been given?'

'Nothing official yet. Just that a grand-scale investigation is taking place and a statement will be made by the Prime Minister later this evening. But they've implied a poisonous gas has drifted in from the sea and caused the disaster in Bournemouth.'

'My God, are people falling for it? What about the eruption?'

'No connection. At least that's the official answer that's been given?'

'The school! What about the school?'

'Er, news of that hasn't been released.'

'But they can't hush something like that up! What have the parents got to say?'

'As far as they know, their sons were killed in an accidental fire. In three major disasters concerning the lives of thousands, the school incident has been easily swallowed up.'

'Three? What are the three?'

'The eruption, Bournemouth and the crash this morning of the 747 into the GPO Tower.'

'How many were killed in that?'

'It hasn't been ascertained yet. It's estimated at least a thousand. There were two hundred and eighty six on the Jumbo alone, God knows how many were in the Tower and the offices around it.'

The air hung heavily in the small hospital-like room for several moments as both men tried to grasp the magnitude of the tragic events that had taken place. It was completely beyond their comprehension, somehow unreal. And it was the unreality of the situation that enabled them to cope.

'Does the public know about the fog?' It was Holman who broke the silence.

'Yes, they're aware. It's hardly a thing that could be kept a secret – a mile wide, a mile high. They had to be informed anyway, to get them to move out of its path.'

'And how have they reacted to that?'

'General hyster – '

The door opened and Janet Halstead entered, interrupting Barrow's answer.

'Hello, John, how are you feeling?' Her smile was a little more strained than it had been that morning.

'I'm fine. Tell me about Casey.'

'Her condition is deteriorating, John. I have to be honest with you, there's been enough evasiveness in this place for one day.' She sat on the edge of his bed. 'But there is a chance.'

He looked up at her, hopefully.

'We are pretty sure we know what is happening. We've had some of the finest minds in the country working on it. The autopsies have provided us with the answers. But we need to know the cause, John. We can't be sure until we know the cause. And that's what I meant when I mentioned evasiveness.'

'Tell me *exactly* what you mean.'

'We all feel – that is, the members of the Medical Research Council – that the Chemical and Microbiological Researchers from the Ministry of Defence are holding out on us. You see, in their tests, they seemed to know exactly what it was they were looking for, as though they were not looking for an answer but for confirmation of an answer they already had.

'We began to realise this as their tests progressed. There was no trial and error in their methods – they knew exactly what they were doing. Well, we let them finish and then we confronted them. But they clammed up, wouldn't say a word. They demanded that they see their Minister as only he had the authority to allow them to reveal their discovery – or affirmation.'

'The bastards – they're covering up!' Holman leapt from the bed. 'Barrow, you get me Sir Trevor Chambers. He'll get some answers for us. If he doesn't, I'm going to blow this thing sky high!'

'I'll get him, Holman, but there's nothing you can do personally. They'll lock you away,' said Barrow in a matter-of-fact voice.

'Just get him! We'll see!'

'Okay, okay. But keep calm, eh?'

'Yes, John,' said Janet Halstead firmly. 'It's no good getting excited, it won't help anyone. The first thing you must do is eat. I think we've found all we need to know from you; some results have still to come in, but I think they'll only confirm our suspicions. Now, let me order you some food while Inspector Barrow gets in touch with Sir Trevor, then I can put you in the picture as to our findings today.'

Fourteen

Two hours later, Holman found himself sitting between Janet
Halstead and Sir Trevor Chambers in one of the spacious con-
ference rooms at the Ministry of Defence. Sir Trevor had
heeded his call from the Research Centre in Alexander Fleming
House and made suitable bellowing noises in the right ears.
They were soon to learn that the fuss was unnecessary; the
Ministry had adopted a new policy of honesty – to a limited
few, anyway. And they hadn't exactly adopted the policy
willingly. They had been instructed to do so by a higher
authority.

As he waited for the meeting to begin Holman looked down
the length of the long oak table and studied the faces deep in
murmured conversation with their immediate neighbours. He
recognised some of them and had been introduced to others on
his arrival. He tried to remember the names and titles while he
waited: the Home Secretary, Charles Lyall-Smith, looking calm
and unruffled as always; the Minister of State for Defence, Lord
Gibbon, and his Principal Private Secretary, deep in conversation with the Parliamentary Under-Secretary of State for
Defence for the Army, William Douglas-Glyne and his Principal Private Secretary; the big, bluff Chief of Defence staff, Sir
Hugh Dowling, bellowing good humouredly across the table at
the Chief of the General Staff, General Sir Michael Reedman,
and his Vice-Chief, Lieutenant-General Sir Keith Macklen; the
Chief Scientific Adviser, Professor Hermann Ryker, silently
studying a document in front of him, underlining certain points
with a pencil. There were others seated away from the table
whose function was not clear to Holman, but three were dressed
in military uniforms.

The Home Secretary rapped the table with his fountain pen
to bring the meeting to order. 'Gentlemen,' he began, 'and lady,'
he smiled briefly at Janet Halstead, 'you all know the facts; this

evening's meeting is to inform you of how it happened and then to discuss a plan of action. I've been in constant touch with the Prime Minister who is at this very moment flying back from Russia. He regrets not being with us in this crisis, but does not wish any action we may take to be delayed because of his absence. It's a great pity his visit to Russia had to be cut short so abruptly – any such trips are of the highest diplomatic importance – but obviously, the safety of the country takes priority over any other matter. He has asked me to inform you that any action we decide upon this evening, he will endorse on his arrival, so there is to be no delay in implementing our plans, whatever they may be.

'His prime instruction is this: there is to be no information withheld by *any* Ministry from the people in this room tonight. I have had private talks with Lord Gibbon and Douglas-Glyne and have passed the facts that emerged from our conversations on to the PM. He is quite explicit that there is to be no cover-up between ourselves. Tonight's meeting *will not* indulge in accusations or blame-shedding; we are here to find solutions! The safety of millions is at stake – let's be quite clear on that issue. The catastrophes that have taken place have not been unrelated incidents. You know of the major disasters, but I can assure you there have been many, many small incidents with the same tragic consequences.

'A few of us in this room now know the cause of these outbreaks; it is my intention that you all know, so that we can combine our various skills to combat this growing – and I mean that literally – threat.'

He looked along the table allowing his words to take their effect. Then he turned to the Minister of State for Defence, seated on his left, and said, 'Richard, will you repeat the information you gave me earlier?'

Lord Gibbon leaned forward, his elbows on the table, his thick hands clasped tightly before him. 'Gentlemen, I'm afraid the Ministry of Defence has to take a large amount of responsibility for – '

'We are not here to apportion blame, Richard. Just tell us the facts,' the Home Secretary snapped irritably.

'Very well.' The big man straightened up as though relieved and proceeded in a brisk, businesslike manner, throwing off his look of guilty admission completely. 'If we are to start at the beginning, we must go back fifteen years, to our Microbiological

140

Research Establishment at Porton Down and a brilliant scientist named Broadmeyer. His speciality was bacteriological warfare.'

Holman felt a coldness grip him. He had been right! The stupid bastards *had* been responsible.

'Professor Broadmeyer was a brilliant man in many ways,' Lord Gibbon continued. 'Perhaps too brilliant. He discovered – or invented – an organism that could affect the brains of man or animal.'

'May we be more accurate than that.' A slightly accented voice interrupted. All eyes swung round towards Professor Hermann Ryker, the Chief Scientific Adviser.

'Yes, Professor Ryker?' said the Home Secretary.

'He did not invent, he did not discover,' Ryker said gravely, 'He mutated. He took an organism known as mycoplasma and mutated it.' He was silent again.

'Perhaps you would like to continue, Professor. You're more of an authority on this kind of thing than I am,' said the Defence Minister.

'Yes,' Ryker admitted dryly. He look around at the assembly. 'Broadmeyer *was* a brilliant man – I studied under him for many years – but he was, what shall we say, a little irresponsible. He mutated the mycoplasma so that if it entered the bloodstream it would attack the healthy existing cells and travel as a parasite to the brain. I am sure Mrs Halstead knows of the Rhesus factor,' – she nodded in acknowledgement – 'where a mother produces a mental defect because of antigenic incompatibility between the mother and foetus. In analogical theory the same process takes place except that the disease is transmitted to the host's brain rather than a foetus.

'The micro-organisms cause inflammation of the brain substance and covering membranes, eventually leading to a breakdown of existing healthy brain cells and a build-up of new, parasitical cells. The stronger the parasites become, the more easily the healthy cells are "devoured". Hence the complete and utter mental breakdown of whoever contracts the disease. Eventually, the victim would become a vegetable, capable of no action at all.'

'But what about me?' Holman exclaimed, unable to hold back. 'Why didn't I become a vegetable?'

Professor Ryker regarded him with a faint smile. 'You have been a very fortunate young man,' he said, then looking at Janet Halstead again. 'I believe Mrs Halstead will have some idea of

141

what saved you by now, but there is a little more to it.'

The Principal Medical Officer spoke up. 'Mr Holman was given a blood transfusion because of an injury he sustained during his attack. I assume this helped clear the bloodstream of the foreign cells.'

'Precisely, Mrs Halstead,' the professor nodded. 'It helped the existing cells destroy the parasites, rather like a regiment that has been sent reinforcements. Luckily for Mr Holman, he received the transfusion before the parasitical cells had a chance to multiply. But he was also lucky in another respect.

'Like most organisms used in germ warfare, the Broadmeyer Mutation, as it was secretly called, was self-reproducing. All it needed was carbon dioxide, the simple element that is contained in the very air we breathe and it could grow and grow, or I should say, multiply itself. Mr Holman was exposed to it in the early stages of its process for it had just been released in its pure form, therefore it was comparatively weak. The vapour, or fog as you have called it, is a by-product of the process it goes through as it draws the carbon dioxide from the air. This in itself is strange, for normally, an organism that lives on carbon dioxide and precious little else must be photosynthetic, and would require sunlight to live and multiply. Now, mycoplasmas lack a cell wall, the mycoplasma being bounded only by the delicate plasma membrane – which means they can only survive and grow in an osmotically protective environment – hence they live as a large group in order to protect their inner core from changes in osmotic pressure. So you see the contradiction: they should need sunlight to exist, yet they surround themselves with this strange mist. Only Broadmeyer, as the creator of this mutation, knew the answer. And unfortunately, he is dead, killed by the disease he made.

'As I have said, he was an irresponsible man. I consider him irresponsible for ever producing such a mutation, but he was also irresponsible in smaller ways. He was careless and allowed himself to be exposed to the mycoplasma. Naturally, he went mad. And in his madness he destroyed all his papers, notes, the work of years, not just on the mutated mycoplasma, but other projects, more admirable conceptions, completely and utterly wasted. He died a lunatic, a victim of his own creation, and with him, he took many secrets.

'The mutation was contained and, like many others produced in the name of germ warfare, was considered too dangerous to

142

use. Perhaps Lieutenant-General Macklen would care to tell you what happened to it?' He raised his eyebrows towards the Vice-Chief of the General Staff.

'We can hardly wait to hear,' Sir Trevor Chambers said caustically.

'Sir Trevor,' warned the Home Secretary.

'Before we do,' Janet Halstead broke in hastily, 'may I ask Professor Ryker a question about the cure? I think it's more important than anything else at the moment, wouldn't you agree?'

The Home Secretary nodded and said, 'Carry on.'

'You confirm that blood transfusion is the answer then, Professor?' she asked Ryker.

'Yes, provided it is given in time. If the parasite cells have taken on too strong a hold in the brain, then new blood will be of no use at all. Mr Holman here was fortunate in that they hadn't been given time to develop; they were easily overcome by the stronger existing cells. But once they have a grip . . . ' He spread his hands and shrugged in a gesture of futility.

'But what if we use radiology to burn out the bad cells?'

'Y-e-s. Yes.' He drew out the words, his mind absorbing the thought. 'It's a possibility. But it's always dangerous; other good cells can be damaged by this method. Extreme care would have to be taken. And remember, nothing can ever be done about healthy cells that have been damaged either by the parasites *or* the x-ray. They will never grow again.'

'No, but it's a chance worth taking,' she said.

'Of course, you could never expect to treat everybody who contracts the disease in this way. I mean to say, there just aren't the resources.' Lord Gibbon shook his head in despair.

'No, we could never treat everyone in this way.' Janet Halstead looked around the room. 'But now it's your job to see that we don't have to. You have to destroy the mycoplasma!'

She allowed no time for them to comment on her last statement. She turned to Holman. 'John, I'm going back to the Research Centre. I want to give Miss Simmons a blood transfusion and if necessary subject her to radiology and, as her father is unable to, I think I should seek permission to do so from you.'

'Go ahead,' Holman answered. 'Whatever she needs – do it!'

She patted his shoulder as she rose from the table. 'Excuse

me, gentlemen, I have some lives to save. And a lot to organise. I trust you'll keep me informed?'

Professor Ryker suppressed an admiring grin as she marched from the room.

The Home Secretary cleared his throat. 'There is another question that I would like to ask; it could have a bearing on something to be discussed later.' He looked at Ryker. 'Once a person has successfully overcome the disease, would that person then be immune from further attacks?'

The professor pondered over the question. Finally he said, 'It would seem likely, although I'd value Mrs Halstead's opinion on this. Once the body's system has beaten off a disease, it builds some, or often total, resistance against it, and in this case, where the mutated mycoplasma would be virtually flushed from the system in the early stages and the unwanted cells in the brain killed before they had a chance to form, as they have in Mr Holman's case, then, yes, I believe one could be made immune from further attacks. The theory would have to be tested, of course, but the body has an acute sense of self-preservation, you know. It builds its own defences.'

'And is this, er, disease infectious?' Sir Trevor Chambers asked, carefully avoiding Holman's eyes. 'Could Mr Holman pass it on to others?'

'Well, that doesn't appear to have happened, does it?' Ryker answered with a restrained smile. 'My opinion is that the DNA – the genetic material – of the organism immediately combines with the DNA of brain cells, in a manner similar to that in which cancer-causing viruses are believed to join up with cellular material. In the case of cancer-causing viruses, of course, the extra genetic material can lie dormant for years until something triggers it off. I suggest that in the case of Broadmeyer's mutated organism, the DNA produces extremely malignant cells almost at once, which cause the untoward effects which make the organism non-infective.

'Our problem is that we do not even know enough about mycoplasma in its normal state, let alone when it has been tampered with. I shall tell you briefly of what we do know. Also called PPLO – pleuropneumonia-like organisms – mycoplasmas include the smallest known cells able to multiply independently of other living cells, some being almost spherical and only 0.001 mm in diameter. The chromosome of many probably contains not more than 650 genes – about one-fifth the

144

number found in common bacteria – and from the physiological and biochemical viewpoint microplasmas are similar to bacteria, with the one important exception I've already mentioned: they lack a cell wall.' Ryker paused to look around at the blank faces.

He continued, his next words cutting through the incomprehension like a knife. 'This means, because they are not restricted by this rigid wall, they can be deformed and are able to squeeze through narrow pores smaller than their own diameter. It also means they are completely resistant to penicillin and any other substances which act by disrupting the synthesis of bacterial cell walls!'

An uneasy silence followed, broken finally by Sir Trevor clearing his throat. 'Er, you mean there *is* no cure?' he asked.

'No, no. We will find one,' Ryker assured them all, 'but to produce a serum, we need to know exactly how the mycoplasma has been mutated.'

'But surely *you* must have some idea?' said the Defence Minister.

'Oh, I have an idea. But do we have the time to experiment with and develop ideas?' He spoke as though to a child who had asked a foolish question and was being given a kind answer. 'No. But we may draw off some of the organism from the living victims. Then we could analyse it, discover its contents, and then develop a serum. But of course, to manufacture it in bulk would take time. And we do not have too much time, do we?' He looked around at them, then added, 'Of course, if we had some of the mutated mycoplasma in its pure state, then it would be an enormous advantage.'

'Well, what's to prevent us from containing some of the fog?' Douglas-Glyne, the Defence Under-Secretary, asked impatiently.

'I said "in its pure state". The fog, apart from being a mutated organism now contains carbon dioxide and various other impurities. I suspect the yellowish colour is due to the pollution in the air – our own man-made pollution. To sort out all these elements to find the mutated mycoplasma in its purest form would take time.'

'This is leading on to our next point, gentlemen,' said the Home Secretary. 'I'd like to get back to Lieutenant-General Macklen. Sir Keith, would you tell us how the virus had been contained?'

'And how it escaped!' snorted Sir Trevor Chambers.

Sir Keith Macklen rose to his feet as though to address the officers on his staff.

'The Broadmeyer Mycoplasma,' he began, purposely avoiding Professor Ryker's name for it, 'was contained in a sealed off room in small glassed steel containers. Broadmeyer had disturbed one of the vials and dislodged its cap while carrying out experiments on an animal – a rabbit I think. Anyway, he noticed the dislodged cap, replaced it and left the sealed room. It took a while for him to become insane. As Professor Ryker said, it was in its purest form and he was only exposed for a few seconds, before it had time to strengthen itself from the air, but when he did, he went under very fast.

'He destroyed his work and killed a fellow scientist in the process. Then he became – a nothing. His brain hardly functioned, he neither saw nor heard anything. He died soon after by his own hand!

'We decided the mutation was too dangerous ever to be used so we had to get rid of it. There were three ways of doing this: destroy it, dump it in the sea, or bury it below ground.'

'My God!' said Sir Trevor, exhaling a long breath. 'And you decided to bury it!'

'Er, not me, Sir Trevor. My superiors at that time. It was fifteen years ago, remember.'

'Carry on, Sir Keith,' said the Home Secretary.

'Well, we couldn't destroy it; we didn't know what it was exactly. And we couldn't dump it in the sea; we considered that was too risky. So we buried it. Very, very deep below ground, in glassed steel vials inside a strong, lead container.'

'Under the village,' said Holman, not a question, but a statement.

'Certainly not! The exact location was a quarter of a mile away from the village.' He looked at Holman with annoyance.

'Go on, Sir Keith,' said the Home Secretary again, keeping a tight rein on the meeting, refusing to allow it to become heated in any way.

'Records were made concerning the mycoplasma's potential and its location, and filed away. Fifteen years ago, as I said. Er, now . . . ' He hesitated, looking at the expressionless faces, reluctant to continue. 'Er, up until a few weeks ago, the army has been carrying out some underground explosive tests –'

'I knew it!' Sir Trevor exploded, leaping to his feet. 'Trust

146

the bloody army! The whole of Salisbury Plain and you have to pick the bloody spot where you planted a deadly disease fifteen years before!'

'We most certainly did not! Our experiment was at least two miles from there!'

'Then how do you account for the eruption in the village?'

'Sir Trevor, please sit down!' the Home Secretary ordered sharply. 'I've already warned you. This meeting will not become a dispute. We are here to find a solution! Sir Keith – please continue.'

'We were experimenting with a powerful new explosive. It was one of many we have carried out below ground for the past twenty years now. Many countries use this method to test the power of their bombs. Would you rather we blew up the countryside?'

'I'd rather you didn't test bombs at all,' Sir Trevor retorted.

'Apparently, the bomb – I'm afraid I can't tell you the nature of the explosive – caused a running fissure below the earth. It was this that caused the eruption and released the mycoplasma.'

'Do you mean to tell me you have a bomb that can cause that sort of damage two miles away,' asked Sir Trevor incredulously.

'Yes. Although we didn't know it at the time,' answered the Vice-Chief of the General Staff, careful to keep any hint of pride from his voice. 'The earth was ruptured severely around the blast, but the fissure that caused most damage ran for several miles. It must have reached the point where the mycoplasma was housed in its lead case, the force of the earth crushed it open, the tremor continued on its way until it found its way to the surface under the village, the mycoplasma being pushed along with it. We assume it was the mutation, already polluted and creating its own gas that was seen emerging from the fissure.'

'Why do you assume that?' asked Holman.

'Because we have been checking through our records most of the day – since we heard a poisonous gas may have been involved – of all our deposited stocks. We found that particular stock was directly in line with the fissure.'

'And you've known all this time it was *your* explosion that caused the earthquake?' asked Sir Trevor accusingly.

He nodded, avoiding the many eyes that glared at him as though he were solely responsible.

The Home Secretary spoke before anyone else had a chance to. '*We* knew and *we* decided no good could come of its disclosure. Until today, that is. Thank you, Sir Keith.' The Vice-Chief of the General Staff sat down, relieved that his statement was over, and the Home Secretary continued: 'Gentlemen, we know most of the facts now. This is not the time for reprisals, but let me stress that *human error* of this magnitude will *not* be tolerated. That is all that is going to be said on that particular issue at this time, but I can assure you,' he looked towards Sir Trevor, 'it will be looked into thoroughly *after* we have made progress in defeating the present threat. Now, let's get on with it.

'We have lost the battle to prevent the fog entering Winchester; fortunately all the residents have been evacuated in time.'

'How did you try to stop it?' Holman asked.

'Perhaps you will tell us, William?' The Home Secretary turned to the Under-Secretary of State for Defence for the Army, William Douglas-Glyne.

'Yes. There are four principal methods of dealing with fog. The method we've been using today, all day, is sprinkling calcium chloride from low flying aircraft, a practice used in San Francisco regularly to clear their fogs. It's a chemical that actually dries up the air, but although we've used tons of the stuff it hasn't had much effect. Very expensive method too, I might add. Some of the vapour was cleared but, as we now know, the gas is self-producing; it just goes on manufacturing itself.'

'Have you tried the other methods?' asked Sir Trevor.

'Not yet, we've had little time. And anyway, the calcium chloride was the most favoured. Let me tell you about the other ways and you'll understand. During the war, our airfields had what was called the F100 system, another expensive process and little used since. With radar, fog isn't much of a problem nowadays, but this is what they used to do: they warmed the air around the airfield with petrol in special devices; as it became warmer it absorbed more moisture and the droplets of liquid turned to invisible water vapour, dispersing the fog and forming a hole above the airfield through which aircraft could land.

'Now, apart from not having enough time to set up such an elaborate system around the town, all we would have succeeded in doing is divert the fog – not get rid of it.

148

'Another method is to use ultrasonic waves. Rapid to and fro movements produced by vibrations in the air tend to cause the tiny water droplets to collect together, forming drops that are large enough to fall as rain. The disadvantage of this method is that the force of the sound waves we would have had to have used could have been harmful to living things. And again, now we know it would be useless because of the self-productive factor.'

He paused, looking down at his notes, reluctant to look at the troubled faces around him.

'And the last method?' The Home Secretary prodded.

'The last method is no good at all. It involves the use of carbon dioxide and of course, the organism thrives on this. If sprinkled on fog, it causes the water droplets to freeze and join together, making them heavy enough to fall to the ground, but in this case the mycoplasma would just "feed" on it.'

'Are you telling us there's nothing we can do?' asked Sir Trevor incredulously.

'We are still looking at other methods,' came the somewhat feeble reply.

'I'm sure we have enough top brains in this country to find a solution,' said the Home Secretary. 'As well as our own, we also have scientific institutes in America, Russia and France searching for the answer. The major powers of the world are working for us. Even China has approached us with an offer of assistance. Remember, there is nothing to prevent the fog from drifting out to sea and reaching other countries; the threat is not with us alone, although we are in the immediate danger.

'The fact that it could virtually depopulate a town the size of Bournemouth has made the danger clear to every country in the world. If it has done any good at all, it's in the fact that the major powers now have a common enemy.

'If we cannot disperse the fog, our only hope is to find the antidote to the disease, fast. And to make that serum, we need a quantity – however small – of the mutated mycoplasma itself, as Professor Ryker says, in its "purest form".'

'But you know it would be impossible to get that,' Ryker said, a worried frown creasing his face.

'Impossible, why?' Sir Trevor looked at the scientist. 'Surely someone wearing some sort of protective clothing, breathing apparatus, that sort of thing, could get close enough to get a sample?'

'It is not a matter of getting close enough,' said Ryker, 'it means going to the very centre of the fog.'

'The centre?'

'Yes,' said the Home Secretary. 'Sensors in our aircraft have discovered a force in the centre of the fog. This is obviously the nucleus of the mycoplasma itself.'

'The glow!' said Holman, half to himself. 'When we were driving through it, Casey saw a glow!'

'Yes, Mr Holman,' the Professor nodded his head. 'It is possible that the organism has taken on a sort of incandescent quality because of the process it is going through.'

Sir Trevor Chambers broke in huffily. 'All right. So the "neat" stuff is in the centre. That still doesn't prevent someone with suitable protection going in to get it!'

Ryker looked towards the Home Secretary askance. He received a sharp nod of acquiescence.

'We said earlier that Broadmeyer was careless,' he said to Sir Trevor. 'But only in small ways. No scientist is careless enough to handle dangerous chemicals or substances without suitable protection. He was covered from head to foot in protective clothing.'

'Good God! You mean there *is* no protection from it?'

'Not the practical protection that would enable a man to move freely. It was one of the reasons it was considered so dangerous, the fact that it could pass through the special heavy material of these suits.'

'Lead-lined suits?' said Holman.

'Too clumsy and cumbersome for an operation of this sort. The wearer would have to travel half a mile to reach the fog's centre in virtual darkness and still have no guarantee he would be safe from the mutated mycoplasma at its strongest.'

A hint of suspicion began to creep into Holman's mind. 'This sort of brings us back to the point about immunity, doesn't it?' he said, looking directly at the Home Secretary.

'Yes, it does,' said the Home Secretary, quite unembarrassed. 'We need someone who is immune to the disease to go in and bring back a sample. You, Mr Holman, it would seem, are that person.'

Fifteen

Four spectral shapes moved through the thick yellow mist. Three were gross, misshapen versions of the human form, lumbering along at a slow, uneven pace, one leading a small trolley containing a dark, oblong box that had several strange attachments to it. The fourth figure was more representative of his species, yet seemed to have a peculiar hump on his back and a face that contained only a pair of eyes.

One of the heavily suited men tapped Holman on the shoulder. This was as far as they dared to go; the rest was up to him. His voice was muffled through the smog-mask as he gave them the thumbs-up sign and said, 'okay'. The three scientists couldn't have heard him anyway through their glass-visored helmets. The aperture for vision was very small and they had to swivel their heads to see one another, and even then the fog was so thick it was difficult to see more than two yards ahead.

It was clearer for Holman who was not wearing a suit, but still the farthest he could see was about five yards. The heavily clad figure who had tapped him on the shoulder handed him the handle to the trolley. By pressing a button in the tip of the handle, the small but heavy motorised vehicle would propel itself along, restricted in its speed by the person who controlled its power. Holman looked into the inscrutable mask of the scientist, trying at least to see the man's eyes, but gave up, unable to penetrate the dark interior of the reinforced glass visor. Instead, he patted the man's arm once in a gesture of thanks.

He watched the grotesque figures turn and disappear into the yellow mist, leaving him with a feeling of utter loneliness, so acute that he had to fight the urge to call after them. But they had taken a risk bringing him this far; they knew the outer

151

fringes of the fog were weak but just how weak, they hadn't yet ascertained.

Holman turned away from the point where they had been swallowed up and faced the direction he himself had to take, remembering the street plan he'd studied during the night. He thought by now he could walk the streets blindfolded and still find his way.

The tiny oxygen tank on his back was uncomfortable but deemed necessary in case the mist became too choking. He pressed the button controlling the trolley and moved forward again, feeling ill at ease and claustrophobic. The test had been positive. They were fairly certain he was immune; certain enough to consider it worth the risk, at any rate. But they had left the choice to him; nobody could force him to enter the fog again.

Of course, there was no choice really. What else could he do? If they couldn't destroy the fog, then millions could die from it. The only answer was the serum. And he was the only suitable person available. It was no good damning the army for their stupidity, the crass stupidity he had suspected all along; now was the time for constructive action. But my God, would they know about it when it was over! If it was ever over.

The small amount of blood containing the disease they had drained from a still-living, but completely insane victim of Bournemouth, had been absolutely rejected and destroyed by his own blood cells when introduced into his system. Whether that small amount was enough to judge the test conclusively or not, they did not know, but in a crisis of this proportion, chances had to be taken. And it was he who had to take them.

He thought of Casey. She had looked so pale last night, so still, and incredibly beautiful in her trance-like state. He didn't want to lose her! He'd rather die himself now than be left without her. Was it just her illness that had brought his love to this crushing, fearful peak? No, he answered himself. It had just made him realise her value, his own incompleteness without her. To lose her now would be the ultimate irony.

He stopped. For a moment he thought he had seen a shadow moving in the fog. Or was it just the swirling mist playing tricks on his eyes? He started walking again, keeping close to the sides of the streets so he could see the buildings and where they ended to allow for other turnings, but he stayed off the pavements because of the contraption trailing behind.

152

The transfusion on Casey had been successful: this morning it would be the turn of therapeutic radiology, the radiation burning out the badness, the angle of the x-ray constantly being moved so as to damage as little as possible of the healthy tissues. He prayed that it would work, expelling from his mind the frightening thought that it might not.

He dreaded the moment he would have to tell her of the death of her 'father'. Simmons had passed away during the night, never having regained consciousness since leaving the house. He had died alone. Holman would never tell Casey she had killed the man she thought to be her father – it might destroy her. And he still wasn't sure if he would tell her of the man's dying confession to him. Would it help diminish her loss? He thought not. It would only confuse her emotions. He walked on through the fog that was becoming thicker, more yellow.

Now, let's see, he thought. This must be the shopping arcade. If I turn right now, it should lead me to the cathedral. He paused for a moment, breathing heavily. He was sure it was more psychological than the fact that the fog was restricting his breathing; he was involuntarily inhaling as little of the surrounding air as possible even though he knew he would be able to use the small oxygen tank strapped to his back if he really needed to. They had told him the source of energy seemed to be coming from somewhere near the old cathedral. The trolley that trailed along behind him like a faithful dog contained a lead-lined box that operated on the same principle as a vacuum cleaner. Attached to its side were several lengths of metal tubing that when assembled and joined to a tough flexible hose from the container could be used as a rod, fifteen feet in length, which could be probed into the nucleus of the mutated mycoplasma and a sample drawn back into the holder. It was a hastily conceived plan, but the only one available to them in so short a time.

Summoning up his courage, Holman turned into the street that would lead him into the lawns surrounding the cathedral. The street was narrow and as he passed by the shops he noticed the window of one had been smashed. Further along, he discovered another had been broken. Looters? Was it possible that there were still people in the town, an unscrupulous few who didn't realise the danger they were in? The public had had to be told of the consequences of contact with the fog; surely no one would risk entering it now for the sake of robbing the unoccupied shops? Perhaps it had been an accident; an army lorry unable to manoeuvre comfortably in the narrow street, or perhaps someone had fallen against it in the rush to leave the town. But two windows? He looked more closely at the shop. It was a jeweller's. Well, that confirmed it. Someone had stayed behind to scavenge, ignoring the risk, heedless of the warnings. Was he, or were they, still around or had they fled having accomplished their easy robbery? He shrugged; it wasn't his problem.

The yellowness was even more dense now as he drew nearer to the historic building and the extent of his vision became even more limited. He passed through the opening to the lawns which housed their few important gravestones and surrounded the cathedral, his eyes constantly narrowed, peering into the murk, trying to make out the path that led to the very doors of the ancient place of worship. Where was the glow? Surely he should have come upon it by now? He would have to make a circuit of the building, they'd insisted the centre was in this particular area. It could have moved on, of course, but there was very little breeze to stir it.

But as he approached the cathedral's entrance, he noticed a faint half-glow.

He stopped dead. Was it possible? Was the nucleus, the heart of the disease, housed within the great church? Could it have drifted into Winchester Cathedral and become trapped inside its ancient but solid stone walls?

Another, more disturbing, thought jarred Holman's mind.

What if it hadn't drifted in by accident? Could it possibly be self-motivated? It was an incredible idea and he tried to dismiss it from his mind. It was too fantastic, too much like science-fiction. But then everything that had happened was too fantastic.

The thought persisted.

He walked on, a coldness creeping through his body, his steps noiseless and cautious. He tried to fight the chill that enveloped him, reassuring himself with the thought that the sinister circumstances, the loneliness and the lack of clear vision were all working together, attacking his imagination, allies to fear.

He saw that the glow – or was it just a brighter tone of yellow? – was definitely coming from the open doorway. Had he the nerve to confront its source lurking inside?

'Fuck it!' It was a soft spoken war cry. He went on.

Lingering at the entrance, he peered into the brighter mist. The air was much harder to breathe in, the acidity burnt his

154

nostrils and throat. He reached for the oxygen mask looped over his shoulder and was about to remove the smog mask when something flickered in the corner of his vision. He froze and studied the spot in the fog from where the movement had come. Imagination again? He saw nothing, only the patterns made by the swirls of the mist. He listened and heard nothing but the imagined beating of his own heart.

Holman looked towards the source of the glow. It was at its strongest at the centre of the cathedral's vast interior, near the altar. It seemed to have no definable shape, its outer edges constantly changing their line and only visible because of the sudden contrast in yellows: the apparently clear, clean yellow of the nucleus itself, against the murkier, greyer yellow of its protective screen, the fog. It was impossible to tell the size of the strangely writhing shape, his vision was too impaired by the surrounding layers of fog, but its very existence seemed to exude a malignancy, a malevolent growth that was frightening, yet perversely fascinating.

It was only with an extreme effort of will that Holman tore his eyes away from the eerie spectacle and knelt down by the machine at his side. He remembered his oxygen mask and placed it over his mouth after removing the smog mask. He drew in several deep breaths and his head immediately became clearer, making him wonder if the fog itself also had a slight drugging effect. Detaching the metal tubes from the vacuum container, he began to screw them together, becoming even more nervous with the action he now had to take.

He still wasn't sure if he had the courage to approach the glowing mass, the mass that looked pure but was in fact made from the deadly, growing mutation, so he closed his mind to it. The moment of truth would be on him soon enough and he would either walk towards it or run like hell away from it. Either way, whichever direction, the movement would be spontaneous, not carefully considered. He concentrated on the rods.

He became aware of their presence more by sensing it than hearing or seeing them. They appeared as three dark shapes in the fog, standing about five feet apart, just beyond reasonably clear visual range, unmoving, silent. He looked from one hazy form to another, their stillness more frightening than if they had been moving, for mobility would have at least given them some form, something he could identify.

155

He rose, apprehensively clutching the section of rods he'd managed to put together before him. One of the shapes moved forward and with some sense of relief he realised it was the figure of a man. But the head was different.

Holman took a step back in horror and raised the metal tubing in defence. As the figure drew nearer, he almost laughed with relief. It was a man, and his head looked so strange because he was wearing a grotesque World War II gas-mask. He held in his hands a long, black candlestick, its wicked looking point, the point on which the base of a candle should have been pressed, exposed and aimed towards Holman.

'What the hell are you doing here?' Holman asked uncertainly, removing his oxygen mask to make himself understood. There was no reply as the man stepped before him.

'This fog is dangerous, you should have cleared out with the rest,' Holman continued, his eyes not moving from the point aimed at his chest. He watched, almost mesmerised, as the candlestick was slowly raised and drawn back, ready to strike.

Holman waited no longer. He jabbed the metal rod hard into the man's stomach and as he doubled up, brought it swiftly down on his exposed head. The man collapsed in a heap.

Holman raised the rod again, ready for the other two. But they'd vanished.

He looked around, his head darting from left to right, the figure at his feet moaning and squirming on the hard, stone floor. He knelt beside him and turned him over on to his back. 'Poor bloody fool!' he muttered. He must have thought the gas mask would be protection against the fog and seized the opportunity to help himself to some of the valuables of the deserted town. But what were he and his companions doing in the cathedral and why had the man attacked him? Had the disease affected them already? Or did they just see him as a threat to their freedom?

He pulled the ugly mask from the groaning man's face and saw that his eyes had the slightly glazed look he'd seen in Casey's; he *had* been infected.

The sound of a footstep warned him of the second man's approach from behind. He whirled around to face him but a glancing blow sent him sprawling back, causing him to lose his grip on the rod. The figure loomed over him and began to laugh, a cackling, hysterical laugh. The third man materialised from the mist and stood by his side and began to laugh with his companion. Suddenly, they reached down and grabbed Holman by his ankles and started to drag him along the stone floor towards the glow. He tried to kick his legs free, but their grips were firm and his efforts made them laugh even louder. His hands scrabbled for a grip but the old stone was smooth from centuries of wear. As he passed the injured man his body came in contact with the heavy candlestick. He snatched at it desperately and thought he'd lost it when it rolled away from him. Fortunately it was stopped by the prone man's foot and Holman was able to seize it. He drew it to him and was about to hurl it at one of his assailants when the man he thought he'd put out of action raised himself to his knees with a demented roar, saw Holman, and threw himself at him, his teeth bared to be used as a weapon.

Holman managed to get an elbow under the man's throat and keep the gnashing teeth away, twisting his own head away at the same time. There were cries of rage from the other two as their progress was halted. They dropped Holman's legs and began to kick at the two struggling bodies, oblivious to friend or foe. One of them grabbed at the first man's hair and yanked his head back beating at his face with his other hand.

It gave Holman the chance he needed. He struck at the exposed throat with his heavy weapon and crushed the man's windpipe, instantly sickened by his own action. But there was only time for momentary regret for the other two now directed their attention completely towards him again.

He pushed the injured man away and pulled at the ankle of one of the others, bringing the startled man crashing to the floor. The third man caught Holman from behind and put his arms around his neck, squeezing his throat, trying to choke him to death. Because of his higher position, his head was above Holman's and saliva from his wildly grinning mouth trickled down on to Holman's gasping face.

Holman felt as though his head was about to explode. As he weakened, he was conscious of the man's insane chuckle and as his vision began to swim, he saw the man he'd brought down raise himself on one elbow and lie there laughing at him. Vaguely, almost remotely, he realised he still held the candlestick. With both hands, he brought its wicked point swiftly up to the only vulnerable spot he could reach. The man's scream and the sudden spurt of blood that gushed down on to Holman's face added new horror to the nightmare. The pressure on his throat was released and he sucked in the foul air greedily as his attacker fell away from him.

The remaining man was pointing a shaking finger at them, laughing hysterically.

It was too much for Holman. He staggered to his feet and ran from the cathedral.

Once outside, he fell to his knees on the gravel path, but the pounding footsteps behind him made him stumble on again into the thick blanket of fog, thankful for its concealing refuge. He found himself running on grass, regardless of the danger of possible collision with hidden trees or gravestones. His only thought was to get away, away from those madmen, away from the mutation, away from the cathedral. To get away from the fog, to be with normal people again. His mission was forgotten, his instinct for self-survival his only driving force. He did not even feel the sudden gustiness of the wind or see that the swirls had become more vigorous in their movements.

He slipped on the wet grass and as he stumbled forward, desperately trying to keep his balance, he ran into a tree. His head struck it with a loud crack and he slowly crumpled against it, sinking to his knees and then sprawling on to the grass.

As his consciousness slipped away from him, he was aware of a shadowy figure appearing from the mist and standing over him. The deep-throated chuckle was the last sound he heard before he blacked out.

They found the lunatic trying to bury Holman alive. The fog had cleared from the town, swept away by a sudden unpredicted force of wind and rain, and the helicopters hovering around the fringes of the thick blanket swooped down to search for him. As one circled the cathedral, it came across the figure of a man digging. At least, that was what the pilot thought the man was doing, but as he swept over him, he realised he was, in fact, filling in a deep hole. A crew member slapped his shoulder vigorously.

'Get down there, quickly!' he shouted above the noise of the helicopter's engine. 'There was a body in that hole. That man's trying to bury it!'

As they landed, the small-time crook who had been amazed at the chance of having the whole town of Winchester to himself to plunder undisturbed with his two cronies, and was now

158

insane because of this ill-seized opportunity, ignored the descending machine and happily continued filling in the pit he had dragged the unconscious man towards. The hole had been left by workmen who had just begun to dig a grave that was to house the remains of an important church dignitary whose last wishes were to be buried in the shadow of his beloved cathedral. The work had been interrupted by the sudden evacuation order and the burial that was to have taken place later on in the day was now replaced by a far less dignified ceremony.

Holman lay at the bottom of the open grave where he'd been roughly dumped. There was a large swelling on his forehead caused by his fall against the tree and only the earth falling on to his body prodded his unconscious state, making him stir, a low moan escaping from his lips. As he raised a hand to his head, his eyes still closed, and opened his mouth to groan even louder, a shovel full of damp earth landed on his face, making his eyes suddenly blink open only to close again instantly as the loose soil ran into them.

He spluttered and choked as the earth fell into his open mouth and ran down his throat. He tried to sit up, but his head was still not clear enough to allow it, so instead, he ran his hands over his face in order to clear off the dirt. He could feel the clumps of earth still landing on his body and his mind struggled to understand what was happening. It was only the chuckling sound that broke through his stupor and brought him fully to his senses.

He opened his eyes again, this time cautiously keeping them covered with his fingers. He saw the edges of the trench above him and then caught sight of the figure that was shovelling the dirt on to him. He suddenly realised where he was and what was happening. The man was burying him alive!

Panic stricken, he clutched at the loose earth at the sides of the pit and pulled himself to an upright position. With a snarl of anger, the man above him raised his shovel to strike down at him to prevent him leaving his premature grave.

He raised an arm to ward off the blow, closing his eyes, knowing there was not room enough to allow him to dodge it. But it never came. He heard voices shouting and then scuffling noises. When he opened his eyes, all he could see through the open rectangle of earth above him was the grey, disturbed sky. He became aware of the rain that was beating down into the hole, its soothing wetness serving to revive his senses even more. He drew his knees up, preparing himself to fight off any further attack.

Suddenly, a face appeared, breaking into the rectangle of sky. It grinned, and its voice said, 'This is no time to lie down on the job, Mr Holman.'

A hand was extended to help him climb from his gruesome resting place.

Sixteen

Holman was filled with apprehension as he walked down the long corridor towards Observation Room 3 in which, he had been informed, Casey was now resting. He hadn't been able to see Janet Halstead on his return to the Research Centre for she'd been working through the night organising her staff as well as hospitals throughout the country for the emergency and still finding time to supervise Casey's treatment, but now she was snatching a necessary few hours' sleep. Another doctor had told him the radiology treatment had gone well and now they were waiting for Casey to come out of a deep slumber before they could tell if it had been successful.

Holman needed sleep too. His experience that morning had left him drained; the memory of regaining consciousness and finding himself in a grave with a madman shovelling in earth to bury him almost outweighed the other horrors he'd been through. Being buried alive was surely a nightmare that most people had had at some time, but very few had actually experienced it.

The army had flown him back to London by helicopter, realising he would not be persuaded to go back into the fog again that day. Professor Ryker, and of course, Barrow, who was still acting as his bodyguard, flew with him. Ryker had naturally been disappointed when he had returned without a sample of the mutated mycoplasma, but had understood the scare he'd been through and did not persist in urging Holman to try again. The unpredicted change of weather was moving the fog too rapidly anyway for him to be able to locate its centre.

Towns that lay ahead of it, directly in its path were being evacuated, but fortunately the direction in which it was moving was not too densely populated. Police and army vehicles, guided by the watchdog helicopters, raced before the rolling grey mass, stopping at small villages and remote houses and bundling their occupants into the vans and trucks, and once full, veering off at a right angle, away from the danger. Then they would unload their human cargo and speed back, using a different route, to repeat the process. It was exhausting and harrowing, and already many serious accidents had occurred, but on the whole, it was proving successful.

Unfortunately, it was a process that could not be maintained indefinitely and the men controlling the operation dreaded the unavoidable moment it would reach a large town. They prayed that the wind would not change its easterly direction and carry the fog towards Basingstoke, Farnham, Aldershot. *London*.

The biggest worry at the moment was Haslemere, the largest town directly in the path of the fog, but already it was being emptied of its occupants, most of the people fleeing north, unwilling to go south because of the fear of being trapped by the sea, the fate of Bournemouth inhabitants influencing their choice. They could not be convinced that their fears were unwarranted – the fog was still only a mile wide and could easily be skirted – and the roads north were jammed with vehicles of every description as well as panic-stricken people on foot.

The Prime Minister had arrived back in London and was directing operations with the help of his chief military, scientific and medical advisers, from a special operational headquarters, a vast, impenetrable underground shelter, less than a mile from the House of Commons, its actual location kept a strict secret from the general public. It was already being prepared for occupation if the fog should head towards London. It had been built as a sanctuary from nuclear bombs, but now it would be used as a shelter from a totally unimagined threat, and its defences against radiation poisoning would serve just as well against the deadly man-made disease.

The proposal to build huge fires in London to disperse the fog if it entered the city was considered and the go-ahead for their preparation given on the understanding that they were only to be used as a last resort; the danger of the whole of London going up in uncontrollable flames was a frightening possibility that could not be ignored. But it was at least a positive action. The demoralising chess game that was being played with the fog further south could not go on for ever and the public had to *see* they were being given some form of physical protection, however crude.

They, the public, were informed an antidote was being prepared and large quantities would soon be available; they were told the disease itself was weakening and would probably soon die or be so diluted with pure air, it would be ineffective; it was confirmed that the experts believed the organism had mysteriously drifted in from the sea and a full inquiry into its source would be put into force as soon as the crisis was over.

They were lied to because the government thought it best; large-scale panic would only increase the danger to lives. The truth could be told – or at least some of it – when the threat had passed.

Those responsible would pay the penalty – but not publicly. Steps would be taken so that a disaster of this nature and magnitude could never happen again.

Holman had discussed with Ryker the fact that the mutated mycoplasma had been trapped inside the cathedral. Or had it taken shelter? Was it feasible, was it remotely possible, that the mutation had some sort of driving force? Could it have – Holman had hesitated to say it – could it have intelligence? After all, it was a parasite that fed on the brain.

Professor Ryker had laughed, but it was without humour. 'Every living thing has some driving force, Mr Holman. Even plant life has some intelligence, it's a matter of degree. But to suggest this organism has a will, a brain. It has a motivation for survival perhaps, just as a flower reaches towards the sun, but a mind of its own? No, Mr Holman, don't let your harrowing experience this morning send you into the realms of fantasy. The mycoplasma does not control the fog; when the wind took the protective cloud away, the mycoplasma had to go too, trapped in its centre, caged by its own protection. It exercised no power over its cloak of fog, it gives no direction. It is a mindless, organic thing, incapable of action by thought.'

'But action by instinct?' Holman had interrupted.

'Yes, perhaps.'

'Maybe it amounts to the same thing.'

Ryker spent the rest of the journey in silence, deep in thought, occasionally shaking his head as though to dismiss a theory, then his forehead wrinkling in concentration as a new thought was processed and again rejected.

Barrow had accompanied Holman to the Research Centre after Holman had given his report to the Home Secretary in person, promising he would attempt to procure some of the mycoplasma as soon as conditions were favourable. They would

163

be in constant radio contact until that moment arrived and when it did, he would be flown to the spot immediately. It was suggested that he be positioned in a place directly in line with the fog's centre so that it would pass right over him, but Holman had rejected the idea vehemently. If there was no other way, then he would do it, but he was damned if he would confront the mutation when it was moving swiftly, giving him little chance to manoeuvre around it.

At another time, he would probably have taken the risk, but at that moment, his nerves were somewhat taut, and he was in no mood to repeat that morning's performance. He was also anxious to see Casey, to find out whether the experiment had worked, to know if she would become a vegetable or return to her normal self.

The Home Secretary wisely but reluctantly refrained from ordering him to carry out his request knowing the man would be more useful in a better condition. In the meantime, gadgets could be set up in the fog's path, containers that could be operated by remote control to close when sensors relayed the message that the source was in the vicinity. It was a hit and miss method, but the only one available at that time.

The rising trepidation Holman felt reached its peak when he turned the handle of the door marked '3'. Through its glass upper portion he could see the pale figure lying still in the bed. A nurse sat at her bedside ready to call in Janet Halstead at the first signs of consciousness. She smiled as Holman entered.

'How is she?' he asked.

'She's been sleeping peacefully enough,' the nurse replied, 'but she had to be heavily drugged for the radiology and the blood transfusion. I'm afraid she was a bit violent.'

'Can I stay with her for a while?'

'Yes, of course.' The nurse rose from her seat, still smiling at him. 'I'll leave you for a little while but if she wakes, press this button. I can promise you, this room will be full of people in a flash. We're all rather anxious to find out the result of the radiology.'

'Are the signs good?'

'Oh, the signs are good, but frankly, Mr Holman, we just don't know. I'm sure Mrs Halstead has explained.'

Holman nodded and sat in the chair she had just vacated. The nurse left the room after checking the girl's pulse for the sixth time since she'd been on duty, her face non-committal to Holman's stare.

He sat watching Casey's face for several minutes, her frailty causing him concern. She had been through so much it seemed impossible that she would ever be the same again even if the parasite had been vanquished. When her eyes opened, would she recognise him or would they still hold that lost, faraway glaze that was so haunting, so terrible? He knew her wrists were strapped to the sides of the bed beneath the white sheets and the knowledge made his own eyes fill with tears he was unable to shed. He wished it were possible for him to cry, to find release for his emotions, but tears were a luxury he hadn't enjoyed for many, many years.

He reached forward to stroke her face, the desire to weep not conquered, but unwillingly suppressed, the incapability a burden rather than a strength.

He touched her lips with his hand, then her cheek, then her throat. She stirred, a slight frown creasing her forehead, but her face relaxed again, and became peaceful. He spoke her name, not to wake her, but because he needed to say it, and for an instant, her eyelids flickered. And then they opened.

They found his, and for an instant, they gave no sign. He froze, and for that tiny second, nothing existed, nothing was real, and there was no time and there were no questions.

Then the eyes became a person's because emotion was filtering through them, feelings reflecting what lay beyond, and they smiled and her lips smiled with them.

'Why do you call me Casey, John?' she asked, and fell back into a deep sleep again.

Janet Halstead was delighted when Holman told her of Casey's words. She couldn't be sure until Casey had recovered consciousness fully, but it seemed fairly certain that her brain would function normally once she had. Janet urged Holman to snatch a couple of hours sleep, promising to wake him as soon as Casey came out of her slumber. She found him a quiet room containing a couch and left him resting while she went back to study Casey's chart.

It was three hours later that Barrow shook his shoulder to wake him.

'She's awake, Holman, and she's fine,' he told him.

165

With a grin, Holman sat up and rubbed his face. 'Hell,' he said, 'I need a shave.'

'I don't think she'll mind.'

'Any new developments with the fog?' he asked the policeman as he hurriedly slipped on his jacket.

'Plenty, but I'll tell you after you've seen the girl.'

When Holman reached Observation Room 3, Casey was sitting up in bed talking to Janet Halstead. Her face lit up as he walked through the door and in a second they were in each other's arms, Holman smothering her face with kisses. Janet smiled at Barrow and they discreetly left the room.

'You're all right!' Holman laughed, breaking away from the tight embrace at last.

'Yes, yes, I'm all right.'

'Do,' he hesitated, 'do you remember anything.'

'A few things, John.' She became serious, her eyes averting his. 'I remember trying to kill you.'

He drew her towards him and said nothing.

'It's all so unclear,' she went on. 'Different images going through my mind, all mixed up, none of it real.' She clung to him, tighter.

'My father . . . ' Her voice drifted off.

'Casey,' Holman began.

'He's dead isn't he?'

Holman was stunned into silence. She remembered that? Finally, he said, 'Yes, Casey, he's dead.'

'He wasn't my father.'

Again, Holman fell into inadequate silence.

'He told me, John, just before I killed him. He told me he loved me . . . but it was more than a father's love. He . . . he wanted me.' She began to weep now, her body trembling, but the tears were of sadness and not remorse. 'I don't feel it yet. I feel sorry for him, but for some reason it's not really affecting me the way it should. Why, John? Am I still mad?' She pulled away and looked at him imploringly. 'Tell me, John, am I still insane?'

'No, darling,' he said, cupping her face in his hands. 'It'll hit you later.' And God help you when it does, he thought. 'You've been through too much. Your mind's protecting you. The pain will find you soon enough. Don't go looking for it.'

She cried out then and buried her head against him, her body now convulsing with her sobs. He held her tightly to him, knowing the hurt was seeping through, his words had spurred it to.

166

'I loved him, I loved him so much! How can I ever live with what I've done?'

'It wasn't your fault, Casey, you weren't responsible.'

'And you, John, I tried to kill you. Can you forgive me?'

'I told you darling, you weren't responsible.'

'Am I really all right now? Am I really better?'

'Yes, of course you are. And I'll help you forget, Casey, I promise I'll help you forget.'

It would take a long time to heal the wound she'd inflicted upon herself, but he knew she was strong enough to get over it. Maybe the fact that Simmons' motives were not entirely pure would help, or maybe it would make matters worse. There was no way of knowing. It would be up to Casey, and up to him to make up for part of that love she'd lost.

He talked to her quietly for a long time, the intensity of his words breaking through her barrier of regret, reaching, searching, until she began to respond with feelings other than self pity. 'What's going to happen now?' she finally asked.

'They want me to go back into the fog for the mycoplasma.'

'Why? Why you? Janet told me about the mutation and how it's causing the madness. But who wants you to get it? And why does it have to be you?'

Briefly, he told her of the events that had passed, of the disasters, of his immunity, and the fact that she would now be immune. He told her of the disease, of its origin, of the blind foolishness that had freed it. He barely mentioned his experience that morning, not wanting to give her cause for even more concern, merely telling her he'd been unable to locate the source.

She listened in quiet horror, occasionally shaking her head in disbelief, the rising fear inside her only slightly quelled by the knowledge that she was presumably now immune.

They were interrupted by Janet Halstead who bustled into the room, a tight smile betraying her tiredness. 'We still have a few more tests to make on Miss Simmons, John, and then I think she should get some rest. Your policeman is anxious to have a word with you, I believe.'

Holman kissed Casey and promised to return as soon as he was allowed. Casey wanted to tell him not to go back to the fog, to stay near-by, to take her away as soon as she was strong enough, but she knew her words would be wasted. And she knew the lives of many others dependend on him. Despite all

167

the technological advances of science, it seemed survival still depended on the action of a man. One man.

Barrow was still waiting for him in the corridor outside. 'They want you to go in again,' he told Holman.

'But what about the contraptions they set up to contain it?'

'Didn't work. The mutation itself just didn't cross their paths. At the moment they're still spraying the fog with calcium chloride, hundreds of tons of it, and it seems to be receding. They want you out there and ready to go in when they've dispersed it as much as they can.'

'What about the wind? Has it dropped?'

'It's not as bad as it was.'

'All right. Since I have no choice, I'll choose to try again.'

The helicopter flew them to a point east of Haslemere where they were met by Hermann Ryker, William Douglas-Glyne and Lieutenant-General Sir Keith Macklen. The men were standing among a group of vehicles that held a high vantage point overlooking the surrounding countryside. Holman was impressed by the constant stream of light aircraft that flew over the distant cloud of fog which looked even more ominous in the evening gloom.

Douglas-Glyne strode towards him, his hand outstretched. 'Valiant effort this morning, Mr Holman,' he said, grasping Holman's hand.

Holman grinned wryly at the insincerity of the words. 'Sorry I couldn't pull it off,' he said.

'Not to worry. Better luck next time, eh?'

Sir Keith Macklen joined them and said bluntly. 'You have to try again. It's absolutely vital that you bring us back some of the bloody stuff.'

'Yes,' said Douglas-Glyne. 'We sent two volunteers in a couple of hours ago out of desperation. They were well protected with suits and used an army scout vehicle to go in. We lost radio contact with them about an hour ago.'

'So it's up to you now,' said Sir Keith.

'Gentlemen,' broke in Professor Ryker's voice as he walked over at a leisurely pace, 'there is nothing Mr Holman can do for the moment. We do not want to stop the spraying now that it seems to be taking effect and Mr Holman could hardly walk into such a heavy concentration of calcium chloride. Unfortunately, we have not dispersed the fog as much as I thought we would and it will be dark shortly which would make his task even more hazardous.'

'But there are thousands of lives at stake,' said Sir Keith gruffly.

'Precisely. That is why Mr Holman is so valuable to us. We cannot take unnecessary risks with his life – particularly now we know there are definitely two lunatics wandering around out there.'

'But we don't know that – '

'Yes we do!' Ryker said angrily. 'It was on your insistence, Sir Keith, that they went in. I advised against it, I told you what would happen. I will not allow Mr Holman to risk his life because of your misjudgement! He means too much to the whole operation.'

'But we can't just stand by and do nothing,' Douglas-Glyne fumed.

'We are not doing nothing. We will spray the fog all night, for as long as our supplies last. By early morning, it should have depleted enough for us to see the actual mycoplasma – if it is still visible without its protective mist. In the meantime, Mr Holman, I suggest you try to sleep and we'll call you when the time is right.'

Once again, Holman found Barrow shaking him into reluctant consciousness in the early hours of the following morning. He had watched the fog for hours the previous night as the fleet of cars and army vehicles had slowly trundled after it like a funeral procession searching for a graveyard, and had finally fallen into a heavy, dreamless sleep in the back of the car he was travelling in, woken only once when shouts of alarm had passed down the convoy. The bodies of the two scientists who had gone into the fog earlier had been found; the signs indicated that they had killed each other with the guns they had carried for protection against attacks from any individuals who had not escaped the fog. Sleep had recaptured him almost immediately, but it had been filled with grotesque figures which his eyes were somehow never able to focus on.

He was confused at Barrow's statement and had to ask him to repeat it, rubbing his eyes in an effort to become fully awake.

'I said the fog has gone,' said Barrow slowly, emphasising each word. 'It's disappeared.'

Seventeen

Corporal Wilcox cursed as he slid down the steep incline in the dark. The damp grass increased the speed of his descent and an unseen root caught his boot, spinning his body at an awkward angle. He heard the hoots of laughter from the two soldiers who had watched his uncontrolled progress from above as he came to an abrupt halt at the foot of the embankment.

'I'll bloody murder you two!' he shouted up at them as he crawled forward to retrieve his fallen torch. He shone it towards the two grinning figures. 'Now get down 'ere, the pair of you!'

'Comin' Corp,' they replied in unison and with a shout, they jumped together, switching off their torches as they did so.

He heard their crashing, giggling descent, swinging his beam away from them so they would be in complete darkness. Let the mad fuckers break their necks, he grumbled to himself.

They arrived at his feet and he had to jump back hastily to avoid being knocked over by their kicking legs. They lay on ther backs, breathing hard and grinning up at him.

'Come on, get up,' he ordered gruffly. 'I don't know what's the matter with you two. You're like a couple of gigglin' fairies on a night out.'

'Sorry, Eddie,' the smaller of the two apologised with a smirk, 'but my friend Bernard' – he over emphasised the 'ard' – 'always gets this way when it's past his bedtime.'

'It's Corporal to you, Evans,' said Wilcox, his dislike for the little Cockney and his Mancunian companion evident in his tone. The pair of them were a constant thorn in his flesh, always taking the piss, but never quite overstepping the mark so he could put them on a charge – or belt one of them. They didn't even have to say anything, their stupid mocking faces were enough to make him feel a cunt.

They picked themselves up, brushing themselves down and groaning at imagined bruises.

170

'What we coom down 'ere for anyway, Corp?' asked Private Buswell, his droning accent a further irritant to Wilcox. 'It's only a bloomin' railway track.'

'Orders are that every square inch of ground is to be covered!' the Corporal snapped, swinging his torch along the lines that were no longer silver but dull and rusty.

'Anyway, it's gone, innit?' Evans stated disgustedly. 'I mean, we been lookin' for two bleedin' days now!'

'They think it's gone. We're lookin' to make sure.'

'Yeah, but that spray stuff cleared it, didn't it?' insisted Evans. 'I told you, they think so.'

'Well, they couldn't 'ave just lost it, could they?' drawled Buswell.

'No, but it was funny 'ow it just vanished,' said Wilcox. 'I mean, they'd been sprayin' it all day and the stuff was workin', but all of a sudden, it wasn't there anymore. The thing in the middle, I mean.'

'Yeah, well, what is it then, this thing in the middle? It's supposed to be a bug, innit?' Evans asked, switching on his own torch, pointing it at the sky to see how far its beam travelled.

'The disease, that's what it is. They want to make sure that's gone an' all.'

'Yeah, well I don't fancy findin' it.'

'Don't worry, we don't have to go near it,' Wilcox reassured him, then added disdainfully, 'Anyway, you two bleeders are potty enough. It wouldn't have any effect on you.'

'Quite right, Corp,' grinned Evans, 'me and Bernard are right nutters, so I'd watch us close seeing as we've got bullets for our rifles.'

'Yeah, Corp,' said Buswell, his smiling expression turning into one of puzzlement, 'why've we got ammunition?'

'Just in case, Buswell, just in case we run into real lunatics.'

'You don't mean we'd 'ave to shoot them?'

'If we found the glow and ran into any trouble that might prevent us reportin' its location, then we're to use our own discretion, of course.'

'Ooh, makes me feel all cold,' shivered Evans. 'Come on, let's 'ave a fag.'

'Always the fuckin' same you two. It's me who cops it if the Sarge finds us. He's around 'ere somewhere,' Wilcox moaned.

'Nah, he's a long way off. Let's walk up a bit, find a nice secluded spot.'

171

Corporal Wilcox stepped into the centre of the lines and began to walk forward, playing his torch along the sleepers ahead of him. The oher two fell in behind him, Evans whistling an off-key tune.

' 'Ere! We not gonna' get run down, are we?' He broke off his whistling to ask the question.

'Don't be bloody daft. This is a disused track. You can see by the grass it hasn't been used for years. And look at the rust on the lines.'

'Just checkin' Corp.'

Wilcox heard Buswell's snigger from behind and snorted with weary annoyance. 'Why the hell do I always get roped in with you two piss artists?'

They marched on to the accompaniment of Evans' tuneless whistle, searching the steep embankments on either side with their torches.

'How coom it glows then, this stuff?' asked Buswell after a while.

'Radiation, innit?' Evans told him.

'Who said it was radiation?' Wilcox stopped and turned to look at him.

'Stands to reason, dunnit?' The amusement never left his eyes. 'It glows, so they tell us. It eats away people's brains. It's driftin' around the country at its leisure and they can't stop it. All adds up.'

'Yeah, well how would radiation come from the sea?' asked the Corporal belligerently.

'Oh gawd! You don't believe that do you?' said Evans, his turn to be disgusted. 'They rely on pricks like you to believe the stories they put out.'

'Watch it, Evans, or you'll be on a charge.'

'All right, Corp, don't get nasty. Come on, let's keep going.'

They continued marching, Evans expounding on his theory. 'You see, they've done it, the scientists. They've 'ad an accident at one of their atomic power plants and now they're doin' a cover up. This bloody fog, in actual fact, is a bloody radiation cloud, right Bernard?'

'Right, Professor.'

'That earthquake, the other day. Now what d'you think that was?'

'An earthquake,' said Buswell brightly.

'Oh, shut up, turd-brain. That, Corp, was an underground

172

explosion. And for all we know, it was an atomic explosion. And for all we know, that's where this radiation came from.' He nodded his head in appreciation of his own theory.

'You do talk rubbish, Evans,' said Wilcox, his attention now directed at the black shape looming ahead of them.

'Yeah,' muttered Evans under his breath, 'and it's silly sods like you that never learn.'

Wilcox stopped abruptly again, causing Evans to bump into him, and Buswell to bump into Evans.

'There's a tunnel up ahead,' he told them.

'Right, let's 'ave a fag now then,' said Evans, already unbuttoning his tunic.

'You'll get me shot, you two,' grumbled the Corporal, the other two interpreting his remark for one of assent. They squatted just inside the entrance to the tunnel, away from the searching eyes of the other soldiers that were heavily concentrated in the surrounding area.

Evans shielded the flare from his match with a cupped hand, lighting Buswell's cigarette first and then his own. 'Oh, sorry Corp,' he apologised insincerely, offering the light towards Wilcox.

Wilcox ignored him and huffily lit his cigarette with his own matches. He sat on the rail opposite the two privates.

'All right, know-all,' he said acidly to Evans, 'tell me something: if this thing we're lookin' for is radiation, why can't they find it with detectors?' He leaned forward, a smile of satisfaction on his face.

'Because, my old fruit, they've already got rid of it,' said Evans returning the smile smugly.

'What, with a bloody spray?' Wilcox sat upright, shaking his head at the private's stupidity.

'That's right. We don't know what the spray was, do we? They said it was to clear the fog, but what they really meant was it was to clear the radiation.'

'Gawd 'elp us,' sighed Wilcox, looking towards the roof of the tunnel.

'No, no,' Evans insisted. 'We don't know, do we? We don't know what they've invented. Stands to reason they'd 'ave thought of something to get rid of radiation. They've 'ad enough time to.'

Wilcox snorted again and Buswell sniggered.

173

'We're the cannon fodder, mate,' Evans went on. 'They've sent us in to make sure it *as* cleared up.'

'Without detectors?'

'Without detectors. They don't want people to *know* it's radiation, do they?'

'Christ!' Wilcox gave up. Evans' absurd logic had been a source of irritation and frustration to him for a long time now, but sometimes it became unbearable. 'I'm gonna' 'ave a quick look up the tunnel then we'll be on our way.' He could have sent either of the two men but couldn't face the protests as to why they shouldn't and besides, he felt the need to be away from them even if it was only for a few seconds.

Bloody misfits, he cursed inwardly, as he trudged down into the blackness. They hadn't joined the army for a career as he had. They'd joined because they wanted an easy life – free food, free lodgings, and someone else to make the decisions for them. The Professionals! The Shirkers was more like it. Any chance they had to get out of doing their job, they'd grab at it. They'd got him into enough trouble in the past, these two, that's why he wasn't a sergeant yet. You'd think after six bloody years he'd have made sergeant! He'd been in line for it this year until these two monkeys had latched on to him. Why him? What was so fascinating about him that they had to make themselves a nuisance around him? The time they'd got him pissed in Germany while they were on guard duty. They'd started off by persuading him to have just a quick one, then another, then another, till he didn't care any more and had got so drunk he spewed up over the NCO's shiny boots when he'd come round on his inspection.

He'd almost got court-martialled over that; it was only the fact that the NCO was being returned to England the next day and didn't want to hang around for the trial that got him off. But he'd been made to pay for it in other ways.

Then there was the 'nice, clean, little tart' they'd introduced him to in Hamburg. She even had a medical certificate to prove she was clean. He'd got the pox from her and the British army frowned on soldiers who get the pox, even though it happened all the time.

In Northern Ireland, they'd taken him to a 'friendly little social club', not far from the barracks and where they'd be well received so long as they were in civvies. The three of them had nearly 'well received' bullets in the backs of their heads on that occasion. It was only his prompt action of hurling a chair through a window, the three soldiers quickly following it, that had saved their lives. Evans had laid out the bitch who had invited them with a bottle before he'd leapt through, and that had cost him a glancing bullet on the side of his arse. It was a pity it hadn't gone right up it! The army hadn't been too pleased about that little episode either.

He supposed he'd been lucky, considering. The incidents – there were many more of them – were never quite enough to cause drastic action against him, but they all served to keep him down at his present rank.

The trouble was, he fell for it every time. They either smarmed their way round him or offered him a challenge. And he always gave in or rose to the bait. He always had to prove he was one of the boys. Christ, this was a long tunnel!

He looked back and realised he must have rounded a bend for the torches of the two privates were no longer visible. He shone his torch ahead but all he could see was its bright reflection against the shiny damp wall. He must be at the centre of the bend, unable to see back or ahead – and unable to be seen. Right, this is far enough, he thought to himself, stepping out of the track and leaning his rifle against the wall. He began to unbutton his trousers, holding his torch between his upper arm and side. That was another thing! He couldn't even piss in front of them. Their mocking faces caused a mental block – or a block somewhere else. They knew the effect they had on him and sometimes would follow him out to the gents if they were in the Naafi or a club, and stand on either side of him, grinning, while his face grew redder and the cock in his hand more apologetic.

Even now, just the thought of them was preventing him from performing his body's natural function. Why did they have to make his life a misery? Just wait till he was made sergeant, then they'd pay for it. Maybe that was it. Maybe they knew that and were trying to stop his progress. Bastards!

As he stared blankly at the wall two feet away from him, his features eerily lit in the throwback from his torch, his legs apart, his hands on his penis, his mind engrossed in bitter thoughts, he failed to notice the thick tentacles of mist that crept around his ankles like a wispy grey vine. The tentacles thickened into a layer of fog as they began to rise and slowly engulf his body.

*

175

'Eddie's a long time,' Buswell commented, his cigarette beginning to burn the insides of his fingers in his effort to waste as little as possible.

'You'll get cancer doing that,' Evans remarked. 'It's the last bit that's got the most nicotine.'

Buswell shrugged his shoulders. He should worry.

'Come on, Corp, what you doing? Having a wank?' Evans shouted into the darkness. There was no reply. 'He's probably sulking,' he said, once more resting his elbows on his knees and flicking his cigarette end into the gloom.

'Poor old Eddie. He takes it serious, doesn't he?' said Buswell.

'Yeah. He's all right though. Just 'asn't really got what it takes. He's good for a laugh though.'

'D'you think he'll ever get to be sergeant?'

'Nah, no chance! Every time there's a possibility, he fucks it up. Every time!' Evans smiled, his face looking evil in the torchlight. 'Don't know how he does it.'

'What d'you think this fog really was then, Ray?' Buswell asked him, knowing Evans always had several theories on any topic.

'Well, I tell you, Bernard, I don't fuckin' know. But I bet you one thing – it's man-made. It's got something to do with the pollution, I reckon. It's like those rivers where they've found thousands of dead fish, all because the bleedin' factories have dumped their rubbish into them. Well, this time, somebody's dumped somethin' into the air, y'see, gas or chemicals, I dunno what, but it's got out of 'and. Like one of those 'orror films.'

'Get away.'

'Nah, I mean it. Somethin' got into the air and it was spreadin'. It ain't really fog, y'know. It's like, er, like vapour . . . '

As he embroidered on his new theory which was occurring to him while he spoke, the fog, unseen in the dark, curled its way along the tunnel towards them. Just inside its fringes walked the figure of a man. He held a loaded rifle thrust before him, as though it were bayoneted and he was advancing on a rioting crowd. He heard the voices that were coming from ahead and something stirred in his disturbed mind.

He saw the figures outlined in the glare of two torches. His own torch lay shattered between the railway lines far back inside the tunnel. He drew nearer to the two men and the words, 'Where you been?' meant nothing to him.

Slowly he raised the rifle and placed it against the forehead of one of the soldiers. Then he pulled the trigger.

The tunnel was filled with the roar from the gun and the scream of the other man. The brief flash lit the scene into a frozen moment that was impressed for seconds after it had vanished on the mind of the soldier who had screamed.

Buswell threw his torch at Corporal Wilcox, who still held the smoking rifle, his fixed gaze on the dead man who was slowly toppling backwards. Still screaming, Buswell ran from the tunnel, leaving his rifle leaning against the dark wall. In his panic he made the mistake of trying to climb the steep embankment just outside the tunnel's entrance, his hands pulling out clumps of grass as he endeavoured to pull himself up, his feet slipping on the damp earth.

His flailing arms caught at a small bush and, miraculously, it held his weight enabling him to scramble up several feet. He heard the sound of a bolt being shot, sharp and clear in the chill night air, and it drove him on to further exertion for he realised the gun was ready to be fired again.

By sheer brute strength and blind defiance of the laws of gravity he almost reached the top of the incline.

His second mistake was to look back.

He saw the still figure at the foot of the slope staring up at him, not moving, not even raising his rifle.

Buswell sobbed and made a desperate lunge upwards stretching his arm in a vain effort to reach the top of the embankment, as though there was another arm ready to grip his and pull him to safety. His hand closed over grass which was instantly torn from the soft earth and his boots were dislodged from their precarious footholds. He began to slither down, his scrabbling hands finding no purchase to halt his descent, his body pressed flat against the damp grass.

Slowly, slowly he slid down until his feet touched the bottom and carried on at right angles to his body so that he was almost in a kneeling position. The Corporal stood over him and raised the butt of his rifle.

The fog flowed from the tunnel, wispy and hesitant at first, but soon thickly and swift. It swirled around the two soldiers and quickly enveloped them.

12

Eighteen

Holman opened his eyes, his brain taking a few seconds to begin functioning normally. He stared up at the ceiling and allowed his thoughts to gather and settle, then turned towards the figure lying in his bed next to him. In the grey light that filtered through the drawn curtains her face looked as it used to be, calm, and hardly touched by life, but he knew, in harsh daylight, the faint beginnings of lines would be there, for she could not possibly have escaped the rigours of the past few days without their leaving some visible mark. And the wound left inside her would be much worse than any physical scar.

How different she looked from the last time she had been in his flat. Would he ever forget that deranged look of hatred on her face, the violence of her attack on him? Would he always be waiting for that look to return, unable to close his mind to visions of the past, dreading that the disease was only lying dormant, lurking deep in the recesses of her brain, waiting for the moment to begin its evil, parasitical journey once again?

Janet Halstead had assured him Casey was completely cured, as was he, and there was no chance of the malignancy ever returning, but it was difficult to rid himself of all his fears. Only time would do that.

He was grateful to the doctor for allowing him to bring Casey home. Although all the tests had been completed, both on himself and the girl, and their usefulness in that particular area had been diminished, she could have insisted that they both remain at the Research Centre in case of any eventuality that might arise. But provided they reported in every day, Janet was happy to let them go, recognising the need for them to retreat into their own privacy, to lick their wounds, to comfort one another. Medical treatment could only reach a certain point; after that, it was up to each individual's natural protective instinct to complete the cure.

178

Holman was on call at any time although they had found no trace of the fog for two days now. The trail of havoc it had left behind it was appalling, for not everybody had been cleared from its path in time. The consequences of the fog were still occurring, for reaction to it took longer to manifest itself in some than in others. For many, the effect was immediate, causing instant madness, their brain cells crumbling rapidly against the onslaught of the mutated parasite. Many people were killed; many killed themselves.

On the first day of quiet, when the fog had inexplicably disappeared, the country had been left in a state of numbness. Then a stirring seemed to ripple through the land as the public demanded answers. What was the fog? Where had it come from? If it had come from the sea, what was its source? Had it really gone, and if so, could it possibly return? Were there still lunatics at large and what were the first symptoms? Had the government acted swiftly enough and what steps were being taken to ensure that a disaster of this kind and magnitude would never happen again? Had a foreign power secretly experimented on Britain and was the country now being held to ransom by that power?

All these questions and many more had been asked and the government had to provide answers – and quickly. Today was the day for answers and reassurances. Even the truth had been considered by the special inner Cabinet who had full knowledge of the source, but the consideration was easily rejected.

Holman's hand found the soft curve of Casey's waist and he dreaded the telephone call that might take him away from her. The thought of going back into the fog was repugnant to him and he prayed it had been finally vanquished.

She stirred and snuggled towards him, a low murmur of peace escaping from slightly parted lips. His hand slid up her back and he pulled her farther towards him until their bodies touched. Still half asleep, she pushed her leg between his and her arm encircled his waist, reaching down until her hand spread out over a buttock. He grew hard against her, slowly and sweetly, his penis pressed between her soft flesh and his own.

Awake now, but her mind still comfortably dulled, her senses racing ahead of it, her hand reached down and casually stroked the back of his leg. She sighed and spoke his name and he whispered his love to her, kissing her hair and forehead. She raised her head and her lips met his, moist, gently demanding.

179

He parted their bodies so he could touch her breasts and her nipples were hard beneath his fingertips, eager to be awakened and risen from their small surrounding islands of flesh. His head came down to take one in his mouth, his lips closing over it, his tongue moistening its tip.

She moaned and her body stretched, her lower limbs pressing tight against him, his thigh filling her inner thighs. There had been no desire for lovemaking for either of them the night before; the memory of her father's death was too dominant in their minds. Their bodies had needed contact, but only to gain each other's warmth and solace, and they had soon fallen asleep, both wearied in body and spirit by the week's events.

Now the tiredness had gone from their bodies and their spirits were on the first step towards recovery, although for Casey, the step was small. She pulled her breast away from him, the very act of its withdrawal heightening her sensuality, and her teeth bit gently at his neck, then harder, drawing his blood towards the spot without breaking the skin.

A flicker of fear passed swiftly through his thoughts but was instantly subdued as her lips moved on, murmuring sounds of love, kissing his chest, closing over his own rigid nipple then moving over to its jealous companion. Her tongue traced a line between the muscles of his stomach, a tiny damp stream that ended in the well of his navel.

His penis rose quivering to meet her parted lips and suddenly it was engulfed in a warm cavern, the soft entrance concealing a sharp ridge of teeth, but its interior containing a silky, ever-moving animal that smothered it in its welcome. Her lips moved down the length of him and back again in a steady, regular motion, her tongue always active, her teeth barely making contact. He shuddered at the sensation and his hands gripped her shoulders, moving with her, controlling her timing.

Before the shudders became frantic and the pleasure too exquisite, he withdrew himself from her and gently pulled her smiling face up to his, kissing her lips hard and passionately, the faint taste of his own body on her tongue exciting him even more.

His hand reached flatly towards her stomach and he ran his fingers downwards through the small, tidy forest of hair until he found her other even more moist cave, silky smooth with its aroused lubricity. Her hips rose slightly and her thighs tautened as her knees bent and her heels dug into the bed. She relaxed

180

then tightened her muscles again, moaning as she twisted her head to one side. His fingers stayed near her entrance and teased her most sensual part, then stroking more firmly, understanding her body's demands.

This time it was Casey who drew him away before the ecstasy became too overwhelming. She pulled at his hip and he slid over her, entering her with measured ease, resisting his own urgency. The passage was smooth and he stopped only when his penis had travelled its full length, her hands tightly clenched on his buttocks, drawing him into her, desperate to claim every inch of him. She cried out as he began to move rhythmically, her lips frenziedly seeking his, then twisting her head away again into the pillow as the pleasure began its swift ascent. Her legs bent but did not close around him, unwilling to restrict his movements or her own upward thrusts. One of his hands reached up for her breast and crushed it cruelly, but the cruelty was derived from passion, and was understood and welcomed.

Her body-stretching release came seconds before his, but the warm fluid that finally flowed from him into her deepened her own satisfaction and she was pleased to receive the heavy weight of his body as it slumped against her when his movements had ceased. They lay still until their breathing had become steady and their hearts had slowed their pace, she stroking the back of his head, he using his elbows to help ease his weight.

After a short while, he lifted himself from her, kissing her chest flushed from her orgasm, and rolled on to his back. She turned sideways towards him, one arm across his chest to clasp his shoulder, one leg raised to rest on his.

She gazed at his relaxed face and drew a finger down his profile, stopping to run it the length of his mouth, then down again over his chin, past his neck to come to rest on his chest where it nestled amongst dark hairs.

'You still haven't told me,' she said after a while.

'What?' He looked down at her in surprise.

'You haven't told me.'

'Told you what?'

'Why you call me Casey.'

He began to chuckle. 'You really want to know, do you?'

'Yes.'

'No. You'll only get angry.'

'Angry? You'd better tell me now!' She raised her head to look down at him.

181

'You're sure you want to know?'

'Yes!' Indignant.

'Well,' he began, smiling and looking at her from the corner of his eyes, 'when I was a kid, I used to have a dog . . .'

'A dog?'

'. . . and I used to call it Casey . . .'

'You called it . . .'

'. . . and when I saw you . . .'

'. . . Casey! You –'

'. . . you had the same sad little eyes . . .'

'. . . you . . .'

'. . . and they made me fall in love with you . . . and I knew I'd found something that would be precious again to me . . . and that's why I called you Casey.'

She fell against him, half-laughing but ready to cry. He hugged her, still grinning, but strangely near to sadness himself.

'Imagine my delight when I found you were house-trained too.'

And now, she did cry. She cried from happiness, sadness, and relief that they were together.

'Is it over now?'

'The fog? The nightmare? I just hope so. If it isn't, well, I just don't know what else they can do about it.'

'Surely they could find an answer.'

'The calcium chloride must have been the answer. They just needed a lot of it.'

'Why are they so reticent about announcing it?'

'Because they don't understand how the chemical could have destroyed the mycoplasma. On Ryker's advice, they've decided to play it cautiously, to wait until they're absolutely certain.'

'And when will that be?'

'Who knows? When they've covered the area thoroughly, I suppose.'

She shuddered and pressed closer to him. 'Or when people stop going insane.'

'They've got the cure now. Provided it doesn't happen again on a massive scale, they can cure anyone they find with the illness.'

'Unless the victims kill themselves first.'

He was silent. They'd been lucky, both of them, but the price they had to pay in memories was harsh. He knew there would be many silences between them now as they both remembered. It would take years for them to detach themselves from the dream, but because of their own personal experiences, they would be able to understand and help each other.

He looked down at her and her eyes met his. She too, had been lost in her own thoughts. She smiled.

'I'm okay,' she said.

He sat up then, resolving never to allow either of them to sink too far into the quicksands of their memories. 'I'll get some coffee.'

'No,' she pulled him down again, 'you stay there. Let me do it.'

He lay back and watched her naked figure slip into his discarded shirt. The shirt flapped large and seductively around her as she bent forward to kiss him, the glimpse of her small breasts beginning to excite him again. She walked around the bed towards the drawn curtains and once more the image of the last time he'd seen her in the darkened room leapt into his mind. But even now, the thought was becoming easier to push away.

She reached up and began to draw the curtains, but she stopped midway and he saw her body stiffen.

'John . . . ' he heard her say, half turning her head towards him but unable to tear her eyes away from the strangely subdued light that came from outside.

He leapt from the bed, already feeling the familiar coldness chilling his body. Reaching her side, he drew the curtain back at one side in a violent sweep, then stopped to stare at the scene that lay beyond.

'Oh God!' he gasped.

For there was no scene beyond. Just a grey blankness. A heavy, still blankness, tinged with yellow.

They stood in awe and dread of its obscuring density and were only dimly aware of the telephone that rang persistently from the room next door.

They had tried to warn the city of the approaching doom. It had appeared suddenly, a small cloud swept onwards by a strong wind. After two days of searching, just when they had begun to relax, it appeared, at first hidden by the predawn mists, but then rising as though it had been lying in wait, mustering its

183

forces, waiting for its new ally, the north-east wind. Many had panicked, for they were directly in the path of the fast-moving cloud, and had scattered in three directions. The bravest remembered to radio their mobile operations base before and as they fled, but the majority were concerned only with self-preservation.

As the fog swept over the countryside, it grew larger. It passed through the smaller towns, then through industrial estates which belched out their filthy fumes even during the night, and it welcomed the polluted air, drawing it to its poisonous womb, growing with it. It reached the suburbs and its size began to make the wind less effective. It drifted inwards towards the city.

The scattered army was regathered and the troops sped ahead of the fog, loudspeakers blaring out their ill-timed warning. They realised it was virtually useless, that by the time the people had rubbed their blurry eyes and the message registered, it would be too late, the growing fog would already be on them.

But they tried. Or at least, two-thirds of the forces tried. The remaining third raced into London to perform other tasks.

Janet Halstead was aroused from her sleep by one of her assistants. She slipped on her robe and went through to the office adjoining her private sleeping quarters. Picking up the phone, she asked the switchboard to put through the call that had been waiting for her. She listened in silence, her expression never changing, only her eyes betraying a sad weariness.

When she finally put down the phone, she stared at it for a few seconds longer. Then her body seemed to draw itself together and she began to snap instructions at her bewildered assistant for the immediate evacuation of the Research Centre. All equipment, notes – anything useful that could be dismantled – were to be moved to another location. A secret location. Transport was already on its way to take them there.

Stan Reynolds, a middle-aged security guard strolled along the lush carpeted corridor towards his favourite room at the very top of the giant oil company building that towered over the black River Thames. It contained the largest boardroom table he'd ever seen, and he'd seen a few over the years in the various companies he'd been employed in as a guard. It was made of the deepest oak and was reputed to have cost over six thousand pounds; sixty people could be comfortably seated round it. He opened the heavy boardoom doors that reached the ceiling and stepped into the room, switching on the lights as he did so.

Walking the length of the table, he stopped behind the magnificent leather chair that belonged to the chairman. He sank into it, removed his boots and placed his feet on the table. With a contented sigh, he lost himself in a colourful reverie of big business deals and boardroom power games.

His nightly dream fulfilled, he swung his legs off the table, put his boots back on and strolled towards the huge windows that looked south across London. It was a view that always filled him with immense pride in the vast city, the lights shining like star clusters on a black velvet universe.

But on this occasion, the view was different. There was an orange glow in the sky and he drew in his breath as he realised the cause of it. He saw a line of fires stretching across South London, huge fires at regular intervals, their flames red and frightening. For a moment, his mind travelled back in time and it was the war and the blitz, the fires caused by the bombs of the enemy.

Then the flames seemed to lose their brightness as though they were being covered, one by one, by a semi-transparent blanket, leaving only a red glow shining dully through.

He thought he heard the sound of a loudspeaker coming from somewhere in the distance, but it was too indistinct and he was too puzzled by the phenomenon before him to concentrate on its message.

He stood and watched the approaching fog as it gradually obscured the million lights, crawling forward, swallowing the town, piece by piece, until it reached the river just below him.

And then the river was gone and the fog was brushing against the large plate-glass window in front of him.

Dawn. McLellan, Holman's colleague at the Ministry of the Environment, stared from his bedroom window out at the fog. His eyes were heavy from unshed tears. He knew it was *the* fog, its yellowish tinge told him that. And he had been expecting it; his faith in his own government in times of crisis had never been great and he had expected them to bungle this.

185

He was much more aware of the danger than most of the general public for he had been closer to the strange occurrences through Holman and the dead Spiers, and many people still did not understand that it was not the fog that killed, but the madness it caused that drove people to their deaths.

He turned to look at his wife still snugly curled up beneath the bedclothes, asleep and vulnerable. As he thought of his children in the adjoining bedrooms, the tears of bitterness and frustration broke. How long would it take for the poison to work on their minds, to make them insane? What would it do to him? Would he be the one to take the lives of his own family? He struck out at the air blindly. There must be a way to protect them.

Sitting on the edge of the bed, taking care not to wake his wife, he tried to calm himself. There had to be an answer! Could he tie them up, or lock them in their rooms? But what about himself? What would protect them from him? Could he make sure they were protected from themselves and then go out and hopefully lose himself in the fog? No, he couldn't leave them; it would seem like desertion. He had to think fast; God knows how long it took for the poison to take effect. For Spiers it had taken a day, for Holman, it was almost immediate.

Then he had the answer! It wasn't ideal, but it could give them a little time; time enough perhaps for the authorities to take some kind of action, time for them to start saving lives.

He went into his daughter's room and took the small toy blackboard from its easel, together with some chalk, carefully closing the door as he left so as not to disturb her. He went downstairs and, sitting on the bottom step, he chalked a message in large capitals on the board. Opening the front door, he placed the message on the doorstep, praying that it would serve its purpose. Then he went back upstairs and into the bathroom, taking the bottle of sleeping pills from the top shelf of the cabinet, the pills his wife sometimes found necessary to calm her from the rigours of raising three lively children. He filled a glass full of water and returned to his daughter's bedroom. He lifted her forward on the bed, ignoring her feeble, half-asleep protests, and forced her to take five of the pills. Kissing her forehead, he laid her down again and tucked her in, then repeated the same operation on the boys next door. Paul had been awkward, but at the promise of a staggering reward, he'd complied. The next part would be more difficult. He would have to wake his wife, Joan, and explain why he was doing this. Was it his imagination, or could he really feel the beginnings of a headache?

Joan wept and at first refused to take the pills, but after much persuasion and then pleading, she agreed. For himself, he took eight, not knowing what the fatal dose would be, but sure that the amount he had given to his family and himself was not too dangerous. Besides, under the circumstances, the risk had to be taken.

He climbed back into the warm bed and drew his weeping wife to him. They lay there, waiting for sleep to come.

Irma Bidmead always rose early. At seventy-three, her days were too short to be wasted on slumber. And her cats would be hungry.

She had thirteen cats, all of them strays that she had adopted. Or perhaps they'd adopted her. She would often roam the streets late at night with a bagful of morsels and scraps for the cats she found in the back streets of Kennington. The cats knew her and recognised her tiny ragbag figure and hissing call as she trundled down the darkened streets and they would follow her until she decided she had a large enough gathering and stopped. Then she would feed them, talking to them, admonishing them for their greed, cackling at their antics to be the first to be fed.

Every few months there would be a van waiting at a pre-arranged spot, and a dozen or so of the cats would be piled into it and driven off to a South London hospital. The man who drove the van, the man she had the arrangement with, took the lion's share of the money paid by the hospital for the animals, but she still earned a nice little sum from it. Animals for vivisection had always been a profitable business even though the RSPCA had got massive support behind their outcry against it, but because it was necessary, and the authorities knew it, they turned a blind eye.

And the money she earned from the deal went towards feeding her own cats. Because she loved her cats.

Irma was oblivious to the smell that leapt from the room as she opened the door; after a lifetime of living with the creatures, their odour was part of her own, and the fact that thirteen of them had been locked up together in a room all night had no effect on her insensitive nostrils at all.

187

'Hello, lovelies,' she greeted them expecting them to run towards her, nuzzling against her ragged dressing gown in which she slept, as they normally did each morning. But this morning, they remained aloof, neither moving nor making any sound.

In her annoyance, she failed to notice the yellowish mist that drifted in through the thin crack of the slightly opened window.

'Now what's the matter with you today?' she demanded to know, her irritation growing. 'Showing off, are you? Well, you can feed yourselves!'

She stamped from the room and into the kitchen where she retrieved two stiff and pungent kippers from the sink. Muttering to herself, she flounced back to the cats' room and threw the kippers in.

' 'Ere,' she shouted, 'an' don't choke on the bones, you're lucky to get 'em!' She trundled back into her room and climbed into bed, pushing the comfortably curled-up cat that always slept with her away from the warm spot. It bristled in annoyance, but soon settled down again. Irma called out to the other cats again: 'Don't you come crawlin' 'round me when you've finished your fish! I don't want to know, I've got an 'eadache,' and then to herself as she pulled the covers up to her chin, 'Ungrateful pigs! I should take them all up the 'ospital, that's what I should do! Except you, Mogs, you love your old lady, don't yuh.' She turned her head and smiled at the cat that purred next to her. 'You're a good old girl, you are. Not like them others – all they want is feedin'! Ooh, my 'ead does ache today!' She closed her eyes to concentrate on the pain.

The cats ignored the fish and silently padded from their room and into Irma's where they waited at the foot of her bed as she began to doze off.

Chief Superintendent Wreford slumped down the stairs and entered the kitchen. Yawning freely, he filled the electric kettle with water and switched it on. God, he was tired! He'd worked long hours because of this wretched fog business and last night was the first he'd been able to take off. Hopefully, it was all over now and he'd be able to take a spot of leave. He congratulated himself on covering himself in the Holman affair. He could have chosen to dismiss the man as a crank, but experience had

188

told him never to ignore warnings, no matter from what source. He'd played it right, not making his enquiries official; at least not until he'd found out there was some truth to the story, and then he'd jumped in feet first, claiming credit for precipitating proceedings before the terrible Bournemouth disaster.

I bet Barrow was choked, he smiled to himself as he emptied stale tea leaves from the pot into the sink. A bit *too* ambitious, that lad, he'd like to see me come unstuck.

He stood with one hand on the kettle and one hand on the pot as he waited for the water to boil, smiling at the wall before him. Still, he's not a bad lad. Bit brutal at times, but he'll mellow with experience and he's useful as he is for the moment. The emergence of steam from the kettle interrupted his thoughts and he poured the boiling water into the teapot, turning the switch off as he did so.

He went to the front door to collect the milk, eager for his first deep lungful of fresh morning air. It was a habit he'd acquired over the years, telling his wife it was the only time one could get a decent breath of fresh air living in London. By nine o'clock the streets would be filled with fumes so he always made the most of his half-past seven deep breathing routine, standing on his doorstep for a full five minutes, taking in great gasps of air, while the tea in the kitchen brewed.

As he opened the door he was already drawing in his breath, and before he saw the fog, his lungs were half full of it.

Detective Inspector Barrow slept. He'd had a heavy week and this had been his first break. Playing nursemaid to Holman hadn't suited him at all; there were better things for him to do in a crisis such as this, chances to prove himself, to make himself felt. Hadn't it been he who had brought Holman in in the first place? The man irritated him. True, Barrow had been rough on him at first, but as soon as he'd realised his mistake, he had tried to make it up to him. He'd protected the man when he'd been assigned as his bodyguard, had worried about him, tried to start up a more friendly relationship with him. After all, as a man immune to the disease, he was quite important, and if anything *had* happened to him while under Barrow's protection, it would have been Barrow who copped it in the neck. But Holman hadn't wanted to be friendly; he'd kept a distance between them, unwilling to forgive him for his past treatment.

189

Well, it probably didn't matter any more, the scare seemed to be over. It had done a lot of damage but at least now it was under control – or so they said.

The thoughts had buzzed around his head the night before, a sure sign of extreme weariness, and he had gratefully sunk into his bed, for once unaccompanied by a girl. He had been too tired even for that.

He had immediately gone into a deep sleep and still slept as the sombre grey light filtered through the fog into his bedroom.

Samson King made his way blindly through the fog. He'd lived in London since he was fifteen, but he'd never experienced fog like this before. It was a good thing he did not live too far from the bus depot or he would never have been able to find it. As it was, he wasn't too sure he was going in the right direction. He did not miss the sun of Jamaica as much as his old folks did for he could hardly remember the warm beaches and the deep green sea they described. No, he was used to the watery sun of England and even found the few days of intense heat that the country sometimes had uncomfortable.

Surely they wouldn't expect him to take the bus out in weather like this. Bernice hadn't even wanted him to report for work but he was afraid it might look bad on his record. He did not want to lose this job as he had many others; it suited him being up there behind the wheel of the big red monster, totally in control, dwarfing and bullying the other traffic on the road.

Now, where was he? 'Goddam' fockin' weather!' he cursed aloud, needing to hear the sound of his own voice. He hadn't passed anyone in the fog and it gave him a peculiar feeling of not being flesh and bone, of being a wandering spirit in a murky void.

The depot should be across the road. The zebra crossing in front of him ran out halfway across the road, but he knew the bus station would be about fifty yards to the right of it. The crossing often helped him to get his bus out into the busy street for the flow of traffic often had to stop to allow people to cross.

He started forward, keeping a wary eye out for any approaching traffic and using the black and white stripes as a guide to the other side. His head ached, from eye strain he thought, from squinting into the fog, trying to catch glimpses of familiar sights. At least the roads should be clearer today. He giggled, not knowing why he did and was still giggling when he reached the opposite pavement. He turned right, keeping close to the shops on his left, using them as a guide.

Soon he reached the garage and turned into it, an occasional giggle jerking his body. He didn't ask himself why the depot was empty, why there was no inspector to check him out, why there were no cleaners preparing to leave, why there was no crew-mate waiting impatiently for him. He asked himself no questions.

He just climbed up into his cabin, still grinning, occasionally giggling, and started his engine. Then he moved the bus slowly forward and out of the depot.

Throughout London, people were waking to discover the yellow-grey fog surrounding their homes, some realising its meaning, some not; many already too insane to care. Thousands had fled during the night, fortunate to have heard the warnings of the loudspeakers or the radio broadcasts. Those had, in turn, informed relatives, friends or loved ones, either by telephone (which, because of the chaos, was the least reliable) or by hurried visits.

But it was a big city, and the thousands who had time to flee were a small proportion compared to the millions who received no warning at all. The huge beacons were lit, but the rolling fog swept right over them, rising from the heat, but immediately descending once it was cleared.

The panic of the night before was nothing compared to the tragic and bizarre pandemonium that was to follow during the ensuing day.

Nineteen

Holman steered the Devastation Vehicle cautiously up the ramp out into the fog and away from the huge underground shelter. A man called Mason, gross and misshapen because of his protective clothing, sat in the seat next to him peering through the small, heavy lead-reinforced window, his face intense with concentration.

'It doesn't seem to be quite as thick as it was,' said Holman, still looking directly ahead.

'It's probably settled in the London basin and now it's spreading out a bit,' Mason replied.

Holman nodded; it seemed logical. London was in a dip, a saucer-shaped bowl, surrounded by hills. The fog would have drifted into it and come to rest at its base, then sprawled out, filling the town. Its probable way out, unless there was a strong wind, was east along the Thames, through the flat county of Essex.

'Go left along the Embankment,' said Mason, checking the instruments on a panel before him. 'If we follow the road into the City, it'll take us towards it.'

Holman turned left, using the pavement as a guideline. He could just about see the opposite pavement now, something he hadn't been able to do earlier that morning as he had made his way to the secret shelter. He shuddered inwardly, remembering the eerie journey through the fog-filled streets.

Even as he and Casey had been looking out at the fog, still in a state of shock and dismay, tentacles of despair spreading through them, the telephone had begun its persistent, strident ringing. He'd broken away from the mesmeric spell the fog was casting to answer it, as though it were some sort of lifeline, a straw to be clutched at.

It had been Douglas-Glyne, the Defence Under-Secretary, at the other end and he'd snapped out instructions, not allow-

192

ing Holman to argue or dissent. He was to make his way to Westminster Bridge where he would be picked up by a vehicle resembling an army scout car, only larger and much heavier and fitted with various antennae.

From there he would be brought to a secret rendezvous, the whereabouts of which could not be revealed to him just yet. He was to avoid becoming involved in any incidents that might occur on the way; his sole purpose was to get to the rendezvous point unharmed and as quickly as possible. He was to protect himself even if it meant killing or hurting others to do so; one or two lives were nothing compared to the millions he could help save if he himself remained unhurt. The girl was to remain where she was for now; it was too risky for both of them to make the journey across town. If anything happened to Holman then they would find a way to reach her. They could have sent their 'special' vehicle to fetch him but this would have taken hours, for it was virtually blind in the fog because of its own restricted vision. If he did not make it, they would have to use this method to bring back the girl.

The phone went dead as soon as Holman said he understood and would carry out the instructions. He told Casey what was happening as he quickly dressed, doing his best to keep his voice calm and assured. She did not cry, nor protest, knowing circumstances were directing their actions, that they could no longer control their own destinies, that they had to move as events dictated. He told her to bolt the door behind him and then lock herself in his bedroom. They wasted little time in saying goodbye for the temptation to lock themselves in, away from the outside world and its madness, was too great; the slightest hint from either one of them would all too easily be succumbed to. Instead, they kissed and, without a word, he left.

He used the stairs to get to the ground, not daring to chance the lift which was unreliable at the best of times. The nightmare took on a new dimension once he was in the street.

It was the feeling of emptiness that was most frightening. A feeling of complete hollowness. Nothing was substantial, nothing quite real. He stayed close to the walls, dreading bumping into anyone, but, at the same time, eager to meet someone of his kind, of flesh and blood. He heard a strange wailing noise and realised it was human. He heard a car pass by, travelling fast, fading into the distance, then a crash, followed by cold silence. He heard a scream, a woman's scream, mingled with a

193

laugh. Hysterical laughter. A madman's laugh. But it was all remote and unreal, the phony rantings of a fairground ghost house.

He was thankful it was still early morning and most people were either asleep or just stirring. In his mind's eye he saw a picture of the bedlam that would come later that day, and he quickened his step almost into a trot. He guessed what the task before him would be, but in a strange way, he now welcomed it. At least it would be positive action and not just stumbling around in the mist waiting for something to happen. And he would be among people again, hopefully normal people. Thank God Casey was immune. If the plan failed, whatever they had in mind (and he had a shrewd idea), he would go back to her and get her away. To hell with them; they'd made the mess, let them deal with it. He'd done enough already.

Too late he saw the dark shadow before him and they collided, the impact sending the other man to the ground. Without thinking, Holman stooped down to help the sprawled figure to his feet. The man reached up and held on to Holman's shoulders and it was only then, when their faces were no more than a foot apart, that Holman noticed the strange grin on the man's face. He backed away, but the man clung to him, a low growling, chuckling noise coming from his wide grinning mouth. Holman tried to push him off, but an arm reached around his neck and his head was forced forward. He struck out in panic and the man's chuckle turned into a snarl of rage as he retaliated with a savage kick at Holman's ankle. Holman ducked forward, releasing himself from the tenacious grasp, then brought the flat of his hand up underneath the man's chin and pushed it back and back, swiftly, moving with it until the back of the man's head connected with the brick wall behind him. There was a loud crack and the man went down on his knees, one hand reaching for the back of his head, a pathetic whining sob coming from him. His other hand groped blindly for Holman's leg, but Holman stepped back out of reach then turned and began to run.

When he stopped, he found himself completely isolated. He must have run into the road for he could see nothing on either side of him. He walked forward briskly, but alert for any danger, hoping he was heading in the right direction. He heard a scream on his left, a long piercing scream that ended in a sickening, squelching thud. Something wet brushed his face and

194

he put his hand to it. When he looked at his fingers, they were smeared with blood. He wiped his cheek vigorously with his coat sleeve, repulsed by the thought of what had happened. Someone, a man or woman, had jumped from a window, and their body had splattered blood for some distance as it broke on the concrete.

His pace quickened. The longer it took him to reach Westminster, the more people there would be out on the streets. He had to move faster. Dare he chance a car? It was risky, he would be driving virtually blind, but it might be worth it. He heard singing, not far away and drawing nearer. It was a man's voice, loud and clear. And happy. He saw the dark shape that suddenly became clearly defined; it was a man on a bicycle, weaving left and right, pedalling slowly, oblivious to anything but his own song. He saw Holman and rode round him in a tight circle, smiling and singing, his eyes never leaving Holman's, neither challenging nor belligerent. Placid.

As the cyclist completed a second circuit, Holman considered relieving him of his vehicle and using it himself, but decided against the idea, for it could be more dangerous than just walking. With a wave of his hand, the man disappeared into the mist again and Holman listened to the voice as it receded into the vacuous distance, leaving him feeling even more isolated.

He whirled as he heard running footsteps, but they carried on right past him without his catching anything more than a glimpse of a shadowy figure. He realised it was no good at all going on like this. His nerves were taut and his progress was slow; it would take him hours to reach Westminster at this rate and long before then the streets would be crowded. He would have to take a car; it wouldn't be too difficult to find one and he knew how to start one without a key. He found his way back to the kerb and used it as a guide. He was bound to run into a parked car soon.

He passed a woman who was pushing an ordinary house broom along the gutter, tutting at the piled up dirt and cursing at the world in general.

He passed a body that lay sprawled across his path. He didn't stop to see whether it was male or female, dead or alive.

He passed a dog feeding on the carcass of another. It looked up and growled menacingly, saliva and blood drooling from

195

its jaws, not attacking, but watching him intently until he'd been swallowed up by the fog again.

Holman's breath was coming in short gasps now and he wasn't quite sure if it was because of the impure air or the tenseness of the situation. He had to find a car soon.

Then, he saw the soft light ahead of him which grew brighter as he approached. He thought it might be a fire at first, then perhaps a shop front because of its steady glare, but, as he drew nearer, he realised its source. It gave him the answer; the way to get across London fast, and with far less risk. It would be frightening, he knew, but not as frightening as it would have been by car. He broke into a run.

Holman emerged from Trafalgar Square underground station just over an hour later, his hands and face black with dirt, a torch still glowing in his hand. The dark journey through the tunnels had been without incident. The station at St John's Wood had been deserted even though all the lights were still working. He had assumed it had been abandoned during the night and nobody had bothered to lock its gates or switch off the power. A door marked 'Private' had been left open and he had soon found a heavy-duty-type rubber torch. As he descended the staircase to the platform, he had wondered if the current had been switched off, but there would be no way of knowing. It was his intention to keep well clear of the lines, but he would have felt better in his own mind if he had known whether they contained their deadly electricity.

Fortunately, the single low-watt lights along the tunnels had been left on too, ready for the night cleaners and maintenance men, but on several stretches further on between stations he had been in total darkness. He had noticed the station itself had been full of the fog although less thick, and even the lower regions of the platforms contained some wispy clouds of it. On one occasion, he had heard muffled voices coming from the tunnel parallel to his and he'd switched off his torch and waited in the dark until they had faded into the distance. His main worry was that a train would come roaring down the tunnel at him, a notion he had a hard time shaking off. Even the black, scuttling shapes of disturbed rats did not bother him as much as that thought.

But he'd made it. The joy of once again emerging into the

daylight, grey though it was, was immense and made him feel quite light headed. The fog seemed slightly less dense, but he wasn't sure if it wasn't just because he'd come from the blackness of the tunnels and the contrast between total darkness and murky grey was deceiving his eyes.

He paused for a moment to get his bearings, switching the torch off and placing it on the ground. He became aware of a puzzling sound off to his right, a curious cooing noise echoing from the mists, continuous and monotonous and somehow, haunting. He realised its source: pigeons. The thousands of pigeons that belonged to Trafalgar Square. Would they be affected by the fog? Their unified call was strange and hypnotic and aroused his curiosity. Forgetting his instructions to avoid any trouble, he walked towards the compulsive ululation, keeping a wary eye out for any sudden shadows that might appear. He crossed the broad road and reached the inner square where he stopped and peered into the mist.

The pigeons were spread like a deep grey carpet before him, disappearing into the mist, but giving the impression that the mass of small bodies covered the rest of the square completely. Occasionally, one would flutter a few feet into the air but would soon settle on to the backs of the others and snuggle its way in between them. Although they huddled together, they did not seem afraid; there was no nervousness about them, no sudden movements among them except for those that were squeezed from their positions and had to manoeuvre their way in again. And all the while, the deep-throated cooing penetrating the poisoned air, sinister and compelling. Holman suddenly noticed there were taller shadows rising from them; the ghostly shapes of people, quite motionless, silent and inhuman.

He backed away. Something was going to happen. He could sense it.

His eyes never left the birds until they had been obscured from his vision by the other enemy, the fog, and only then did he turn and begin to walk away at a brisk pace. He knew that a sudden movement from any of the people who stood among them – and there must have been many others for he had counted at least five within range of himself – and the pigeons would be galvanised into action. Whether or not they would attack he did not know for sure, but instinct had told him to get away; the menace that pervaded from them was an almost tangible thing.

197

Hoping he was headed in the right direction, he hurried on. The fact that he now appeared to be in a sort of no man's land, without a kerb or building to guide him, caused him even more anxiety. If his sense of direction was correct, Whitehall would be ahead of him, the Strand to the left and the Mall just off to the right; he was at the junction of all the roads.

He heard the car before he saw it. Its engine was roaring, the tyres screeching which, fortunately for Holman, gave him plenty of warning of its approach. Standing perfectly still, he tried to judge with his ears exactly where the car would appear. The noise was coming from the direction of the Strand, but seemed to be alternating from left to right; the screeching of tyres told him the driver was weaving some crazy pattern from one side of the road to the other. And then it was no more than twenty yards from him, sweeping through the mist like a demon from hell.

He was rigid from the shock of it for even though he had been expecting its emergence from the fog, the suddenness of its appearance had an almost paralysing effect on his limbs. His keen instinct for survival took command and moved his legs just in time as the vehicle, a bright red sports car, sped past, just catching the side of his leg, sending him spinning into the road. He had caught sight of its driver just as the car bore down on him: it had been a middle-aged man, naked – at least from the waist up – and gross, a maniacal grin on his face; beside him was an equally naked woman, also middle-aged, also gross, and she stood with her large breasts flopping over the windscreen, shrieking and laughing.

Holman lay in the road, not hurt but stunned, watching the car as it disappeared into the mist again. As he got to one knee, he heard one elongated screech of tortured tyres, silence, and then the awful sound of impact as the car struck something immovable. This was followed at once by the beating of thousands of wings, the cooing now becoming a shrill cry as the pigeons rose en masse into the fog-laden air. Human screams mingled with those of the birds and Holman knew he had been right; the pigeons were attacking.

He rose to his feet and pulled up his trousers to check his leg. He would have a nasty bruise later but the skin hadn't broken. All too conscious of the danger just beyond his vision, he ran away from the noise, limping only slightly, sure that if just one bird found him, others would soon follow.

He thanked God when he found the pavement and thanked Him again aloud when he discovered he was in Whitehall. The rest of the journey to Westminster Bridge was hazy and unreal, a fantasy of sounds and sudden visions that appeared briefly and vanished just as abruptly. He later remembered many people rushing past him towards the noise, like lemmings seeking destruction; a huge fire to his right (he had no idea of which building it had been, famous or otherwise); two more cars racing neck and neck, smashing into each other's sides as they went; a group of people engaged in a scuffle beneath the War Memorial. It had meant nothing to him as he fled; his only thoughts were to reach safety of some kind and the only safety he would find would be with sane people.

Finally he found the turn-off he sought. The bridge was just ahead. And so were the religious freaks.

He was among them before he'd had a chance to retreat. He had often seen them around London, dressed in long, brightly coloured saffron robes, the men's heads shaved, chanting their monotonous litany to the discordant accompaniment of crashing tambourines, shuffling along in a peculiar hopping-dance motion. Secretly, he had always been fondly amused by them, for there was an engaging freshness about them, and their religion seemed harmless and happy. But now, their appearance took on a more sinister aspect.

They were seated on the ground in a wide circle which he had unwittingly broken into.

'Welcome, Brother!' One of them, who had been standing in the centre leading the chant, spread his arms wide in greeting. 'Today is the Beginning! Join us in our thanks.'

Holman warily looked around; the others were on their feet now and advancing on him with their hopping gait, the gaps between them closing as they drew nearer.

'Come, Brother. Now is the time!' The man before him was only two feet away and Holman was impressed and a little intimidated by his size. He placed two huge hands on Holman's shoulders while the dirge coming from the others grew louder. He tried to pull away but the grip on his shoulders tightened.

The man leaned forward until his pointed face was touching Holman's and whispered, 'If you try to run, I'll break your fucking back.'

Holman was transfixed more by the harsh words than by the hold on him.

'To your knees, Brother. Humble yourself so that you might be saved.'

Holman tried to resist but more hands clasped his shoulders and forced him down. The big man stayed with him so they were both on their knees facing one another, the immense hands still holding him. He looked into the big-boned face and saw dark brown eyes that looked glazed yet cruel. A thin stream of saliva drooled from the corner of the man's mouth. His voice boomed out, 'I love you, Brother! We love you!' And then in a whisper, 'I'm going to kill you, you fucking creep.'

He grinned at Holman, bringing his forehead down and kissing it.

'Today is your Beginning. And to Begin, you must first die,' he said, as others leaned forward to kiss Holman. Now they were all kneeling, packed tightly up against the two men in the centre.

'You – you've got to let me go,' Holman said, looking around anxiously. 'I'm the only one who can do something about the fog.'

'The fog, Brother? There is no fog. All you see around us is the spirit of mankind. Today is the Beginning. The mist is only the *Being*, the souls who have already begun the journey.'

'Let me go!'

'Peace! The bridge you are about to cross is short, and the brief pain you will feel will be nothing compared to the eternal happiness that waits beyond.' And again, the whispered words, 'You'll be the fifth today, bastard. I'll snap your neck like a fucking matchstick.'

His hands closed on Holman's neck, but before the thick fingers could form into a stranglehold, Holman brought his fist up into the man's lower stomach. The blow had no other effect than to tighten the religious leader's smile into a grimace. He rose to his feet bringing his victim up with him, held by the neck. The fingers began to squeeze.

In a desperate move, Holman went limp so that his body dropped, then pushed forward. It was fortunate for him that the other followers were still kneeling around them for the momentum forced the leader to step back thus tripping over the bowed head of one of his flock. They went down in a heap of struggling arms and legs, Holman managing to break free of the grip around his throat. He lashed out again with his fist, and with some satisfaction, drew blood from the big man's nose.

200

The long robes of the religious sect hampered their movements and put Holman at an advantage. Instead of trying to rise above the clutching leader, he rolled forward over him, his shoulder cracking the man's head hard against the pavement. His feet accidently kicked into the chest of one of the female members, sending her backwards and gaining him a free area to rise. Hands grabbed for him, voices screamed in dismay, but he was moving through them, slapping the hands away, pushing half-risen bodies back down. He heard the roar of the big man behind him and redoubled his efforts to get away. Just as he thought he was clear, a hand closed on his ankle, tripping him and sending him rolling across the pavement to crash against a restaurant front.

He rose as quickly as he could, but already the big man was coming for him, lifting his legs high to stride through the startled bodies as though wading through a stream, mouthing obscenities at Holman, the blood from his nose covering his face, giving him a red mask of pure hatred. Most of his confused followers were trying to gain their feet, and just as he was nearly through, one rose up in front of him. The big man pushed him viciously, sending him sprawling across the pavement to land at Holman's feet.

Holman's back was pressed up against the large window of a restaurant, the palms of his hands flat against it, ready to give him leverage to push himself away. The big man was only a few feet from him and still rushing forward, his arms outstretched to embrace him in a hug of death. But the frightened man at Holman's feet was now scrabbling around on hands and knees, and the leader's eyes were so intent on their prey that they failed to see him. Holman sprang to one side as the big man pitched forward, tripped by his follower on the ground.

Holman heard the scream and crash of shattered glass as the big man's bare head and upper body fell through the window, scattering the fancy cakes and expensive confectionery that lay just inside. The heavy glass descended on him like a guillotine, cutting into his neck and breaking across his back.

Splinters and shards of glass flew out at Holman, but they did little damage for he was already running away, now using the fog as an ally, trying to hide in it, seeking refuge in its murkiness. But the religious fanatics came after him, several picking up long slivers of glass to be used as weapons against him. Heedless of what lay ahead, he ran blindly on, spurred by their cries of vengeance, but unable to find the speed that would take him out of their vision.

He knew the bridge was near-by and prayed that the government vehicle would be there waiting for him. His chest heaving, he reached the corner where the road branched off along the Embankment. My God, he suddenly thought, on which side would the vehicle be? Could it be on this corner, just out of sight in the mist, or would it be on the other side, the bridge corner? Without hesitating, he ran off the kerb and into the road, hoping his judgement was correct. He didn't much like the idea of dashing around in the fog trying to locate the car with the crowd of lunatics so close on his heels.

He reached the island in the middle of the road and kept going, trusting luck and his instinct for survival to pull him through. To have stopped to look around would have been more than pointless; it would have meant his death.

And then, two bright circles lit up before him, behind the circles, the shadowy shape of an odd-looking machine. He heard the roar of its engine and suddenly it was coming towards him. It must be the one! It had to be.

But to his dismay, it curved around him, gathering speed, going past. With a sickening feeling, he realised the driver's intention. The heavy, bulky vehicle ploughed into the following pack of bodies, sending them flying, crushing some beneath its broad wheels, scattering the luckier ones. Then it reversed and came back towards Holman. It didn't have the appearance of having speed, but the tyres screeched as they tried to grip the ground when the driver braked. He had to move fast to avoid being run down himself.

A small door at its side sprang open and a strange metallic voice said: 'Sorry, sir. But you're a bit more important than those people at the moment. I had to do it, it was your only chance. Now please get in, we haven't got much time!'

Crouching low, he clambered into the vehicle and was confronted by a heavily garbed figure, the suit similar to those worn by the men in Winchester, but much bulkier and more clumsy looking. The man wore a large helmet and Holman failed to see his eyes through the dark, narrow visor. The metallic voice came from a small mouthpiece positioned in the centre of his helmet.

'Close the door, sir. We don't want any of those lunatics or any more of the fog getting in.'

202

Holman did as he was told and turned to face the figure again.

'Where are you taking me?' he asked.

'You'll see, sir,' came the reply. 'My name is Mason – can't really shake hands, these gloves don't allow for it. I must say, you had me worried. I've been waiting ages.'

'I had a few problems on the way,' said Holman dryly, slumping back breathlessly in his seat. 'Where are we going?'

'Just a moment, sir. Must let them know I've picked you up.' He pressed a switch and spoke without the use of a hand speaker, reporting that his mission had so far been successful and they would soon be returning to base. He turned back to Holman.

'Now, sir, I'd like you to drive. These vehicles aren't really meant for travelling in thick fog as you can see by the tiny apertures. And my wearing this suit doesn't help much, either. Had a devil of a time reaching this spot even though I wasn't wearing a helmet then. Now that I've had the door open, I daren't risk taking it off again because some of the fog is bound to have got in.'

'The suit's lead-lined?'

'Yes, sir. That's what makes it so bloody cumbersome. Meant to be protection against radiation, y'see. The whole car is.'

'Radiation?'

'Yes. We call it the Devastation Vehicle. You'll find out why, later.'

Glancing around, Holman saw it was fitted with a mass of instruments, gauges and switches.

'I'm not sure I *can* drive it,' he said.

'Oh, don't let all those gadgets put you off,' Mason assured him. 'They're nothing to do with the running of the thing. In fact, it couldn't be simpler; just like driving a dodgem. The whole thing's operated on electricity, y'see. You push down on one pedal to go, another to stop, that's all there is to it. C'mon, there're a lot of people rather anxious to see you!'

Holman had followed Mason's instructions and driven slowly along the Embankment, turning left on command into what appeared to be an underground car park belonging to one of the large government office buildings. It was in darkness, but Holman had seen many cars crammed together in the glare of the vehicle's headlights. A lane had been left clear, and this he followed, going deeper and deeper below ground. It ended in a solid, concrete wall. Mason pressed a switch and began saying several words that sounded senseless to Holman; he realised they must have been in code. The wall before them suddenly rose into the ceiling and he saw a long box-shaped room beyond.

Mason touched his arm and the huge helmet nodded towards the opening. Holman drove forward and stopped once inside. The wall behind was lowered again and they sat in silence for a full minute until, quite abruptly, the wall before them swung open and they were faced with a long, dimly-lit corridor which again seemed to end in a blank wall. As they passed through, Holman saw that the wall which had just opened was in fact made of grey metal and was at least eighteen inches thick.

The corridor sloped downwards and they passed through two more doors before they entered a large, open area. Holman estimated they had travelled at least a quarter of a mile to reach this point. He noticed another vehicle looking identical to the one he had been travelling in parked in a far corner. A group of grey-suited men who had been waiting for them, each holding a long cannister which was connected to a central box, stepped forward, pointing the cannisters' nozzles at the vehicle, and then began to spray it with an almost invisible substance.

'Sit tight just a moment longer, sir,' said Mason. 'We were decontaminated when we first entered the tunnel, but this is a final going over. As a further precaution, they'll spray us as we get out.'

'Spray us against what?'

'The whole complex is sterile; there's not a germ down here. Everyone and everything that comes in is decontaminated. You see, it's built to contain at least three hundred people for anything up to ten years. If any bug got loose in such a confined space, well, it'd spread like wildfire.'

'Ten years?' Holman looked incredulously at the hooded figure. 'Just what the hell is this place?'

'I thought you knew. I thought you'd been told.'

Holman shook his head slowly.

'This,' said Mason, 'is a fallout shelter. A government fallout shelter.'

Mason waited for a comment from Holman, but none came so he continued. 'They started building it in the early 1960s and are still adding to it. If the country were ever to reach the point of crisis – the point where atomic war was inevitable – this is where the most important VIPs will come. There's a tunnel that leads directly to the Houses of Parliament, another that leads to the Palace.'

Holman's smile was cynical. 'Are there any others like it? For the ordinary people, I mean.'

'Er, I don't know about that, sir. These things are kept pretty much a secret. I know there isn't another in London, but I've visited one in Manchester and I assume some of the other major towns have them.'

'But all for "special" people.'

'Well, they could hardly cope with the whole population of Great Britain, could they, sir?'

Holman sighed. 'No, I suppose not. But I wonder how you qualify to be a "special" person.'

Mason changed the subject. 'Time to get out now,' he said.

Holman was led along more corridors by a young, unexcited man, who, despite the crisis, was dressed immaculately and tastefully in a dark blue pin-stripe suit, deep red tie and spot-lessly white collar. He spoke quietly and efficiently, explaining to Holman exactly what had happened during the night and how it was now being coped with. The Prime Minister was there, together with most of his Cabinet; they had been the first to be warned along with the Royal Family who were now safe in Scotland. The PM had decided to stay in London and direct operations from there, for the shelter was ideal for that purpose: it was impenetrable, contained virtually unlimited resources, had contact with any point on the globe, and had a large and well-equipped 'war' room. It had its own source of power, even its own telephone exchange which had proved invaluable when London's had broken down (Holman realised now that that was how they had been able to contact him). The army was mustered just outside London, mobile and ready for whatever action was demanded of them, but most of the Chiefs of Staff were inside the shelter helping the PM draw up a plan of campaign. Professor Ryker was there along with many other notable scientists and they were already hard at work on a new theory of Ryker's regarding the rapid growth of the fog – a possible clue to its make-up. Janet Halstead was there with her research team and some of the victims of the fog whom she'd been treating. Many people skilled in various aspects of life had been brought into the vast underground shelter, from

205

doctors to religious ministers, from naturalists to carpenters and plumbers; all had been previously earmarked for survival (mostly unknown to themselves) and their names and current address were kept on a list which was reviewed every three months.

As they walked, Holman recognised many familiar faces, familiar only because he'd seen them in the media. He was puzzled as to what possible value most of them could have in this situation. The fact that most were very wealthy made him extremely suspicious. Had they bought their way in? Or had they done certain favours for government officials, their price a ticket for survival on the Doomsday?

A lot of the people, both men and women, seemed to be in a daze. Ashen faced, many of the women in tears, they looked at him uncomprehendingly as he passed, some hoping to recognise a friend or relative, others envying him because he seemed to be going somewhere, had a task to perform, something positive, something active.

'How did you manage to get so many people in here in time?' he asked the young man he was following, walking briskly to keep up.

'A decision was made,' came the curt reply.

'What decision?'

'It was seen that the whole population of London could not possibly be saved and even if it was tried, the panic that would have ensued would have seriously disrupted rescue operations for certain key people.'

Holman caught his arm and brought him to a halt. 'You mean they didn't try? They just let people lie in their beds while the fog . . . ?'

'Of course they tried!' the young man snapped. 'But they used common sense. A third of the force was deployed to warn certain people and bring them here, the rest did as much as they could. Thousands escaped into the surrounding suburbs because of the army, but London is a big place, you know. Common sense had to prevail!' He pulled his arm away and marched on, leaving Holman staring open-mouthed after him. Grimly, he followed.

They entered a large hall thriving with people, each of whom had some particular task to perform, and filled with electronic equipment, brightly lit maps, television screens. Despite the activity, there was an air of calm throughout the hall as though whatever turmoil was now taking place above ground was a world away, unreal because it was largely unseen, for the television screens showed only a grey blankness, an occasional shadowy figure appearing to be quickly swallowed up again.

They don't know, Holman thought. They don't know what it's like up there: the complete madness that would have now gripped the town, the chaos that lay beyond those mists shown on the screens. They felt shock, he was sure, but not true, deep-felt sorrow, for how could they? It was an unreal situation. They knew of the tragedy of Bournemouth of course, and of the aeroplane crash; but how could minds possibly accept the fact of one of the world's largest cities gone mad? Only he could realise its full horror because he had seen it at first-hand, had even experienced it. But perhaps they would have still acted in the same way if it had been the holocaust the shelter had originally been intended for. It was those who had nothing to do who were affected, those who could only watch and wait. And wonder.

'This way, Mr Holman,' the young man's voice cut through his thoughts. He was standing by a doorway guarded by an armed soldier. Holman walked towards them, a questioning look on his face.

'This is the Planning Room,' the young man told him. 'The Minister is waiting to brief you himself.'

As he guided the Devastation Vehicle along the fog-bound street, Holman kept a wary eye out for groups of people. These would be the most dangerous; the ones that travelled in packs, like wolves searching for lone and defenceless victims. Most of the people ignored the strangely shaped car, for today everything was strange. Mason was now helmetless because the vehicle hadn't yet been opened above ground. They were using the reserve vehicle while the interior of the other was being carefully decontaminated. Mason grinned nervously at Holman. 'How are you feeling?' he asked, more to make conversation than out of actual curiosity.

'Sick,' replied Holman. 'I feel like driving on till we reach open country, away from this.'

'I know what you mean,' said Mason. 'But a lot depends on us, sir. I need you to guide me. I won't be able to see a thing once I get out there, not with this gear on.'

'The fog doesn't seem to be as bad now.'

'No. As I said, it's spreading out, thinning. But our reports say it isn't moving on yet. Look, we won't be out in it for long; just time enough for me to suction some of the bastard into our container and then we'll be off. If I didn't need your eyes, I'd do it on my own.'

Christ, you don't know the half of it, brooded Holman. He was armed with a revolver carried in a concealed shoulder holster and his instructions from the Prime Minister himself were that he was to protect his own life at all costs, even if it meant killing his companion to do so. It wasn't known yet if the protective suit was adequate against the mutated mycoplasma which was still an unknown entity and if Mason began to behave in the least threatening way, he was to be disposed of immediately and Holman was to carry out the misson on his own. He had balked at the order, but the PM had talked long and hard at him, telling him the choice was not his, that one life meant little compared to the millions that were in danger. A promise that he would carry out the order in the event was extracted from Holman, but he knew that only when the moment presented itself – if it presented itself – would he be able to decide.

Ryker had been present at the meeting and had assured Holman that the danger was getting worse. Because of the fog's rapid growth overnight, he now suspected that this was Broadmeyer's intention for the mycoplasma: to feed and grow on polluted air, thus the bigger the city, the more industrial, the more effective the disease was. The fog itself was a mere side effect of the gathering of impure air, deadly only because of the microbes that floated within it. It had given Ryker a clue to its source, but it would take time to investigate and come up with answers. In the meantime, the quickest way to probe the mutation was still to obtain a large sample of it. He had every faith in Holman that this time he would succeed. Holman wished he had as much faith in himself .

On his way back to the vehicle he had met Janet Halstead. Her cheeriness had gone, her face showed rigid lines of strain: she looked old. She, too, had urged him to succeed this time; only if he did could they begin to undo some of the terrible damage that had already been perpetrated. If she could inoculate against the disease, then men would be free to go into the disaster area and prevent others from destroying themselves and each other. He had left her without saying a word. How could he promise to succeed? There were too many other forces involved; he had thrived on risks before, but they had never been of this nature nor so numerous. All he could do was try.

'My God, look at that!' Mason was pointing ahead at four blazing cars that had piled up in the centre of the road. The flames were too thick to see if anybody occupied them, but a large crowd of people had gathered round the blaze, silently watching. As Holman and Mason drew nearer, the blood froze in their veins at the horror of what was happening. As the crowd watched, individuals would break from the ring and rush forward to throw themselves into the fire. The crowd cheered and then fell silent until another repeated the action.

'We've got to stop them!' Holman shouted, unable to take his eyes from the scene.

'No, we've got our orders,' said Mason firmly. 'We're not to interfere in any way. We *mustn't* get involved!'

Holman knew it was useless to argue. And Mason was right; they were not to jeopardise the mission. If they were to involve themselves in every incident that occurred along the way, then the odds were that they would never reach their destination.

'All right,' he said evenly, 'if there's nothing we can do, let's get away from it as quickly as possible.'

Mason was relieved. 'We'll go around,' he said. 'Back up, there's a turning to the left – goes towards the Strand. We'll go that way.'

Holman reversed the vehicle, narrowly missing a heavy truck that thundered past them, headed directly towards the burning cars and people. They heard the crash, for although the vehicle itself was soundproof, it was equipped with receivers on its exterior to pick up noise, a function that was necessary because of the lack of vision.

'Oh, Jesus,' breathed Mason, 'this is terrible.'

'It's only just beginning,' Holman told him cruelly. 'It'll get worse.'

And it did get worse. They passed many burning buildings, more blazing cars; scores of people roaming the streets, insanity evident in their faces; individuals curled up in corners, occasionally staring around with wide, fearful eyes. They passed bodies that had obviously fallen or jumped from the surrounding tall buildings; they heard screams, laughter, chanting; they saw people on their knees praying. And, strangest of all, they saw people behaving normally: queuing at bus stops, walking along briskly as though on their way to work, swinging umbrellas or carrying briefcases, entering the buildings that were open, waiting patiently outside others whose doors had not yet been unlocked, chatting to one another as though it were an ordinary working day, ignoring the chaos that was taking place around them. But that was *their* abnormality.

They drove slowly on down Fleet Street towards Ludgate Circus, steeling themselves against the sights, resisting the almost overwhelming urge to stop the vehicle and help those in particularly perilous plights. Holman was thankful they had passed no children. He realised they probably would later on when they passed through the more residential districts, but he hoped they would remain hidden from his eyes behind the veiling mist, for he doubted whether he could prevent himself helping a child in distress.

Suddenly they found themselves surrounded by a mob of workmen at the bottom of Fleet Street. The men began banging on the sides of the vehicle, trying to peer into the small but wide windows. They rapped on the glass, trying to break it. Holman and Mason heard heavy footsteps clunking overhead as some of the men scrambled on to the roof.

'Christ! Must be all the bloody printers in Fleet Street!' said Mason.

'Yes, they must have been working through the night,' Holman agreed. 'But surely they would have been warned?'

Mason shrugged his shoulders. 'We'll have to drive through them!' he said.

Just then the vehicle began to rock from side to side.

'They're trying to turn us over!' shouted Holman above the noise.

'Drive!' Mason commanded, leaning forward to switch off the sound. He didn't want Holman to hear the screams as they mowed their way through the crowd.

Holman pressed his foot down hard on the accelerator, sorry for the action he had to take but knowing it had to be done. He remembered Winchester and had less sympathy for the men and more interest in his own survival.

The car leapt forward and the startled men jumped back. Others were slower and disappeared beneath the wheels. Holman felt the car bump as it passed over their bodies, but he kept his foot down hard on the pedal, gathering speed, sending

the men on the roof flying off. It ploughed through the throng-
ing mass and Holman closed his mind from thoughts of his unfortunate victims. Perhaps it was because he regarded them as a
threat rather than human beings. Perhaps he thought they were
less human because of their madness. Or perhaps it was because
he didn't have time to think at all that enabled him to carry on.

At last, they were clear of the mob and travelling up the hill
towards St Paul's. Only then did Holman's hands begin to shake.

Mason noticed and said, 'Here, let me take over. You've had
enough.'

'No,' said Holman, 'I'll be all right. I'd rather drive than sit
and think. You check your instruments; make sure we're still
going in the right direction.'

Mason clapped a steadying hand on his shoulder then turned
his attention towards the panel of instruments in front of him.
He reported their position back to the underground base and
related some of the incidents they had run into and the fact that
the fog seemed much thinner. Holman glanced at his watch
and saw that they had only been out for thirty-odd minutes. It
seemed like hours.

He heard over the speaker a voice telling Mason that people
were fleeing from the town in their thousands; large internment
camps had been set up and police and troops from all over
the country had surrounded London with blockades, and were
trying to hold everyone who was leaving, imprisoning them for
their own protection. It was an impossible task, of course, to
save everyone, but fortunately, most of those that had fled were
unaffected as yet by the disease and willingly turned themselves
over to the authorities in the hope they would be protected when
the madness struck them.

Helicopters above the cloud had reported that the fog seemed
thickest around the river and thickest of all around the dockside
area past the Tower of London. Although it had spread further,
they confirmed that it did seem to be thinning, particularly on
its outer fringes. They could also see the glow of many large
fires all over London.

The voice informed them that aircraft from all over the
country were already on their way, loaded with calcium chloride
in an attempt to avalanche the city with the chemical, but it
would take hours for the operation to be put into effect.

It promised to send any further information that would help
them and wished them both good luck.

Mason switched off and said to Holman, 'It all checks. We're going the right way – it's somewhere down by the docks.'

They were now passing St Paul's Cathedral and were amazed to see scores of people sitting on its steps, their faces expressionless, their lips unmoving.

'Switch on the sound again,' said Holman.

Mason did so but they heard no noise from the gathering.

'They remind me of a flock of birds,' said Mason. 'One loud noise and they'll be fluttering all over the place.'

Holman remembered the pigeons in Trafalgar Square and told Mason of it.

'Christ!' said Mason. 'It gives me the creeps – let's move a bit faster.'

He increased the speed as much as he dared and they soon left the historic building behind.

'You notice how they seem to be mostly grouping together,' observed Mason.

'Yes. It's as though with the breaking down of their brain cells, they're losing their individuality, flocking together the way animals do. Look how they're gathering at bus stops, a natural grouping place for people. At first, I thought in their shocked state they were queuing, but now I realise they're grouping together at spots that are familiar to that idea.'

'Look at him!' Mason was pointing at a figure that had suddenly emerged from the fog ahead of them. The man was completely naked and was brandishing a long, curved sword. He advanced on the vehicle.

Holman turned the wheel sharply and swerved around him, narrowly avoiding running him down. Mason swung his head around to watch him through the rear windows, but he had disappeared into the mists again.

'It seems, even in total madness, there are a few individuals though,' he commented.

They passed fewer people as they drove through the City, but when they left its grey canyons behind they were faced with a spectacular scene.

Across the road in front of them was a mass of white-pink bodies, a sea of writhing limbs. As their eyes narrowed to focus, they saw it was made up of small groups of people, but packed so tightly together they represented a solid mass. All were engaged in copulation.

'Jesus!' said Mason slowly. 'Look at them! A bloody street orgy!'

'It probably started with one couple and others just joined in,' said Holman.

'But there's some there that must be in their sixties.'

'And others not more than kids.'

'What do we do?' asked Mason, tearing his eyes away from the scene to look at Holman.

Holman smiled thinly, a faint feeling of satisfaction at his companion's sudden perplexity causing the smile. Mason's calm throughout had bothered him.

'Well, we don't join them,' he said, and then, more grimly, 'we go around, of course.'

He turned the vehicle and found a narrow side street. As he drove away, Mason craned his neck to keep the spectacle in sight for as long as possible, cursing at the fog when it obliterated it.

'Incredible,' was all he could say.

Holman turned into another, wider street to get them back on their original course. They had travelled no more than fifty yards when he stopped the vehicle with a sudden jerk.

'What's wrong?' asked the startled Mason who had been checking his instruments.

'Look,' said Holman, pointing ahead.

Mason narrowed his eyes and peered into the fog. He heard her screams before he actually saw the girl. She looked to be no more than fifteen and she was backed into a doorway. Even at that distance, they could see her eyes were wide with terror and her screams echoed round the cramped interior of the vehicle.

Advancing on her were two men, both heavy set, both wearing clothes that were in tatters, both grinning at the girl. Their faces and hands were black with filth giving them an even more menacing appearance. But most frightening of all was their actions upon themselves for it made their intent obvious. Each had unbuttoned his trousers and was slowly stroking his penis, calling out to the girl, mouthing obscenities, informing her of their intentions upon her small body. She crouched in the doorway – whether she, herself, was mad yet was not apparent – whimpering, holding her hands up to her face as if to hide the sight from her mind.

'Oh God,' said Holman.

'Look, we can't go out there. In this suit, I'd be no help to

213

you at all. And you're too valuable to risk your life. And if we stopped to help everybody we see in trouble, we'll never get to the nucleus.'

'Shut up,' said Holman quietly. He stabbed his foot down hard on the accelerator and the vehicle leapt forward with a jolt. As it gathered speed it mounted the kerb and sped towards the two men, two wheels on the pavement, two wheels in the road. The two men just had time to see it coming, their grinning faces barely registering the fear that had begun its swift climb, before the vehicle hit them. One disappeared beneath the wheels, the other was tossed into the air to slam against the merciless concrete of a building. Their short screams, and the longer, more shrill scream of the girl, spun around in Holman's head even when the sound had stopped. He brought the vehicle to a screeching halt, throwing the astonished Mason forward on to his instruments. Holman swung around in his seat and looked through the rear apertures just in time to see the girl running into the fog, her face still hidden in her hands in an effort to block the horror.

He saw the crumpled figure of one of the men lying in the road, lifeless and somehow withered. The other lay propped up against the foot of the wall he'd smashed into, his neck twisted so that his open eyes seemed to be staring after the vehicle which had inflicted such a terrible death upon him.

Holman turned away from the sight and leaned forward on the steering wheel, rubbing a hand across his eyes then staring blankly downwards.

Mason pushed himself upright and silently placed a hand on Holman's shoulder, giving it a little shake of comfort. Without a word, Holman looked up and started the vehicle rolling forward again, guiding it back into the roadway and slowly building up a steady speed.

As they continued their journey, their minds became more numbed to each new incident, whether horrifying or just bizarre: the sight of an elderly woman pushing the obviously dead body of a man in a pram, leaving a stream of blood trickling from the carriage on to the road behind her, barely penetrated their consciousness; three men sitting by the roadside drinking from what looked like a can of paraffin, waving dirty handkerchiefs at the vehicle as it passed meant nothing to them. For Holman, it was probably the fact that he had just killed other human beings; nothing could surpass the horror of deliberately taking the lives of other men, whether they were mad or not. Remorse had not yet set in, but repulsion for the act had and, because he had been forced to take such measures, his resolution to find the means of destroying the disease was stronger than ever. For Mason, it was the mere consistency of the strange happenings, consistency being the steadiest ally to acceptance.

The scenes had not become unreal to them, but they, in their enclosed mobile compartment, had become remote from the scenes, observers moving through a strange, cloudy world, like explorers in a diving capsule on a seabed.

From time to time, Mason reported back to the underground base, coldly describing the scenes around them: the fires, the havoc, the waste of human life. Suddenly, he asked Holman to stop the vehicle. Holman had no idea of their exact location, but he guessed they must be somewhere near the East London docks by now. He looked askance towards his companion.

'We've lost it,' said Mason. He checked his instruments again then reported back to base speaking sharply and urgently.

'How could we have lost it?' asked Holman.

'We're being guided by a helicopter above the fog,' Mason told him. 'They have sensors that have been keeping track of the mycoplasma's centre; they relay the information back to headquarters who operate our directional finders from there. It has to be that complicated because obviously the chopper can't see which area it's over through the fog. But now, nothing's happening; our finder's just gone loose.'

A voice came over the speaker and echoed round the small apartment: 'Hello, D.V.1. Base here again. Do you read?' Mason acknowledged and the metallic voice went on, 'Trouble I'm afraid, D.V.1 Charlie 2 says they've lost the nucleus. Nothing at all shows on their instruments but they're going to scout around the area until they find it again. We don't understand how it's happened unless the bloody thing's gone into the river – you're near it – but that's hardly likely. Anyhow, sit tight for a while until you receive further instructions. Won't be long, I'm sure. Over and out.'

Mason sat back in his seat. 'Sod it!' he said, then added, 'We were close.'

'D'you think they'll find it again?' Holman asked.

'Who knows? They lost it before.' He glanced nervously around, looking through the apertures out at the fog-shrouded

215

streets. 'Must say I don't much like sitting around in the open like this.'

'Nor me,' said Holman. 'It's too vulnerable. Let's get over against a building. It'll give us some shelter, at least.'

He moved the vehicle forward more slowly this time, angling it across the wide road, looking for a building that might give it some protection.

It was just then that the bus emerged from the fog like a huge red monster, its lights appearing a split second before it like two glaring, searching eyes. Its front was splattered with a darker red, the bloodstains of the many victims it had struck down in the course of its frantic journey. It swerved towards their vehicle and, guessing the driver's intention, Holman pressed down hard on the accelerator in an effort to get clear, but he was too late.

The bus struck their vehicle side on, towards the rear. They felt themselves lifted violently as the vehicle was pushed into the air and then over on to its back. The grey world became suddenly black.

For the second time that morning, Janet Halstead felt the room spin dizzily around her. She was beyond the point of exhaustion, she knew. What little sleep she had had during the past few days had been fitful and disturbed and last night's had been interrupted by the fresh, major crisis. But she had to keep going; countless lives depended on the work she and her colleagues were involved in. She realised Professor Ryker and his team of scientists, microbiologists and virologists were close to the answer and wondered if it had really been necessary to send Holman out into the fog once again. She sighed wearily, wondering if it was just her concern for the man himself that caused these thoughts; she had grown fond of him in a maternal way and it made her uneasy to see him used as a pawn, an instrument, by the great body of officials that ruled the country.

It was they who had made the mistake. The great, faceless *they* and now they were using one man, one man who had had nothing to do with their mistake, to help rectify it.

But, she supposed, it *was* necessary. There was a chance he could save them valuable time, be it hours, or days, and his life was expendable because of it.

She tried to focus her attention on the report before her: the

216

latest patient they had treated was responding immediately to the blood transfusion and the radiology. Fortunately, they had got to him in time; others would not be so lucky. And this was just the beginning, the first few of the thousands, probably millions, to come. The world was standing by to give assistance, for Britain was no primitive, backwater country inhabited by people dying because they lacked civilisation. Because it was a country populated by educated Westerners, other countries were eager to help, not just because of a kinship with another race, but because if it could happen to Great Britain, it could happen anywhere, on any continent, to any country. And if it, or something equal to it, ever did happen to another country, the country concerned wanted to be sure they would receive such help as they were now giving.

Still, Janet thought, the help, from whatever source and for whatever reason, would be sorely needed over the next few weeks.

Stan Reynolds, the Security Guard for the giant oil company building that stood towering over the Thames, again sat with his huge boots on the oak boardroom table smoking a fat cigar, sipping an expensive brand of Scotch.

'If it's good enough for the Chairman, it's good enough for me,' he chuckled, puffing away at the cigar while the flames from the room directly below heated the floor beneath him.

Earlier, he had visited many offices in the vast, complex building and empied their desks and filing cabinets of paper on to the floor. He hated the building because it represented a life style he had never experienced himself, nor ever would. He was expected to protect the executives' offices, to guard them with his life if necessary, and for what? A pittance of a salary and the privilege of having snot-nosed execs bidding him 'Good morning' or 'Good night' when they felt like it. That was why he had set fire to their 'confidential' papers, their 'strictly private' files. Besides, he liked fires; they reminded him of the blitz. He'd been something in those days; a sergeant in the army, respected by privates *and* snot-nosed young officers alike. And when he'd been home on leave during some of the worst bombing of the war, his neighbours had come to *him* for help. He'd been respected then.

By now, half the bottle of Scotch had gone and he took a

long, stiff swallow of the remainder. As the heavy boardroom doors burst into flame, he rose unsteadily to his feet.

'Gen'men,' he said, looking along the table at the two rows of empty seats. 'I wish to perprose a toast.' He climbed on to the black leather chair, then on to the table, his boots making ugly scratch marks on its smooth surface. He raised the bottle high. 'Fuck the Chairman!' he shouted and took another swig from the bottle, nearly choking when he began to cackle with laughter.

Looking down, he saw the deep impressions his boots had made on the table and again went into fits of laughter. He dug a heel hard into the wood and was pleased with the result. He did it again with his other heel then clomped his way to the end of the table, stopping and turning to study his trail of scars. He lifted the bottle to his lips and drank, then threw it at the picture of the previous chairman which hung near-by, and, with one final whoop of exhilaration, ran back down the length of the oak table and jumped over the leather chair towards the huge window behind it.

He was well past his prime and his jump did not have much momentum, but half his body went through the glass and its weight toppled the rest over the edge behind him. He couldn't see the ground as he fell; all he could see was a soft, yellowish-grey blanket ready to receive him.

McLellan and his family slept soundly. Outside his house, in the normally quiet Wimbledon street where he lived, was pandemonium. His neighbours were in combat, using bottles, pokers, anything that came to hand; scratching at each other's eyes, tearing at each other's throats. They kicked, they punched, they pulled the clothes from one another. No one knew why and no one bothered to ask themselves; they were too far gone with the madness.

McLellan was lucky for they ignored the sign he'd left on his doorstep which said: PLEASE HELP. HAVE GIVEN FAMILY OVERDOSE TO KEEP FROM HARM. PLEASE HELP. He knew when he'd chalked the message on to his child's toy blackboard it was a slim chance, but there had been little choice anyway. Better to die in their sleep than be at the mercy of a dreadful madness.

So far, they had been left undisturbed and their neighbours

218

were too intent on killing each other to break in and search them out. They slept on.

Irma Bidmead, the old woman who had loved cats yet sold their bodies for vivisection was already dead. The cats she had fed and housed still gnawed away at her cold flesh mixed with bits of material from the garments she had worn. They had clawed and scratched at her eyes first, then when she had been blinded and weakened, they had sat on her face and smothered her. When her feeble struggles had ceased, they had begun to eat her.

Now they were full, eating out of greed, not hunger, but later they would go out and seek younger, more tender flesh. It wouldn't be hard to find.

Chief Superintendent Wreford laughed at the rantings of his wife. He had locked her in a bedroom cupboard and sat on the end of their bed watching the doors as it bulged when she tried to force it open from inside. Her moans had a peculiar rasping tone to them, for earlier that morning he had climbed the stairs from the kitchen holding a kettle full of boiling water in one hand. He had stood over his wife and poured the contents of the kettle into her upturned, open mouth. Her snoring had always sickened him.

Then, as she had screamed and screamed, he had bundled her up in the bedclothes and locked her away in the cupboard. Soon now, her struggles would grow weaker and he would let her out. She would see the joke when he explained it to her and if she didn't, if she began to nag at him like she had in the past, well, he would show her the kitchen knife he held in his lap. He had seen what you could do to a person with a kitchen knife; he had seen many pictures of victims at the Yard. They were funny those pictures; fascinating what you could do to a human face. You could make the lips smile permanently if you wanted to. He would show her when he let her out – if she whined at him.

He waited patiently, smiling at the cupboard door.

Detective Inspector Barrow had only just woken. He stood by
219

the window, wearing a loose-fitting bathrobe, and gazed out at the fog. Abruptly, he turned away and walked towards the wardrobe. He took out his best suit and laid it carefully on the bed. Then he opened a drawer and took out a clean shirt which he laid on top of the suit. He walked back to the wardrobe again and reached up into the high shelf inside and brought down a wide cardboard box. It was his own private, and strictly against regulations, 'Black Museum' of weapons used in various cases in which he had been involved. He studied its contents for a while, then removed one particular object. He replaced the lid, and returned the box to its resting place.

He went into the bathroom and turned on the bath taps. While it was filling, he carefully shaved.

Samson King had enjoyed his bus ride immensely. He didn't know where he was for he had left his normal route, but it didn't matter. He felt free as a bird and a million times more powerful. He had smashed down anything that had got in the way of his charging red beast. People, cars – anything that had stood before him. The passengers on his bus had enjoyed it too; even now they were laughing gleefully, pointing out of the windows, calling out at the blank faces that stared after them. There were at least fifty people on his bus now for he had stopped twice at bus stops to let them on.

Samson giggled as he remembered the bus stop he hadn't stopped at. Instead, he had driven into the queue, encouraged by his passengers, fascinated by the bodies that disappeared like skittles beneath his wheels.

He couldn't see too far in the fog, and had crashed into quite a few traffic islands and signs. He had been using the kerb as a guide but occasionally he would switch to the other side of the road, and for a brief time would be driving blind in a no-man's-land. He had enjoyed that. He had also enjoyed the moments when he had found himself at a broad junction and had sent the bus spinning round and round, almost toppling it over.

But most of all, he had enjoyed crossing the river over Tower Bridge. There had been quite a few people on the bridge and he had swerved the bus from side to side, making them run before him, chasing them to the very edge where they had been forced to climb the parapet and jump into the filthy water. That had been best!

And now he raced down the wide road, not knowing where he was going and not caring, picking up speed, the excitement rising inside him, heedless to his lack of clear vision, regardless of anything that got in his way.

Then he saw the vehicle. It was an odd looking thing, grey-coloured with strange-looking objects sticking out from its sides. He ignored its oddity for his mind had already determined to ram it. It was moving directly across his path and it suddenly gave a spurt of speed as though the driver had spotted him and was trying to get clear.

Samson laughed aloud. It couldn't escape him! He pressed down even harder on the accelerator and two seconds later the bus was on the vehicle, catching it at its rear, lifting it up and over, pushing it on to its back, knocking it aside. He lost control of the bus for a moment but didn't try to regain it. He was too busy laughing.

The bus sped across the road and ploughed into a shop-front.

Twenty

Holman shook his head to try to clear the haze. It made it worse so he stopped.

He lay there for several moments longer, giving his body time for feeling to return again, for the shock of the crash to wear off. Slowly, he opened his eyes and was surprised to find himself in daylight, grey though it was. He could hear a strange voice speaking from a distance. Unreal as it sounded, it managed to convey urgency, anxiety.

Lifting his head slightly, he tried to look around to find out where it was coming from, and, to his surprise, discovered he was lying in the road with the Devastation Vehicle on its back a few yards away from him. The voice was coming from the open doorway to its cabin and he realised it was the voice of the radio. Base was demanding to know what had happened.

He must have been thrown clear from the vehicle, but as yet, could not ascertain whether he had been fortunate or not. The door must have been smashed by the bus as it had hit it, and then swung open as it turned over, spilling him out into the road. He didn't feel as though anything was broken: his face felt raw as if he had skidded along the road on it and both his knees hurt like hell, but apart from that, he seemed to be all right. He tried to lift himself and found he could, although it made him feel a little giddy.

Mason! Where was Mason? Holman's senses were returning rapidly now and he sat up, turning his body towards the vehicle, using one hand for support. He must be still inside, he told himself. God, he mustn't be hurt too badly! Trembling, he got to his feet, then staggered forward to the open doorway.

'Mason!' he called out, poking his head into the dim interior. It was empty.

Holman spun round, leaning back against the vehicle for

support. 'Mason!' he called out again, this time louder. Then he saw the grey-clad figure.

Mason was stumbling away from the vehicle, leaning forward at the waist, both hands to his face as though in pain. He was making for the red bus, whether by intent or because he was walking blind, there was no way of knowing, and as he drew nearer, several people were alighting from its platform and staring silently at him. One of them pointed at him and began to giggle.

'Mason, come back!' Holman shouted, realising that without his helmet, his companion was exposed to the fog.

But Mason hadn't heard him. He fell to one knee as he reached the crowd that was still climbing off the bus. Several of them began to laugh now, pointing down at him, calling out to their fellow passengers to come and see the ridiculous looking man. The front of the bus was embedded in a shop window, but now a figure was emerging from the wreckage, crunching through the shattered glass, leaning against the side of the bus to steady himself. He was wearing the uniform of a London Transport driver and blood trickled in a thin line from his crinkly scalp down his brown face. He was grinning broadly.

Holman started forward to warn Mason, but he was still unsteady on his feet and fell painfully on to his knees. He called out again, one hand reaching outward towards the crowd, but nobody seemed to hear him.

The driver was now standing over Mason, who was still on one knee, rocking his body backwards and forwards in pain, low moans coming from deep down in his throat. The black man swung a foot at him then stepped back and roared with laughter as the clumsy figure toppled. Someone else stepped forward and aimed a kick, retreating when the blow had been accomplished. The rest of the crowd joined in the laughter. At once, as if by some silent, mutual agreement, they all gathered around the prone body and began to kick at it.

'Don't, don't!' Holman screamed at them, but they took no notice, absorbed in their own violence. To his amazement, he saw the figure of Mason emerge from the tangle of legs, crawling on all fours protected from the worst of the blows by the heavy suit he wore. His eyes met Holman's and they registered recognition, but his hands were kicked from beneath him even as he opened his mouth to cry out. His exposed head hit the pavement with a loud thud and he lay motionless in the road.

The crowd's laughter took on a new, more hysterical pitch as they leapt upon his body, using their feet to stomp the life from him.

With a shout of pure rage, Holman gained his feet and staggered towards them, his anger pumping adrenalin through his body, helping his strength to return. He leapt into the throng, taking several people down with him and was on his feet again instantly, swinging punches, kicking out at them. For a moment they cowered away from him, afraid of his anger, afraid because they sensed he wasn't like them.

All except the driver. He wasn't afraid of anybody. He roared at Holman for spoiling the fun and threw himself at him. Holman went down under the weight and found his face pressed hard against the road's surface and his eyes staring into those of a dead man.

Mason's face lay a foot away from his own and it was turned towards him, the eyes unseeing, the expression rigid. A thread of blood came from one corner of his mouth, an indication that some of his ribs had torn into his lungs. Whether it had been caused by the accident or the cruel kicks of the lunatic mob, Holman would never know; all he felt was despair and the urge to lie there on the ground until the crowd left him alone. But he knew they would not leave him alone until he too was dead. The heavy weight was suddenly released from his body as the black man stood up and a boot kicked Holman viciously over on to his back. He saw nothing but the greyness above him at first, the eddying, drifting clouds of fog, tinged with yellow, filled with man-made impurities. A ring of grinning, evil-looking heads intruded upon the periphery of the soft grey picture as the crowd gathered round him, looking down at him as though he were an animal about to be slaughtered for the sheer fun of it. They reminded him of the faces of his school friends when, many, so many years ago, they had trapped a wasp in a jam-jar and had begun to fill the jar with water through a small hole in the top. The ring of expectant faces had smiled gleefully at the wasp's struggles to get free as the water rose, frantically buzzing around the inside of the jar, its circuit becoming smaller and smaller, its tiny legs beating against the smooth glass in an effort to grip it, all to no avail. To Holman, the smiles had seemed to turn into sadistic leers as the water crept up, inch by inch, the space between the top of the water and the roof of the jar physically encapsulating the wasp's remaining lifetime. The grinning lunatics reminded him of the incident, for their expressions were not unlike those of the schoolboys and the circumstances now were not dissimilar. But this time there would be no one to save his life as he had done for the wasp by stepping forward and knocking the jar from the ringleader's hands so it shattered upon the ground, giving the insect its small existence back. He had paid for that action with a beating, but it had been worth it for the astonished, cheated looks on his companions' faces alone.

One head came closer to his, bringing his fleeing mind back to the present, and he saw it was the black man's. The bus driver's hand shot forward and grabbed him by the hair, pulling his head up and forward, the large brown eyes looking into his own. Holman recognised the slightly glazed look of the madness, even though the eyes were filled with cruel amusement. He remembered the revolver.

Carefully, he reached for the shoulder holster beneath his coat, flicked the gun's hammer free of its retaining loop, drew it out steadily, clicking off the safety catch as he did so, put the short barrel under the man's chin, and pulled the trigger.

The driver's head exploded, spattering the crowd with blood and brains, tiny bone fragments flying into the air acting as shrapnel. The force of the blast sent the body reeling back away from Holman, the grip on his hair tightening so some of it came away at the roots. He jumped to his feet, holding the gun forward, ready to use it again, but the mob was too stunned to attack him. They stood looking at the twitching body on the ground, their crazed minds unable to understand exactly what had happened.

Holman began slowly to back away, his eyes never leaving the faces of the crowd, waiting for the first sign of hostility towards him to resume. Several were wiping blood from their faces and looking at their hands in amazement. He saw one middle-aged woman, a woman who normally would have probably fainted at the sight of blood, lick the red stains from the fingers of one hand, then repeat the process with the other. Her glazed eyes looked around her at her companions, then at the bodies on the ground, then over towards the cautiously retreating Holman. A snarl broke from her lips.

Holman turned and fled. Away from the bus, away from the crowd, away from the dead bodies, away from the vehicle. Into the fog.

He heard a cry from behind and knew they were following. His legs hurt and still felt unsteady as a result of the crash, but he refused to succumb for if he stopped running, he would have to kill again. And then they would kill him.

From nowhere, a car appeared, screeching to a halt in front of him, pitching him forward on to the bonnet although it hadn't actually hit him; it was the momentum of his own pace that had sent him sprawling. The car was an old Ford Anglia, rusty with age but obviously still having some life in it. Holman rolled off the bonnet and ran round to the driver's door. He yanked it open and was about to haul its occupant out when the startled man said: 'Please let me go. I've got to get away from these lunatics!'

Holman hesitated and then bent forward to get a closer look at the man behind the wheel. He appeared to be in his early forties, fairly well dressed and most important of all, his eyes, although frightened, did not appear to have the glazed look that was a symptom of the disease. He looked up at Holman, a pleading expression on his face and said, again, 'Please let me go.'

'Get over!' Holman commanded, pushing his way in, using his weight to get the trembling man into the passenger seat. He revved up the engine and engaged first gear, pulling the door shut as the car shot forward. He was just in time, for outstretched hands clutched at the windows but were knocked aside by the sudden jerk of the car. A figure ran into their path and was sent spinning back into the road. He swerved to avoid another and skidded violently when he was confronted with the overturned Devastation Vehicle. The Anglia did a screeching U-turn, mounted the kerb on one side of the road and sped on along the broad pavement for fifty yards or so, leaving it with a resounding thump only when Holman saw he would not get through the gap ahead caused by a concrete street light and its neighbouring wall. When he considered he was far enough from the pursuing crowd, he reduced speed, afraid that he might run into another vehicle in the fog. He became aware he was still holding the revolver in one hand and the man he had pushed roughly into the passenger seat was staring at it apprehensively. He shoved it back into its shoulder holster and heard the man breath a sigh of relief.

'You're not the same as the rest, are you?' the man asked nervously.

Holman took his eyes off the road for a moment to look at him. He was backed away as far as he could get against the door, one hand on the dashboard, the other holding on to the back of his seat to steady himself. He looked white and frightened.

'As the rest?' Holman asked cautiously.

'You know, mad. Everyone's gone mad. It's the fog. Please tell me you're not, you're okay. Like me.'

Was it possible? Holman stole another quick glance at the man; was it possible the disease hadn't affected him? He seemed normal enough. Scared, his eyes were frightened, but he seemed rational under the circumstances.

'I'm sane,' Holman said, but wondering if he still was. Could anyone remain sane after all he'd been through?

The man smiled. 'Thank God for that,' he said. 'I've been living through a bad dream. I thought I was the only one left. You've no idea what I've been through.' He rubbed a hand across his eyes that were becoming moist with self pity. 'My – my wife tried to kill me. We were having breakfast; we didn't realise what the fog was, what it meant. I don't know why, we just didn't associate it with the fog we'd heard about, the Bournemouth fog. I looked up and she was just sitting there, staring at me, a sort of smile on her face. I asked her what she was smiling about and she didn't answer. Just smiled even more. Her eyes – her eyes were different somehow. Wide. Not really seeing.' He began to sob quietly. 'It was horrible,' he said brokenly. Taking a deep breath, he continued: 'She got up from the table and walked around it until she was behind me. I didn't know she'd picked up the breadknife. I turned around to ask her what was wrong and saw her bringing the knife down. I – I was lucky: it caught my shoulder and the blade snapped. It was only then I realised what was happening. The fog. I realised it was *the fog*! I jumped up and we struggled. I didn't want to hurt her but, God, she was so strong. She, she's only a tiny thing, my wife, you know, but suddenly, she was so strong. She pushed me back across the table and we fought there, over the breakfast things, until we rolled off on to the floor. She cracked her head, knocked herself out. I didn't know what to do.' His body began to shake and once more he had to stop talking until he had calmed himself.

'Take it easy,' said Holman soothingly, feeling pity for the man. How many countless others had gone through the same

227

thing that morning? How many loved ones had turned on one another, tried to kill, to maim the people that meant most to them? How many had killed themselves so far? Was this man lucky because the disease had not affected him or was he unlucky because he'd had to witness what had happened to his wife, to watch her go insane, to fight her to save his own life? 'Don't talk about it anymore,' he said. 'I'll try to get you to a safe place.'

The man looked up at Holman, his tears under control again. 'No, I want to talk about it. You're the only normal person I've spoken to. I tried to get help from others, but they're all the same; they're all mad. Why not us, why haven't we gone mad? Why hasn't it done anything to us?'

Holman hesitated. Should he tell him the chances were that eventually the disease would destroy his brain cells and he, too, would become insane; that the time varied from person to person, that the parasite cells took longer to multiply in some than they did in others? Perhaps he could get him back to base in time for Janet Halstead to go to work on him. He was only one, one life, but at least it was something positive amongst all this carnage. The mission was scrapped now, there was nothing he could do on his own; perhaps he could come back in the other vehicle once they'd located the nucleus again, but in the meantime, he could try to save this one life.

Fortunately, he did not have to answer the man's question, for he was talking again, reliving the horror of that morning. 'I tied her up. I didn't know what else to do, I was afraid of her, afraid of my own wife. She came out of her daze as I was tying her. She didn't struggle, didn't say anything at first – just stared at me with those eyes. Those terrible eyes. I was afraid to look at them; they were so – so hate filled!' He shook his head as though to erase the memory. 'And then she began to speak. Such filth! I couldn't believe it. I'd never known her even to swear before, but the filth, the obscenities that came from her! I couldn't believe such thoughts could exist in someone, especially not her! She's always been so good, so gentle. I couldn't stand it; I couldn't stand to listen to her, I couldn't stand to look at her eyes! Oh God, I didn't know what I should do!

'I knew I had to get away, to get out of London, and I knew my only chance would be in the car; I didn't know what it would be like out on the streets, but I knew I couldn't stay there. The drive was terrible. I couldn't go too fast in the fog, I was afraid of crashing, and the people that I saw . . . lunatics. Some were like vegetables; just standing by the roadside, not moving. I saw people crawling along the gutters. I saw some sitting in burning cars, others making love in the streets. One man I saw was stabbing himself; standing in a doorway stabbing his own body with a knife. Oh thank God I met you! I think I would have gone mad myself if I hadn't. I got lost, you see. I didn't know where I was going and things just seemed to be getting worse and worse.'

'Did you make sure your wife was securely tied before you left her?' asked Holman, still keeping a wary eye on the road ahead, knowing he would have to make a turn soon if he were to go in the right direction back towards the underground base. 'Did you make sure she wouldn't be able to harm herself?'

'Oh, I didn't leave her,' the man replied. 'I couldn't have left Louise. I love her too much to have left her there alone at the mercy of anyone who might break in. But it was her eyes, you see, and the things she was saying. I couldn't stand it. I had to stop her from looking at me like that and saying those horrible things. And I couldn't leave her, not Louise, she's too precious to me. So I brought her with me; she's in the back. I stopped her saying those foul things and stopped her looking at me that way and put her in the back seat. There she is, my Louise, behind you, in the back.'

Holman quickly glanced over his shoulder and found himself transfixed, the car moving ahead unguided, picking up speed as his foot involuntarily pressed down on the accelerator.

On the back seat was slumped the bound figure of a woman, recognisable as a woman only by her clothes, for the body ended in a bloody stump at the neck. She had been decapitated.

'I couldn't leave her, you see,' the man went on,' and I couldn't stand the things she was saying and the way she was looking so I used a saw. It was terribly messy, I must say. The kitchen was in a terrible state and I had to change my clothes. And, you know, she kept talking, even while I was doing it, but she had to stop in the end.' His voice grew sad. 'But I couldn't stop her eyes looking at me like that, even when the head came right off. She just kept glaring at me in that lunatic way. Look, she still does.'

He reached behind him, half kneeling on his seat, stretching for something that lay on the floor at the back. He brought his hand up again, his face looking seriously into Holman's. 'Look,' he said.

He held the blood-dripping head by the hair, pushing it towards Holman's face. He was right – the eyes *were* still staring.

A cry of horror escaped from Holman's lips as he backed away, the hairs on his body stiffening, the vertebrae of his spine seeming to contract and lock together. He thrashed out with his hand knocking the disembodied head aside, causing the car to swerve violently across the road. His fight to control it gave his mind a brief respite from the shock it had just received.

The man beside him was astonished that Holman had smashed his wife's head aside. 'Don't do that to Louise, you bastard!' he shouted, placing it gently on his lap. He reached behind him again, careful not to dislodge the head between his legs, and this time, his hand came up with a bloodstained saw. 'I'll kill you!' he screamed. 'You're the same as all the rest!'

He tried to bring the sharp-toothed blade down on the back of Holman's neck, but the car bumped over a kerb, mounting a narrow pavement which ran along the centre of the broad road, knocking him back against the door on his side, the saw falling harmlessly against Holman's shoulder blades. Even as he tried to control the car's skid when it thumped down on to the other lane of the road, Holman struck out with his fist at the figure beside him, catching the man on the side of the jaw. His foot was jammed down hard on the brake pedal and the tyres burnt into the road, struggling for a grip. He thought the car was bound to smash into a building on the other side of the road, but to his surprise and relief he found the way clear; there was a side road dead ahead. The road dipped and the car skidded down its incline finally stopping broadside across it, the sudden jolt throwing the man forward against the windscreen. Before he had a chance to recover, Holman had leaned across his back and pushed the doorcatch down and shoved the door open. Still in one motion, he pushed the man's rising figure out of the car and into the road, raising his foot and using it to clear the man's legs. His efforts were helped because the car was slightly angled on the slope of the road, and the man's body easily fell forward. Holman saw the woman's head, with its ghastly staring eyes, begin a slow roll down the incline.

Not bothering to pull the door shut again, he restarted the stalled engine and swung the car round, heading down the slope, narrowly missing the head that had come to rest in the middle of the road. He corrected his turn and held the car steady, the

230

door on his other side swinging shut with the momentum. He didn't want to stop; he didn't want to think. He just wanted to get away.

A black hole opened up ahead of him and he suddenly found himself swallowed up by darkness. Once again, his foot hit the brakes, and the car screeched to a halt. He looked around in panic but could see only blackness ahead and to his sides. He remembered the decapitated body behind him and turned swiftly as though to assure himself that it was still lying prone. Grey light flowed in from a high square arch about thirty yards back and he saw that the body had slumped to the floor behind the front seats. He looked up again at the light and then he realised what had happened. He had driven into a tunnel! He should have realised it instantly, but because of circumstances, everything that happened seemed abnormal.

A tunnel! And suddenly it came to him which tunnel.

'The Blackwall Tunnel,' he said aloud. It had to be; they'd been driving in that direction, into the City, through Aldgate, down Commercial Road towards Poplar. The road he had just driven down must have been a ramp leading into the tunnel from the main road. The long winding tunnel stretched beneath the Thames to the south side of London, cutting out miles of snarled-up roads for motorists who would otherwise have had to use distant bridges. There were two tunnels in fact, running parallel to one another but completely separated; the old, built in the 1890s, and the new, completed in the late 1960s, one for the northbound traffic, the other for southbound. Holman was in the old tunnel, used for access to the north. He would use it himself now and get back to Westminster by following the rive along its southern side. For a full minute he debated whether to go back to his flat, collect Casey, and get the hell out of London, but he finally dismissed the thought because he knew really there was no choice.

Before he made his way back, there was one thing he would have to do: get rid of the grotesque figure on the floor behind him. He opened the side door and got out, pulling the driving seat forward so he could reach the body, the old car being a two-door model. He could have switched the car's headlights on to give him more light, but he had no desire to see too clearly what he was doing; the dim light from the opening further back would suffice for his purposes. He groped around until he found the tied ankles and gave the body a tug, finding it surprisingly light as it came out smoothly. He avoided touching anything but the woman's ankles; the thought of coming in contact with her headless shoulders made him feel nauseous. He pulled the body to the side of the tunnel then straightened up and wiped his hands down the sides of his jacket to rid himself of the feel of her cold flesh. Looking down into the depths of the tunnel as he did so, he was forced to blink his eyes to clear them.

Was it his imagination, or was it lighter down there? The underground passage was filled with fog but much less than there was above ground so his vision was not seriously hindered, and his eyes had become fairly accustomed to the gloom. He was sure, there was light coming from ahead, from around a bend, but it couldn't be daylight, for the exit would be at least a quarter of a mile away on the other side of the river and there were more bends that would diminish any daylight coming from that source. The only other possibility was that there was another car down there with its headlights full on. Before he drove any further into the tunnel, he would have to investigate; he was reluctant to run into more trouble again. Cautiously, quietly, he began to walk down the tunnel towards the eerie light.

It grew brighter at his approach, a strange yellowish light, reminding him of the light he'd come across before, in Winchester. The familiar dread crept through him again; he began to suspect the source of the light. His heart seemed to be pounding almost painfully as he neared the bend and he had to take short, shallow breaths to combat the acrid smell that was growing stronger. He kept close to the wall, one hand touching its rough surface with every step he took, and then he was at the first curve of the tunnel.

The bend was casual, not sharp, and there was no need to go to its apex to see what lay beyond. The whole tunnel further ahead was filled with the glow, the strange incandescence peculiar to the mutated mycoplasma. He had found it! Now he knew why the instruments of the helicopter above had lost it: it had literally gone to ground, slunk into a hole beneath the ground almost as though it remembered the hole it had been buried in for so many years. Could it be possible? Had it actually sought shelter like an animal searching for a lair? No, it was too ridiculous. And yet he *had* found it lurking inside the cathedral, and they *had* lost it once before. Could it really have drifted accidentally into these enclosures, into these man-made shelters?

He stood gazing into its hypnotic shine for several minutes, leaning back against the tunnel's wall, suddenly realising he was actually resisting walking towards it, that it seemed to be pulling him forward, that a small part of his mind was urging him to envelope his body in the glow, but the fact that he had become conscious of its mesmeric influence made him back away. He felt certain his immunity would not hold if he were to enter the mycoplasma in its strongest form.

As soon as it was out of vision, the magnetic pull on his mind was broken and suddenly he wasn't sure if it had been his imagination or not. He hurried back towards the car, his brain racing with new thoughts and, by the time he had reached the car, an idea had formed in his mind.

He jumped into the Anglia, switched on the engine and, without turning on its lights, he began to reverse it towards the entrance. Looking over his shoulder through the rear window, he saw a shadowy figure silhouetted in the cloudy entrance and, as he drew nearer, he saw it was the man he'd thrown from the car. In his arms he cradled the head of his dead wife.

Twenty-one

Holman crouched in the dark interior of the shop away from the eyes of the groups of lunatics roaming the streets, but positioned so that he could see the overturned Devastation Vehicle lying in the middle of the road. The fog seemed much clearer now, although there were still thick pockets of it drifting through and the very air seemed to carry the yellow tinge to it. Holman had taken extreme care in driving back to the vehicle for everything depended on his reaching the radio; he needed help from the base if he were to carry out his plan. And certain materials.

He had driven slowly and every time he came across a menacing individual or mob, he had speeded up until he was a safe distance away from them. Twice he had had to mount the pavement to avoid recklessly driven cars and once he'd deliberately run over a dog that was running amok attacking people, but that was the only time he'd allowed himself to interfere in the surrounding chaos and only because the dog had presented itself directly in the path of the car. If he had had to chase it, he wouldn't have bothered. He had detached himself from the nightmare and had become a mere observer. He knew it was the self-protection of his own mind: he'd always had that ability (or perhaps misfortune) to allow his feelings to go cold, remote, whenever circumstances became intolerable. He could either bury himself in action or retreat into insensitive logic; it wasn't callousness, for emotion always flooded through him after the event. It was a natural ability to survive.

He no longer felt any strong sympathy for the people out there; his feelings were more akin to fear. It was strange how madness, which, after all, was only an illness of the mind, was so repulsive to the 'normal'. Was it due to fear? Even with Casey when she had been under restraint, he'd felt the tension, the urge to get away from her, to shut her from his mind, and she must have experienced the same feelings when it had been he who

234

was insane. That was what made madness so cruel for the relatives or friends of its victim: the fear of the person they loved. And now, there was a whole city full of the insane.

And yet, his detachment wasn't complete: it was the sight of the children, infants some of them, who were walking the streets, many on their own, still clad in pyjamas and nightclothes, that lost dazed look on their tiny faces. It was this that stirred his emotions most. He wanted to help them, to gather them up and lead them to safety, to keep them from harm until help was at hand, but he knew the best way he could help them was to carry out his plan.

The idea was simple: the mutated mycoplasma had been locked away below ground for many years, trapped and contained by tons of earth; now it had returned to another underground sanctuary, a man-made open womb that could be made into a prison if both ends were sealed. So he had returned to the vehicle and, with relief, found it untampered with; the radio was still buzzing (a voice had been calling in every ten minutes, desperate for a reply from the two passengers of the vehicle) and he'd used it to tell headquarters of his plan. There had been great excitement and relief at the sound of his voice, but the men on the other end were professionals and had soon acknowledged his instructions. He asked for explosives, the 'brisant' kind, the type used for quarrying and demolition work because of its shattering power. He asked for as much as could be loaded into the second Devastation Vehicle in case the first attempts failed, and an explosives expert because his own knowledge was extremely limited in that field. He gave them directions as to his exact location, for he had checked on the names of the streets on his way back to the vehicle: they would find him and the overturned vehicle at a point along the East India Dock Road close to a turning called Hale Street. He told them to hurry.

The voice at the other end urged him to sit tight and wait, no matter how long it took them to get there, and to avoid any trouble. If he were to be attacked, he was to use the gun without hesitation.

He had smiled grimly. He had little compunction about killing now, for he thought of the people out there as hardly human any more, their hostility helping to negate his compassion. He had remembered the demented man clutching his wife's disembodied head at the entrance to the tunnel; he had

235

backed the car right into him, repugnance at what the man had done filling him with hatred – unreasonable hatred, he knew, for the man could not help the actions of a sick mind. The impact had killed him, Holman was sure, and he felt no regret. Perhaps later, when he had time to reflect, he would feel pity, but now he had become quite ruthless; partly because of fear of the illness, but mostly because he had a mission that he couldn't allow to be jeopardised.

Two hours went by before he saw the other vehicle appear from the fog and halt beside its ill-fortuned twin. He rose from his hiding place behind the shop's counter, amid shelves filled with confectionery, and walked towards the door, unbolting it and stepping outside into the misty street. He had found the door wide open when he'd arrived and assumed the owner had left it so on leaving the premises. He walked over to the second vehicle just as one of its side doors began to open. A heavy-suited figure clambered out carrying what appeared to be an ordinary rifle except that its trigger was at least three inches long and had a wide, looping guard to accommodate it. The figure wore a helmet fitted with a dark, narrow visor for vision, and he had to swing his whole body around from the waist in order to see about him. The black visor came to rest in the direction of Holman as he walked forward, his arm slightly raised in a gesture of greeting turning into one of apprehensive placation as the rifle swung up to meet him. The four fingers of the clumsy glove tightened on the long trigger and a voice with its familiar metallic tone said sharply, 'Stay there!'

'It's all right,' said Holman wearily, 'it's me, Holman.' He stopped nevertheless.

Another grey-suited figure was now climbing from the car. 'Yes, Captain, it's Holman. Put your gun down.'

'Sorry, sir,' the man holding the gun said, 'but I'm a bit jumpy after what we've seen coming here.'

'It's okay,' said Holman, 'I know what you mean.'

The second figure pushed by the Captain and advanced on Holman. 'Well done, Mr Holman,' said a voice, familiar although distorted by the helmet's speaker. 'Let us hope we are in time to carry out your plan, eh?'

He recognised the slight German accent. 'Professor Ryker?' he asked.

'Yes,' came the reply, 'I decided to see the mutation first hand before we sealed it off. Once it is trapped, the fog itself should be easy to disperse. Later, we will be able to drill holes and draw the mycoplasma off into containers. It should in itself provide us with enough vaccine to cure a large majority of the people we catch in time. But first, I must have that sample for I'm afraid we still do not know exactly what the mutation is.'

'But you must have some idea by now,' said Holman.

'Brain cells perhaps, broken down, crystallised in some way, infected with the mycoplasma, multiplying, somehow feeding on impurities and carbon dioxide from the air. Yes, we have some some idea,' said Ryker, 'but that is not enough. We still need the thing itself. And soon, if it is to be of any use.' He pointed towards the vehicle he'd just arrived in. 'Now, please, let us go to this place, this tunnel. We must not waste any more time.'

He walked back to the vehicle, pulling Holman gently by the arm along with him. 'This is Captain Peters, our explosives expert,' he said as they passed the figure still clutching the gun.

'Sir,' the Captain said to Holman, 'you didn't say what had happened to Mason when you reported back.'

Holman pointed towards the two dead figures lying beside the bus across the road. 'One of them's Mason. He was injured in the crash and ran into a mob. They kicked him to death.'

He thought he heard the Captain cursing softly as he climbed into the vehicle. Inside, he was surprised to find the figure of another man, also clad in the usual grotesque garb.

'This is Sergeant Stanton,' the Captain introduced him as he squeezed in behind Holman. The Sergeant's helmet nodded towards him.

'Did you find room for the explosives?' Holman asked, quite seriously. The small cabin was fairly cramped with all four of them, especially with the other three's suits making their bodies even more bulky.

'I think you'll find we have enough, sir,' the Sergeant replied, equally seriously. They had all seen enough distressing sights that day to dismiss any joviality they might normally have. 'Blasting gelatine we brought. Enough to blow up the 'ouses of Parly. You're sitting on most of it!'

Holman shifted in his seat uncomfortably.

'Don't worry, sir,' the Captain said, 'it's quite safe for the moment.'

'So long as nobody bashes into us,' Stanton remarked dryly.

'Yes,' agreed the Captain. 'I think it might be better if Mr Holman drives providing he feels up to it; he'll have a clearer view than any of us. We daren't take off these helmets now that the door has been opened.'

Holman struggled forward into the driver's seat and the Sergeant squeezed back into the place he had vacated.

'Of course, we still do not know if these suits are strong enough to resist the mycoplasma,' said Ryker. 'At least not near its centre, in its purest form. That is why it is still you, Mr Holman, who will have to draw off the sample.'

As Holman shuddered, Ryker went on reassuringly, 'Don't worry, my friend. You will not have to go too near; we have long tubing which you will only have to direct into the nucleus. And one of us will come as far as possible with you to see that you come to no harm.'

The vehicle moved on and once again the four men were subjected to the wretched sight of fellow human beings in the depths of degradation. Holman noticed they were banding together more now, solitary figures becoming less and less frequent. He remarked on it.

'Yes, we have seen it too as we drove here,' said Ryker. 'There were thousands of them by the river. We had to take an alternative route to get through.'

'Oh, God, you don't think – ' Holman began, remembering Bournemouth.

'It's possible,' said Ryker gravely, guessing Holman's meaning. 'That's why it is essential that we are successful this time and can clear the fog.'

'Why, what can you do? Thousands, millions more likely, are going to commit mass suicide. They'll throw themselves into the river. The Thames will be full of bodies – there'll be so many you'll be able to walk across it!'

'Calm yourself, please Mr Holman,' Ryker placed a gentle hand on Holman's arm. 'We are going to spray the city, the whole town, with sleeping gas.'

'What? That's impossible!'

'No, it isn't,' Ryker answered quietly. 'Ever since the crisis began in London, small aircraft and helicopters – commercial as well as military – have been loading up with two things: calcium chloride and nitrous oxide, a gas you might describe as knock-out gas. The intention is to send the city to sleep for as

238

long as it takes to find and administer a serum. And remember: many will not have been affected by the disease yet for it varies from body to body as to how long it takes for the infection to begin its work; these people will have the best chance of all. Hundreds will still die, of course – thousands, perhaps – but we will save the majority. *Provided we have a serum and provided we are in time!*'

Holman picked up speed. It was plausible; countless lives could be saved! They had to succeed, no matter what they came up against, they had to succeed this time.

Soon, by carefully skirting likely trouble spots, they arrived at the black entrances to the twin tunnels. He stopped the vehicle and they clambered out, the two soliers going first, each clutching their rifles, ready to use them if necessary.

'There's a body over there just inside the tunnel,' the Sergeant said flatly, pointing towards the recumbent figure of the man Holman had knocked down.

'I killed him,' he told them, and they accepted it without comment, as though he had told them he'd stepped on a bug.

'Now,' said Ryker, who was emerging last from the vehicle, 'we have to make sure the nucleus is still there and if it is, then you know what you must do Mr Holman.' And then he added, in surprise, 'But there are two tunnels!'

Holman nodded. 'Yes, one is the old tunnel – the right hand one – used by northbound traffic; the other, more recent one, is the south. The nucleus is in the old one.' He indicated with his hand, adding, 'At least, I hope to God it's still there.'

The four men walked into the entrance, three lumbering along, small oxygen tanks strapped to their backs, one, unencumbered, but looking humanly frail beside the others.

'It's pretty solid,' the Captain remarked, peering up at the roof of the entrance. 'Lovely solid chunks of concrete to come down and fill up the hole. Yes, should do very nicely.'

'Fuck me,' said the Sergeant through clenched lips, 'there's a bloody 'ead lyin' over there.'

'Forget it,' said Holman coldly.

He walked into the blackness for about six yards, then stood there, allowing his eyes to grow accustomed to the darkness. 'It's there,' he said after a while.

The two soldiers returned to the vehicle and unloaded a lead container mounted on wheels from its side, similar to the one Holman had used in Winchester, only bigger. The Sergeant un-

239

strapped a long length of flexible steel tubing, narrower at one end. He coiled it over his shoulder and followed the Captain who was leading the motorised container back towards the tunnel's entrance.

'You know how to use the machine, Mr Holman,' Ryker said, facing him and placing one hand on his shoulder as though contact would make his words more intelligible. 'As I told you, there is no need to go too near the nucleus. You have sixty yards of steel tubing that is just stiff enough for you to push into the mycoplasma and by switching on the machine, it will be sucked back into the container. I will come with you myself; I want to get a closer look at this monster.'

'Take this with you, sir,' the Captain said, handing Holman a small oxygen tank, 'you may find you need it. And here's a torch.'

Holman thanked him and put his arm through the strap of the tank, sliding it on to his shoulder. Switching on the torch, he took the arm of the mobile container in his other hand and said, 'I'm ready, Professor.'

They walked down the slope of the tunnel towards the first curve and Ryker stiffened as for the first time he became aware of the light shining from ahead.

'I can see it now,' he said to Holman.

Holman didn't bother to reply; he could feel his nerves tensing at every step nearer to the bend and the now-familiar clammy coldness creeping up his back. He kept the torch shining on to the ground just ahead of him, knowing it would only reflect back at him if he shone it directly at the fog in the tunnel. He moved to the side of the tunnel as if to keep out of vision from the brightness ahead, as if it were a seeing thing. Strangely, Ryker followed suit.

They reached the bend and stopped for a moment, Holman turning to look at the scientist as though seeking reassurance. Ryker nodded and pointed ahead. 'I'll come with you around the curve so I can get a better look at it, but that's as far as I think I should go.'

Holman took a deep breath, then was forced to cough to clear his throat from the fumes. It wasn't too bad yet, but he would soon have to use the breathing apparatus as he went deeper into the tunnel. He moved on, Ryker following.

They were a long way down the next straight run before

Holman said, 'You'd better stop here, Professor, the light's getting much stronger.'

'Yes, yes, I think you're right,' came the reply. 'I cannot see too well through this visor, but I think we must be very close to the main body of the mycoplasma.'

'The worst of it seems to be around the next bend; I can see the light shining brilliantly at its corner. I'm going forward, you stay here. I won't go out of your sight around the curve if I can help it.'

Once again, he felt the compulsion to approach it, but he did so only because he had to. The fog seemed thicker but he guessed it was only because of the light bouncing off its particles that made it more difficult to see. He turned his head to make sure Ryker was still in view; he didn't want the Professor to lose sight of him! He soon reached the next gently sweeping curve, this one bending to the right as opposed to the first which had bent to the left, but he sayed on the same side of the tunnel, hoping he would be able to reach the nucleus from as far back in the curve as possible.

The light was dazzling as he reached the point of the bend that allowed him to see further up the tunnel. Either it was just the confined space creating an illusion or the nucleus was growing larger; he was sure it hadn't been as bright as this in Winchester. True, he hadn't been as close as this there, but because of the old cathedral's vastness, he had been afforded an unhindered view. He began hastily to assemble the machinery, pushing the end of the steel tubing into its cavity and clicking the switch to release grips that would hold it securely; the sooner he had completed his task and could get away, the better he would like it. Before he began to push the tubing towards its goal, he placed the mouthpiece of the oxygen cylinder over his mouth for the acrid smell was becoming stronger. Then he began unwinding the coil of steel, placing its rigid end on the ground and slowly sliding it along the centre of the tunnel's flat surface. It began to go off course after a while, but that didn't matter; the side wall would guide it forward into the glowing mass ahead. Beads of perspiration broke out on Holman's forehead, due to the clammy heat inside the cavernous tunnel and the tension that had gripped him.

Finally the tubing began to disappear into the light, meeting no resistance, a fact that surprised Holman; he had almost expected the nucleus to have some substance, at least some kind of resilience, but he realised again it was an organism he was probing, millions of tiny microbes. He pushed the steel tube to the limit of its extension then pressed the switch on the container which would operate the suction unit. The machine began to buzz and draw off the deadly mutation into its reinforced container, the snaking coil of steel stiffening and straightening out as it did so. Previously, at Winchester, he had been instructed to leave the machine on for at least two minutes to allow the container to fill itself with the mutated microbes, but as this container was larger, he decided to leave it on for at least three minutes. He crouched on one knee, bathed in the yellow glow, studying the phenomenon before him.

He had come to regard it almost as a living, thinking thing. Ryker had called it a monster. It seemed apt. The feeling that it was protesting in some way against this violation against it still persisted but, of course, it was only the high-pitched humming of the machinery, the quivering stiffness of the steel tubing combining with his imagination that produced and heightened the effect. At least, that was what he told himself.

The urge to go closer to the source was becoming stronger and several times during that long three minutes he found himself staring blankly into the bright mass. At last, with a sigh of relief, he switched off the machine, pushed another button to effectively seal the container, then detached the tubing, leaving it lying limply along the ground. He stood up and once again looked into the radiance. Perhaps he *should* get a closer look at it. Perhaps behind the veiling mists that swirled in front of it he would find some clue to its beginnings; some idea of its structure he could inform Ryker of, who would perhaps, recognise a vital factor in the progress of his theory. He was immune, after all; it couldn't harm him.

He began to walk towards it.

A gloved hand clamped down heavily on his shoulder, when he had only gone ten yards, spinning him round roughly.

'What do you think you are doing?' Ryker demanded to know, his body heaving with the exertion of running in the cumbersome suit.

Holman could only stare at the darkened visor.

'I could barely make out your figure through the fog,' Ryker went on, 'and when it disappeared altogether, I knew something was wrong. It has been a long time since I have run so fast. Now tell me: what are you up to?'

242

Holman rubbed a hand across his forehead. 'Christ,' he said, 'I don't know. I was walking into it. I just had a compulsion to get nearer to it.'

'Yes,' said Ryker slowly and thoughtfully. 'Well, do not look at it again. Turn your back on it and let us return to the machine. Did you complete your task?'

'Y-yes. Yes, it should be full. But you shouldn't be this close – your suit may not be enough protection.'

'I know, I know, but you had to be stopped. Come along, let us get away from here.'

They collected the machine and made their way back to the tunnel's entrance, much to the relief of the two soldiers who had been growing more anxious by the minute.

'Everything okay, sir?' enquired the Captain, stepping forward to take the machine.

'Everything is fine,' Ryker told him. 'Now, we will not waste any more time; we must seal the tunnel entrance immediately. Take the container back out of harm's way – we will worry about loading it on to the vehicle later, when our next job is done.' He looked up at the arch of the tunnel and smiled inside his helmet.

'It is very fortunate that they thought of building another tunnel. Captain Peters and I will take explosives through the southbound passage and plant them at the other end. We must seal both openings at the same time so that the mycoplasma will be trapped; we will time our blasts so they occur simultaneously.'

They went over to the vehicle and the Sergeant began to unload three cases of explosives. 'This will be more than enough,' he told them. 'If we fail the first time, we've plenty more for as many goes as we like.' He reached in and brought out another box, smaller than the others. 'Detonators,' he explained.

They turned as they heard the lumbering figure of the Captain returning. 'I've put the container halfway up the in-cline,' he said, 'where the road branches off to the ramp we've just come down. It'll be quite safe there for now; it's virtually indestructible and nobody can move it unless they know how to operate it.'

He poked his head inside the cabin of the vehicle and emerged again holding a small two-way radio. 'We'll keep in touch con-stantly,' he said. 'You take this, Mr Holman. It's simple to operate, and you can speak to us while Sergeant Stanton is setting up his explosives.' He handed the radio to Holman who examined it briefly, then nodded.

'It should take us about twenty minutes to get through the tunnel and set ourselves up, providing we don't run into trouble on the way,' the Captain went on, glancing at his watch. 'But we'll radio through and synchronise our blasts that way. All set?' he turned towards Ryker.

The figure nodded and clambered into the vehicle. Before he was completely through, he turned and said, 'Good luck to all of us. And may God help us.'

Holman stood well back while the Sergeant went about setting his explosives thirty feet inside the tunnel, even though he was assured it was quite harmless until it had been 'primed'. 'In fact,' Sergeant Stanton had explained, 'it's the blasting caps that are more dangerous. Highly explosive, they are.' He had shown him the small metal tube that was the primer. 'There's a little bit of lead azide in there, with a larger amount of trinitro-toluene – TNT to you. Very sensitive.' He had grinned through his mask at Holman, enjoying the man's discomfort. 'Don't worry, sir, you'll be all right with me.' He had gone into the tunnel whistling tunelessly, happy now that he was at last doing something positive, something he was an expert at.

Holman dragged clear of the entrance the dead body of the man he'd thrown from the car, some illogical reason not wanting it to be buried beneath tons of concrete. After a short while, the Sergeant came out of the tunnel, unwinding a long thin cable from a spindle behind him. 'That should do it,' he said, almost cheerfully now.

The radio crackled in Holman's hand. 'Hello, can you hear me, Mr Holman?' It was Ryker's voice sounding distant and even less human than it had through the mask's speaker. Holman acknowledged. 'The Captain is inside the tunnel now,' the voice went on. 'The southbound passage was clear. Filled with the fog of course, but not the nucleus. We had to take it steady – our vision was not too good – but we used dipped headlights and stayed close to the wall. As yet, we've seen no people over this side and I must admit, we have no desire to. The exit – or should I say entrance – at this end is perfect for our purposes. It is enclosed by heavy concrete slabs all the way along the incline leading from the tunnel. We have parked our vehicle on the opposite road of the other tunnel which is much higher than its sister road. That is where I am perched at this moment, looking straight down into the exit; we will move back to a safer position as soon as we are ready. How are things at your end?'

'Sergeant Stanton is just running out the fuse. We should be ready at any time.'

'Good. Captain Peters asked me to tell the Sergeant he will place one charge as near to the roof as possible, another at the bottom of the opposite wall. Could you pass that on to Sergeant Stanton please.'

Holman shouted the message after Stanton who was now some distance away up the incline. He looked up at Holman, nodded, pointed at his chest and gave the thumbs up sign.

'The Sergeant's done the same,' Holman said into the mouthpiece.

'Good, good. Now I suggest we find cover. The Captain is coming out of the tunnel now so we should soon be ready to proceed. I will speak to you again in a few moments.'

The radio went dead and Holman walked back towards Sergeant Stanton who had now climbed the parapet on to the small side road that overlooked the incline leading down to the black hole.

'We'll be all right up here, sir,' the soldier said as Holman scrambled up after him. 'I've set it so that the tunnel will come down causing very little to come our way – but we'll have to be wary of a few flying rocks.'

'What about the container.' Holman pointed towards the mobile box that stood further down, closer to the entrance.

'Oh, that'll be all right, sir. There's not much that can harm that thing.' He connected the plastic-sheathed fuse to a small handbox. 'One twist of this knob here, sir, and we'll have that entrance down in no time.'

'No plunger?' asked Holman, feeling naïve.

'Not for this.' The Sergeant grinned, his enjoyment increasing as the time for his blast grew nearer.

The radio crackled into life again and a voice said, 'Captain Peters here. Can you hear me Sergeant?'

The Sergeant leaned towards the speaker. 'I can hear you, sir.'

'Right. We're in position here. We'll give it a countdown of one minute. Check your timer.'

Holman saw the soldier look at a small clockface on the detonation box he held in his hand. His gloved finger poised above a catch at its side. The voice from the radio said, 'Start it after three.' The seconds were counted and the Sergeant's clumsy finger pushed the catch down, starting a tiny red second hand on its circular course.

'All right, Sergeant. I'm handing the radio back to Professor Ryker now,' the Captain's voice said. 'Be ready on the stroke of sixty. Good luck and keep your bloody heads down.' The radio went silent again.

Holman watched in fascination as the red hand crept round the dial. Several times he thought it had stopped but realised it was only an optical illusion. As it reached the forty-five second mark, he felt the urge to blow his nose, but he knew it was only nerves and rubbed it with a shaking finger instead. Ten. His throat felt dry. Seven. He cleared it. Five. He remembered to breathe. Three. Would the blast be powerful enough to completely block the entrance? Two. It had to be. One.

He buried his head in his hands as he sensed rather than saw the Sergeant briskly turn the knob.

He felt the whooshing of air before he heard the explosion, sweeping his hair back, dragging at his clothes. He thought the ground had actually trembled beneath him. Then he heard the roar, a split second behind the actual blast, muffled at first then developing into a loud, rumbling crack of thunder.

He kept his head down close to the concrete surface, expecting to feel fragments of rubble descending upon them, but none came. Still, he lay there, covering his head until the Sergeant's hand prodded him on the shoulder.

'It's all right now, sir. A nice clean one, that.'

The Sergeant was on his knees looking towards the tunnel's entrance, nodding his head in self-admiration. Holman looked up, deafened by the blast, but anxious to see its results.

Dust was swirling around the entrance, mixed with the fog, but after a few seconds, it began to drift away. Holman managed to smile at what he saw.

Tons of broken concrete and rubble had completely filled the high entrance – if one could call it an entrance any more. For some inexplicable reason, he had expected just to see the entrance blocked up, but of course, the beginning of the hole had now moved back forty feet or so and a steep slope of broken rock led up to its broken roof.

He clapped the grinning Sergeant on the arm and picked up the radio. 'Hello, Professor Ryker,' he said into it and was puzzled as to why he couldn't hear his own voice. Then realised his head was still ringing with the blast so he placed the radio on the ground while he studied the wreckage more thoroughly. The Sergeant had already dropped down on to the incline and was now walking towards it. He reached its foot and stood there, examining the damage. At last satisfied, he turned and waved at Holman and once more gave him the thumbs up sign.

By now, Holman's head was clearing so he picked up the radio again and spoke into it. 'Hello, Ryker, can you hear me?'

There was a few moments of static then the professor's voice came through. 'Hello, hello, Mr Holman. Can you hear me?'

'Yes, I can, Professor.'

'Quite a blast, eh? Well, it seems to have done the job at this end. Captain Peters has just gone for a closer look, but from here it looks fine. How about your side?'

'It's completely sealed at this end. Sergeant Stanton is just climbing the slope to the top, but he's already indicated everything's fine.'

'Excellent, excellent. I shall move forward myself now along the top road, and examine the damage from there. The dust is settling and the air over here seems to be clearer than on your side, so I am getting a pretty clear picture of the results of our little blast. Yes, yes, the nearer I get the better it looks. I can see Captain Peters directly below me; I think he will be satisfied with his work. He is looking round for me – ah, yes, he sees me. He is waving. Good, good, I think he is happy – he is shaking hands with himself.' Holman heard a strange metallic rasping through the receiver which could only have been the Professor chuckling to himself. The voice went on: 'I am moving past the blockage now and I must say it looks very, very solid to me. There is one enormous concrete slab at an angle at the top, it must be at least twenty feet across, that is – ' the radio went silent for a few moments, then the voice continued, and Holman could sense a sudden tension in it, even through its distortion. 'There is something wróng. There – there is dust spewing from the top of the concrete – no, from behind it. Is it dust?' There was a long pause. 'Or is it just the disturbed fog? No, the fog is clearer over here, it must be dust. I will look closer. It seems to be coming out rapidly, like steam. I am near to it now, I can see behind the con – ' again his voice broke off. 'There is a gap!' Holman started at the sudden exclamation. 'There is a gap in the roof! The fog – it is escaping from it! But this is impossible. It must be the force of the blast. The air inside the tunnel must be forcing the fog out. It must be that, surely the fog couldn't – God! There is a light! The hole is beginning to glow. The light is coming out. It is the light we saw in the tunnel, the yellow light. No, no, the mycoplasma is escaping. It is emerging with the fog! I must get away from here! I must get away.'

The radio went dead, except for the sharp crackle of static, and Holman, for the first time in many years, broke down and wept.

'Holman! Sergeant Stanton! Can you hear me?' Holman raised his head at the sound of the voice and made a grab for the radio. He had no idea of how much time had elapsed since the receiver had gone dead: it might only have been seconds, but more likely it had been several minutes for his tears of frustration had blotted out all sense of time. Was there no answer to this nightmare? Was there no way to succeed in destroying it?

'Hello, this is Holman,' he said hastily into the speaker. 'Ryker?'

'No, this is Captain Peters. Professor Ryker is beside me in the vehicle; I don't think he's too good.'

'What happened?'

'The mycoplasma: it got loose. I heard Professor Ryker shouting and scrambled up to the top of the slope to see what was wrong. He was down the road a piece, near the vehicle, lying in the road. Ahead of him, I could see a – I can only describe it as a solid mass of light, although that hardly fits. It seemed to be drifting away with the fog; *it must have passed right over him!*'

Holman drew in his breath slowly. 'Is he all right?'

'I don't know, he seems sort of dazed. I dragged him into the vehicle, but couldn't risk taking his helmet off to examine him. I think it's more fright than anything; the sight of that thing escaping and coming towards him. Anyway, he seemed to come out of it a minute ago; he told me to follow it, said we mustn't lose sight of it this time, and then he just slumped back and seemed to black out. I think he's coming round a bit now.'

'Peters, be careful,' Holman urged. 'He may have been infected.'

'No, I don't think so; these suits are pretty bloody tough. I think it's just shock. Anyway, I'm following the thing, the nucleus, whatever it is, just keeping it within visual range. We haven't got far yet, but it seems to be heading due east towards – ' again, the agonising silence. 'Holman, there're two enormous buildings rising up ahead of us in the fog,' the voice broke in again. 'They look like – yes, they are. Gas holders. Giant gas holders!'

Holman's mind raced back to the occasions he had used the three-lane motorway leading from the Blackwall Tunnel. He remembered the last time had been late at night, and on his left, just as he'd emerged from the southbound tunnel, he'd seen a fantastic sight that had resembled a scene from a science-fiction movie. It had been a vast gas refinery, its silver towers and tanks floodlit at night giving it an awesome and spectacular appearance. There were two main gas holders (those Peters had just seen presumably) and rows of smaller tanks farther back. The refinery had been built on the river bank to give it easy access for the coal that was brought up the Thames in barges to be processed for the manufacture of town gas. He knew it was one of the largest plants of its kind in England, for it helped serve a vast area of the South East.

'Holman, what is this place?' It had sounded like Ryker's voice.

'Professor, is that you?' he asked anxiously. 'Are you okay?'

'Yes, yes, I'm a little bit dizzy, but otherwise fine. Now, quickly tell me, what is this place ahead?'

Holman told him all he knew of the huge gasworks and how, if necessary, they could get into it.

'I think it is necessary,' the voice came back. 'The nucleus is making straight for it. How strange: it is the large quantities of carbon dioxide and sulphur dioxide that are formed in the combustion of gas that add greatly to the pollution of our atmosphere; and now, the mutated mycoplasma is seeking it out, going to it as if it knows it is under threat and needs replenishment, needs to grow stronger.

'Ah, Captain Peters has seen the side road you spoke of; we are turning into it. We are close to the holders now, they are looming above us. There is a gate ahead; we will go through. I can see the nucleus.'

'Where is it, where is it now?' Holman shouted into the receiver.

He thought he heard a dry laugh at the other end. 'Why, where you would expect it to be, Mr Holman, nestled between the two gas holders, like a tiny child between two monstrous parents.'

Holman stared at the receiver. Ryker's voice had sounded almost whimsical. 'Ryker?' he said.

The voice that returned was brisker, sharper. 'Do you know what town gas is comprised of Mr Holman? Let me tell you: it is a toxic mixture comprising fifty per cent hydrogen, twenty to thirty per cent methane, seven to seventeen per cent carbon monoxide, three per cent carbon dioxide, eight per cent nitrogen and two per cent hydrocarbons. Furthermore,' Ryker went on, as though lecturing an inquisitive student, 'it contains ammonia, sulphur, hydrocyanic acid, benzene and other substances. In other words, a highly combustible mixture. I think the mutation has provided us with another answer, don't you agree, Mr Holman?'

The radio went frustratingly dead again before he had time to answer. My God, he thought, he means to blow the tanks up and the mutated mycoplasma with them! But what sort of damage would an explosion of that force do to the surrounding area? But he was right; it was worth the risk!

Holman scrambled to his feet, intending to cross the river through the tunnel that was still intact and give help to the two on the other side. Hanging the radio over his shoulder by its strap, he raised a hand to his mouth to call the Sergeant, who was still unaware of what had happened. It was then that he discovered he had problems of his own.

Before he could utter a sound, Holman became conscious of the fact that he was not alone. A crowd, attracted by the noise of the explosion, had gathered behind him; there seemed to be a couple of hundred of them, filling the road leading to the tunnel. Whether the crowd had already assembled before and were mindlessly roaming the streets en masse, he had no way of knowing, but their complete silence was more disturbing than if they had been yelling and screaming. Somehow, he knew, they sensed he was different.

He backed cautiously away from their cold, staring eyes, not wanting to make any sudden movement that would alarm them and jerk them into action. But there was a stirring in the crowd and a small boy of about fourteen pushed his way through and said in a quavering voice: 'Please tell me what's happening mister?'

Holman looked down at him in surprise. The poor kid, he

250

thought. He hadn't been affected yet. He's wandering around with the pack wondering what the hell's going on. He stepped towards the boy and said, leaning forward, 'Listen, son – ' He got no further. The crowd suddenly surged forward like a human tidal wave at the sound of his voice. The boy went down instantly, and Holman knew he was lost. Hands grabbed for him and he was swept backward with the motion of the people; striking out at them, trying to break their grips on him. He felled one man directly in front of him with his knee, back-handed a woman who was grabbing for his hair, struck another man who was trying to choke him with a hefty blow from his elbow. But there were too many of them. He felt himself going down, his breath being crushed from his body.

Then a shot rang out. A body close to him screamed and fell forward. He couldn't tell by the scream if a man or a woman had been hit, but at that stage, he couldn't have cared less. The crowd froze, then fell back, scrambling over one another to get clear. It was the noise of the rifle shot that had frightened them more than anything else.

'Quick, sir, make a break for it!' he heard the mechanical voice of Sergeant Stanton call out.

In a flash Holman was on his feet and, using one hand for support, cleared the iron balustrade that ran along the road overlooking the ramp, dropping six feet on to the incline. He fell forward on to his knees, but the Sergeant allowed him no time for pause. 'This way, sir, quickly,' he shouted, and another shot rang out.

Holman sprang to his feet and ran towards the grey-suited soldier. 'Thank God you hung on to your gun,' he gasped.

'After what I've seen today, mate, I wouldn't go anywhere without it.' He fired into the crowd again. 'Not very accurate in this get-up, but with this mob, who needs accuracy.' He raised it again and fired. 'Quick now, into the tunnel. I won't be able to keep up with you, so you go ahead, get to the Captain. I'll be able to hold them as I beat a slow retreat.'

It was pointless to tell him what had happened at the other end of the tunnel so he said, 'I'll stay with you, I'll help you.'

'What you gonna do, spit at them?'

'I've got a gun.' Holman showed him the revolver.

'They'd have to be on top of you for that squirt to work, and if they're on top of you, well, that's not going to help much, is it? No, you go on, sir, I can hold 'em. Look at 'em now, cowering like animals. They won't come any nearer.' To show Holman what he meant he raised the rifle and shot at the nearest figure, a woman who was crawling forward towards them on all fours. As she screamed, the crowd moved several feet back. 'You be on your way, mate,' he said, and Holman could almost imagine him grinning beneath the mask.

He was staggered by the soldier's cruelty: he knew they were in a dangerous predicament and his feelings for the demented people were becoming less and less sympathetic by degree, but he could not understand the Sergeant's inhumanity. He was taking potshots at the mob as if they were diseased sheep that had to be slaughtered. Had the madness touched him, too?

'What about the container?' was all he could manage to say.

'That'll be all right. They can't harm it and they can't move it. We'll collect it later when we come back in the vehicle. Now for the last time: *will you get into that fucking tunnel . . . sir?*'

Holman turned, and with one last look at the intimidated, but still slowly advancing crowd, he disappeared into the tunnel leaving the Sergeant at the foot of the broken concrete slope he had created. As his running footsteps echoed around the walls of the tunnel, and he sank deeper into the blackness of its interior, he heard two shots ring out in rapid succession. He hoped the Sergeant would retreat into the tunnel where he would be safer; the crowd might not even follow him into the darkness.

But Sergeant Stanton had been foolhardy in his contempt of the crowd, for as he had shot at them, taking his time, picking off the more dangerous looking of them, one had climbed around behind him to the top of the twin tunnels; madmen have a special kind of cunning. The man picked up a solid rock of concrete from the many scattered around the top of the bridging structure of the tunnels, and, almost nonchalantly, hurled it down at the unsuspecting Sergeant. Even the tough helmet could not prevent Sergeant Stanton's head from caving in under the impact. The grey-clad figure crumpled and the mob surged forward again, screeching with delight, grabbing the dead body and holding it aloft, throwing it high into the air and letting it drop to the ground with bone-shattering thuds. Then they stripped it of its clothing and ran into the tunnel with it, holding it high above their heads.

252

Holman heard the noise of the crowd behind him. He listened for gunshots but when none came, he knew what had happened; they'd got the Sergeant.

He was in total, frightening darkness now, halfway down the tunnel he guessed, but both ends out of sight because of its many curves. How he prayed to see that patch of grey light ahead that would mean the tunnel's exit, for the blackness made him feel as though he were in a void, without a body, inside his own mind, his fears intensified because his imagination had no barriers of vision now. At least earlier that day (God, had it been the same day, it seemed like an eternity away) in the Underground tunnel, he'd had a torch; he had been able to relate to what he actually saw, but now he only had the touch of the rough concrete wall and the feel of the road beneath his feet to tell him he still existed as a living person. He barely took his groping fingers off the wall for fear of it not being there when he reached for it again. He moved along at a careless speed, trusting to chance that he would not meet an unexpected obstacle in the dark. Ryker had said the tunnel was clear, but then he had been travelling in the vehicle.

He could hear the frenzied mob behind him, sounding much closer than he knew they actually were because of the confined space, but, nevertheless, he increased his pace. He felt the wall curve gently and the road begin a subtle ascent. Were his eyes playing tricks, or was the blackness really less solid to the right of his vision? He blinked his eyes, knowing he had only by the flexing of his small eye muscles. Yes, there was definitely a greyness ahead. There would be another bend, the incline would become steeper, and there, at the end, would be daylight! He was breathing heavily and the muscles of his thighs ached abominably, but the effect of the dull light and anticipation of the brighter light to follow gave him new stamina. His fatigue wasn't overcome; it was just ignored.

It took him another five minutes to emerge from the tunnel, the cries of the demented mob behind and the promise of daylight ahead continuing to keep his weary legs pumping away, refusing to slacken their cruel pace. The fresh air, fog-filled though it was, managed to revive him a little, which was fortunate, for the final slope leading on to the motorway above ground, was the most exhausting. He was almost at the top when the radio hanging from his shoulder began to crackle into life again. Several times, in the tunnel, he had been tempted to dump it as an unnecessary encumbrance, but now he was glad he hadn't.

'Can you hear me, can you hear me?' a voice asked urgently.

He pressed the transmit switch. 'Hello, yes. This is Holman! I can hear you. Ryker? Peters?'

'Thank God,' the voice said. 'It's Captain Peters here.'

He slumped down against the wall which sloped down towards the tunnel. 'Have you planted the explosives yet?' he asked, trying to make his words intelligible through gasping breath.

'Yes, I've done that. As much as I could beneath each gas holder. They're made of steel those things, but they'll crack like eggs with the amount of gelignite I've used. I'm going to set the timer for five minutes which will give us plenty of time to get back into that tunnel. We're going to need all the shelter we can get.' Before Holman could tell him of the mob in the tunnel, the Captain went on, 'Here comes Ryker now. He was just getting a last look at the bloody thing while I was setting up the wires here. I think he's still in a state of shock, you know. One minute he's quite rational, the next he seems to go off into – my God! *He isn't wearing his helmet!*'

Holman heard the Captain calling out Professor Ryker's name, then the radio went dead. He raised himself and looked over the top of the wedge-shaped wall, narrow at his end, but deep by the tunnel's exit. He could just about make out the huge structures of the gasworks through the fog which, he noticed, was thinning out considerably.

'Peters, Peters!' he shouted into the receiver. 'What's happening? For Christ's sake answer!'

He was still shouting into the speaker when he realised it *was* answering. Again, it was the Captain's voice, but his words sounded even more distant. The brisk, military coolness had gone, and the words carried an edge of panic to them. 'H-he's taken the detonator box from me. He's become infected by the fog, I'm sure and yet . . . ' The voice struggled to control itself, 'He seemed quite rational. He said we couldn't wait for five minutes, the risk of the nucleus moving away was too great – it had to be destroyed now while we had the chance. I refused, but h-he pushed me back and grabbed the box. I didn't dare struggle with him in case the mechanism was jolted and it went off there and then. He's – he's walking back now, into the fog, into the nucleus! Holman, wherever you are now, try and find shelter.

254

Get into the tunnel if you can. I'm coming out! I'm beside the vehicle – I may just have a chance!' Static, then silence.

Holman knew better than to try to call the Captain again; the poor bastard needed all the time he could get! He looked towards the vast refinery, shaking at the thought of what was about to happen and then he thought he saw movement. He couldn't be sure because of the drifting fog, but yes, it looked like the Devastation Vehicle! He might *just* make it!

Then two things happened at the same time: the mob poured from the tunnel below, carrying what looked like a bloodied naked carcass above their heads, and, as he turned their way, a searing flash, followed by a deafening explosion, and then in turn followed by a thunderous whoosh of exploding gas, rocked the very earth.

Holman curled up into a tight ball, trying to make himself as small as possible. He could feel the hot air burning into his back, his hair crackling as it was singed from his scalp; he thought his eardrums would burst with the noise, he could feel the trickle of blood as it ran from his nose. The roar seemed to be going on forever, the concrete was cracking beneath him. Although he could not hear them with his deafened ears he could feel fresh blast-waves sweeping over him, more violent trembling of the ground, and he knew the other smaller tanks were going up one by one. He was afraid to look even had it been possible, for he knew the world above him was now a blazing inferno and if he raised himself, the heat would scorch his eyes. He was luckier than most of the people below at the tunnel's exit; he was tight up against the solid wall which was reinforced by the width of the road running along its top, but they, although sheltered from the worst of the blast, were relatively exposed. Many were burnt to death instantly by the scorching blast of dry air; others were swept back into the tunnel, the bodies shattered by fragments of flying steel and masonry; and many more were crushed to death by the falling concrete slabs as parts of the tunnel caved in.

It was a long, long time before Holman had the courage to uncover his head from his blistered hands and look up. He saw that the ramp he had crouched in was littered with debris, much of it solid pieces of rock and metal that, if they had struck him, would have killed him instantly. He did not look down towards the tunnel for he had no desire to see the carnage to human bodies the explosion would have wreaked; instead, he slowly and painfully raised himself to his knees and cautiously, inch by inch, lifted his head so that he could see what lay beyond the wall.

The whole area before him seemed to be a gigantic ball of flame. He could no longer see the structures of the gas plant or any buildings at all for that matter; anything that had been left standing – *if* anything had been left standing – was completely obscured by the billowing fire. He couldn't hear the rumble of new, smaller explosions, but he could see the sudden bursts of yellow flame among the deeper orange and red billowing fire. He ducked down again for his eyes were already becoming sore with the heat and he blinked rapidly to moisten them. After a minute had passed, he looked over the top again.

The fire seemed to stretch from the river for at least a quarter of a mile to his right, covering the whole of the plant and most of the smaller factories nearby. He turned his head and saw that even the buildings across the wide motorway had been completely gutted. The devastation was appalling: the gas holders had obviously been full, the steel containers raised to the limits of their height for the use of gas that day would obviously have been small, and the two explosions beneath them had cracked them both wide open, igniting the highly combustible gas they held, setting off a chain reaction among the surrounding refining tanks, spreading the destruction with rebounding swiftness.

A few hundred yards away he could see what must have been the broken shell of the Devastation Vehicle lying on its side, almost completely burnt out now. He sank back down, his head against the wall, and closed his aching eyes. What a terrible price to pay. His thoughts were no longer angry – not even at those who had first instigated the malignancy then set it free by their stupidity – nor were his thoughts filled with fear of the madness it had caused. He was drained of feelings of that extremity; all he felt now was a deep, wearying sadness. He knew the mutation was gone, destroyed by the intense heat, the enemy and the ally of mankind. Nothing could have withstood that destructive but purifying inferno, not even the man-inspired disease, the mutated mycoplasma that seemed somehow more than just a formation of malignant and parasitical cells. Had its deviousness been imagined? Had it really possessed the power to evade its would-be destroyers, or had its movements been controlled merely by the drifting air currents? Had its mesmerising quality only been the imagination of man, part of the subconscious will for self-destruction every mind possesses, hidden deep down in the darkest recesses of the brain, but always ready to be brought to the surface? Had Ryker really gone mad, or had he seen it was the only sure way? Perhaps he had known the disease had already got a grip on his brain and was steadily duplicating itself, destroying his healthy brain cells one by one, gaining control of his mind. Perhaps he had known this and decided in his last rational thoughts to end it both for himself and the disease. Or perhaps his suicide had been a combination of the madness and the compulsive drawing power of the nucleus itself. There was no way of knowing the answers to any of these questions now, and at that moment, Holman had no wish to know. All he wanted was to rest.

A sudden rush of colder air stirred him from his apathy. His hand stretched to the top of the wall and he pulled himself up once again. The fire was rising, drawing itself together in a great mushroom shape, spreading out with fire and black smoke at its head, the flames at its base almost white in their intensity. As it rose into the air, terrifyingly awesome in its furious beauty, the warm air rose with it, drawing in the cooler surrounding air, the heat repeating the process, creating an ascending maelstrom, reaching into the sky. He could see the fog being drawn in and sucked up, the streaking yellow-grey vapour making the fast currents of air visible, sweeping over him in swirling drifts, soaring upwards with the flames to be dispersed into the sky. Holman knew all the fog would not be cleared in this way, but at least a vast area would be free of it; the rest would be thinned and then dispersed by the wind now that its core, its nucleus, the mutation that had been creating and feeding from it, had been destroyed.

He sat, back against the wall, his hands hanging loosely over his raised knees, staring into the sky, waiting for the first clear blue patch to appear,

Twenty-two

Holman had moored the small launch beside the jetty near Westminster pier. He had left the lead container in the boat; they could send men in protective suits from the underground headquarters to collect it, he was too exhausted to attempt bringing it to dry land. He had waited by the tunnel exit for more than an hour before summoning up his reserves of power to make the journey back. He'd gone through the tunnel again, this time using the narrow catwalk at its side slightly above the level of the road, intended for motorists whose cars had broken down, using its rail as a guide, ignoring the moans of torment and pain from the people in the darkness below him. On the other side he had found the trampled body of the boy who had come forward from the crowd, lost and afraid, wondering what had happened to the world around him. Holman's mind had gone back to the beginning to the little girl he had rescued from the earthquake in the village, the first victim to die from the disease. He tried to contain the sorrow for there was more for him to do.

He had found the container where they had left it and he led it towards the river. There, he had soon found a small rowboat which he had used to reach a motor launch moored further down. Starting the launch had caused no great problem for it had a self starter and by the simple trick of touching wires and completing the circuit, the engine had soon been running. With satisfaction he had noted its tanks were half full, more than enough for his purposes. He had run the mobile container off the dockside on to the deck and it lay there on its side, undamaged and, for him at least, immovable.

As he had guided the launch out into midstream and begun his journey up the long, winding river, the sun had been breaking through the patchy grey sky above, its rays, where they managed to strike the brownish water, reflecting schools of bobbing silver light shards. He could see both banks of the river and knew an enormous hole was being created in the fog. The fire behind him raged, its blazing column still rising and its base spreading outwards. The fire would last for days, consuming more lives, more property but, most important, the fog. Then it would burn itself out, finally subdued by its own ferocity.

All along the river banks, he could see people staring towards it, white-faced, shocked by its enormity, the sight filling their sick minds to the exclusion of all else. The blaze would be seen for miles and he hoped it had the same paralysing effect on many more; at least this way they had no thoughts of harming themselves or others. He avoided the floating bodies in the water where he could, but others were knocked aside by the launch, their stiff, puffed-up limbs turning lazily in the water.

The fog had been thicker near Westminster, but not as thick as before. He had left the launch and found his way back to the underground car park. They had seen him coming through their television scanners, but had not recognised him at first because of his scorched hair, his blackened and bruised face, his tattered and bloody clothes, but when he began pounding on the blank concrete wall at the back of the basement car park, they had realised who he was and immediately opened the massive door.

He had told them of all that had happened: of the journey through the city; the death of Mason; the sealing off of the Blackwall Tunnel; the final destruction of the mycoplasma with the destruction of the gas plant. They had fired questions rapidly at him and he did his weary best to answer them all. Finally, they had congratulated him, praised him, but he had told them it was Professor Ryker and Captain Peters who deserved the thanks; it had been their combined efforts that had finally destroyed the disease.

Janet Halstead had examined him quickly, but not before she had smothered his grimy face with kisses of relief. She had found nothing seriously wrong, although many of his cuts and the burns on his hands would need special attention, and the enormous bruise on the side of his face, caused when he had been thrown from the overturned vehicle, would give him a lot of pain in the days to follow. She had urged him to rest, insisting he was in a state of near collapse, but he had refused, telling her there was one more thing he had to do before they began spraying the town with sleeping gas: he had to reach Casey.

He had begged her for a shot of something that would keep his fatigued body going and seeing that he was determined to leave anyway, she agreed, warning him she did not know how long the effects of the drug would last in his exhausted condition. He had assured her they would last long enough for him to get to Casey and that he would then gladly lie down and sleep while the city was sprayed with gas. His resolve had been strengthened and his anxiety aroused when they had tried to reach his flat on their internal switchboard, but power throughout London had finally gone dead and their only communication with the waiting outside world was through their transmitters. They had promised him the spraying operation would begin in the southwest and northeast areas, the aircraft working their way in sections across London, leaving the area in which he lived till last. To help him, they had given him the use of a military vehicle, a stocky, solid army scout car, but obviously, and to their regret, they could not risk sending anybody with him; the fog might still contain enough of the disease to penetrate the protective suits. As it was, they would need volunteers to collect the container, but that was a justifiable risk.

Finally, after Janet Halstead had quickly cleaned his face and hands up and he had borrowed a leather jacket from someone to cover the gun and shoulder holster he still wore, he had driven from the underground shelter, feeling the drug already beginning to revitalise his exhausted system.

He climbed the stairs and by the fourth flight, he could feel the weariness creeping back through his limbs; the drug was wearing off already. It must have been the drive back that had begun to drain him again, for the horror was still going on. Somehow he had half expected it to be all over with the destruction of the nucleus, but he soon realised the trail of misery it had left in its wake. There were still many of the individually gruesome and macabre incidents, but now the majority of the people had formed themselves into large marching crowds. Marching towards the river! It seemed that there would be a recurrence of the Bournemouth tragedy unless the gas reached them first. He had used the car's transmitter to inform the base of what was happening and they reported back they would now concentrate the dropping of the gas along the river's edge, on both sides, before dealing with the rest of London. Where he could, he had skirted the main groups of people, but several times he had had to drive carefully through them. Fortunately they ignored him, their minds filled now with only one thought. Self-destruction.

Even as he climbed the stairs, he could hear the low-flying aircraft in the distance, swooping down, spewing out their life-saving and hopefully for many, mind-saving gas. In other parts of the town, where the fog seemed fairly low, helicopters were being used, their pilots breathing through oxygen tanks in case gas from the aeroplanes drifted their way.

When he reached his floor, he breathed a sigh of relief to see the door to his flat was still firmly closed. As he pounded on it with his fist, calling out Casey's name, he failed to see the shadowy figure sitting on the stairs leading to the roof where it had been patiently waiting for most of the day.

Holman heard her muffled voice from behind the door, 'John is that you?'

'Yes, darling,' he shouted back, managing to coax his aching face into a wide grin, 'it's me. Everything's going to be okay. Open up.'

He heard the scraping of furniture, the heavy bolt being shot back, the latch clicking, then her face appeared in the small gap governed by the safety chain, stained with dried-up tears, fresh ones about to flow.

'Oh, John,' she cried, 'I didn't know what had happened to you. I've been so worr – ' her words were cut off as she fumbled with the safety chain. 'Somebody's been trying to get in all – ' but again her words were cut off as he pushed the door wide and pulled her towards him, enveloping her with his arms, relaxing his grip slightly only to kiss her face.

She was crying with relief and happiness as he pushed her back into the hall and kicked the door with the heel of his foot.

She broke away to look into his face and her eyes instantly clouded with anxiety. 'John, what's happened to you? What have they done to you?' she asked.

He smiled wearily. 'It's a long story,' he said. 'First, you and I are going to have a stiff drink. Then we're going to bed and I'll tell you all about it. And then, we're going to sleep. We're going to go into a long and glorious sleep.'

She smiled back at him, her expression curious but full of happiness. And then it froze into rigid lines of fear as she saw something over his shoulder, something that had prevented the door from closing fully. Puzzzled by her frightened look, Holman turned to see what had caused it. He caught his breath.

Barrow was standing in the doorway, a strange grin on his face.

Holman turned his body so that he was facing the detective and Casey was behind him.

'Hello Barrow,' he said warily.

There was no reply, no movement.

Casey touched his shoulder and said in an urgent, hushed voice, 'John, it must have been him. Somebody's been trying to get in all day. Banging on the door, trying to force it. When I called out, there was never any answer but the pounding would stop then start again an hour or so later. He must have been out there all this time.'

Holman tried to get an answer from him again. 'What do you want, Barrow?' he said.

Again, there was no reply, just the odd, disturbing grin. Strangely, Holman noticed, he was immaculately dressed: dark brown three-piece suit, white stiff-collared shirt, deep green tie. It was only his distant eyes and the humourless smile that gave any signs of his demented state. Holman tensed as Barrow suddenly put his hand into the right hand pocket of his jacket and drew something out. He couldn't make out what it was at first, but as Barrow began to unwind it, he saw it was a length of thin wire, two small wooden handles attached to each end.

'Get into the bedroom, Casey, and lock the door,' he said quietly, keeping his eyes on the figure in front of him.

'No, John, I'm not leaving you,' she said.

'Do as you're bloody told,' he said evenly through clenched teeth. He sensed her move away from him and heard the click as the bedroom door closed.

'What do you want, Barrow?' he said again, not expecting a reply but this time receiving one.

'You,' Barrow said. 'You, you bastard.'

He had the handles of the wire in either hand now, holding it up at chest level, drawing it out so that the wire was taut. Holman knew how the macabre weapon was meant to be used: as a garrotte. Twisted around the victim's neck, it would cut into the windpipe and jugular vein, killing within seconds,

262

Barrow took a step towards him.

Holman had been through too much that day to waste time trying to appease him and Barrow was already too near for him to risk reaching for the gun – so he attacked first.

He flew at the detective, charging low, ducking under the threatening wire, and both men went crashing back through the open doorway, falling in a struggling heap in the hall outside. Holman had landed on top but found himself being lifted completely off his opponent and then thrown to one side. The policeman's strength was incredible and, as he rolled over in an effort to get to one knee, Holman knew he would not stand much chance against him, especially in his own weakened condition. He saw Casey suddenly appear in the doorway, a hand to her open mouth as she saw the weapon Barrow held. The policeman was on his feet, moving in for the kill, a dry chuckling noise coming from his throat, but he turned his head when Casey screamed.

It gave Holman the fraction of time he needed to get to one knee and launch himself forward again from that position. His head struck Barrow in the midriff, knocking the wind from him, sending him reeling back along the hall. Holman found himself lying on Barrow's legs and he received a vicious kick under his chin from the detective's knee. He fell back against the wall, his senses spinning for precious moments. He tried to push himself up by using the wall for support, but he was too late. He felt the icy sharp wire go around his neck and just managed to get an arm up to prevent it closing completely. Barrow had crossed the two handles and was kneeling in front of Holman pulling them in opposite directions with all his strength.

Holman could feel the wire cutting into the back of his neck, and his arm, fortunately protected by the borrowed leather jacket, which was preventing him from being choked, although he was near to it. His hand was pressed up against the side of his face held there by the wire at his wrist, and he tried to push it away, resisting the tremendous pressure Barrow was exerting, but it was no use; he could feel his strength deserting him. His vision seemed to be dimming, the excruciating pain was sending waves of white heat through his head. He began to lose consciousness.

Then, by some miracle, the pressure was released slightly. His eyes began to clear as he fought his way up from the deep well of unconsciousness, but it seemed an age before he could focus

them, and when he could, he saw that Casey had Barrow by his
hair and was pulling his head back, tears streaming down her
face, her body trembling with the effort. Barrow was forced to
let go of one of the handles to use a hand to free himself. He
reached up and grabbed one of her wrists, trying to break her
grip, but she hung on grimly, pulling him backwards, forcing
him to lose his balance.

He came up again with an enraged roar, turning on her,
forgetting Holman for the moment. He lashed out at her
viciously with the back of his hand, sending her flying back
against the opposite wall, bringing blood to her lips. She stood
there sobbing, a hand to her face where he had hit her and he
stepped towards her and slapped her again, knocking her body
upright, her eyes blazing into his. He looked down at her, breathing heavily, his gaze completely blank for a few seconds. Then
he began to grin again. He reached out and gripped the top of
her flimsy blouse then pulled down with one swift motion, ripping it open, the sight of her small, exposed breasts causing him
to pause, his smile becoming wider, his eyes more cruel.

He stared at Holman almost incomprehendingly when he was
roughly swung round by his shoulder, his expression barely having time to change into one of fury before the fist smashed into
his face. He went crashing back against the girl, but retaliated
instantly, using his feet as he had been taught to – as weapons –
catching Holman a painful blow on his thigh. He lashed out with
his fist, catching Holman only a glancing blow on the forehead,
but enough to send him spinning across the hallway. He made as
if to follow, but Casey courageously hooked an arm around his
neck and tried to pull him back. He whirled around in her grip
and pushed her back against the wall, his body tight against
hers, pressing into her. One hand reached up for her shoulder,
ripping the blouse from it, then groping towards her breasts, his
other hand sliding down towards her thighs. His head was close
against hers, and she could feel the wetness on his lips on her
cheek. She tried to cry out but found she couldn't, her terror
paralysing her vocal chords.

Holman staggered towards him again, knowing he had to
finish it soon or Barrow would kill them both. His anger when
he saw the detective's intention gave him just the added strength
he needed to launch another attack. His fingers encircled
Barrow's head and found his eyes. He dug his fingers in and
pulled back with all his might.

Barrow screamed and came away from the girl, his hands flying to his face, trying to break Holman's merciless grip. He pushed himself back, crushing Holman against the opposite wall but even though the grip was released, he found he couldn't see through his bruised eyeballs. He struck out blindly but Holman easily dodged the blow, using the opportunity himself to send a vicious hook into Barrow's stomach, doubling him up. He kicked him in the face, the back of Barrow's hands taking the worst of the blow, but nevertheless, the force of it sending him staggering back down the corridor.

Even as Holman went after him, the detective was straightening his body, shaking his head, his sight returning. A smile was just beginning to spread across his face again when Holman charged into him, using his shoulder in an attempt to knock him flat. Barrow almost avoided the attack by twisting his body, but Holman just caught him, spinning him round, both of them falling to the floor again. Both men raised themselves to their knees at the same time and faced one another, but it was Barrow who reacted first. He used the hardened edge of his hand on the side of Holman's neck, bringing it down in a short sharp chopping motion. Again if it hadn't been for the collar of the leather jacket, Holman would have been seriously injured; as it was he fell forward on to his face, the whole of his left shoulder and the top of his arm completely numbed with pain.

He lay there gasping, his body heaving with the exertion, and he heard the dry insane chuckle of Barrow as he got to his feet.

The Detective Inspector looked down at his weakened opponent, his face a mask of sadistic pleasure. Casey was farther down the hall, collapsed on her knees, leaning against the wall, her blouse hanging in tatters around her. She wept for Holman, but knew she could do no more to help him, the madman was too strong. Barrow raised a foot to bring it crushingly down on the back of Holman's head.

As he did, Holman looked up and their eyes met: gloating victory showed through Barrow's crazed glare; defeat showed in Holman's. But the detective hesitated a moment too long in relishing his triumph and the defeat in Holman's eyes was replaced by a look of hope.

They had moved so far down the hall that Barrow now stood with his back to the stairs. Holman's right hand snaked out and grabbed for Barrow's foot, the one that supported his weight. He gripped the ankle and yanked it forward, using the last of his remaining strength to do so. The detective fell back and crashed down the stone stairs, over and over until he reached the bottom and bounced off the facing wall.

Holman's head sank to the floor and he lay there, his body heaving, too exhausted to move. He could hear Casey sobbing farther down the hall, but he could not summon the strength to go to her just yet. She called his name and slowly began to crawl towards him.

He lay there, his mind buzzing with thoughts as it does when too tired to concentrate on anything specific. He had been through so much in the last few days: his mind had had to adapt to so many strange factors; he'd had to accept death, not just individual but multiple death; *he'd had to accept killing.*

He heard a scraping noise coming from the stairs; a slithering, dragging noise. He looked up and saw that Casey had heard it too; she had frozen against the wall, her eyes looking at him in terror. He turned his head towards the stairs. The slithering noise continued, growing louder, now coupled with the sound of breathing. Holman stared at the empty space at the top of the stairs, unable to move, transfixed by the sounds, dreading what he would see. A hand appeared on the top stair, the fingers whitening as they pressed against the floor to grip and pull. Holman looked at them in disbelief, his head only two feet away from them. And then suddenly, he was staring into the evil, grinning face of Barrow! Blood was flowing from his nose and a deep cut above his eyebrow, giving his face an even more frightening aspect, but he grinned at Holman, his broken body shaking with exertion. He began to chuckle, his mouth opening in a wide grimace, the sound rasping from the back of his throat. He began to pull himself forward, over the top step. He wanted to reach Holman.

Holman slowly lifted his body, reached for the gun in his shoulder holster and clicked off the safety catch with his thumb. Then he put the barrel inside Barrow's grinning mouth, and pulled the trigger.

He knelt beside Casey, pulling her away from the wall and cradling her in his arms. Overhead, he could hear the hum of the low-flying aircraft and he knew they had reached his sector.

'The worst is over for us now, darling,' he told her, holding her close, rocking her gently back and forth. 'We'll never be the same, too much has happened to both of us, but we can help each other. I love you so much, Casey.'

He pulled her to her feet, and she wept against him.

'When this is finally finished, when they've done all they can for those who've been harmed, the people are going to find out exactly how it happened. I'm going to make sure of it and, I think, there are others who will too. But now, Casey, we're going to sleep. We're going to lie down together, and drift into a long, long sleep.'

She managed to smile up at him and they walked towards his flat, his tired and aching body leaning on hers for support.

He closed the door behind them.

FLUKE

by James Herbert

The story of a dog who thinks
he's a man ... or a man who
thinks he's a dog

NEW ENGLISH LIBRARY

THE RATS
by James Herbert

London is struck by an invasion. Women, children, old and young, none are safe from the deadly menace. The attacks are swift and sure, escape is impossible.
A state of emergency is declared. Evacuation seems the only solution in the face of a growing panic and mounting death toll. War is declared on the public enemy number one. The Rats!

NEW ENGLISH LIBRARY

THE SURVIVOR
by James Herbert

A TALE OF DEATH, AND
OF AN EVIL WHICH
TRANSCENDS DEATH

NEW ENGLISH LIBRARY